The Navigator

Clive Cussler is the author or co-author of thirty-one previous books, most recently the Dirk Pitt® adventure *Treasure of Khan*, the Kurt Austin novel *Polar Shift* and the *Oregon* Files novel *Skeleton Coast*. He is also the author of the non-fiction *The Sea Hunters* and *The Sea Hunters II*; these describe the true adventures of the real NUMA®, which, led by Cussler, searches for ships of historic significance. With his crew of volunteers, Cussler has discovered more than sixty ships, including the long-lost Confederate submarine *Hunley*. He lives in Arizona.

Paul Kemprecos has co-authored all six previous NUMA® Files novels with Cussler and is a Shamus Award-winning author of six underwater detective thrillers. A certified scuba diver and a former reporter, he lives in Massachusetts.

The Navigator

A Kurt Austin Adventure,
a Novel from the Numa® Files

CLIVE CUSSLER

with PAUL KEMPRECOS

MICHAEL JOSEPH
an imprint of
PENGUIN BOOKS

MICHAEL JOSEPH

Published by the Penguin Group
Penguin Books Ltd, 80 Strand, London WC2R ORL, England
Penguin Group (USA) Inc., 375 Hudson Street, New York, New York 10014, USA
Penguin Group (Canada), 90 Eglinton Avenue East, Suite 700, Toronto, Ontario, Canada M4P 2Y3
(a division of Pearson Penguin Canada Inc.)
Penguin Ireland, 25 St Stephen's Green, Dublin 2, Ireland (a division of Penguin Books Ltd)
Penguin Group (Australia), 250 Camberwell Road,
Camberwell, Victoria 3124, Australia (a division of Pearson Australia Group Pty Ltd)
Penguin Books India Pvt Ltd, 11 Community Centre,
Panchsheel Park, New Delhi – 110 017, India
Penguin Group (NZ), 67 Apollo Drive, Rosedale, North Shore 0632, New Zealand
(a division of Pearson New Zealand Ltd)
Penguin Books (South Africa) (Pty) Ltd, 24 Sturdee Avenue,
Rosebank, Johannesburg 2196, South Africa

Penguin Books Ltd, Registered Offices: 80 Strand, London WC2R ORL, England

www.penguin.com

First published in the United States of America by G. P. Putnam's Sons,
part of the Penguin Group (USA) Inc. in 2007
First published in Great Britain by Michael Joseph, 2007
This hardback edition published in 2008

2

Copyright © Sandecker, RLLLP, 2007

The moral right of the author has been asserted

Printed in Great Britain by Clays Ltd, St Ives plc

A CIP catalogue record for this book is available from the British Library

TRADE PAPERBACK ISBN: 978–0–718–14977–2
HARDBACK ISBN: 978–0–718–18154–141

www.greenpenguin.co.uk

Mixed Sources
Product group from well-managed
forests and other controlled sources
www.fsc.org Cert no. SA-COC-1592
© 1996 Forest Stewardship Council

Penguin Books is committed to a sustainable future
for our business, our readers and our planet.
The book in your hands is made from paper
certified by the Forest Stewardship Council.

PROLOGUE

THE MONSTER EMERGED FROM the morning mists in the pearly light of dawn. The massive head, with its long snout and flaring nostrils, advanced toward shore where the hunter knelt, bowstring taut to his cheek, eyes focused on a deer grazing in the marsh. A rippling sound caught the hunter's ear and he glanced out at the water. He uttered a fearful moan, threw the bow aside, and leaped to his feet. The startled deer disappeared into the woods with the terrified hunter close on its tail.

The tendrils of fog parted to reveal a giant sailing ship. Curtains of seaweed fringed the vessel's two-hundred-foot-long wooden hull of reddish brown. A man stood on the ship's upswept stem behind the carved figurehead of a snorting stallion. He had been gazing into a small wooden box. As the ghostly shoreline materialized, the man raised his head and pointed to the left.

The helmsmen at the twin steering oars brought the ship around in a graceful turn that sent it on a new course parallel to the densely wooded shoreline. Deckhands expertly adjusted the vertically striped red-and-white square sail to compensate for the change in direction.

The captain was in his mid-twenties, but the serious expression on his handsome face added years to his appearance. His strong nose was curved slightly at the bridge. His thick black beard was arranged in rows around a full mouth and square jaw. Sun and sea had tanned his skin to a mahogany hue. The unfathomable eyes that scanned the shoreline were a deep brown that was so dark the pupils were almost invisible.

The captain's high station in life entitled him to wear a purple robe dyed with the valuable extract from the murex snail. He preferred to go bare-chested, and wore the cotton kilt of an ordinary crewman. A floppy, conical knit cap covered the close-cropped, wavy black hair.

The briny smell of the sea had faded as the ship left the open ocean and entered the wide bay. The captain filled his lungs with air that was redolent with the scent of flowers and green growing things. He savored the prospect of freshwater and ached to set foot on dry land.

Although the voyage was long, it had gone well, thanks to the handpicked Phoenician crew, all seasoned deepwater mariners. The crew included a scattering of Egyptians and Libyans, and others from the countries bordering the Mediterranean. A contingent of Scythian marines provided security.

The Phoenicians were the finest seamen in the world, adventurous explorers and traders whose maritime empire extended throughout the Mediterranean and beyond the Pillars of Hercules and the Red Sea. Unlike the Greeks and the Egyptians, whose ships hugged the shore and dropped anchor when the sun set, the fearless Phoenicians sailed day and night out of sight of land. With a fair wind from astern, their big trading ships could cover more than a hundred miles a day.

The captain was not Phoenician by birth, but he was well versed in the sea arts. His command of navigation and seamanship and his cool judgment during bouts of bad weather had quickly gained the crew's respect.

The vessel under the captain's command was a "ship of Tarshish," built specifically for long-range commerce on the open ocean. Unlike the more-tubby short-haul traders, the vessel's lines were long and straight. The deck and hull timbers were hewn from tough Lebanese cedar, and the thick mast was low and strong. The square Egyptian-linen sail, quilted with leather belts for strength, was the most efficient deepwater sailing rig in existence. The curved keel and upswept stem and stern presaged the Viking ships that would not be built until centuries later.

The secret behind Phoenician mastery of the sea went beyond technology. Organization aboard their ships was legendary. Each crewman knew his place in the well-oiled machinery that was a Phoenician sea venture. Rigging was neatly stowed in an easily accessible room that was the responsibility of the captain's assistant. The lookout man knew the location of each piece of tackle, and constantly tested the ship's rigging to make sure it would work if needed in an emergency.

The captain felt something soft brush against his bare leg. Allowing himself a rare smile, he set the wooden box in a receptacle and reached down and picked up the ship's cat. Phoenician cats had their origins in Egypt where the animals were worshipped as gods. Phoenician ships carried cats as trade items and for rat control. The captain stroked the orange-and-yellow-striped cat for a few times, then gently set the purring feline back down on the deck. The ship was approaching the wide mouth of a river.

The captain called out a command to the lookout man.

"Prepare the riggers to drop sail, and alert the oarsmen."

The lookout man relayed the first command to a pair of crewmen, who scrambled like monkeys up the mast to the yardarm. Two other sailors tossed lines attached to the lower corners of the sail to the riggers, who used the ropes to reef the big linen square.

Brawny-armed rowers arranged in two ranks of twenty were already at their benches. Unlike the slave rowers on many vessels, the oarsmen who powered the ship forward with quick, precise strokes were trained professionals.

The helmsmen steered the ship into the river. Although the river was swollen with spring runoff from snow melting in the hills and mountains, its shallow waters and rapids would prevent the ship from moving farther upstream.

The Scythian mercenaries lined the ship's rail, their weapons at the ready. The captain stood on the prow, surveying the riverbank. He saw a grassy promontory that projected into the river and ordered the oarsmen to hold the ship against the current while the deck crew dropped anchor.

A muscular man with prominent cheekbones and a face as weathered as old saddle leather strode up to the captain. Tarsa commanded the Scythian marines who protected the ship and its cargo. Related to the Mongols, the Scythians were known for their skill as horsemen and bowmen, and for their peculiar habits.

In battle, they drank the blood of their vanquished enemies and took scalps that they used as napkins. Tarsa and his men painted their bodies red and blue, cleansed themselves with vapor baths, and wore leather shirts and trousers tucked into soft leather boots. Even the poorest Scythian adorned his clothes with gold ornaments. Tarsa wore a small horse pendant that the captain had given him.

"I'll organize a scouting party to go ashore," Tarsa said.

The captain nodded. "I'm going with you."

A smile came to the Scythian's stony face. As a landsman he had had little faith at first in the young captain's ability to keep the ship afloat. But he had watched the captain command the massive ship and had seen that there was iron behind the young man's patrician features and soft-spoken manner.

The wide-bodied utility boat normally towed behind the ship was brought alongside. The Scythian and three of his toughest fighters got into the boat with the captain and two strong rowers.

Minutes later the boat bumped against the promontory with a hard, grating sound. Under the grass overgrowth was a stone quay. The captain tied the boat up to a bollard that was all but hidden by weeds.

Tarsa ordered one man to stay with the rowers. Then he set off with the captain and the other Scythians along the overgrown stone-paved road that ran inland from the quay. After weeks spent on a rocking deck, they walked with an unsteady gait but quickly recovered their land legs. A few hundred feet from the river they encountered a weed-choked central plaza lined on all four sides by dilapidated buildings. Tall grass grew in the open doorways and alleys.

The captain pictured the settlement as it was on his first visit. The plaza had bustled with activity. Hundreds of workers had occupied the flat-roofed dormitories and toiled in the warehouses.

The landing party methodically searched every building. Satisfied that the settlement was deserted, the captain led the way back to the river. He walked to the end of the pier and waved. As the crew hauled anchor and the rowers powered the ship toward the quay, the captain turned to the Scythian commander.

"Are your men ready for the important task that lies ahead?"

The question brought a snort from the Scythian. "My men are ready for *any*thing."

The captain was unsurprised at the answer. He had spent many hours talking to Tarsa during the long voyage. The captain's unquenchable thirst for knowledge about people of all races had led him to question Tarsa about his homeland and people, and he had come to like the tough old warrior in spite of his blue-and-red skin and his odd habits.

The ship tied up to the quay and the crew lowered a wide gang-plank. Hooves pounded on the deck as two draft horses were led from their stable beneath the stern and down the ramp. The animals were nervous at being out in the open, but the Scythians quickly calmed them with soft words and handfuls of honey-soaked grain.

The captain organized a work party to take on freshwater and forage for food. Then he descended into the hold and stood next to a crate made out of sturdy Lebanese cedar. The container seemed to glow in the light streaming through the deck hatch. He called up to the crew to use great care in hoisting it from the hold.

Thick ropes were attached to the crate and affixed to the boom hook. The boom creaked under the heavy weight. The crate was lifted slowly from the hold and lowered onto the deck. The hook was detached, and oars were passed through holes in the sides and ends of the container, to be used as carrying poles. Men shouldered the poles and moved the crate down the ramp onto the quay.

The crate was lifted onto a low-slung cart that rested on sturdy, ironbound wooden wheels. The horses were harnessed to the cart. The marines slung their shields and bows over their shoulders, and, with spears in hand, formed protective flanks on each side. The captain and the Scythian commander took the lead. The procession surged forward with a clatter of weapons.

They marched through the abandoned settlement to a road that had been cut through the forest along the course of the river. Grass had grown up in the track, but the road still afforded rapid progress through the dense woods. The procession stopped each night to set up camp. On the morning of the third day, the marchers came to a valley between two low mountains.

The captain stopped the column and removed from his pack the same wooden box he had consulted on the ship. As the soldiers took a rest break and tended to the horses, he lifted the cover, poured in a small amount of water, and peered into the box. He glanced from the box to a scroll of vellum that he carried in a cloth sack. Then he pushed on with the unerring determination of a migratory bird.

The procession marched through the valley and eventually came to a field where remnants of round millstones were visible through the tall grass. The captain remembered the field when teams of sweating men had turned the stone wheels. Workers had poured baskets full of rocks into the mills, which ground the contents into powder. The powder had been carried over to fire pits. Bellows had stoked the blazes to white-hot intensity. Workers tilted clay crucibles and poured the glowing yellow molten contents into brick-shaped molds.

The expedition pushed on and came upon two stone idols. Each statue was twice the height of a man, and depicted a more or less human form from the neck down. The idols had been carved to frighten natives away. The nightmarish heads were a combination of animal and human, taking the worst features of each, as if the sculptor intended to create the most hideous and frightening face imaginable. Even the tough mercenaries were ill at ease. They nervously switched their spears from one hand to the other and cast wary glances at the evil-looking idols.

The captain consulted his magic box and vellum scroll, and plunged into the woods. The procession followed in the artificial twilight created by the canopy of foliage. Thick tree roots were a frequent obstacle, but after about an hour of marching the procession emerged from the woods. They approached the smooth face of a low rock wall at the base of the ridge. Two more idols, identical to the first pair, barred the way.

Using the idols for reference, the captain triangulated a point on the rock wall. He groped along the vertical face like a blind man who had encountered an unexpected obstacle. His probing fingers found a barely visible set of handholds, which he used to climb up the side of the wall.

About a dozen feet above the ground he turned his body and sat in a rock hollow. He borrowed a spear, which he inserted in a crack as a lever. The soldiers tossed a rope up, which he attached to the spear shaft. The other end of the rope was tied to a horse. The captain called out a signal, and the horse pulled while he pushed with his feet against a slight outcropping. A rock slab about a foot thick detached itself and slammed down with a thud, revealing a cavity about six feet wide and ten feet high.

After descending from the rock wall the captain started a fire in a nest of dry grass, then transferred the smoldering blaze to a bundle of brush. Holding the torch high, he led the way through the opening. The Scythians had hitched themselves to the harnesses and proceeded to pull the cart through a smooth-walled tunnel, which extended for about fifty feet before it opened up into a chamber.

The captain lit several oil lamps set into sconces along the wall of the chamber. The blazing ring of light revealed a large circular gallery, with tunnels leading off from it. In the center of the room was a circular section of rock about three feet high and six feet in diameter. The captain directed the Scythians to raise the crate to the dais. At his order, they removed the lid and stepped back.

The captain leaned into the crate and lifted the cover on a slightly smaller, more-ornate chest of gold and dark wood. As he peeled away layers of blue cloth, his heart hammered against his rib cage. He stared, transfixed; his face glowed in the reflection coming from the box. After a moment, the captain carefully rearranged the blue cloth and cover. Tarsa's men replaced the lid.

"Our mission here is done," he said, his words echoing in the chamber.

He led the way outside. The clean, cool air felt good against his sweaty face and cleansed the dust from his lungs. The captain directed the Scythians to lift the stone slab back in place. He studied the wall. No one would suspect that the slab hid the opening.

The column set off the way it had come. The procession moved at a brisk pace, without the weight burdening the cart, and marched directly to the river. Built along the sloping shore of the river was a wooden building whose large doors faced the water. The captain inspected the interior of the building. When he emerged, he seemed pleased. He told Tarsa and his men to prepare a fine meal and get a good night's sleep.

At dawn, the tireless captain awoke them. The horses dragged a wooden boat from the storehouse and down to the river. The open-decked craft was half boat, half raft, around fifty feet long and a dozen or so feet wide, and drew only a few feet of water. A long tiller operated the rudder.

The horses were led onto the boat, and it was pushed and poled into the river to catch the currents. The ride downriver was more hair-raising than their sea voyage. The boat encountered shallows, rapids, drifting trees, whirlpools, and rocks. The Scythians cheered when the boat popped out of the mouth of the river and they saw the ship at its mooring.

The ship's crew welcomed the new arrivals and helped drag the riverboat onto shore. While the captain wrote in his log, the crew celebrated late into the night. They were astir well before dawn, and the sun was just peeking over the trees as they cast off the mooring lines. Powered by the ranks of oarsmen and the wind, the ship moved swiftly out into the bay, the rowers putting their backs into their work. Like every other man on board, they were impatient to return home.

The exuberance on board the vessel was cut short by an unexpected development. As the ship passed an island, another vessel pulled out and barred their way.

✦ ✦ ✦

THE CAPTAIN shouted a brisk order to ship oars and drop sails. He climbed onto a large water urn in the bow to better study the vessel. There was no sign of life on board, but the deck was obscured by a wicker fence for cargo protection that ran along the sheer strake, as the highest hull plank was called.

He was looking at a ship of Tarshish.

The craft had the same functionally graceful lines as the captain's ship. The deck was long and straight, and the curving stern and horse-head-sculpted stem rose high above the water. The captain's razor-sharp eyes picked out important differences between the two ships. The strange craft had been built for trade and modified for war.

The stranger's bow was bound with bronze rather than wood, creating a beak that could tear the heart out of the strongest-built ship. The massive scull and prow oars clamped to the hull could serve as battering rams.

The Scythian commander came up to the captain. "Should we send a boarding party?"

The captain pondered the question. A Phoenician ship should pose no threat, but there was no reason for the vessel to be where it was. Its actions, while not hostile, were certain not friendly.

"No," the captain said. "We wait."

Five minutes passed. Then ten. After twenty minutes, figures could be seen climbing down a ladder into the warship's utility boat. The boat approached to within earshot. There were four men at the oars. A fifth stood with legs wide in the prow, his purple cloak billowing out behind him like a loose sail. He cupped his hands to his mouth.

"Greetings, my brother," he shouted across the water.

"Greetings to you, brother," the captain said with surprise. "How came you here?"

A look of mock incredulity appeared on the man's face. He pointed to the warship. "I came as you did, Menelik, in a ship of Tarshish."

"For what purpose, Melqart?"

"To join forces once again, dear brother."

The captain's face betrayed no emotion, but his dark eyes smoldered with anger. "You *knew* of my mission?"

"We are family, are we not? There are no secrets among kin."

"Then make no secret to me of your wishes."

"Yes, of course. Come aboard my ship and we'll talk."

"My ship's hospitality is open to you as well."

The man in purple laughed. "It's obvious that we lack brotherly trust."

"Maybe that's because we are only *half* brothers."

"We share the same blood, nonetheless." Melqart pointed to the island. "Let us stop this childish discussion and meet on neutral ground to talk."

The captain studied the island. Unlike most of the heavily treed shoreline, the sandy riverbank was flat for a few hundred feet before rising into a low, grassy ridge.

"Very well," he shouted.

The captain told Tarsa to round up a landing party. Tarsa picked four of his most battle-hardened men. Minutes later, the utility boat nudged up to the riverbank. The Scythians stayed with the boat while the captain strode up the sloping beach.

His half brother stood a hundred feet from the shore with arms crossed. He was dressed in full Phoenician regalia, with a richly patterned two-piece tunic under his purple cloak and a conical cap on his head. A gold collar encircled his neck, and his arms and fingers were adorned with gold.

He was the captain's equal in height, and his handsome face bore a sharp resemblance to his brother's, with its prominent nose, dark complexion, wavy hair and beard. There were major differences, however. The captain's regal bearing came across as imperious and arrogant while his half brother's features were brutish rather than strong. His dark eyes had no depth or softness. His prominent chin hinted at stubbornness rather than determination.

"How wonderful to see you after all these years, dear brother," Melqart said, with an engaging smile that had more slyness than charm in it.

The captain was in no mood for insincere niceties. "Why are you here?" he demanded.

"Perhaps our father decided that you needed help on your mission."

"He would never have trusted you."

"He obviously entrusted you, and you're a thief."

The captain's cheeks burned at the insult, but he held his anger in check. "You haven't answered my question."

His half brother shrugged. "I learned that you were on the move. I tried to intercept you, but your ship was too fast and we fell behind."

"Why has your ship been fit for war?"

"These are dangerous waters."

"You defy our father by coming here. This would not be his wish."

"Our *father.*" He spit out the words. "Our father was a womanizer who slept with your whore of a mother."

"And *your* whore of a mother as well?"

Melqart pulled his purple robe back. His hand started toward the pommel of his sword, but he thought better of it and drew his hand it back. "We are foolish to quarrel over family matters," he soothed. "Let us go back to my ship. I will serve you refreshments, and we can talk."

"There is nothing to talk about. You will turn your ship back. We will follow."

The captain spun on his heel and strode back toward the river. He kept his ear cocked for footfalls, in the unlikely event that his brother found the courage to attack him. But the only sound he heard was Tarsa, who cried out:

"Captain! Behind you!"

The Scythian had seen a dozen or so figures rise from the grassy ridge behind the beach.

The captain wheeled as the men sprinted in his direction. Tattoos decorated their shoulders and chests.

Thracians.

Another fierce-eyed race that hired out its skills with the sword and javelin to the Phoenician navies. The Thracians swept by his half brother, who urged them on:

"Kill him! Kill him!"

The captain drew his short broadsword as the screaming Thracians quickly encircled him.

He pivoted to face his attackers, but he couldn't guard his back. A Thracian moved in with his javelin in throwing position, only to stop short and drop his weapon. Clutching at the feathered shaft protruding from his throat, he let out a wet cough, sank to his knees, and fell forward face-first into the sand.

Tarsa calmly notched another arrow to his bowstring. With no more effort than taking a breath, he killed a second Thracian. The others scattered.

Tarsa's bowmen unleashed a deadly rain of arrows that found their mark in the backs of the fleeing Thracians.

The captain let out a mighty war cry and ran up the beach. He swung his sword in a powerful blow that would have decapitated his half brother if Melqart hadn't sideslipped the blade in a desperate parry. Under the flurry of blows that followed, Melqart tripped over his robes and fell in the soft sand.

He rolled onto his back and threw his sword aside. "Don't kill me, my brother."

The captain hesitated. Evil as he was, Melqart was still a blood relative.

Tarsa shouted another warning.

A second wave of Thracians had appeared on the ridge to reinforce the first line of attackers.

The captain backed off and dashed for the boat, leaping over the dead bodies of the attackers.

The Scythians unleashed their last arrows. The hastily aimed shots slowed the Thracians' advance but didn't stop it.

Tarsa threw his bow aside, grabbed the captain in his powerful arms, and lifted him into the boat. The rowers pulled at the oars and put the boat quickly out of range of the javelins, which splashed harmlessly into the water behind them.

The captain climbed onto the deck of his ship. The lookout man was handing out spears and swords, which he had neatly organized in an on-deck weapons room.

Melqart's boat pushed off from the beach with the last of the Thracians. The wicker fence on board the warship dropped to reveal at least a hundred men on a raised combat deck.

The sun glinted off their spear tips. Their shields were hung over the balustrade to create a defensive wall. The captain saw plumes of smoke rising from the deck and ordered urns of water placed around the ship.

Trailed by thin streaks of smoke, flaming arrows dipped in pitch rose from the ship and arced down from the skies in a fiery shower.

No arrow found a human target, but some stuck in the sides and deck of the ship. The flames were doused with water from the urns, but another volley followed the first, and some of the flaming arrows landed in the furled sail.

Crewmen pulled the sail onto the deck and stamped on the blazing cloth, ignoring the glowing embers that burned their feet and legs.

The captain barked an order to lift anchor. As the Scythians unleashed a deadly volley of arrows for cover, the rowers moved the ship backward out of range of the fire arrows. But the awkward maneuver left the ship broadside to the other vessel.

Flames from the sail were spreading. The captain knew that his vessel was doomed. Ships were made of wood, hemp, pitch, and cloth. Within minutes, the vessel would become a huge flaming torch.

The warship was preparing to come in for the kill.

The large oars at both ends of the ship were being used to swing the vessel rapidly around in a hundred-eighty-degree turn that would bring the bronze battering ram into play.

The ram would punch a hole in the burning ship. Once the ship foundered, it would be peppered with more fire arrows. Grenades filled with flaming oil would be suspended from the bow on poles.

The captain ordered the helmsmen to turn the ship. When the bow pointed downstream, he yelled to the rowers.

"Full speed ahead!"

The ship lurched like a lazy whale and gained speed. The enemy vessel was still turning, and would never be in a more-vulnerable position. Although the prow of the captain's ship was not sheathed with metal, the thick Lebanese timbers could be used with deadly effect.

Hooves thundered amid the shouts of men. The horses had broken loose from their stable and had climbed up a ramp onto the deck. The Scythians dropped their bows and tried to drive the horses back below. The animals reared and rolled their eyes, more frightened of the smoke and fire than of the noisy human beings.

The ships were yards apart. The captain could see a figure in purple striding from one end of the deck to the other as Melqart urged his crew to move faster.

The burning vessel crunched into the warship. The captain lost his footing and fell to his knees but quickly climbed back to his feet. The horse-head figurehead hung at an angle. The ship had bounced back and was swinging so that its hull would be side by side with the other vessel. Enemy archers could pick them off at will. Spear-carrying warriors would swarm aboard to finish the job.

Discipline had broken down on his ship. Men ran about the burning deck trying to avoid being cremated or trampled by the rampaging horses.

The ships crunched up against one another.

A gust of wind cleared the smoke for an instant. The captain saw the grinning face of his brother staring at him from only a few yards away.

Galvanized, the captain waded along the main deck through clouds of smoke and tried to rally his panicked crew.

A horse reared up on front of the captain, and he had to draw back to avoid being crushed. Suddenly inspired, he plucked a shred of burning sail from the deck and waved it at the horse. The animal reared, and pawed the air with its sharp hooves. He yelled at the Scythians to follow his lead.

A ragged line formed. Shouting and brandishing pieces of flaming cloth or leather shirts in the air, they herded the horses against the low ship's rail.

Tattooed Thracians lined the rail on the other vessel, their eyes glittering in anticipation of the massacre to come. But then the horses half leaped and half climbed over the rail and onto the deck of the warship. The animals crashed through the line of warriors and raced madly from one end of the deck to the other, trampling anyone in their way.

The captain vaulted over the rail, with the Scythians close behind. A quick thrust of his sword dropped the first man he encountered. Then his entire crew swarmed aboard. The Thracians drew back in confusion under the fierce attack.

The captain's face was black with soot. He was bleeding from several nonfatal sword and spear wounds, but he moved inexorably toward Melqart, who had seen the tide of battle turn and was trying to find safety at the raised aft end of ship. Menelik climbed a short ladder to the stern where his half brother cowered.

This time he would not hesitate to deliver the fatal blow.

As his sword struck living flesh, however, something hard crashed into the captain's skull, and he crumpled to the deck, a curtain of blackness falling over his eyes.

LATER, when the last trace of the battle had bubbled to the surface, the silent witness who had been hiding in the grass made his way cautiously along the beach not far from where he had first seen the horse-head monster.

All was quiet. The cries of pain and agony and the clash of weapons had faded. There was only the soft ripple of water along the riverbank, which was littered with the dead. He went from body to body, ignoring gold ornaments in favor of more-useful items.

He was bending over to pick up more booty when he heard a pitiful meow. The soggy mass of yellowish orange fur had its claws dug into a charred board. The hunter had never seen a cat before, and, for a moment, he considered killing it. But he relented and instead wrapped the animal in a soft leather cloth.

When he could carry no more, he stole away, leaving only his footprints in the sand.

THE WHITE HOUSE, 1809

THE EXECUTIVE MANSION ON Pennsylvania Avenue was dark except for the study, where a crackling fire in the hearth kept the winter chill at bay. The flickering yellow firelight bathed the high-nosed profile of the man who sat at a desk, humming as he worked.

Thomas Jefferson glanced at the wall clock with the bright blue-gray eyes whose intensity often startled those who met him for the first time. It was two in the morning; he usually retired at ten. He had been working in the study since six o'clock in the evening, having risen at dawn.

The president had taken his afternoon ride around Washington on his favorite horse, Eagle, and still wore his riding clothes: a comfortable, worn brown jacket, red waistcoat, corduroy pants, and woolen socks. He had exchanged his riding boots for the slippers without heels that had shocked foreign envoys who'd expected more-regal footwear gracing the presidential feet.

The president's long arm reached out to a cabinet. The doors flew open at the touch of his finger, a feature that appealed to Jefferson's love of gadgetry. Stacked neatly inside the cabinet were a cut-glass goblet, a decanter filled with French red wine, a plate of cakes, and a night candle used to navigate the corridors back to his bedroom. He poured half a glass of wine, held it dreamily to the light, and took a sip that brought back fond memories of Paris.

Tomorrow could not come too soon. Within hours, the onerous burden of office would be shifted to the narrow but capable shoulders of his friend James Madison.

He savored another sip and returned to the papers spread out on his desk. Written in the same flowing hand that had penned the Declaration of Independence were specimens, arranged in columns, of more than fifty Indian vocabularies collected over a thirty-year period.

Jefferson had long been obsessed with the question of how the Indians came to North America and had spent years compiling lists of words commonly used in Indian languages and dialects. His theory was that similarities between words from the Old and New World might offer a clue to the Indians' origin.

Jefferson had shamelessly exercised his presidential power in pursuit of his obsession. He had once invited five Cherokee chiefs to a White House reception and quizzed them about their language. He had instructed Meriwether Lewis to collect vocabularies from the Indians the explorer encountered on his historic journey to the Pacific Ocean.

The book Jefferson planned to write on the origins of the Indian would be the culmination of his intellectual career. The tumultuous events of his second term had temporarily stalled the project, and he had put off sending the lists to the printer until he could write digests of the reams of new material Lewis and Clark had brought back from their trek.

Vowing to tend to the task as soon as he was back at Monticello, he stacked the papers into a neat pile, tied it with string, and placed it with the other vocabularies and stationery in a sturdy trunk. It would be transported with his belongings to the James River and loaded onto a boat that would take his baggage to Monticello. He placed the last packet of documents in the trunk and snapped the cover shut.

His desk was clear now except for a pewter box that had his name embossed on the lid. The president opened the box and removed a rectangular piece of vellum about ten by twelve inches in size. He held the soft animal hide close to an oil lamp. The pebbled surface was covered with strange writing, wavy lines, and Xs. One edge was ragged.

He had acquired the vellum in 1791. He and his Virginia neighbor "Jemmy" Madison had ridden on horseback to Long Island, New York, to meet some impoverished remnants of the Unkechaug tribe. Jefferson had hoped to find someone who knew the ancient languages of the Algonquin tribe, and, in fact, three elderly women could still speak the old language. Jefferson had compiled a glossary from them that he hoped would help prove his thesis about the European origin of the Indians.

The chief of the tribe had presented Jefferson with the vellum, saying it had been passed down from generation to generation. Touched by the gesture, Jefferson had asked a rich landowner and fellow signer of the Declaration to provide for the Indians.

Looking at the vellum now, an idea occurred to him. He took it over to a table, where a horizontal wooden easel had two pens suspended from a framework that allowed them to move simultaneously. Jefferson regularly used this copying machine, known as a polygraph, for his voluminous correspondence.

He copied the vellum markings and added notes asking the recipient to identify the language in which the words were written. Then he addressed and sealed the envelopes and placed them in a basket for outgoing mail.

The Unkechaug word lists were packed with the other papers in

the trunk. Jefferson wanted to keep the vellum close, and he placed
it back in the box. He would carry the box in his saddlebags on the
ride to Monticello. He glanced at the wall clock again, drained his
wineglass, and rose from his chair.

At the age of sixty-five, Jefferson hadn't an ounce of surplus flesh
on his farmer's body. His thick hair was going from reddish blond
to sandy gray as he aged. With his square-shouldered, musket-barrel
posture and six-foot-two-inch height, he would always be an imposing figure. Inflammatory arthritis was making inroads, but, after
he worked the stiffness out of his limbs, his movements were flexi-
ble and easy, and he moved with the grace of a younger man.

He lit his night candle and made his way along the silent White
House corridors to his bedroom.

Up at dawn, he rode to the new president's inauguration with his
usual lack of pomp and ceremony. With a touch of his hat, he simply galloped past the waiting cavalry escort, dismounted near the
Capitol, and hitched his horse to a picket fence. He sat with the public during the inauguration. Later, he paid a farewell visit at the
White House. At the inaugural ball he danced with Dolley Madison.

The next day he finished packing, making certain in particular
that the trunk with his Indian material was on the wagon that would
take it to the James River. Setting off on horseback for Monticello,
he rode eight hours through a driving snowstorm in his eagerness
to resume life as a country gentleman.

*The watcher stood in the shadow of a snow-covered oak tree near the
edge of the James River, where several cargo boats were tied up for
the night. Raucous laughter emanated from a nearby tavern. The
voices were growing louder, and he judged from personal experience
that the boat crews had reached the last stage before drinking themselves senseless.*

He emerged from the protection of darkness and made his way over the snow-covered ground to a boat that was outlined faintly in the flickering light of its stern lantern. The fifty-foot-long bateau was a narrow, flat-bottomed craft designed to move tobacco along the river.

He stood on shore and called out, receiving no answer. Enticed by the prospects of drink, a warm fire, and female company, the captain had gone ashore with the two pole men who worked the riverboat. Crime was practically unknown in this remote part of the river, and none of the boats felt the need to leave crew aboard on this cold night.

The watcher padded up the ramp and used the lamp hanging from the stern to light his way as he ducked under an arched awning covering the central part of the deck. The awning sheltered more than two dozen bundles stenciled with the initials TJ. He set the light down and began to go through the baggage and boxes.

He pried a trunk open with a knife and pulled out a handful of the papers neatly packed inside. As he'd been instructed, he stuffed the papers into a large sack and threw a handful onto the riverbank. He tossed more papers into the river, where they drifted out of sight on the swift currents.

The man grinned at his accomplishment. With a quick glance toward the noisy tavern, he crept silently down the gangway onto the riverbank and melted like a ghost into the darkness.

SOON AFTER, Jefferson was returning to Monticello with friends and saw his house slaves unloading boxes from a wagon drawn close to the mansion's columned entrance. As he rode closer, he recognized a stocky, bearded figure as the captain of the James River boat carrying his baggage from Washington.

He dismounted and strode to the wagon, but, in his excitement at seeing his baggage arrive, he didn't notice the boatman's stricken expression. He rapped his knuckles on the side of the wagon. "Good work, Captain. All arrived safe and sound, I see."

The captain's round face crumpled like an overripe pumpkin. "Not all, I'm sorry to say, sir," he mumbled.

"What do you mean?"

The captain seemed to shrink into himself. Jefferson towered over the riverman by several inches and would have been a formidable figure even if he hadn't been the former president of the United States. He seemed to bore holes right through the hapless captain with eyes almost luminous in their intensity.

As the riverman told his story, he wrung his hat so tight it was a wonder that he didn't tear it into pieces.

Jefferson's trunk had been vandalized on the last leg of the boat's journey while ascending the river above Richmond. The thief had boarded the boat while it was tied up and the crew was sleeping on shore, the captain said. A trunk had been emptied. The captain handed Jefferson some mud-smeared papers, explaining that they had been found on the riverbank.

Jefferson stared at the wet wad in his hand.

Barely able to get the words out, he said, "Nothing else stolen?"

"No, sir." The captain brightened at the opportunity to point out the silver lining. "Only the one trunk."

Only the one trunk.

The words echoed in Jefferson's ears as if they were being spoken in a cave.

"Tell me where you found this," he demanded.

Moments later, Jefferson and his friends galloped off, and rode until they came to the river, then fanned out along both sides. After an intensive search, they fished out some papers that had floated ashore. Except for a few sheets, the mud-caked specimens of Indian vocabularies were water-damaged beyond use.

Later that summer, a petty thief and drunk was arrested and charged with the crime. The man claimed he had been hired by a stranger to steal the papers and pretend they were destroyed.

Jefferson was glad the culprit had been caught and might be hanged. He took no interest in the man's fate. The scoundrel had caused him an irreparable loss. Jefferson had more pressing problems, such as tending his long-neglected fields and trying to figure out how to pay his mounting debts.

That was all changed months later when a letter arrived in the mail.

Jefferson had received several replies from the notes he had mailed from the White House to members of the Philosophical Society. All expressed their puzzlement at the word lists Jefferson had transcribed from the vellum. Except for one.

Professor Holmberg was a linguist at Oxford University. He apologized for not answering Jefferson sooner but he had been traveling in North Africa. He knew exactly what language the words were written in and enclosed translations.

Jefferson's eyes widened as he read Holmberg's findings. With the letter in hand, he roamed his library and plucked volume after volume from his bookshelves. History. Language. Religion.

He spent the next several hours reading and making notes. When he had pushed away the last book, he sat back in his chair, tented his fingers, and stared into space. After a moment lost in thought, Jefferson silently mouthed a familar name.

Meriwether Lewis.

FATE HAD NOT dealt kindly with the man who had led the expedition that opened the floodgates of the American West to United States expansion.

Lewis was a man of extraordinary talents. Jefferson had been aware of his fellow Virginian's qualities when he'd asked Lewis to lead the exploratory expedition to the Pacific Coast in 1803.

Educated, intrepid, versed in the sciences, tough physically, Lewis was an outdoorsman familiar with Indian customs, and possessed of a sterling character. He'd been a well-respected army captain before he had come to work for Jefferson in the White House, where he added diplomacy, statesmanship, and politics to his quiver of talents.

The expedition had been successful beyond belief. After Lewis returned to Washington in 1806 with William Clark, the expedition's coleader, Jefferson appointed him as governor of the Louisiana Territory.

Lewis had reason to wonder, however, whether the appointment was a reward or a punishment. Even with all his talents and energy, Lewis had a hard time trying to tame the wild frontier. The explorer's political enemies were relentless.

One night, after Lewis had spent another wearying day dealing with charges that he'd spent government money on a fur company in which he had an interest, he saw a sealed packet on his desk and immediately recognized Jefferson's handwriting. Lewis had a smile on his hawk-nosed face as he slid a knife blade under the seal and carefully unwrapped the stiff paper that enclosed a stack of documents. The note inside said:

My Dear Mr. Lewis. Your gardens might benefit from the information contained within. TJ

The next page was entitled "The Cultivation of Artichokes." The pages contained a detailed treatise, complete with planting tables and a garden diagram.

He spread the contents of the packet on his desktop, his brow wrinkled in puzzlement. Lewis knew of Jefferson's interest in gardening, but it seemed strange that he would take the trouble to send information on artichoke cultivation halfway across the continent. He must have known that Lewis's crushing responsibilities left no time for gardening.

Then the light of comprehension dawned on Lewis's long face and his pulse quickened. He pawed through the shelves of a cabinet where he had stored the reports from the Lewis and Clark expedition and found what he was looking for within minutes.

Sandwiched between two bundles of documents was a sheet of heavy paper, which he extracted and held up to the light. The sheet was perforated with dozens of small rectangular holes, and, with trembling fingers, he placed the matrix over the first written page in the artichoke file and copied the letters that showed through the holes onto a separate sheet of paper.

When Jefferson had conceived the idea for the Pacific expedition, he knew that Lewis would be in a diplomatically sensitive position exploring territory held by France and Spain. Behind Jefferson's sphinxlike imperturbability was a mind as devious as any to be found in the courts and palaces of Europe. In corresponding with his minister to France, he had often used a cipher, which he described as "a mask when we need it."

While Lewis was in Philadelphia preparing for his journey with leading scientists from the Philosophical Society, Jefferson sent him a cipher he had worked up for the expedition. He based the encryption method on the Vigenere cipher widely used in Europe. The system involved an alphanumeric table and was unlocked with a key word.

Artichokes.

It had not been necessary to use the cipher during the expedition, which was why Lewis had been baffled at seeing it utilized. Casting questions aside now, he attacked the enciphered message with the enthusiasm he brought to all challenges. As he deciphered each letter from the gibberish, the words began to form before his eyes.

Dear Mr. Lewis: I hope this missive finds you well. I have taken the liberty of submitting this report to you in the enciphered form upon which we had agreed, with the goal that it should be for your eyes only, and for your sole disposition. I fear that the information enclosed, whether true or not, would excite certain passions, cause men to go into territory where they were ill-prepared to survive, and create problems with the Indians. I understood that you are fully engaged in the formidable task of placing a harness on the Louisiana stallion, but plead your assistance in resolving this matter.

Y'r ob'd'nt s'v'nt, TJ

Lewis deciphered the balance of the encrypted message. Then he went back to the garden diagram. The lines, Xs, circles, and words penned in an ancient language began to make sense of sorts. He was looking at a map—and something about it struck him as familiar. He pawed through dozens of his charts and documents and found what he was looking for.

Taking up pen and paper, he wrote a brief note. He thanked Jefferson for his gardening advice, and said he had located an ideal spot for his crop to flourish, then he told Jefferson that he would discuss gardening when he came to Washington to clear his name. Lewis planned to start down the Mississippi River early in September 1809. He would let Jefferson know when he had arrived in Washington.

It was not to be. Late that fall, Jefferson received a note from a

Major Neelly saying that Lewis had died of gunshot wounds on the Natchez Trace wilderness road. He was only thirty-five.

The loss of the talented young man was incomprehensible to Jefferson. It almost seemed as if an ancient curse hovered over the Indian vocabularies. Several weeks later, Major Neelly arrived at Monticello with Lewis's young slave. While Neelly was cleaning up from his ride, the slave timidly handed Jefferson a packet and whispered a message.

Instructing his staff that he not be disturbed, Jefferson locked himself in his study and studied the packet's contents. Then he compiled a thorough written analysis of the events leading to Lewis's death. The dawn's light was streaming through the windows as he summed up the synopsis in a single underlined word.

Conspiracy.

What if his Indian word lists had been *stolen,* as the thief had claimed? What if someone knew that Jefferson's research held the key to an age-old secret? What if the death of Lewis were not a suicide but murder?

Jefferson spent several more days working in his study. When he emerged, brandishing a list of instructions for his staff, he seemed like a man possessed. One night, under cover of darkness, he rode off on his horse, followed in a wagon by his most trusted slaves. Weeks later, they returned, looking tired and disheveled, but there was a glint of triumph in Jefferson's eye.

He considered the implications of his discovery. He had done everything in his power to keep the United States from being contaminated by the deadly alliance of church and state that had spawned the religious wars which had raged on the continent. He feared that if this information were made public it could shake the foundations of the young country and even destroy the fledgling republic he had helped create.

Without pausing to clean up or change, Jefferson plunged into his study and penned a long letter to his old friend and sometimes nemesis, John Adams. As he sealed the envelope, a smile crossed his weary face.

He could play at the conspiracy game as well as anyone.

CHAPTER

1

BAGHDAD, IRAQ, 2003

CARINA MECHADI WAS INCANDESCENT with rage. The young Italian woman threw off sparks like a Roman candle as she surveyed the rubble that littered the administrative offices of the Iraqi National Museum. Cabinets had been overturned. Files were scattered as if they'd been caught up in a whirlwind. Desks and chairs had been smashed to splinters. The vindictiveness of the destruction was appalling.

Carina unleashed a withering outburst that dissected the parentage, sexual orientation, and prowess of the vandals who had wreaked such senseless havoc.

The wave of blue language washed over the young U.S. Marine corporal who had been hovering protectively nearby cradling an M4 carbine in his arms. The only two Italian words the marine knew were *pepperoni* and *pizza*. He didn't need a lexicon to tell him that he'd witnessed a display of razor-edged invective worthy of a longshoreman with a sore back.

The muscular language was all the more amazing considering its source. Carina was a foot shorter than the marine. The battle gear the military people had insisted she wear made the slender woman appear even smaller. She looked like a turtle too small for its shell in the borrowed flak jacket. The desert-camouflage uniform was meant for a small man. The helmet that concealed her long sable hair sat so low it almost hid her cornflower blue eyes.

Carina noticed the marine's astonished grin. She blushed with embarrassment and brought her tirade to a halt. "Sorry about that."

"No problem, ma'am," the corporal said. "You ever want to be a drill instructor, the Marine Corps would be glad to have you."

The heat faded from her dusky face. Full lips that seemed better suited for seduction than for swearing widened in a broad smile that revealed perfect white teeth. With the fire in her words extinguished, her voice was low and cool. Speaking with a slight accent, she said, "Thank you for the offer, Corporal O'Leary." She glanced at the rubble at her feet. "As you can see, I'm quite passionate when it comes to this sort of thing."

"Don't blame you for being pissed—" The marine's cheeks flushed and he glanced away. "Excuse me, I mean for being *mad,* ma'am. Hell of a mess."

Saddam Hussein's elite Republican Guard had set up a defensive position in the eleven-acre museum complex in the heart of Baghdad on the western bank of the Tigris. The Iraqi troops had run for their lives in the face of the American advance, leaving the museum unguarded for thirty-six hours. Hundreds of plunderers had rampaged through the complex until they were chased out by the senior staff.

The Republican Guards had shed their uniforms and burned piles of identity cards in their hurry to return to civilian life. In a last gasp of defiance, someone had scrawled DEATH TO ALL AMERICANS on a courtyard wall.

"We've seen all we need to see here," Carina said with a grimace.

With Corporal O'Leary trailing a few paces behind, she plodded out of the administrative offices. Her leaden-footed gait was only partly the fault of the army boots on her feet. She was weighed down by a feeling of dread at what she would find, or *not* find, in the public gallery, where the museum's prize holdings were exhibited in more than five hundred display cases.

The walk down the long central corridor only served to heighten her fears. A number of sarcophagi had been cracked open and statues decapitated.

Carina set foot in the first gallery and the air involuntarily escaped from her lungs. She wandered from room to room as if in a daze. Every case looked as if it had been vacuumed clean.

She entered a gallery that had held Babylonian artifacts. A portly, middle-aged man was bent over a smashed cabinet. Standing next to him was a young Iraqi, who raised his AK-47 when they entered.

The marine brought the carbine to his shoulder.

The heavyset man looked up and stared through thick lenses at the marine. There was disdain rather than fear in his eyes. His glance shifted to Carina and his face lit up in a fourteen-karat smile.

"My dear Miss Mechadi," he said with undisguised warmth.

"Hello, Dr. Nasir. Glad to see that you're all right." Carina turned to the marine. "Corporal, this is Mohammed Jassim Nasir. He's senior curator here at the museum. "

The marine lowered his weapon. After a pause to show that he had not been intimidated by the American, the Iraqi did the same with his gun. They continued to eye each other warily.

Nasir came over to clasp Carina's hands in his. "You shouldn't have come so soon. It is still dangerous."

"*You* are here, professor."

"Of *course*. This institution has been my lifeblood."

"I understand completely," Carina said. "But the area around the museum is secure." She nodded toward her marine escort. "Besides, Corporal O'Leary is keeping close watch on me."

Nasir's brow clouded over. "I hope this *gentleman* is a better guard than his friends were. If not for my brave colleagues the disaster would have been total."

Carina understood Nasir's anger. The American troops arrived four days after the museum's curators had told the commanders about the looting. Carina had tried desperately to have them move in sooner. She had waved the UNESCO identification card hanging around her neck under the noses of the American officers only to be told that the situation was too fluid and dangerous.

Carina saw no use arguing over who was to blame. The damage had already been done. "I've talked to the Americans," she said. "They said there would have been a bloody battle if they came in earlier."

Nasir shot a drop-dead glance in the marine's direction. "I understand. They were too busy guarding the oil wells." The unsympathetic expression on his nut-brown face suggested that he would have preferred bloodshed to looting.

"I'm as sickened as you are," she said. "This is terrible."

"Well, it's not as bad as it seems here," Nasir said with unexpected optimism. "The artifacts taken from this case were minor items. Fortunately, the museum had put together a contingency plan after the 1991 invasion. The curators moved most of the artifacts to safe rooms known only to the five most senior museum officers."

"That's wonderful, Professor!"

Nasir's sunny mood was short-lived. He tugged fretfully at his beard. "I wish the rest of the news were as good," he said with a doleful note in his voice. "Other parts of the museum did not fare as well. The thieves looted the greatest treasures of Mesopotamia. They took the sacred vase and the mask of Warka, the Bassetki statue, the ivory of the lioness attacking the Nubian, and the twin copper bulls."

"Those objects are priceless!"

"Unlike the petty thieves we chased out of the museum, the people who removed the more-valuable antiquities were sophisticated. They bypassed the Black Obelisk, for instance."

"They must have known that the original is in the Louvre."

Nasir's lips tightened in a grim smile. "They didn't touch *any* copies. They were very organized and selective. Come, I'll show you."

Nasir led the way to the aboveground storage rooms. The shelves lining the walls were empty. Dozens of jars, vessels, and shards littered the floor. Carina kicked away an army uniform.

"The Republican Guards spent time here as well," she said. "Any idea of how much is missing?"

"It will take years to assess the loss. I'm estimating around three thousand or so pieces gone. I wish I could say that was the worst of it."

They walked into a gallery that displayed Roman antiquities. The professor pushed aside a corner shelf to reveal a hidden door whose glass paneling had been smashed and steel grate bent back. He fumbled in his pocket for a candle and a cigarette lighter. They descended the narrow set of stairs to metal doors that were wide-open, with no sign of forced entry. A wall sealed the space beyond the door. The concrete bricks had been pried away to make a large opening.

They climbed through the opening into a hot and airless room. An acrid stench assaulted their nostrils. Footprints on the dusty floor had been cordoned off with yellow tape placed at the crime scene by a team of investigators.

Carina glanced around. "Where are we?"

"The basement storage area. There are five rooms down here. Few people in the museum even know this place exists. That's why we thought the collection was safe. We were wrong, as you can see."

He moved the candle in an arc. Its yellow light fell upon dozens of plastic fishing boxes thrown willy-nilly around the room.

"I've never seen such absolute chaos," Carina whispered.

"The boxes held cylinder seals, beads, coins, glass bottles, amulets, and jewelry. Thousands of items are missing." He brought the candle over to dozens of larger plastic boxes that lined the walls. "They didn't bother with these. Apparently, they knew they were empty."

Corporal O'Leary surveyed the wreckage with a street fighter's eye for entrances and exits. "If you don't mind my asking sir, how'd they know how to find this place?"

Nasir's heavy features drooped and he gave a glum nod of his head. "You Americans aren't the only ones who have reason to be embarrassed. We suspect someone on our staff with intimate knowledge of the museum alerted the thieves to this room. We have fingerprinted our staff, except for the head of security, who has not come back to reclaim his job."

"I was wondering why I didn't see any evidence of the door being forced," Carina said.

"The thieves came into the basement the same way we did, but they had forgotten torches or never expected they would need them." He picked up a piece of burned rubber foam. "They used this material from upstairs for torchlight. The stuff burns quickly and the fumes would have been terrible. We found a set of keys on the floor. They probably dropped the keys and couldn't find them. They missed thirty cabinets with our best cylinder seals and tens of thousands of gold and silver coins. I'd guess about ten thousand excavated artifacts are missing. Hundreds of boxes were left intact, praise Allah."

They filed through a doorway into a larger space filled with antiquities of every size and shape. "These are objects that were given a preliminary identification and were to be absorbed into the main collection as work allowed. Some have been stored here for years."

"The footprints lead in here," Carina said.

"The thieves evidently thought there was something of value

in this room. We would have no way of knowing until we go over our inventory. We are far too busy trying to retrieve more precious items."

"I heard there was an amnesty," she said.

"That's right. It has somewhat restored some of my faith in human nature. People have brought in thousands of items, including the mask of Warka. I expect that objects will continue to be returned, but, as you know, the most valuable ones are probably in the possession of some wealthy collector in New York or London."

Carina sighed in agreement. The thefts had been carefully planned. The invasion took weeks to gear up. Unscrupulous dealers in Europe and the United States could take advance orders for specific objects from rich clients.

The antiquities business had become almost as lucrative as drug trafficking. London and New York were the main markets. Stolen antiquities from illegal excavations in Greece, Italy, and South America were often laundered through Switzerland, where objects can gain legal title after only five years in the country.

Carina stood in silence amid the empty boxes, apparently lost in thought. After a moment, she said, "Perhaps I can speed up the amnesty process."

"But *how*? We have spread the word far and wide."

She turned to the marine. "I'll need your help, Corporal O'Leary."

"I was ordered to comply with any request you asked for, ma'am."

Carina spread her lips in a mysterious smile. "I was *counting* on that."

CHAPTER

2

THE PAVEMENT SHOOK UNDER the treads of the twenty-five-ton Bradley Fighting Vehicle, warning of the troop carrier's approach long before it rumbled into view. By the time the vehicle had turned the corner and rolled down the boulevard, the man who'd been making his way along the deserted storefronts had slipped into an alley. He ducked into a doorway, where he would be invisible to the vehicle's night vision scope.

The man watched the vehicle until it disappeared around another corner before he ventured from the alley. The thud of bombs that had presaged the advance of the American-led forces had stopped. The rattle of small-arms fire was constant but sporadic. Except for the firefights that ensued as the invaders mopped up pockets of resistance, there had been a pause in the battle as the coalition and the remnants of the defenders considered their next step.

He passed a defaced statue of Saddam Hussein, and walked another ten minutes until he came to a side street. Using a penlight that cast a thin red beam, he studied a city map, then he tucked the map and light back into his pocket and turned down the street.

Although he was a big man, several inches over six feet, he moved through the pitch-dark city as silently as a shadow. His stealth was a skill he had developed through weeks of training at a camp run by former members of the French Foreign Legion, U.S. Delta Force, and British Special Ops. He could infiltrate the most heavily guarded installation to carry out his mission. Although he was adept in the use of a dozen different methods of assassination, his weapon of choice was the crushing strength in his large, thick-fingered hands.

He had come a long way from his humble beginnings. His family had been living in a small town in the south of Spain when his benefactor found him. He'd been in his late teens and working in a slaughterhouse. He enjoyed the work of dispatching everything from chickens to cows and tried to bring some creativity to the task whenever he could, but something in him yearned for greater things.

It almost hadn't happened. He had strangled an annoying coworker to death over a petty argument. Charged with murder, he had languished in jail while headlines made much of the fact that he was the son of the man who had been Spain's official garroter back in the days when strangulation was the state-approved method of execution.

One day, the man who would become his benefactor arrived at the jailhouse in a chauffeur-driven car. He sat in the cell and told the young man, "You have a proud and glorious past and a great future."

The youth listened with rapt attention as the stranger talked about the family's service to the state. He knew that the youth's father had been put out of work after the garrote machine was retired in 1974, how he had changed his name and retreated to a small farm, where the family pursued a pitiful, subsistence living, and died, penniless and brokenhearted, leaving a widow and child.

His benefactor wanted the young man to work for him. He paid off the jailers and the judge, gave the grieving family more money than the dead chicken plucker could have earned in a hundred lifetimes, and the charges against the young man disappeared. He was sent to a private school, where he learned several languages, and, after he graduated, he was trained in military skills. The professional killers who took him under their wing recognized, as had his benefactor, that he was a talented student. Soon he was being sent on solo missions to remove those who were selected by his benefactor. The phone call would come with instructions, the mission would be carried out, and money would be deposited in his Swiss bank account.

Before coming to Baghdad, he had murdered an activist priest who was stirring up opposition to one of his benefactor's mines in Peru. He'd been on his way back to Spain to meet his benefactor when he got the message to slip into Iraq ahead of the American invasion, and there he had taken up residence in a small hotel and made the necessary contacts.

He had been disappointed to learn that his assignment was not to kill but to arrange for the removal of an object from the Baghdad Museum. On the positive side, however, he had virtually a front-row seat to the invasion, with its resultant death and destruction.

He studied the map again and grunted with satisfaction. He was minutes away from his destination.

3

WITH ELECTRICAL POWER OUT in the city, Carina had a hard time finding the squat concrete building in the older section of Baghdad. She had been there once before, in daylight, and not in the middle of a war. The building's windows had been boarded over, giving it the aspect of a fortress. As she strode up to the thick wooden door, she could hear the pop of small-arms fire in the distance.

She tried the heavy cast-iron handle. The door was unlocked, and she pushed it open and stepped inside. The gauzy glow of oil lamps illuminated the faces of men hunched over backgammon boards and glasses of tea. The thick choking smoke produced by dozens of cigarettes and water pipes had taken only a slight edge off the sweaty odor of unwashed bodies.

The low murmur of male voices halted, as if a switch had been turned off. Although most of the unshaven faces were cloaked in shadow, she knew that she was the target of hostile eyes.

Two figures detached themselves from a dark corner like creatures crawling out of a swamp. One man slipped around behind her, shut the door, and cut off any possible escape. The other man confronted her head-on. Speaking in Arabic, he growled, "Who are you?"

His breath was foul with stale tobacco and garlic. Resisting the natural impulse to gag, Carina stood to her full five-foot-five-inch height. "Tell Ali that Mechadi wants to see him."

Female assertiveness had its limits with Arab males. An arm snaked around her neck from behind and squeezed tight. The man standing in front produced a knife and held it so close to her left eye that its sharp point was a blur.

She croaked out a feeble call for help.

The door opened with a crash. The arm relaxed around her neck. Corporal O'Leary stood in the doorway, the muzzle of his carbine pressed against the base of the door guard's skull. The marine had heard Carina over a walkie-talkie tuned to the same channel as the one clipped to her vest.

A Humvee was parked across the street. The vehicle's top lights were on, and those inside the teahouse had a clear view of the long barrel of the M2 machine gun mounted on the vehicle's roof. The gun was aimed at the door. A squad of marines stood in the street with rifles in attack position.

The marine kept his eyes on the man with the knife. "You okay, ma'am?"

"Yes, thank you," she said, rubbing her neck. "I'm fine."

"Crash course I took in Arabic didn't teach me how to tell this guy I will splatter his brains around the room if his friend doesn't drop the knife."

Carina did a rough but effective translation. The knife clattered to the floor, and the marine kicked it out of reach. The thugs almost tripped over themselves as they retreated back into the murk that had spawned them.

A voice called out in English from behind a curtain at the back of the teahouse.

"Peace be upon you."

Carina responded to the traditional Arabic greeting. "Peace be upon you, Ali."

A man emerged from between the dingy sheets of cotton that served as curtains and wove his way around the close-packed tables. The light from the Humvee fell on his pudgy face and fleshy nose. A circular knit cap covered his shaven head. His NEW YORK YANKEES T-shirt was too short for his ample body, exposing his hairy belly button.

"Welcome, Signorina Mechadi," he said. He clasped his palms together. "And to your friends, the same."

"Your man was about to stick a knife in my eye," Carina responded. "Is *that* how you welcome guests?"

Ali's small, cunning eyes surveyed Carina's body and lingered on her face. "You're wearing a military uniform," he said with an unctuous smile. "Perhaps he thought you were an enemy soldier."

Carina ignored Ali's comment. "I want to talk to you."

The Iraqi scratched a scraggly black beard that had bits of food caught in it. "Of *course*. Let us step out back and have some tea."

The marine spoke up. "Do you want me to go with you?"

"I'll be all right." Carina surveyed the room. "I wouldn't mind some insurance, however. As you can see, Ali's place doesn't attract the finest clientele."

The corporal grinned. He poked his head out the door and gave a wave. Several marines piled into the room and took up positions along the walls.

Ali held aside the grubby curtains, opened a metal door, and ushered Carina into a room bright with electric lights. A generator purred in another part of the building. Richly colored rugs covered the floor and walls. A television screen connected to an exterior security camera showed images of the street outside the building. The Humvee was clearly visible.

Ali gestured for Carina to take a seat on a platform piled with large velvet cushions. He offered her tea, which she refused. He poured a glass for himself.

"What brings you out for a visit in the middle of an invasion?"

She met his question with a hard gaze. "I came from the national museum. It's been looted of thousands of antiquities."

He lowered his glass in midsip. "That's *outrageous*! The national museum is the heart and soul of Iraqi's cultural heritage."

Carina laughed out loud at Ali's feigned shock. "You should have been an actor, Ali. You'd easily win an Academy Award on that line alone."

Ali had learned his acting skills as a professional wrestler. He had even wrestled in the United States under the name of Ali Babbas.

"How could you *think* I'd be involved in a heist like that?" He still used some of the American slang he had picked up from his wrestling days.

"No antiquity of value moves in and out of Iraq without your connivance or knowledge."

Ali had established a worldwide network of procurers, dealers, and collectors. He had cultivated the Saddam Hussein family, and was said to have acquired many objects for the collection of the psychopathic sons, Uday and Qusay.

"I only deal in *legal* objects. You can search the place if you want to."

"You're dishonest but not stupid, Ali. I'm not demanding the return of the minor artifacts. They're useless for museum purposes without reliable provenance." She drew a piece of paper from her pocket and handed it to Ali. "I want these objects. There's an amnesty. No questions asked."

He unfolded the paper with his thick fingers. His lips widened in a smile.

"I'm surprised you don't have the Brooklyn Bridge on this list."

"I already own it," Carina said. "Well?"

He handed the paper back. "Can't help you."

Carina tucked it back in her pocket and rose from the cushion. "Okay."

"Just *okay*? You're disappointing me, signorina. I expected you to be your usual pit bull self."

"I don't have time. I have to go talk to the Americans." She headed for the door.

He called after her. "The Americans will have their hands full trying to get the power and water back on." Carina kept walking. "They left the museum unguarded. Do you think they care about a petty thief like me?"

She put her hand on the doorknob. "I think they'll care a *great* deal when they learn of your ties to Saddam Hussein."

"*Everyone* in Iraq had ties to Saddam," Ali said with a guffaw. "I was careful to leave no record of my dealings."

"That doesn't matter. The Americans have had itchy trigger fingers since 9/11. I'd suggest that you vacate this building before they target it with one of their smart bombs."

Ali vaulted from his cushion and lumbered over. The sneer had been replaced by an expression of alarm. He reached out for the paper. "I'll see what I can do."

Carina pulled the list out of reach. "I've raised the ante. Make your calls now. Don't tell me that the phones are out. I know you have your own ways to communicate. I'll wait while you call your people."

Ali frowned and snatched the list from her hand. He went over and reached under his cushion and pulled out a portable radio. He made several calls, using innocuous language that didn't betray their purpose. After the last call, he clicked off the radio and set it down on the tea table.

"You will have what you want within forty-eight hours."

"Make it twenty-four hours," Carina said. "I can find my way out." She opened the door and flung a final taunt over her shoulder. "You should stock up on your supply of flashlight batteries."

"What do you mean?"

"While the idiots you hired were floundering around in the dark getting their fingers burned, they missed thirty cabinets with the museum's best cylinder seals and tens of thousands of gold and silver coins. *Ciao*." She gave a light laugh and disappeared through the curtains.

As Ali slammed the door behind her, a rug hanging on the wall pushed aside and a man stepped through a doorway into the room.

He was tall and powerfully built. His cherubic face seemed out of place with his cruel physique, as if his close-shaven head had been attached to the wrong body. Although there was plenty of room for his features on the broad face, eyes, nose, and mouth were squeezed close together, creating an effect that was childlike and grotesque at the same time.

"A formidable woman," said the man.

Ali spat his words out. "Carina Mechadi? She is nothing but a UNESCO busybody who thinks she can push me around."

The stranger glanced up at the television monitor and smiled mischievously as he watched the Humvee drive off with Carina and the marines. "From what I heard, she did exactly that."

"I survived Saddam and I can survive the Americans," Ali said with a fierce grin.

The man shifted his gaze back to the Arab. "I trust your difficulties won't endanger the matter we were discussing before she interrupted our negotiations."

"Not exactly."

"What do you mean?"

"There's been a glitch."

The man moved closer until he loomed over the Iraqi. "What *sort* of glitch?"

"The *Navigator* has been sold to another buyer."

"We ordered its removal from the museum, and paid you in advance. I came to Baghdad to close the deal."

"A buyer has come forth with a higher bid. I'll return your deposit. Perhaps I can persuade the buyer to part with the object, although the price is likely to be greater than the one we discussed."

The man's gaze seemed to drill through Ali's skull, but he maintained his smile. "You wouldn't be holding me up for more money?"

"If you don't want to make a deal, tough."

Ali was still fuming over his confrontation with Carina. His anger had dulled his street smarts; otherwise, he might have sensed the menace in the quiet tone when the man whispered, "I must have the statue."

For the first time, Ali noticed the disproportionately large hands that dangled from long, powerful-looking arms.

"I was just giving you a hard time," Ali said with a toothy smile. "Blame it on that Italian bitch. I'll call the warehouse on my hand radio and have the statue sent over."

He started toward the sitting area.

"Wait," the man said. Ali froze in midstep. The man's grin grew even wider as he picked up the pocket radio Ali had left on the table. "Is *this* what you're looking for?"

Ali lunged toward the seating platform and slipped his hand under a cushion. His fingers closed on the grip of his Beretta and slipped the pistol out from its hiding place.

The man moved with the swiftness of a hunting cheetah. He tossed the radio aside, grabbed Ali under the chin from behind, and twisted his arm. The pistol dropped from Ali's hand, his body bent backward like a horseshoe on an anvil.

"Tell me where to find the *Navigator* and I'll let you go. If you don't, I'll snap your spine."

Ali was a tough man but not a particularly courageous one. He needed only a few seconds of exquisite pain to convince him that no piece of art was worth his life. "Okay, okay, I'll tell you," he gasped. He spit out a location.

The man stopped twisting his arm. The pain eased up. Ali's hand drifted down to the dagger in his ankle sheath. As soon as he got free, he'd carve this creep like a pig. He never got the chance. The man's free hand joined the other under his chin and the fingers began to squeeze. The knee came up at the same time and dug into the small of his back.

"What are you doing? I thought we had a deal," Ali said, barely able to get the words out.

He was almost unconscious when he felt a dull snap. The grip on his chin loosened. Ali's head lolled on his chest like a rag doll's and he slumped to the floor. The man stepped over the still-twitching body and pushed aside the hanging rug that hid a back door to the building. Moments later, he disappeared in the maze of alleyways. It took him almost to dawn to make his way back to his hotel. He stood in the window, watching the smoke rise over the wounded city, and made a call on his satellite phone.

His benefactor's mellifluous voice came on the phone immediately.

"I've been waiting for your call, Adriano," he said.

"Sorry for the delay, sir. There were unexpected difficulties."

Adriano described every detail of his encounter with Ali. His benefactor would know if he were lying or shading the truth.

"I'm very disappointed, Adriano."

"I know, sir. I was under orders not to let the *Navigator* fall into anyone else's hands. This seemed to be the only way."

"You were absolutely right to follow orders. It is important that we find the object first. We have waited nearly three thousand years. A little more time won't matter."

Adriano breathed a sigh of relief. He had been trained not to feel pain or fear, but he was well aware of the fate of those who displeased his benefactor. "Do you want me to try to track it down?"

"No. I'll try to go through international channels once more. It's becoming too dangerous there for you."

"I've made arrangements to leave the country through Syria."

"Good." There was a pause at the other end of the line. "This woman, Carina Mechadi, may prove useful."

"In what way, sir?"

"We shall see, Adriano. We shall see."

The line went dead.

He grabbed his bag and closed the hotel-room door behind him. He planned to meet an oil smuggler who had promised to get him out of Iraq. In accordance with his standing orders to leave no trace of his passing, he would, of course, dispatch the man to Allah once he was safe across the border.

He smiled as he savored the prospect.

CHAPTER

4

FAIRFAX COUNTY, VIRGINIA, THE PRESENT

THE RED CORVETTE CONVERTIBLE swung off the road, with its stereo speakers blasting salsa music like a Tijuana jukebox on wheels. The car breezed along a driveway that ran past a Victorian mansion and lawns which looked as if they had been clipped with manicure scissors. Joe Zavala pulled his car up in front of an ornate boathouse built on the banks of the Potomac River and was about to slide out from behind the steering wheel when he heard the gunshot.

As a brilliant designer of undersea craft for the National Underwater and Marine Agency, Zavala ordinarily carried nothing more lethal than a laptop computer. But his years working for NUMA's Special Assignments Team had taught him the wisdom of the Boy Scout adage to be prepared. Zavala reached under the car seat, his fingers closed on a quick-release holster, and his hand came out with a Walther PPK handgun.

He got out of the car and made his way around the boathouse, moving with the stealth of a deer hunter. Pressing his back to the exterior wall, he edged his way to the corner and popped out into the open, gun extended with both hands and ready to find a target.

A broad-shouldered man dressed in tan shorts and white T-shirt was standing on the riverbank with his back to Zavala. The man held a pistol down by his thigh and was inspecting a paper bull's-eye pinned to a tree. A cloud of purple smoke hung in the air. The man slipped a pair of ear protectors off his head just as Zavala stepped on a twig. He turned at the snapping sound and saw Zavala creeping around the corner with the gun clutched in his hands.

Kurt Austin, Zavala's boss on NUMA's Special Assignments Team, grinned and said, "Going on a turkey shoot, Joe?"

Zavala lowered the gun and walked over to the tree to inspect the hole that had been punched slightly off the center ring of the target.

"*You're* the one who should be hunting turkeys, deadeye."

Austin removed his yellow protective shooting goggles to reveal blue eyes the color of coral under water. "I'll stick to stationary targets for now." He glanced at Zavala's pistol. "What's with the SWAT team imitation?"

Zavala tucked the gun into his belt. "You didn't tell me you'd turned your expensive riverfront property into a shooting gallery."

Austin blew the smoke away from the pistol barrel like a gunfighter who'd beaten his opponent to the draw.

"I couldn't wait to try out my new toy at a shooting range."

He handed the flintlock dueling pistol to Zavala, who inspected the walnut stock and the engraved octagonal barrel.

"Nice balance," he said, hefting the weapon. "How old is it?"

"It was made in 1785 by Robert Wogdon, a London gunsmith. He fashioned some of the most accurate dueling pistols of his day. You test a dueling pistol by dangling it down at arm's length. Then you bring it up quickly and hold it just long enough to check the sights and squeeze off a shot. It should be right on target."

Zavala aimed for another tree and clicked his tongue to simulate gunfire.

"Bull's-eye," Austin said.

Zavala handed the pistol back. "Didn't you tell me your pistol collection was complete?"

"Blame it on Rudi," Austin said with a shrug. Rudi Gunn was the assistant director of NUMA.

"All he said was to decompress after our last assignment," Zavala said.

"You make my case. Idle time is a dangerous thing in the hands of a collector." Austin ripped the target off the tree and tucked it into his pocket. "What brings you to Virginia? Run out of women to date in Washington?"

Zavala's quiet-spoken charm and dark good looks made him much in demand on the Washington dating scene. The corners of his mouth turned up slightly in his trademark smile.

"I won't say I've been living a monk's life because you'd never believe me. I stopped by to show you a project I started months ago."

"Project S? You can fill me in while we work on a couple of beers," Austin said.

He put the shooting gear in a bag, wrapped the pistol in a soft cloth, and led the way up a staircase to a wide deck that overlooked the river.

Austin had bought the boathouse near Langley when he was with a clandestine undersea unit of the CIA. The purchase was beyond his budget, but the panoramic view of the river had closed the deal, and he got the price down because the boathouse was a wreck. He had spent thousands of dollars and countless hours transforming it from a run-down repository for boats to a comfortable retreat from the demands of his job as director of the Special Assignments Team.

Austin got couple of cold Tecate beers from the refrigerator, went out to the deck and handed one to Zavala. They clinked bottles and took a swig of the Mexican brew. Zavala took a sheet of computer paper from his pocket, placed it on a table, and smoothed out the folds with his hand.

"What do you think of my new wet submersible?"

In a wet submersible, the pilot and passenger wore scuba gear and sat on the outside of the vehicle rather than inside an enclosed cockpit. Wet submersibles commonly echoed the shape of their dry counterparts, with propellers at one end of a torpedo-shaped vehicle, the pilot at the other end.

The vehicle that Zavala had designed had a long, sloping hood, tapering trunk, and a wraparound windshield. It had dual headlights, white, so-called cove panels on the side, and a two-toned interior. The submersible had four thrusters instead of wheels.

Austin cleared his throat. "If I didn't know this was a submersible, I'd swear it looked like a 1961 Corvette. *Your* 'Vette, in fact."

Zavala pinched his chin between his thumb and forefinger. "This is turquoise. My car is red."

"She looks fast," Austin said appraisingly.

"My car can do zero to sixty in about six seconds. This is a little slower. But she'll move out on or under the water and handles the curves as if they weren't there. She'll do everything a car can do except peel rubber."

"Why the departure from more, uh, conventional submersible models, like the saucer, torpedo, or bulbous shape?"

"Apart from the challenge, I wanted something I could use on NUMA assignments that would be fun to drive."

"Will this thing work?"

"Field trials have gone well. I've designed a complete vehicle transport, launch, and recovery system too. The prototype is on its way to Turkey. I'm going over in a week to help out with an underwater archaeological dig of an old port they found in Istanbul."

"A week should give us plenty of time."

"Time for *what*?" Zavala said, suddenly wary.

Austin handed Zavala a science magazine that was open to an article describing the work of a ship that lassoed and towed icebergs threatening Newfoundland oil and gas rigs.

"How would you like to join me on a cruise to Iceberg Alley?"

Zavala scanned the magazine article.

"I don't know, Kurt. Sounds mighty cold. Cabo might be more appealing to my warm-blooded Mexican American nature."

Austin gave Zavala a look of disgust. "C'mon, Joe. What would you be doing in Cabo? Lying on the beach sipping margaritas. Watching the sun set with your arm around a beautiful señorita. Same old same old. Where's your sense of adventure?"

"Actually, my friend, I was thinking of watching the sun come *up* as I sang my señorita love songs."

"You'd be pressing your luck," Austin said with a snort. "Don't forget, I've *heard* you sing."

Zavala harbored no illusions about his singing voice, which tended to be off-key. "Good point," he said with a sigh.

Austin picked up the magazine. "I don't want to push you into this, Joe."

Zavala knew from past experience that his colleague didn't push; he *leaned*. "*That* will be the day."

Austin smiled and said, "If you're interested, I need a quick decision. We'd leave tomorrow. I just got the okay. What do you say?"

Zavala rose from his chair and gathered up his submersible diagrams. "Thanks for the beer."

"Where are you going?"

Zavala headed for the door.

"*Home*. So I can pack my flannel jockstrap and a bottle of tequila."

CHAPTER
5

OWN THERE, MISTER, is tomb of queen."
The wizened Bedouin jabbed the air, his bony finger pointing to a fissure about a yard wide and two feet high in the side of the pockmarked limestone hill. The rough-edged layers of strata above and below the opening were like lips afflicted with a bad case of trench mouth.

Anthony Saxon got down on his hands and knees and peered into the hole. He pushed aside thoughts of poisonous snakes and spiders, unwound his turban, and pulled off his beige desert robe to reveal long pants and a shirt. He flicked on a flashlight, probed the darkness with its beam, and took a deep breath.

"Down the rabbit hole I go," he said with a carefree jauntiness.

Saxon dove into the opening, wriggling his lanky six-foot frame like a salamander, and disappeared from sight. The passageway sloped downward like a coal chute. Saxon experienced a claustrophobic moment of panic when the chute narrowed and he pictured himself stuck, but he shimmied his way through the tight squeeze with the use of creative finger-toe coordination.

To his relief, the passageway widened again. After crawling for about twenty feet, he popped out of the chute into the open. Mindful not to bump his head on a low ceiling, he slowly stood erect and explored his surroundings with the flashlight.

The bull's-eye of light fell on the mortared-stone-block wall of a rectangular space about as big as a two-car garage. There was an opening with a corbeled arch about five feet high on the opposite wall. He ducked through the breach and followed a passageway for around fifty feet until he came to a rectangular room about half the square footage of the first.

The dust that covered every surface started him on a coughing fit. When he recovered, he saw that the room was bare except for a wooden sarcophagus that was tipped on its side. The lid lay a few feet away. A vaguely human form swathed in bandages from head to toe was half tumbled out of the ancient casket. Saxon cursed under his breath. He had arrived centuries too late. Grave robbers had stripped the tomb of any valuables hundreds of years before he was born.

The sarcophagus lid was decorated with a painting of a young girl, probably in her late teens. She had dark, oversized eyes, a full mouth, and black hair tied back from her face. She looked vibrant and full of life. With gentle hands, he rolled the mummy back into the case. The dissected corpse felt like a dried bag of sticks. He righted the sarcophagus and slid the lid back on.

He ran the flashlight beam around the walls of the tomb and read the letters carved into the stone. The words they formed were in epigraphic Arabic of the first century A.D. Off by a thousand years. *"Crap,"* he muttered.

Saxon patted the sarcophagus cover. "Sleep well, sweetheart. Sorry to disturb you."

With a last, sad glance around the tomb, he followed the corridor back to the chute opening. He grunted his way through the tight spot and pulled his dust-covered body out of the hole into the hundred-degree heat. His pants were ripped, and his knees and elbows were scraped and bleeding.

The Bedouin had an expectant expression on his dark face.

"Bilqis?" he said.

Anthony Saxon responded with a belly laugh. *"Bilked,* is more like it."

The Bedouin's face fell. "No queen."

Saxon recalled the portrait on the sarcophagus. "A princess, maybe. But not my queen. Not Sheba."

A car horn beeped at the bottom of the hill. A man standing next to a beat-up old Land Rover had one hand in the car and the other waving in the air. Saxon waved back, slipped into his desert robe and turban, and led the way down the slope. The man blowing the horn in the sandblasted vehicle was an aristocratic-looking Arab whose upper lip was hidden under a luxuriant mustache.

"What's up, Mohammed?" Saxon said.

"Time to go," the Arab said. "Bad people come."

He brandished the barrel of the Kalashnikov automatic rifle toward a point about a half mile distance. An oncoming vehicle was kicking up a dust cloud.

"How do you know they're bad people?" Saxon asked.

"They *all* bad people around here," the Arab said with a gold-toothed smile. Without another word, he got behind the wheel of the car and started the engine.

Saxon had learned to respect Mohammed's skill at keeping him alive in the Wild West atmosphere of Yemen's backcountry. Every chieftain in the area seemed to have his own private army of brigands, and larceny and murder in his heart.

He slid onto the passenger seat. The Bedouin piled into the back.

Mohammed mashed the accelerator. The Land Rover kicked up dirt and sand. As the driver ground through the gears, he managed somehow to steer and hold on to his weapon as well.

Mohammed kept checking his rearview mirror. After several minutes, he patted the dashboard as if it were the neck of a trusty steed.

"We're okay," he said with a wide grin. "You find your queen?"

Saxon told him about the sarcophagus and the mummy of the young girl.

Mohammed jerked his thumb at the Bedouin in the backseat. "I told you. This son of a camel and his village are all crooks."

Thinking that he was being praised, the Bedouin displayed a toothless grin.

Saxon sighed and shifted his gaze to the barren countryside. The locale changed, but the scene was always the same. A native con man would tell him in excited tones that the queen he was looking for was literally beneath his nose. Saxon would make a hair-raising crawl into the middle of an ancient necropolis that the con man's forebears had looted hundreds of years before. He couldn't count the number of mummies he had encountered. He had met a lot of nice people along the way. Too bad they were all dead.

Saxon dug a few riales out of his shorts pocket. He handed the coins to the delighted Bedouin and declined the man's offer to show him another dead queen.

Mohammed dropped the Bedouin off at a cluster of desert tents, then he drove to the old city of Ma'arib. Saxon was staying at the Garden of the Two Paradises Hotel. He asked Mohammed to come by the hotel the next morning and they would decide on his plan.

After a hot shower, Saxon changed into long cotton slacks and shirt and went down to the lounge, his mouth feeling as if he'd swallowed a pound of desert sand. He sat at the bar and ordered a

Bombay Sapphire martini, and the drink's astringent sweetness washed the grit out of his throat.

He chatted with a couple of Texas oil company rednecks. A second martini revived his spirits, until one of the oilmen asked him what he was doing in Ma'arib.

Saxon could have responded that it was the last leg of a doomed quest to find the fabled Queen of Sheba among the ruins of old Ma'arib, the city that was said to be her home base.

He said simply, "I'm here to test the waters."

The oilmen exchanged puzzled glances and then broke into hearty laughter. Before they headed back to their quarters, they bought Saxon a third martini.

Saxon was at that wonderful point where all brain activity was clouded by an alcoholic haze when an elderly bellhop shuffled into the bar and handed him a sheet of hotel stationery with a brief message scrawled on it:

I believe I can introduce you to the man of the sea. If you are still interested in meeting him let me know soonest.

He blinked the blurriness from his eyes and read it again. The sender was a Cairo antiques finder named Hassan, whom he had spoken to by phone before coming to Yemen. He scrawled an answer at the bottom of the note and handed it to the bellhop with a tip and instructions to arrange transportation for a morning departure. Then he ordered the first of several pots of strong black coffee and buckled down to the job of getting sober.

CHAPTER

6

Z AVALA HAD HIS DUFFEL BAG packed and was ready to go when Austin swung by the former library building in Alexandria, Virginia, that his friend had converted to a bachelor pad with a southwestern flair. The two men caught a morning Air Canada flight, and their plane touched down on the tarmac at St. John's, Newfoundland, late in the afternoon, after a stop-off in Montreal.

A taxi took them to the busy waterfront, where the two-hundred-seventy-foot-long *Leif Eriksson* was tied up. The forty-six-hundred-ton vessel was a brawny ship, less than five years old, its hull reinforced for protection against the punishing North Atlantic ice.

The captain, a native Newfoundlander named Alfred Dawe, knew when their flight was coming in and was waiting on deck in anticipation of their arrival. As the men came up the gangway, he introduced himself and said, "Welcome aboard the *Eriksson*."

Austin extended his hand in a bone-crushing grip. "Thanks for having us, Captain Dawe. I'm Kurt Austin, and this is my colleague, Joe Zavala. We're your new iceberg wranglers."

Dawe was a compact man in his fifties who liked to brag that he'd been born in a place with the forlorn name of Misery Cove, and

that his family was so dumb they still lived there. Schoolboy mischief
lurked in his clear blue eyes, and he had a dimpled grin that came
easily to his ruddy face. Despite his self-deprecating humor, Dawe
was an accomplished skipper with years of experience running ships
in the cantankerous waters of the Northwest Atlantic. He had often
encountered NUMA's distinctive turquoise-hulled research ships,
and knew that the American agency was the most highly respected
ocean exploration and study organization on the globe.

When Austin had called and asked to go on an iceberg cruise, the
captain had checked with the ship's owners for permission to have
guests aboard. He'd gotten a go-ahead and called Austin back with
the date for the ship's next departure.

Dawe had been eager to meet the two men ever since Austin had
faxed him a copy of their résumés. Austin had wanted Dawe to
know that he and Zavala were not landlubber dilettantes who'd
need constant watching for fear they'd fall overboard.

The captain knew about Austin's master's degree from the
University of Washington, his training as an expert diver proficient
in a variety of underwater specialties, and his expertise in deepwater
salvage. Long before former NUMA director James Sandecker had
hired Austin away from the CIA, Austin had worked on North Sea
oil rigs and with his father's Seattle-based ocean-salvage company.

Zavala's curriculum vitae said that he was an honors graduate of
New York Maritime College, a skilled pilot with hundreds of hours
on, above, and under the sea, and a brilliant engineer with expertise
in the design and operation of underwater vehicles.

Given his guests' impressive academic credentials, the captain was
intrigued when he met the NUMA engineers in person. Austin and
Zavala came across more like gentlemen swashbucklers than the
scientific types he'd expected. Their soft-spoken manner couldn't
mask a barnacle-like toughness and a brass balls brashness that was
only partly tempered by their veneer of politeness.

His guests were obviously rugged physically. Austin was over six feet tall and around two hundred pounds, without an ounce of fat on his sturdy frame. With his broad shoulders and powerful build, the brawny man with the mane of prematurely gray, almost-white, hair looked like a one-man wrecking crew. His chiseled face was deeply tanned from constant outdoor exposure, and the ocean winds and sun had given his skin a metallic burnishing. Laugh wrinkles framed intelligent, coral-hued eyes that calmly gazed out at the world with an expression that suggested nothing they saw would surprise them.

Zavala was a few inches shorter. He was flexibly muscular, and he moved with the catlike lightness of a matador, a holdover from his college days when he had boxed professionally as a middleweight. He had earned his tuition with a devastating right cross–left hook combination. With his movie star good looks and athletic build, he looked like the male lead in a pirate saga.

The captain showed his guests to their small but comfortable cabin.

"I hope we haven't crowded anyone out," Austin said as he tossed his duffel on a bunk.

Dawe shook his head. "We've got a crew of twelve on this cruise—two short of our normal contingent."

"In that case, we'll be glad to lend a hand," Zavala said.

"I'm *counting* on it, gentlemen."

Dawe conducted a quick stem-to-stern tour of the ship, and then they went up to the bridge, where he gave the order to get under way. The deckhands cast off the mooring lines, and the ship steamed out of St. John's harbor. After passing between Fort Amherst and Point Spear, the most northeasterly spit of land in North America, the ship headed up along the Newfoundland coast under layers of slag-gray clouds.

Once the ship hit the open sea and settled on its course, Dawe turned over command to his first mate and spread a satellite photo out on a chart table.

"The *Eriksson* delivers food and equipment to the drilling rigs in the warm months. From February to July, we're looking for big stuff floating down from Baffin Bay." He tapped the photo with his forefinger. "This is where most of our North Atlantic bergs originate. Got around a hundred glaciers in West Greenland that turn out some ninety percent of the Newfoundland icebergs."

"How's that translate into the actual number of icebergs?" Austin said.

"I'd guess that about forty thousand medium-to-large bergs calve in Greenland. Only a fraction of that total comes this far south. Between four hundred and eight hundred make it to Iceberg Alley, the area forty-eight degrees north latitude off St. John's. They drift for around a year after calving, and then they pass through the Davis Strait into the Labrador Current."

"Smack into the great circle shipping lanes," Austin said.

"You've been doing your homework," Dawe said with a grin. "Yep. That's where the trouble starts. You've got a steady flow of ships between Canada, the States, and Europe. The shipping companies want the voyages to be short and economical. The ships pass just south of the boundary of all known ice."

"Which is where the *Titanic* discovered *unknown* ice," Austin said.

Dawe's genial smile dissolved. "You think a lot about the *Titanic* when you're out here. It's a constant reminder that bad seamanship can fetch you a one-way ticket to Davy Jones's locker. The *Titanic*'s grave is near the Grand Banks, where the Labrador Current meets the Gulf Stream. There's a twenty-degree water temperature difference that creates fog that's as dense as steel wool. The ocean circulation in the area is pretty complex as well."

"That must make your job hair-raising at times," Austin observed.

"I wish it was something I could put in a bottle for bald-headed men. A berg can wander around the ocean like a drunk on his way home from a bender. North Atlantic icebergs are the fastest moving in the world. They'll travel up to seven knots an hour. Fortunately, we've got a lot of help. The International Ice Patrol makes regular flights. Passing ships keep tabs on icebergs, and the *Eriksson* works with a fleet of small spotting planes hired by the oil and gas companies."

"How'd you get into towing?" Zavala asked.

"We tried using water cannon to move bergs. That works with 'growlers,' chunks of ice about the size of a big piano. There isn't a hose big enough to move a five-hundred-thousand-ton mountain of ice. Towing them to warmer water seems to work the best."

"How many bergs do you actually lasso?" Austin said.

"Only those that are headed for an oil or gas drilling platform. Two or three dozen. Once a ship hears about a berg, it can adjust its course. A five-billion-dollar world-class rig doesn't have that option. The floating platforms can move, but it takes time. There was a near collision a few years ago. Berg wasn't sighted until it got about six miles from the platform. It was too late by then to tow the berg or evacuate the platform. The supply boats pulled it off at the last second. The berg went right over the wellhead."

"With all the surveillance, I'm surprised the berg got that close," Austin said.

"As I said, their course can be erratic, depending on shape, size, and wind. That one snuck by us. We'll be keeping any eye out for a big lunker that disappeared in the fog after being sighted a few days ago. I've been calling her Moby-Berg."

"Let's hope that we're not Captain Ahab chasing white whales," Austin said.

"I'd prefer a white whale to an iceberg," Dawe said. "By the way, did I ever tell you why Newfoundlanders like to drive in winter?"

Austin and Zavala exchanged blank looks at the odd shift in conversation.

"The snow fills in the potholes," Dawe said. He laughed so hard that tears streamed down his cheeks. The captain had a seemingly endless supply of "Newfie" jokes that poked fun at his heritage. The jokes continued through dinner.

The *Leif Eriksson*'s cook served up a meal that would have been worthy of a five-star diner. As Austin and Zavala dug into rare roast beef, canned green beans, and garlic mashed potatoes, covered with a layer of thick gravy, the captain unleashed his joke repertoire on his captive audience. Austin and Zavala weathered the barrage of marginal humor until they could take it no longer and excused themselves to turn in.

When they climbed to the bridge early the next morning, the captain must have felt sorry for them. He dispensed with the jokes and poured them mugs of hot coffee. "We're making good time. We've seen a lot of growlers. That's our first 'bergy bit.' "

Dawe pointed to an iceberg floating about a quarter of a mile off the starboard bow.

"That's bigger than any burger bit I've ever seen," Austin said.

"It's nothing compared to the stuff we'll see later," the captain said. "It isn't considered an iceberg unless it's nearly twenty feet above the water and fifty feet long. Anything smaller is a bergy or growler."

"Looks like we'll have to learn a whole new vocabulary out here," Zavala commented.

Dawe nodded in agreement. "Welcome to Iceberg Alley, gentlemen."

CHAPTER

7

Saxon picked up his rental car at the Cairo Airport
and plunged into the automotive anarchy that passed for traffic flow in the ancient city of the Pyramids. The cacophony of beep-
ing horns and the choking impact of dust and car exhaust was
a strong antidote to weeks spent traveling in the lonely deserts
of Yemen.

He drove to the outskirts of Cairo and parked on the *Sharia Sudan*.
Pungent barnyard smells and inhuman sounds came from a nearby
fenced-in area, the *Souq al-Gamaal.* The old Cairo camel market.
The corrals that had once been surrounded by green fields were
hemmed in by apartment houses.

Saxon had suggested the rendezvous. He wanted to meet Hassan
in a public place for security. The dung-spattered oasis of old Egypt
appealed to his sense of drama as well.

Saxon paid the small entrance fee required of non-Egyptians and
strolled among the corrals. Hundreds of camels brought up from the
Sudan awaited the slaughterhouse or an even worse fate carrying
overweight tourists at the Pyramids.

Saxon paused to watch a protesting dromedary being loaded into
the back of a compact pickup truck. He felt a gentle tug at his hand.

One of the dirty-faced urchins who haunted the market begging for *baksheesh* was trying to get his attention.

Saxon followed the boy's pointing finger. A man was standing under a makeshift awning near a group of haggling camel buyers. Saxon gave the boy a tip and walked across the corral. The man had a café au lait complexion typical of many Egyptians, and a neatly trimmed beard decorated his chin. He wore a circular knit cap and a matching white *gallibaya,* the long cotton gown favored by many Egyptian men.

"*Sabaah ilkheer,*" Saxon said. Good morning.

"*Sabaah innuur,* Mr. Saxon. I am Hassan."

"Thank you for coming."

"You want to do business?" Hassan said. The offer should have made Saxon suspicious. Egyptians liked to linger over tea before talking business. But his eagerness overpowered his judgment.

"I'm told you might be able to help me find a certain lost property."

"Maybe," Hassan said. "If you can pay the price."

"I will pay whatever is reasonable," Saxon said. "When might I see this property?"

"I can show it to you now. I have a car. Come with me."

Saxon hesitated. The Cairo underworld sometimes had ties to shadowy political groups. He thought it prudent to size Hassan up before he put himself in the stranger's hands.

"Let's go to Fishawi's. We can talk and get to know each other," he suggested. The popular outdoor café was near Cairo's main bazaar and its oldest mosque.

Hassan frowned. "Too many people."

"Yes, I *know,*" Saxon said.

Hassan nodded. He led the way out of the market to a battered white Fiat that was drawn up to the curb. He opened the door for Saxon.

"I'll follow you in my car," Saxon said.

He walked across the street and slipped behind the wheel of his rental car. He inserted the key in the ignition to start the engine just as another car squealed to a stop next to his.

Two men in black suits jumped out of the car and bulled their way into his vehicle. One sat in the back and the other next to Saxon. Both leveled guns at Saxon's head.

"Drive," said the man in the front passenger seat.

Saxon's innards turned to ice water. But he reacted with characteristic calm. He had experienced many close calls in his years as an explorer and adventurer. He started the car, pulled away from the curb, and obeyed the order to follow Hassan's car. He kept his mouth shut. Questions would only antagonize his uninvited passengers.

The Fiat drove across the traffic-snarled city toward the Citadel, a complex of mosques and military buildings. Saxon's heart fell. An army would not be able to find him in the labyrinth of narrow streets around the Citadel.

Hassan's car pulled up to the entrance of a nondescript building. The sign out front said, in English and Arabic, POLICE STATION.

Hassan and his men hustled Saxon out of the car, through a dimly lit lobby into a small windowless room smelling of sweat and stale cigarette smoke. The only furniture was a metal table and two chairs. Light came from a single overhead bulb.

Saxon was only partially relieved. He knew that in Egypt people who go into police stations sometimes didn't come out.

He was told to sit down and hand over his billfold. He was left alone for a few minutes. Then Hassan appeared with a balding, grizzled man who had a cigarette dangling from his thick lips. The newcomer unbuttoned the suit jacket that was tight across his ample belly and eased into the chair to face Saxon. He mashed his cigarette into an ashtray filled with butts and snapped his fingers. Hassan handed him the billfold, which he opened as if it were a rare book.

He looked at the ID. "Anthony Saxon," he said.

"Yes," Saxon replied. "And you?"

"I am Inspector Sharif. This is my station."

"May I ask why I am here, Inspector?"

The inspector slapped the billfold down. "*I* ask the questions."

Saxon nodded.

The inspector jerked his thumb at Hassan. "Why did you want to meet with this man?"

"I *didn't*," Saxon said. "I talked to somebody *named* Hassan. This is obviously not he."

The inspector grunted. "Correct. This man is Officer Abdul. Why did you want to see Hassan? He is a thief."

"I thought he might be able to lead me to property stolen from the Baghdad Museum."

"So you wished to receive stolen goods," the inspector said.

"I would have returned the property to the museum. You can talk to the real Hassan if you want to check my story."

The inspector shot a knowing glance at Abdul. "Not possible," he said to Saxon. "Hassan is dead."

"Dead? I talked to him yesterday on the phone. What happened?"

Carefully watching Saxon's reaction, the inspector said, "Murdered. Very big mess. You're sure you don't know about this?"

"Yes. Very sure."

The inspector lit up a Cleopatra cigarette and blew twin plumes of smoke through his nostrils. "I believe you. Now you may ask questions."

"How did you know I was going to meet Hassan?"

"Simple. You are in his appointment book. We look up your name. You're very famous writer. Everybody reads your books."

"I wish *more* people read them," Saxon said, with a faint smile.

The inspector shrugged. "Why is a big writer interested in a thief?"

Saxon doubted whether the inspector would understand the obsession that had launched him on a journey throughout Europe, the Middle East, and South America in his quest to solve one of the puzzles of the ages. There were times he didn't understand it himself. Choosing his words carefully, he said, "I believed that Hassan could have helped me find a woman."

"Ah," the inspector said. He turned to Officer Abdul. "A *woman*."

"Hassan had an antiquity that could have helped me with a book I'm writing and a film I hope to produce on the Queen of Sheba."

"*Sheba,*" the inspector said with disappointment. "A dead woman."

"Dead and not dead. Like Cleopatra."

"Cleopatra was a great queen."

"Yes. And so was Sheba. As beautiful as the day."

The door opened to admit another man. Unlike the rotund and grubby inspector, he was tall and slim. He was dressed in a pale olive suit that had razor creases in the trousers. Sharif got up from his chair and stood at attention.

"The man said, "Thank you, Inspector. You and your officer may go."

The inspector snapped off a salute and left the room with the officer.

The man eased into the inspector's chair and placed a manila file on the table. He stared at Saxon with amusement on his narrow face.

"I'm told you like the camel market," the man said in perfect English.

"I admire the way camels hold their heads high. They remind me of aristocrats who have fallen on hard times."

"Interesting," the man said. "My name is Yousef. I am with the Interior Ministry."

Saxon knew that the Interior Ministry was synonymous with national security.

"You're very kind to come out here."

"Kindness had little to do with this situation." He opened the folder. "This is the file of the *real* Hassan." His manicured fingers extracted several sheets of paper stapled together, which he slid across to Saxon. "And this is the list of antiquities."

Saxon read the list, which was in English. "This corresponds to the list published by the Baghdad Museum."

"Then I am afraid you are too late." Yousef sat back and tented his fingers. "The items were removed by the army. They are in the possession of a representative from UNESCO. The day after the transfer, Hassan was tortured and murdered." Yousef drew his finger across his throat.

"If he didn't have any antiquities, why did he tell me he had them?"

"A thief steals more than once. He may have felt he could dupe a rich foreigner."

"Do you know who killed him?"

"We are working on it."

"Who was the UNESCO representative?"

"An Italian woman. Her name is Carina Mechadi."

"Do you know if she is still in Cairo?"

"She left on a ship with the antiquities some days ago. She is taking them to the United States under an arrangement with the Baghdad government."

The wind went out of Saxon's sails. He had been *so* close to his goal. "May I be allowed to go now?"

"Anytime you wish." Yousef rose from his chair. "There is always a woman at the heart of every case."

"Miss Mechadi?"

He shook his head. "Sheba."

The Egyptian flashed an opaque smile and held the door open. Saxon drove back to the Marriott Hotel. Back in his room, he made some telephone calls and reached a contact at UNESCO, who confirmed that Carina Mechadi was on her way to America.

Saxon went over to the window and looked out on the timeless Nile and the sparkling lights of the ancient city. He recalled Yousef's smile at the mention of his quest for the ghost of a woman who died three thousand years ago.

After a moment of thought, he picked up the phone again and made reservations for a flight to the United States. Then he began to pack.

His long journey in search of the perfect woman had carried him to the most remote and dangerous places on the globe. He wasn't about to give up now.

8

THE CONTAINERSHIP *Ocean Adventure* could hold nearly two thousand cargo containers, but even at seven thousand tons and a length of five hundred feet it was a pygmy compared with newer box ships that were as long as three football fields laid end to end. The finer points of spatial relativism were lost on Carina Mechadi as she strode along the ship's long deck huddled against the bone-chilling rawness of the North Atlantic.

Since boarding at Salerno, Carina had arisen early each morning and descended from her cabin on the third level of the bridge house to go on a brisk walk before breakfast. Her compulsion was fueled by an unnecessary obsession with keeping her lithe figure in shape and to sooth her impatience at reaching her destination. The number of laps varied according to the weather, which ranged from raw dampness to the bitingly cold air off the coast of Newfoundland.

The *Ocean Adventure* inspired little of the romance immortalized by Joseph Conrad's tales of the doughty tramp steamers that plied the world's oceans in a bygone age. The ship was a seagoing platform that carried steel container units twenty feet long by about eight feet tall. They were stacked six high and covered most of the deck, except for fore and aft, and narrow aisles on either side. Hundreds more containers were stored belowdecks.

As Carina made her way along the starboard rail, she recalled the chain of events that had brought her to a ship plowing its way across the Atlantic. The murder of Ali Babbas some years before in Baghdad had shocked but not surprised her. Violence always lurked behind the scenes in the high-stakes trade in illegal antiquities. It was a shadowy world where enormous sums of money flowed and gentlemen were rarely found. Ali had probably double-crossed the wrong person.

She had mourned his death nonetheless. Without Ali, it was doubtful she would ever recover the lost cache of antiques. Ali had been the middleman who moved stolen goods to market. He had committed nothing to paper. The names of his buyers and sellers had been in his head. With the sleazy dealer out of the picture, the antiquities she had sought had been scattered to the four winds.

Carina had had plenty to keep her busy once she left Iraq and returned to her UNESCO office in Paris. Months after leaving Baghdad, she'd been was on the trail of a rare Etruscan statue when Auguste Benoir visited her office and presented his card. Benoir was a prim, perfidious man who reminded Carina of Agatha Christie's fictitious detective Hercule Poirot.

Benoir was a partner in a prestigious Paris law firm, and he got right to the point. "My firm has been retained to represent the Baltazar Foundation," he said. "Mr. Baltazar is a wealthy businessman and philanthropist. He was quite saddened when he heard about the looting of the Baghdad Museum. Mr. Baltazar had read an article describing your efforts to find a cache of stolen antiquities, and he is hopeful that with funding from his foundation you could devote your talents to restoring these objects to the Iraqi collection."

"That's very kind of Mr. Baltazar," Carina had replied. "However,

I believe I can be more valuable working with a worldwide organization like UNESCO."

"Forgive me for not being clear about Mr. Baltazar's proposition. You would not be required to leave UNESCO."

Carina glanced at the folders piled up on her desk. "As you can see, I am buried in UNESCO work."

"Understandable." Benoir produced a single sheet of paper from his briefcase. "This is the agreement that is being proposed. The foundation would donate an ongoing grant in a bank of your choice. You could draw on the bank account at any time for any purpose, with one stipulation: The money must be spent to recover the Iraqi artifacts. There is no current limit on the funds available."

Suddenly interested, Carina considered the offer. "Mr. Baltazar is most generous."

Benoir beamed. "Well, Mademoiselle Mechadi?"

Carina was in a quandary. She was balancing several UNESCO assignments, but she couldn't let a chance like this pass. She scanned the agreement. "Let me study this proposal and I'll call you tomorrow with my answer."

The next day she called Benoir and told him her answer was yes. In her UNESCO job, Carina had worked with governments, international police, museum people, and archaeology experts, but the possibilities of unlimited funding opened up whole new worlds. With wads of cash in her hand, she would be able to buy access to the unsavory characters who populated the antiquities trade. And so it was. Soon she developed an effective network of police and underworld informants who often gave her leads on antiquities missing from countries other than Iraq.

One of her more reliable sources was a crooked Egyptian army officer she knew only as the Colonel. Less than a week before, he had called her out of the blue with the news that the cache of Iraqi objects she had been looking for was being put up for sale by a petty thief named Hassan. She told the officer that she would see him within forty-eight hours, wired him a deposit, and told him to make the buy sight unseen.

The agreement with the Baltazar Foundation required that she keep it informed of immediate developments. She called Benoir with the news about Hassan, and Benoir said he would pass the news along. Before flying to Cairo, she called Professor Nasir in Baghdad and told him that she was close to recovering the cache.

Nasir was delighted, but conditions were still chaotic in Iraq and he was worried about the safety of the collection. He was trying to find funds to set up an efficient record-keeping system for the museum's existing collection. Nasir enthusiastically embraced Carina's suggestion that the artifacts be used to leverage donations. He would sign a waiver allowing her to keep the artifacts temporarily in her possession and would contact the Iraqi embassy in Washington to alert the diplomatic staff to the possibility of a tour.

Events moved quickly when she got to Egypt. Over lunch at the Nile Sheraton Hotel, the Colonel said he had already acquired the collection. He gallantly bought her lunch after she had paid him his full fee. That night, in a warehouse on the docks of Port Said, she had waited with growing excitement for the truck that pulled in shortly after midnight.

The artifacts in the truck were covered with dirt, but they were in more or less decent condition. She did a quick inventory by flashlight, writing down a description and number for each item. One of the larger pieces was a tall statue of a man wearing a kilt and conical cap. The bronze surface was caked from grime from the bearded face to the cat at the feet of the figure. The statue didn't appear on her original artifact list, but a wrinkled paper tag affixed to one arm by a string identified the work as the *Navigator*. After spreading more of Baltazar's wealth around the waterfront and the customs office, she had the load put on a freighter that was leaving for Italy.

Flying ahead of the freighter to Salerno, she arranged for the transshipment of the cargo to the United States on the *Ocean Adventure,* and, during the nervous wait, she nailed down the tour plans with Nasir and the embassy. When the freighter finally arrived, she called Benoir and told him she had taken possession of the antiquities in preparation for a tour. He sounded strangely disappointed but called back later, saying he had consulted with Baltazar, who congratulated her on the find. Carina decided not to let the artifacts out of her sight again and had booked a cabin on the containership.

She stopped during her walk now and peered down an alley between stacks to make sure that the blue-painted container was still there. She continued on to the bow, where a blast of icy air hit her as she stepped out onto the open deck.

The captain had told her over dinner the night before that the ship's cruising speed was eighteen knots. He would reduce that as they neared Newfoundland and entered the area known as "Iceberg Alley." The warning made her more curious than fearful.

She paused at the bow to look for icebergs. Only trunk-sized chunks floated in the gray sea. Several layers of clothing were still not enough to keep the icy fingers of wind from tickling her ribs. Hot coffee and scrambled eggs would be waiting in the mess hall. She turned her back to the open sea and headed along the ship's port side.

Carina was about two-thirds of the way to the bridge when she heard a beating sound above the swash of the hull through the sea. She looked up and saw a pair of helicopters flying close together a couple of hundred feet above water level. They were rapidly approaching the ship. No markings of any kind were visible on the black fuselages.

Carina was surprised at their sudden appearance. The ship was a hundred miles from land. She remembered the captain's mention of oil and gas rigs in the area. The helicopters must belong to a drilling platform.

The helicopters buzzed the ship barely above mast level, banked around in a tight formation, and circled the moving vessel like birds of prey in an ever-tightening spiral before disappearing out of the line of sight. The sound of spinning rotors faded. The helicopters evidently had landed on top of the container stacks.

Carina was sure she'd learn the identity of the visitors when she got to the mess hall. She resumed her walk, only to suddenly stop in her tracks. Ahead of her, a figure dropped down from a container stack at the end of a rope and landed on the deck. Three more figures rappelled down the rope and stood in her way. Masks hid their faces except for the eyes. They were dressed in tight-fitting black uniforms and armed with short-barreled automatic weapons.

Carina turned and ran, but four more armed figures had descended from the stacks behind her, and they closed in on her. One of the strangers grabbed her by the arm and spun her around, and her wrists were roughly tied behind her back with duct tape.

She was shoved in the direction of the bridge house and a gun muzzle was jabbed hard between the shoulder blades. More figures were coming in their direction. Carina recognized two Filipino crewmen. She saw their smiling faces and the situation became crystal clear. The Filipinos were working with the hijackers.

The raiding party split up into two groups. One crewman set out toward the bridge house with four hijackers. The other man led the way along the deck. The whole operation had been conducted in silence. These men knew what they were doing and what they wanted, Carina thought. But she was dumbfounded when the crewman directed her to the container box holding her artifacts and rapped his gloved knuckles on the metal surface.

The container door was hemmed in by other boxes. A hijacker opened a metal suitcase and removed a torch and oxygen tank. He assembled the torch, ignited the flame, and adjusted it to a fine point. He donned a pair of goggles to protect his eyes from the shower of sparks and methodically began to cut a hole in the side of the container.

An involuntary cry of protest escaped Carina's lips. Her outburst brought an instant response. One of her captors grabbed her arms and kicked her in the ankle at the same time. Catrina, having lost her footing and unable to use her arms to break her fall, hit the deck. Her forehead smashed against a hard surface and she blacked out.

When she regained consciousness, she was lying on her back in semidarkness. Her head throbbed with pain. She rolled over on her side and saw that she was wedged between two wooden cartons inside the container. Light streamed into the space from a rectangular hole framed by ragged edges from the cutting torch.

She tried to stand, but it was difficult to get her feet under her with her hands bound behind her back, and the effort made her dizzy. As she lay on the cold steel floor with her chest heaving from exertion, she saw a shadow against the crates. A man peered in at her through the hole. His face was slightly plump around the cheeks, but the round eyes that stared out of the cherubic face had a demonic intensity.

Carina's blood ran cold. It was one of the most frightening faces she had ever seen.

Her expression must have mirrored her thoughts because the man smiled.

Carina was almost grateful when she passed out again.

CHAPTER

9

THE ORANGE-AND-WHITE HERCULES 130HC long-range surveillance aircraft had taken off at dawn from St. John's and headed east on a seven-hour flight for the International Ice Patrol. Cruising at three hundred fifty miles an hour, the high-wing aircraft would cover a thirty-thousand-square-mile expanse of ocean before its patrol ended.

The Coast Guardsman at the plane's radar console was daydreaming about his upcoming date with a young Newfoundland woman. He was working on a plan to get her into bed when he saw the suspicious blip on the plane's radar screen.

Training set in. The radarman put aside his prurient thoughts and focused on the radar screen. The four-engine turboprop carried radar that looked forward and sideways. The side-looking radar, or SLR, had picked up the large object in the water around twenty miles to the north.

Iceberg detection had come a long way since 1912, when the ice patrol was created to prevent a repeat of the *Titanic* disaster. Despite the technological advances, identification is considered more of an art than a science.

The radarman tried to decide whether the object was an iceberg or an anchored fishing boat. A smooth-edged moving target would denote a vessel. The blip was almost stationary and showed no sign of a wake. His practiced eye picked out the radar shadow, where there was no radar return on the far side of the target, a phenomenon that indicated that the target was taller than a ship.

Iceberg.

He notified the cockpit of the sighting and its location, and the plane veered off on a northerly course change.

The fog hanging over the ocean surface prevented visual identification until the very last minute. The plane dropped down until it was several hundred feet above the water. The mists cleared to reveal an iceberg with a tall, narrow pinnacle at one end. Then the fog closed in again. The brief glimpse was all that was needed.

The plane sent the iceberg data to the ice patrol's operations center in Groton, Connecticut. There, a computer figured out the iceberg's probable drift. A warning was broadcast over the radio as a bulletin to the maritime community. The report was picked up by a Provincial Airlines Beech Super King that had been patrolling the Grand Banks under contract to the offshore drilling industry.

The two-engine plane homed in on the broadcast coordinates. The fog was clearing, and the plane found its target with no trouble. After making a couple of low-altitude passes, the plane radioed a confirmation of the sighting to the drilling platforms and vessels in the vicinity.

THE *Leif Eriksson* had been cruising at a lazy meander when the vessel received the urgent message. Immediately, the ship's twin ten-thousand-horsepower diesels flexed their muscles in a noisy display of power. Leaving a creamy wake in the gray seas, the vessel raced off like a motorcycle cop chasing a speeder.

Austin had been in the bridge poring over a chart with Zavala when the report came on over the radio's speaker.

"Our missing Moby?" Austin asked the captain.

"Could be," Dawe said. "She fits the description. We should know soon enough."

Dawe ordered the ship's engine room to cut speed. Cottony wisps of fog were curling around the ship's plunging bow. Within minutes, a colorless miasma wrapped the ship like a wet dishcloth. Visibility was reduced to spitting distance. The ship groped its way along relying entirely on its electronic eyes.

The captain kept close tabs on the radar screen and called out commands from time to time for the helmsman to adjust course. The ship was moving at a crawl, and the tension on the bridge was thicker than clam chowder. The ship was traveling through the haunted waters near the grave of the *Titanic*. Even with electronics that could pinpoint a toy boat in a rain puddle, ship collisions with ice were not uncommon, and sometimes fatal.

The captain emitted a cryptic grunt and looked up from the radar screen.

He grinned and said, "Did I ever tell you what a Newfie uses for mosquito repellant?"

"A shotgun," Zavala said.

"The mosquito will crash when you shoot out its landing lights," Austin added.

"Guess you heard that one. Don't worry; we'll make Newfies out of you yet."

With the tension broken, the captain turned his attention back to the radar screen. "Fog's let up a bit. Keep an eye out. Any second now."

Austin scanned the grayness. "We've got company," he said, breaking the cathedral·quietness on the bridge.

The ghostly outlines of an enormous iceberg loomed ahead like something in a dream. Within seconds, the mountain of ice became more solid and less spectral. The berg angled up from one end to a lofty pinnacle that rose as high as a fifteen-story building. A stray shaft of sunlight had penetrated the fog. Under the glare of the heavenly spotlight, the berg glowed with a bone white sheen except for the sky blue crevasses where the refrozen meltwaters were free of bubbles that reflected white light.

The captain slapped Austin and Zavala on the back. "Grab your harpoons, boys. We've found Moby-Berg." He gazed in rapture at the enormous berg. "Real pretty, eh?"

"Quite the little ice cube," Austin said. "And we're only seeing about an eighth of the berg above water."

"There's must be enough ice there for a billion margaritas," Zavala said with undisguised awe.

Dawe said, "She's a castle berg. Like the one that sunk the *Titanic*. The average berg in this neighborhood runs a couple of hundred thousand tons and maybe two hundred feet in length. This one is around three hundred feet plus and maybe five hundred thousand tons. The *Titanic* iceberg was only around two hundred fifty thousand tons."

The captain ordered the helmsman to circle the berg, coming no closer than one hundred feet. "We've got to be extra careful," he explained.

"Those projections poking from the water look as if they could scrape the barnacles off our hull," Austin said.

The captain kept a level gaze on the berg. "It's the obstructions we *can't* see that I worry about. Those blue cracks are weak spots. A gigantic piece of ice could break off at any time and the splash alone could sink us." Dawe flashed a quick grin. "Still glad you hooked a ride with us?"

Nodding in agreement, Austin tried to absorb the deadly beauty of the majestic ice mountain.

Zavala had shed all his reservations about the trip and stared spellbound at the huge berg. "Fantastic!" he said.

"Glad to hear that, my friends, because his baby belongs to you. A NUMA ship helped me out of a jam some years ago. This is my way of paying you back. The ship's owners say liability won't be a problem as long as you sign on as temporary members of the crew, which you've already done. You showed yourself to be naturals rounding up bergy bits."

Dawe had let his guests lend a hand lassoing the smaller bergs, loosely misnamed after the fast-food specialty. Their teamwork and the way they quickly picked up the technique had impressed him.

"Those bergy bits were the size of houses," Austin said. "That thing out there is as big as the Watergate complex."

"The principle's the same. Spot 'em. Encircle 'em, rope 'em, and tow 'em. I'll be watching over your shoulder in case you get into trouble. Get into your foul weather gear. Meet you on deck."

Austin and Zavala grinned like kids getting their first two-wheeled bike. They thanked the captain and headed to their cabin. They pulled on extra layers of warm clothing and slipped into full suits of bright orange foul weather gear. By the time they stepped out onto the open, the wind had picked up. The patched surface of the sea was as rough as alligator skin.

The captain watched closely as the two men worked with the crew to shackle together twelve-hundred-foot-long sections of eight-inch-thick polypropylene towrope. The towrope was attached to a cylindrical bollard on the aft deck and was paid out through a wide opening in the stern rail. An orange buoy was attached to the free-floating end. Austin used a portable radio to contact the bridge to say all was ready.

The ship moved in a big circle, staying about two hundred feet away from the berg, stopping to allow the crew to shackle sections to the towline.

When the *Eriksson* came back to its starting point, a crewman grappled the buoy end floating in the water and hauled it on deck. Austin directed the seamen to attach a wire towline to keep the rope low in the water. The line might slip off the slippery surface of the berg otherwise. The captain inspected the setup.

"Good job," Dawe said. "Now comes the fun part."

He led Austin and Zavala back up to the bridge. About half a mile of open water separated the ship and the berg; Dawe considered this the minimum distance for safe towing.

"I'll let you take over from here," Austin said.

He knew that this was no place for an amateur. Towed bergs have been known to turn over, and there was always the danger of the towline being tangled in the propellers.

Under the captain's direction, the ship increased power. The towline went taut. The water behind the boat boiled in a white, foamy patch. The berg reluctantly overcame the inertia holding it in place. The huge ice mountain became unstuck from the sea, and they began to make slow headway. It might take hours to reach a speed of a single knot.

With the iceberg under tow, Austin excused himself and came back from his cabin a few minutes later. He presented a cardboard box to the captain. Dawe opened the box and his mouth widened in a grin. He lifted a broad-brimmed Stetson from the box and placed the cowboy hat on his head.

"A little large, but I can stuff newspaper inside to make it fit. Thanks, guys."

"Consider it a small token of appreciation for having us on board," Austin said.

Zavala was staring at the iceberg, which dwarfed the ship. "What are we going to do with that thing?"

"We'll tow it to a current that will take it away from the oil rig. It could take a few days."

"Captain—" The radarman called Dawe over to the radar monitor. "I've been tracking a target. Looks like it's heading toward the Great Northern."

The radar man had drawn three Xs with a grease pencil on a transparent plastic overlay and connected them to show the object's course and time. The captain took a straightedge and lined it up with the markings.

"This isn't good," he murmured. "We've got a ship on a straight-line course for the oil rig. Moving fast, too."

He radioed the Great Northern platform. The oil rig's radar operator had spotted the oncoming ship and had tried to contact it. No one answered. He was about to call the *Leif Eriksson* when Dawe hailed him.

"We're getting a little worried," the radarman said. "She's headed right down our throat."

"That's what it looks like," Dawe said. "I figure she's about ten miles out."

"Too damn close."

"We'll dump the berg we're towing and try to make an intercept. How long will it take to move the rig off the wellhead?"

"We've already started, but that ship could get here first if it stays at its present speed."

"Keep trying to make radio contact. We'll wave her off." He turned to Austin and Zavala.

"Sorry, guys, but we'll have to cut your berg loose."

Austin had been listening to the radio exchange. He pulled on his foul weather top and clamped the cap down on his head. Zavala followed suit.

The release procedure was the reverse of the lassoing. The deck team detached the buoyed end of the rope to let it float free. Dawe maneuvered the ship back around the iceberg, and the crew reeled in the thousands of feet of line. When the last foot of line was on deck and pulled safely away from the propellers, the captain gave the order to move out at full speed.

Zavala stayed on deck wrapping up and Austin returned to the bridge. The microphone was clutched in the captain's hand. "Still no luck?" Austin said.

Dawe shook his head. He looked worried, and he had clearly lost his patience. "We should be alongside those idiots before long."

The captain went over to the radar screen. Another X had been drawn and connected to the previous course line. A second, intercepting course line had been drawn for the *Eriksson*.

"What are the chances the rig could sustain a direct hit?" Austin said.

"Not good. Great Northern is a semisubmersible rig. The legs offer some protection but nothing like the Hibernia platform, which is anchored in the bottom and protected by a thick concrete barrier."

Austin was familiar with drilling platforms from his North Sea days. He knew that a semisubmersible rig is more of ship than a platform, used mostly for deep water. Four legs rest on pontoons that act as a hull. The platform is designed to be towed through the water, although some rigs can move on their own power. Once the rig is on a drilling site, the pontoons are flooded. Several massive anchors hold the rig in place.

"How many workers are on the platform?" Austin asked.

"It's got accommodations for two hundred thirty."

"Will they have time to move out of harm's way?"

"They're pulling anchors, and the service boats will start towing soon, but the rig is geared to move out of the path of slow-moving bergs that get past the ice patrol. They're not built to dodge a runaway ship."

Austin wasn't so sure of the captain's use of the term *runaway,* which implied that the vessel was out of control. His own impression was that this ship was very *much* in control and that it was being aimed directly at the Great Northern rig.

A sharp-eyed crewman pointed to the sea off the starboard bow. "I see her."

Austin borrowed the crewman's binoculars and adjusted the focus knob until the profile of a containership came into view. He could make out the tall letters painted on the red hull that identified the ship as belonging to a company called Oceanus Lines. Painted in white letters on the ship's great flaring bow was the name: OCEAN ADVENTURE.

THE SHIPS moved abreast on a parallel course about a quarter of a mile apart. The *Eriksson* blinked its lights and blasted its horn to attract the ship's attention. The *Adventure* plowed through the sea without slowing. The captain ordered the crew to keep trying to make contact visually or over the radio.

The oil rig was coming into view. The platform squatted on the sea like a four-legged water bug. Its most prominent features were a towering oil derrick and a disk-shaped helicopter pad.

"Does the rig have a chopper?" Austin asked the captain.

"On its way back from making a hospital run. Too late to do an air evacuation, anyhow."

"I wasn't thinking about evacuation. Maybe the chopper could put someone aboard the ship."

"There won't be time. The best it will be able to do is pick up some survivors, if there are any."

Austin raised the glasses. "Don't bring out the body bags just yet," he said. "Maybe there's still a chance to save the rig."

"*Impossible!* The platform will sink like a stone when the ship slams into it."

"Take a look around midships," Austin said. "Tell me what you see."

The captain peered through the lenses. "There's a gangway hanging down almost to the waterline."

Austin outlined his plan.

"That's crazy, Kurt. Too dangerous. You and Joe could be killed."

Austin gave Dawe a tight smile. "No offense, Captain, but if your Newfie jokes didn't kill us, *nothing* will."

The captain gazed at Austin's determined face and his expression of utmost confidence. If anyone could pull off the impossible, it would be this American and his friend.

"All right," Dawe said. "I'll give you everything you need."

Austin slipped into his foul weather jacket, yanked up the zipper, and headed down to the deck to fill Zavala in. Zavala knew his friend well enough not to be surprised at the audacity or the risk of Austin's idea.

"Pretty simple scheme when you think about it," Zavala said. "The odds aren't the greatest."

"Slightly better than a snowball's chance in hell by my reckoning."

"Can't get much better than that. The execution could be a little tricky."

A pained expression came to Austin's rugged face. "I'd prefer it if we didn't use the word *execution*."

"An unfortunate slip of the tongue. What does Captain Dawe think of your idea?"

"He thinks we'd be crazy."

Zavala fixed his eyes on the massive containership plowing through the gray seas on a parallel course and his agile mind calculated speed, direction, and water conditions.

"The captain's right, Kurt," Zavala said. "We *are* crazy."

"Then I assume you're in."

Zavala nodded. "Hell, yes. I was bored lassoing icebergs."

"Thanks, Joe. The way I see this thing, it all comes down to risk assessment versus reward."

Zavala understood exactly what Austin was getting at. "How many guys are on the oil rig?"

"Captain says two hundred plus, in addition to those on the ship."

"The math seems pretty simple. The risk is high but not insurmountable, and we might be able to save more than two hundred lives."

"That's the way I look at it," Austin said. He slipped on a flotation vest and tossed another to Zavala. They sealed the deal with a firm handshake. Austin gave a thumbs-up to the captain, who'd been watching their discussion from the bridge.

UNDER CAPTAIN DAWE'S tight command, the ship came around and stopped at an angle to the wind that would allow Austin and Zavala to launch the bright red, sixteen-foot inflatable boat on the lee side of the ship. The ship cut the full impact of the wind, but the boat still tossed on the mounding seas like a rubber duck in a bathtub.

Austin was fitted out with a pocket radio attached to a hands-free microphone and earpiece. Captain Dawe would keep him up to date on the progress of the oil rig's anchor-hauling crews. If the platform got all its anchors up in time to move out of the way of the oncoming ship, or if there were any deviation in the ship's course, he would call Austin, who could then abort his plan. If the ship–platform collision seemed imminent, Austin could go from there.

Austin hung from the ladder with the wave crests splashing at his feet, then stepped off and landed square-footed in the boat. It was like jumping onto a wet trampoline. He would have been bounced out, but he grabbed the safety grips on the pontoons and hung on to the violently pitching boat.

When the inflatable had stabilized under his weight, Austin started the seventy-five-horsepower motor. With the outboard grumbling and snorting in the waves, Austin gripped the ship's ladder and steadied the boat so Zavala could join him. Zavala stepped into the bouncy inflatable with his usual catlike grace, cast off the bow and stern lines, and shoved the boat away from the ship.

Austin turned the tiller over to Zavala, who goosed the throttle and pointed the blunt bow on a course to intercept the *Ocean Adventure*.

CHAPTER
10

FROM THE SIX-STORY-HIGH BRIDGE of the *Ocean Adventure*, Captain Irwin Lange had a gull's-eye view of almost the entire length of the ship under his command. He had been at his lofty post when the helicopters had dropped out of the sky and landed on top of the container stacks. His initial reaction had been one of astonishment. That quickly changed to anger as he gazed through the big windows that overlooked the long deck.

The captain took pride in his Teutonic imperturbability. His stolid character was mirrored in firmly set facial features that almost never changed from their expression of genial self-competence. This was different. His lantern-jawed frown deepened. The helicopters had landed without *his* permission. His logical mind quickly dismissed the possibility that the helicopters were in trouble. One helicopter, maybe. But not *two*.

This was not right. Not proper. Peering through his binoculars, the captain became even more incensed as a dozen or so figures jumped from the helicopters and fanned out under the whirling rotors. All were dressed in black. He only caught a glimpse of the interlopers before they disappeared over the edge of the stack. But in that brief instant he saw that they were carrying weapons. His anger turned to dismay.

Pirates!

Lange took a hard swallow. *Impossible.* Pirates operated in far-off places like Sumatra and the China Sea. There had been pirate attacks off the coast of Brazil and West Africa. But he found it inconceivable that sea marauders would operate in a frigid, fogbound area like the Grand Banks.

In his many years of sailing the Europe-to-America route, the captain's only brush with pirates had been a video produced by an insurance-trade group. The shipping company that owned the ship under his command had distributed the video to its captains with instructions to watch it with their officers. The video showed fierce-eyed Asian pirates attacking a tanker in small, fast boats.

Lange desperately tried to recall the lessons the video tried to instill.

Vigilance is the best defense against piracy. No one warned about pirates dropping from the sky!

Turn the ship into a citadel. Too late to lock all the doors.

Don't fight the pirates. Not a chance. There was nothing more lethal than flare guns on board. None of the German officers or largely Filipino crew was trained in weapons use.

Stay calm. Well, that was *one* thing he was good at.

He turned to the bridge crew, which had been equally as startled at the sudden arrival of the helicopters.

"I believe the ship is being attacked by pirates," he said with the same unemotional tone he might have used to announce that a squall was imminent.

The stricken face of his first officer suggested that the younger man had none of his captain's composure. "*Pirates!* What should we do?"

"Do not offer resistance under any circumstances. I'll call for help."

He picked up the radio microphone but the ship's radio speaker crackled as he was about to make a distress call.

"Calling the captain of the *Ocean Adventure,*" a voice said. "Do you hear me?"

Lange said, "This is the captain speaking. Who is this?"

The speaker ignored Lange's question. "We are rounding up your crew. We are monitoring your radio transmissions and advise you not to call a Mayday. Do you understand me, Captain Lange?"

How did they know his name?

The captain gulped out the words. "Yes, I understand you."

"Good. Wait where you are."

The captain's immediate thought was for the welfare of his twenty-man crew. Maybe if he warned his men they could hide. He picked up the ship's telephone and called the engine room. No answer. He tried the ship's mess hall. Silence. He fought back a growing sense of panic and tried the officers' lounge. Again no answer.

Heavy footsteps pounded on the bridge wing. A gang of armed men burst into the cabin. Four men wore identical black uniforms, caps, and masks hiding their faces except for their hard eyes. The fifth man was dressed in jeans and a foul weather jacket, and his face was uncovered. The captain recognized him as a Filipino named Juan who worked in the engine room.

The captain assumed Juan was a captive until he noticed the pistol in the crewman's hand. The Filipino saw the consternation in the captain's face, and his mouth widened in a gap-toothed grin. The captain realized that Juan was working with the pirates. That's how they managed to take control so quickly. That's how they knew his name. Juan must have guided the attackers directly to the engine room and other parts of the ship.

One man went over to the control panel and pushed the helmsman aside.

"What are you doing?" Captain Lange said.

The man punched coordinates into the ship's computer, using numbers printed on a piece of paper. The captain saw that he had put the ship on autopilot. The man finished his task and barked a command.

"You and others. Down to the deck."

Lange stuck his prominent jaw out in defiance, but he did what he was told and ordered the rest of crew to do the same. The cold breeze sweeping the open deck easily penetrated the captain's light jacket. He would have been chilled in any case by the sight that greeted him. The rest of his crew was being herded along by armed men. A second Filipino crewman, like Juan, seemed to be working with the pirates.

Prodding the crew with their weapons, the pirates marched the frightened group to the aft deck. More pirates were gathered there around an object about as tall as a man. It was wrapped in canvas and was being trussed with several lengths of heavy rope.

Lange's eyes went to the pirate who was examining the knots in the rope. He was tall, several inches over six feet, dwarfing the other hijackers, and he had arms that seemed too long even for his powerful body. The man turned around and Lange saw that his face was uncovered. He gazed at the captain with angelic eyes.

"You did well to follow my orders, Captain," the man said. Lange recognized the voice that had warned him against calling a Mayday. The tone was surreal in its jovial warmth.

"Who are you?" the captain said. "Why are you on my ship?"

"Questions, questions," the man said with a shake of his head. "It would take much longer to explain than we have."

The captain tried another tack. "I will cooperate with you, only, please, do not harm my crew."

The mouth that was almost feminine in its softness widened in a smile. "Don't worry. We intend to leave you and this ship much as we found it."

Lange was no dummy. The fact that the man had chosen to bare his face meant he wasn't worried about witnesses identifying him later. At a nod from the gang's leader, a hijacker jabbed the captain with his gun and told him to lie facedown on the deck with his crewmen. His hands and feet were tightly bound with tape.

"What about the woman?" Juan asked the baby-faced man. "What should we do with her?"

"Whatever you'd like," the lead hijacker said. "She has caused us a great deal of trouble. Just make it fast." He seemed to lose interest in the subject and turned his attention back to the canvas-wrapped object.

Juan stroked the handle of a knife hanging from his belt and strode off along the deck on his dark errand. He walked quickly in anticipation of his task. For days, he had watched Carina with lustful eyes, trying to imagine what she looked like under her layers of clothing. He licked his lips as he recalled the soft warmth of the supple female body that he had lifted into the container. He would only have a few minutes, but it would be long enough for her to experience a real man before he killed her.

As he broke into a trot, he glanced out to sea and was startled to see that a vessel had emerged from the fog and was pacing the containership. An inflatable boat with two men in it was bouncing over the waves toward the *Ocean Adventure*.

The Filipino thought about calling for help, but that would not leave him enough time with the woman. Lust won out over good sense. He would handle this himself.

He crouched low and made his way along the deck. The boat seemed to be headed to a point amidships. The Filipino got there ahead of it. He drew his knife, flattened himself belly down on the deck like a crocodile waiting for its prey, and watched the boat as it drew nearer.

This was going to be a special day.

11

THE FLAT-BOTTOMED RUBBER BOAT bounced across the corrugated surface of the sea in a series of teeth-clacking belly flops. Zavala could have cut short the spastic flying fish leaps by reducing speed, but he had to keep the boat moving to stay with the containership.

"This thing feels like it's got four flat tires," Austin yelled over the high-pitched whine of the outboard motor.

Zavala's reply was drowned out by a detached wave top that hit him full in the face. He blinked the water from his eyes and spit out a mouthful. "Damn potholes!"

He expertly steered the boat closer, jogging the tiller to counter the artificial surf stirred up by the huge hull. His steering arm felt as if it was being wrenched from its socket. The boat lost way with each turn. Within minutes, it had dropped back, until it was almost halfway down the length of the ship. But Zavala's quick hand and steady eye had drastically cut the distance to the vessel.

The containership seemed like the legendary unstoppable force as it plowed through the seas that crashed against the high, flared bow. The flow of water against the hull created a barrier of white water that stood between Austin and his goal: the pilot ladder hanging down from the deck almost to the waterline. The *Adventure*'s deck was high above the water. The rope ladder was meant to provide access from a harbor pilot's boat to a fixed gangway that slanted down the ship's side.

From the deck of the *Leif Eriksson*, the task Austin had set for himself had looked difficult but not impossible. But the *Ocean Adventure* was as long as a skyscraper placed on its side. Even worse, this skyscraper was *moving*. As Austin looked up at the fortress-steep ramparts he hoped to scale, he wondered whether he had bitten off a bigger mouthful than he could chew.

He pushed the dangerously distracting thought from his mind, crawled up to the boat's prow, and dug his fingers into the slippery-wet surface of the rubber pontoons. When he was ready, Austin lifted one arm and signaled Zavala to make his move. Zavala angled the inflatable in toward the ladder. The rolling white water knocked the boat back like a cow brushing away a fly. Zavala had to play catch-up again.

Austin clung to the bow as Zavala tried to keep pace without going broadside to a sea that could easily flip the boat over. Cold spray stung his eyes and blurred his vision. The noise created by the rush of water, the outboard motor, and the ship's engines made communication, and even thought, nearly impossible. Just as well. If Austin thought about what he was about to do, he would not do it.

He was starting to tire from the constant beating. If he didn't make a move soon, his biggest obstacle would be sheer exhaustion. Pluck and determination would come off second best against the simple laws of physics.

A voice crackled over his walkie-talkie.

"*Kurt*. Come in." Captain Dawe was calling him.

"No can do," Austin shouted into the mouthpiece. "Busy."

"I know. I'm watching you. Just heard from the rig. The last anchor line is tangled. A collision looks like a sure thing. You'd better move away from the impact area or you could get caught up in a hell of a mess."

Austin made a snap decision. He pointed at the containership and shouted over his shoulder.

"Oil rig's stuck, Joe. We're going in."

Zavala gave him a thumbs-up and smoothly cranked the tiller to move the boat within yards of the ship. Once more, the small craft was buffeted by artificial surf. Zavala kept the boat riding the roiling hull wash like a Hawaiian surfer until it was slightly ahead of the boarding ladder.

The rope ladder had become entangled in the "man lines," the safety ropes that hung down from either side. Zavala brought the motor up to full throttle and went in at a shallow angle. The boat tipped on its side like a heeling sailboat. Zavala and Austin threw their body weight on the higher side. The boat rode the rushing water until it was within reach of the ladder slapping against the side of the ship.

Austin felt like a salmon swimming upstream as the boat danced on the churning water. With the ladder finally in reach, he wedged his feet under the pontoon sides of the inflatable, slipped out of his flotation vest, and rose in a semicrouch. He needed full freedom of movement, and the vest would be of little use if he screwed up. He would have only one chance and if he missed he would land in the water, get swept back alongside the ship, and likely be ground to pieces in the ship's propeller.

He felt the boat falling away and he reached up, his fingers still inches from the bottom of the rope. He was extended out over the bow, clawing for air. The chasm that yawned between his fingers and the ladder was widening beyond the point of no return. Then the rope snapped closer, and he grabbed the bottom rung like an acrobat in flight.

As Austin's fingers closed on the rung, Zavala swung the boat back away from the ship to avoid flipping over. Austin dangled at the end of the ladder, reached up blindly, and grabbed the next rung. The hard rubber step was slippery with seawater. He almost lost his grip when a wave washed up around his waist and dragged him down, but he held on and pulled himself higher.

The ladder had stabilized slightly with Austin's body weight on it, but the double rope was still twisting on itself. He almost let go when his hand scraped against the steel hull. His knuckles felt as if they had been dipped in acid. He had no choice but to ignore the pain and keep climbing.

He tilted his head back to see how far he was from the gangway that angled against the hull. He was encouraged by what he saw. He was halfway up the ladder. Only a few more rungs and he'd be able to reach the small platform at the bottom of the metal steps.

He grabbed on to a couple of rungs, pulled himself higher, and glanced up again. Someone was peering at him from between two thin metal posts that extended vertically from the deck where those climbing the ladder could use them as handholds. A crown of unruly hair framed the dark-skinned face of a man. His gap-toothed mouth was set in a wide grin.

The face disappeared, and an arm reached over the side. The hand at the end of the arm clutched a knife whose long blade was sawing through the rope ladder.

"Hey!" Austin called out, for want of anything more appropriate.

The knife hesitated, but went back to work and quickly severed the rope. The rope ladder dropped a short distance. Austin was slammed against the hull. The impact almost jolted his hands loose from the ladder. He held on and looked up again. Aw, hell, he muttered. The knife was sawing the second ladder rope.

He reached for a man line that had blown free and was twisting in the wind and got both hands on it as the knife went through the second rope. The severed ladder dropped into the crushing sea and instantly disappeared.

Austin's head slammed against the side of the ship like a clapper in a bell. Galaxies whirled before his eyes. He clung tenaciously to consciousness aware that a single swipe of the knife blade against the line would send him to his death. He reached over and grabbed the bottom step of the gangplank, then swung under the platform, where he hoped he would be invisible to the happy knifeman.

He stayed there for a few moments. When he could hold on no longer, he pulled his body onto the platform and crawled on his hands and knees up the steps until he was at the opening in the deck rail. He leaped onto the deck in a clumsy defensive stance and was glad to see that no one was waiting in ambush.

Austin waved at Zavala, who was running a parallel course to the containership. Zavala waved back.

The captain's frantic voice crackled in the walkie-talkie. "You okay, Kurt?"

Austin felt like newly ground hamburger, but he said, "Finest kind, Cap. I'm on the ship. How long do I have?"

"You're about five miles from the rig. You'll have to allow time for the ship's momentum to stop or turn."

Austin sprinted for the sterncastle, but a terrible sound stopped him in his tracks. Coming from a space between container stacks was a woman's scream, and there was no mistaking the terror in her voice.

12

CARINA HAD REGAINED CONSCIOUSNESS only minutes before Austin had climbed aboard the ship. Her return to the land of the living had some drawbacks. Her head throbbed with pain. Her vision was squirrelly. Waves of nausea sloshed around in her stomach.

The ache and discomfort kept her from sliding back into oblivion, and she became aware that she was still in the container, her body lodged between packing crates. Her arms were bound tightly behind her back. In their haste, the hijackers had left her legs untied.

Combining sheer force of will with a lean physique strengthened from hours of working out at the UNESCO gym, Carina rolled onto her belly. Using her tight abdominal muscles to the max, she leveraged her body into a kneeling position. She stood on wobbly legs and waited until the dizziness passed. Then she backed up to a packing crate and rubbed the duct tape binding her wrists against the corner.

Splinters stabbed at her skin, but she ignored the pain. After a few minutes of self-inflicted torture, she slipped one hand free. She was prying the tape off her wrists when a figure appeared in the opening the hijackers had cut into the container.

Carina recognized the man's face. She didn't know his name, only that he was one of the Filipino crewmen she had seen working around the ship.

"Am I glad to see you," she said with a sigh of relief.

"I am *very* glad to see you, *senorita*," the man said with a wolfish gleam in his eye.

Carina's feminine antennae picked up the suggestion of danger in his voice.

She glanced past the crewman's shoulder. "Are the hijackers gone?"

"No," he said with a grin. "We are still aboard."

We.

Carina tried to step past him. The Filipino shifted position to block her way.

"What do you want?" she said, regretting the words the instant they left her mouth.

The Filipino's lips curled like slices of liverwurst in a frying pan. "I come to kill you. But, first, we have a little fun."

He grabbed Carina's shoulders. He was several inches shorter than she was but much stronger. He stuck his foot out behind her ankle and pushed against her chest. She fell backward. The crewman crashed down and pinned her to the floor. As Carina struggled to push him off, he produced a knife and slashed away the thin leather belt around her waist.

She beat at his face with her fists, scoring a few light punches on his unshaven chin that were more an annoyance than a defense. He stuck the knife into the side of a crate to free both hands—and Carina screamed at the top of her lungs. There was no one on the ship who could come to her aid, but maybe the piercing shriek would distract her attacker.

He backed off, and she lunged for the knife. He saw the move and smashed her in the jaw with his open hand. The blow nearly knocked her out. She stopped struggling. She could feel him jerking her jeans down to her knees, smell his foul breath, and hear his heavy breathing. She could only make feeble efforts to push him back. Then she heard a low, male voice.

"I wouldn't do that if I were you," the voice said.

The Filipino snatched the knife from the crate. He scrambled to his feet and whirled to face the intruder.

A broad-shouldered man stood in the jagged-edged rectangle of light, legs wide apart. His pale, almost-white hair looked like a halo in the backlight.

The Filipino sprang forward with his knife extended. Carina expected to hear a cry of pain as the blade plunged into flesh, but the only sound was a clink and a scrape, as if someone were sharpening a kitchen knife.

Austin had picked up a cuneiform clay tablet he'd seen lying on the deck. He was holding the flat stone down by his knees when he stepped into the container and saw the drama unfolding. When the man turned, Austin recognized the face that had peered out over the deck as he was climbing the rope ladder. With a speed that surprised his attacker, he had hitched the tablet up to his chest to shield against the knife thrust.

As the blade slid harmlessly off to one side, Austin lifted the tablet high above his head and brought it down as if he were beating a rug. The clay broke over the crewman's head and shattered into dozens of pieces. The Filipino miraculously stayed up for a few second, then his eyes rolled back into his head and he folded like a concertina.

Austin stepped over the twitching body and offered his hand to the woman. She reached out and pulled herself to a standing position. With trembling fingers, she hoisted her jeans back up to her waist.

"Are you all right?" he said. There was concern in the coral blue eyes.

Carina nodded. She glared at the crewman's body. "Thank you for saving me from that animal. I hope you killed him."

"I probably did. Are you part of the ship's crew?"

"I'm a passenger. The ship was hijacked. They came in helicopters. They took the *Navigator*."

Austin thought she was talking about one of the ship's crew. "Who?"

Carina saw Austin's confusion. "The *Navigator*. It's . . . it's a statue."

Austin nodded. The woman's reply made about as much sense as anything. He picked up the knife that had fallen from the crewman's hand. "Sorry to hit and run. I've got to tend to a few errands. See if you can find another hiding place. We'll talk later over dinner."

He slipped through the hole in the container and was gone. Carina stood there in a daze. She wondered whether she had dreamed up this avenging angel who could save her life, coolly dispatch her attacker, and suggest having dinner, all in one breath. She didn't know who he was, but she decided to take his advice. She glanced without sympathy at the Filipino, then beat a hasty exit from the container and lost herself in the labyrinth of cargo stacks.

As AUSTIN'S FEET pounded on the enormous deck, he knew that he was facing long odds. His detour to save a damsel in distress was going to be fatal to both of them. There was just too much horizontal and vertical distance to cover on foot. The deck stretched out ahead of him. He still had to get to the top of a bridge house as tall as an apartment building.

He pumped his legs in a touchdown sprint. He was moving so fast that the metal gleam glimpsed between stacks didn't register in his brain until he was several yards past it. He turned back and poked his head into the opening. The gleam had come from the chrome handlebars of a bicycle leaning against a container. Austin would have preferred a Harley-Davidson, but the battered old Raleigh three-speed used by crewmen to get around the giant ship would do.

He pulled the bike out, threw a leg over the seat, and started pedaling, using all the power in his muscular legs. As he sped along the deck, he noticed several bodies on the deck at the base of the bridge tower.

As he got closer, he could see that the men were still alive but tied hand and foot and lying facedown. He tossed the bike aside and went over to a heavyset man who was struggling against his bindings. Austin told him to hold still and sliced the wrist tape with one swipe of the knife.

The man used his freed hands to push himself over onto his side. Austin saw that he was middle-aged, and his weathered face was framed with heavy jowls. The man's eyes went to the knife blade, but he seemed to relax when Austin cut his leg bindings and asked if he were a ship's officer.

"I am Captain Lange, master of the *Ocean Adventure*."

Austin helped the captain to unsteady feet. "What happened to the hijackers?" he said.

"I don't know. They came on helicopters." Lange pointed skyward. "They landed on top of the containers. Who are you?"

"A *friend*. Introductions later." Austin braced the captain by his shoulders to make sure he had his attention. "Your ship is on a collision course with an oil platform. You've only got a few minutes to stop or change course or you won't *have* a ship. "

The blood drained from the captain's face. "I saw them set the autopilot."

"You'll have to disable it as soon as possible. I'll free your men."

"I'm on my way," the captain said, wobbling toward the bridge on stiff-kneed legs.

Austin quickly cut the tape binding the other crewmen and told them to follow the captain to the bridge. He wasn't worried about running into the hijackers. They would be unlikely to stick around after putting the ship on its disastrous course. He knew his instincts were on target when he heard the threshing sound of helicopter rotors above his head.

WITH THEIR MISSION accomplished, the hijackers had been preparing to abandon ship. Their baby-faced leader had finished inspecting the lines securing the canvas-wrapped object when the second Filipino who'd been embedded in the ship's crew ran over.

"Juan isn't back," said the man, whose name was Carlos. "I don't know what he's doing."

The leader smiled. "I know *exactly* what your friend is doing. He's disobeying orders." He climbed through the door into the nearest helicopter.

"What should we do?" Carlos said.

"Keep him company, if you'd like." He smiled and closed the door.

A panicked look came to the Filipino's face. He dashed for the other helicopter and clambered into the cabin as the rotors reached takeoff speed. The helicopter rose slowly from the containers. Dangling from the fuselage was a line with a hook attached to the end of it. The helicopter moved around to stern.

The helicopter hovered over the object wrapped in canvas. The chopper dropped down and engaged the hook of a rope loop at the top of the object. Austin watched the maneuver from around the corner of the bridge house.

In the brief time Austin had known the hijackers, he had come to dislike them intensely. Bending low, he ran toward the object and undid the hook attached to the end of the helicopter's Kevlar line. He wrapped the line around a bollard and hooked it to itself.

He was running back to the shelter of the bridge house when he felt as if a hot iron had been plunged into his ribs. Someone was shooting at him and he'd been hit. Ignoring the pain, Austin hit the deck and rolled over several times.

A second before he made a prairie dog dive into an open hatchway, he looked up and saw the second helicopter. A gun barrel protruded from the open door.

With all the confusion, the pilot of the other helicopter was unaware that his aircraft was attached to the deck. He tried to gain altitude and gave the helicopter extra power to compensate for the weight. The chopper reached the end of the line, came to a jarring halt, and began to gyrate like a kite on a string.

The line caught in the rotor blades, which severed the connection. Spinning crazily, the helicopter arced out over the waves and crashed into the sea with an impact that sent up a monumental splash.

Austin peered from the hatchway. The other helicopter circled over the expanding circle of foamy bubbles. A man stood in the helicopter door, looked down at Austin, and they locked eyes for a second. A smile spread across the man's cherubic face. A second later, the helicopter banked off and flew away from the ship.

Austin climbed back onto the deck and saw why the helicopter hadn't bothered to make another pass. The Great Western oil rig loomed directly ahead.

With the wind whipping at his clothes, he gazed up to the bridge, silently cheering the captain on. He could imagine the desperate struggle in the pilothouse as the captain tried to avoid a calamity. The ship was still moving at full power. Austin put himself in the captain's place. Even if Lange killed the engines, the ship would continue moving on its momentum. The captain would want to maintain even the tiniest shred of control that the engines would allow.

As the ship closed in on the platform, Austin detected a shift of a few degrees to the right. The ship was finally going into its turn. It would need sea room to miss the rig. Austin knew that a ship the size of the *Ocean Adventure* didn't turn on a dime.

He leaned over the rail and saw crewmen scrambling on the oil platform like ants on a floating leaf. A couple of service boats strained against the lines attached to the platform. Icy fingers grabbed at his heart as he pictured the inevitable collision.

Someone was calling Austin as if from afar. He realized that the voice was coming from the walkie-talkie earpiece dangling at his side. He stuck the plug in his ear.

"Kurt, can you hear me? Are you okay?"

Austin cut into Dawe's frantic soliloquy.

"Just dandy. What's happening with the rig?"

"They've untangled the last anchor."

The sentence was barely out of the captain's mouth when Austin saw a burst of foam where the rig's anchor had pulled free of the water. White water boiled around the rig's legs. The wakes forming behind the legs indicated that the platform was on the move.

The rig's evasive action would still fall short. The ship would strike the front right leg within seconds. Austin braced himself for the impact.

At the last instant, the ship's bow moved slightly more to starboard. There was a tortured scraping of metal on metal as the side of the ship grazed the leg. The platform was free of its anchors, and, instead of resisting, which would have spelled its doom, the rig gave way to the force of the impact.

The oil platform rocked from the blow, then slowly stabilized and continued moving out of the danger zone.

A ship's horn was blowing madly. The *Leif Eriksson* had been keeping him company.

Zavala's voice came over his earpiece.

"That's one way to scrape the barnacles off your hull. What do you do for an encore?"

"That's easy," Austin said. "I'm going to make a dinner date with a beautiful woman."

13

THE ASSISTANT LIBRARIAN IN the archives division of the American Philosophical Society in Philadelphia was a slightly built young woman named Angela Worth. Day after day spent hoisting cases filled with documents and files had given her strength that would have been the envy of a professional arm wrestler.

With little apparent effort Angela slid a heavy plastic container off a shelf and placed it on a cart. She wheeled the cart out of the manuscript vault into a reading room. A man in his midthirties sat at a long library table, his fingers tapping at a laptop computer. The table was piled high with files, papers, and documents.

She set the file box on the table. "Bet you didn't know there was so much historical material about artichokes."

"Fine with me," said the man, a writer whose name was Norman Stocker. "My contract calls for a fifty-thousand-word manuscript."

"I don't know much about the publishing business, but would *any*one want to read that much about artichokes?"

"My *editor* thinks so. These single-subject historical books on everyday things are a trend in the publishing biz. Cod. Salt. Tomatoes. Mushrooms. You name it. The trick is to show how your given subject changed the world and saved mankind. You've got it made if you can mix in some sex."

"Sexy artichokes?"

Stocker opened a file folder containing copies of old manuscripts. "Sixteenth-century Europe. Only men are allowed to eat artichokes, which are considered to enhance sexual power." He opened another folder and slipped out a photograph of a pretty young blond woman wearing a bathing suit. "Marilyn Monroe. 1947. California's first Artichoke Queen."

Angela lifted the box off the cart and deposited it on the table. She blew a strand of long blond hair off her face. "Can't wait to see *Artichoke: The Movie.*"

"I'll get you a ticket to the Hollywood premiere."

Angela smiled and told Stocker to let her know when he wanted to get rid of the files. Stocker opened the box and dug into the contents.

Writing books on commodities wouldn't have been his first choice, but the pay wasn't bad, the travel could be interesting, and the books gave him visibility. As long as he wrote, he didn't have to teach to pay his bills. He rationalized that as a subject, artichokes were better than kumquats.

Stocker had come to the American Philosophical Society to look for the type of obscure anecdotes that could spice up an otherwise dry topic. The Georgian-style building that housed the society's library around the corner from Independence Hall in Philadelphia was one of the nation's major repositories of manuscripts on many scientific disciplines from the 1500s to the present.

The organization had been founded in 1745 by an amateur scientist named Benjamin Franklin. Franklin and his friends wanted to make the United States independent in the fields of manufacturing, transportation, and agriculture. The society's early members included doctors, lawyers, clergy, and artisans, as well as presidents Jefferson and Washington.

Stocker was riffling through the carton when his fingers touched a hard surface. He pulled out an envelope that contained a box bound in maroon-and-gold animal skin. Inside the box was a thick packet of crackly paper tied with a black ribbon that had been sealed at some point. The wax seal had since been broken. He untied the ribbon and peeled off the blank cover sheet to reveal words written in a tight longhand that identified the contents as a treatise on the cultivation of artichokes.

The material was an unexciting recitation of growing seasons, fertilizer and harvest times, with a few recipes scattered among the pages. One sheet of parchment was marked with Xs and wavy lines and several words of script in an unknown language. On the bottom of the packet was a thick cardboard sheet perforated with dozens of small rectangular holes.

The assistant librarian was passing by the writer's table with a load of books. He waved her over.

"Find something of interest in that last box?" she said.

"I don't know how interesting it is, but it's certainly old."

Angela examined the hidebound box, and then she went through the pages from top to bottom. The handwriting looked familiar. She went to the stacks and came back with a book on the American Revolution. She opened the volume to a photo of the Declaration of Independence and held one of the papers next to the page. The similarity of the flowing, tightly written script on both samples was remarkable.

"Notice anything?" Angela said.

"The handwriting is practically identical," Stocker said.

"It *should* be. Both these documents were written by the same person."

"Jefferson? It *can't* be."

"Why not? Jefferson was a gentleman farmer, a scientist, and a meticulous keeper of records. Look here, in the corner of the title page. Those tiny letters are TJ."

"This is great! There isn't much here that would interest the average reader, but the fact that a Jefferson document on artichokes ended up with all this other stuff is worth at least a couple of paragraphs."

Angela wrinkled her brow. "It must have landed here by mistake."

"How could someone misfile original Jeffersonian material?"

"The society has an incredible filing system. But we've got eight million manuscripts and more than three hundred thousand volumes and bound periodicals. My guess is that someone saw the title, didn't notice who had written the treatise, and tossed it in with the other agricultural material."

He handed over the diagram. "This was in the file. It looks like a garden that was laid out by a drunk."

The assistant librarian glanced at the diagram, then picked up the perforated cardboard and held it to the light. An idea occurred to her. "Let me know when you're through. I'll want to make sure that it goes back in with the other Jefferson material."

She returned to her desk. As she worked, she glanced impatiently from time to time at the writer's table. It was near closing when he stood and stretched and slid the laptop into its bag. She hurried over.

"Sorry for the mess," he said.

"Not a problem. I'll take care of everything," she said.

She waited for the other patrons to leave and took the Jefferson file over to her desk. Under the light of her desk lamp, she placed the cardboard on top of the first page of writing. Individual letters showed through the small rectangles.

Angela was a crossword buff and had read a number of books on codes and ciphers. She was sure that what she held in her hand was a cipher grille. The grille would be placed over a blank sheet of paper. The message would be written in the holes by letter. Innocent-looking sentences would be built around the letters. The person on the receiving end would place an identical grille over the message and the words would pop out.

She tried the grille on a number of pages, but all she got was gibberish. She suspected that there was another level of encryption that was far beyond her amateur skill to decipher. She turned her attention to the parchment with the wavy lines and Xs. She stared at the words accompanying the strange markings and then called up a lexicon site on her computer. She sometimes went to the research site as a cheat to find obscure words that were used in the crossword puzzles.

Angela typed the words from the parchment onto the site's search function and hit the ENTER key. There was no immediate translation, but the site referred her to its ancient-language section. She requested a translation once more and this time the program responded with an answer that both startled and puzzled her.

She ran off a printout and copied it, along with the Jefferson material. Leaving the copies in her drawer, she gathered up the original files and walked down the hallway to her supervisor's office.

Angela's boss was a middle-aged professional named Helen Woolsey. She looked up from her desk and smiled when she saw her younger protégée.

"Working late?" she said.

"Not exactly. I came across something unusual and thought you might be interested." She handed the packet over.

As the librarian examined the papers, Angela explained her theory about its authorship.

The librarian let out a low whistle. "It gives me a thrill just to touch something that Jefferson held in his hand. This is an *incredible* find."

"I *think* it is," Angela said. "I'm just guessing that Jefferson encoded a message in those papers. Jefferson was an accomplished cryptographer. Some of the systems he devised were used decades after he died."

"Obviously, it was sensitive material he didn't want made public."

"There's more," Angela said. She handed over the printout from the language website.

The librarian studied the sheet for a moment. "Is this website reliable?" she said.

"I've always found it to be," Angela said.

The librarian tapped the Jefferson packet with her long fingernail. "Does your writer friend know the significance of this material?"

"He knows the Jefferson connection," Angela said. "But he thinks it's what it seems to be, a manual on how to grow artichokes."

The librarian shook her head. "This isn't the first time Jefferson's papers have gone astray. He lost some ethnological material having to do with the American Indians, and many of the documents he willed to various institutions simply vanished. Did you come up with even a *suggestion* of what's in here?"

"Not a clue. This needs a code-breaking computer and a cryptologist who knows how to use it. I have a friend at the National Security Agency who may be able to help."

"Wonderful," the librarian said. "But before we contact him I'd better run this by the society's board of directors. We'll keep this discovery between the two of us for the time being. This could mean a lot to the society if it's authentic, but we don't want to be embarrassed if it turns out to be a fake."

Angela agreed with the need for secrecy, but she suspected that her boss wanted the opportunity to take full credit if the material proved to be an historical blockbuster. The librarian wasn't the only one who harbored ambitions. Angela didn't want to be an assistant for the rest of her life.

She nodded in agreement. "I will do everything I can to honor Mr. Jefferson's apparent wish for discretion."

"Very good," the librarian said. She opened a desk drawer, slid the file in, and shut the drawer. "This goes under lock and key until I can talk to the board. If this is a go, I'll see you're recognized for the find, of course."

Of course. You'll hog the limelight unless it's a fraud, then you'll blame me.

Angela's smile disguised her seditious thoughts. She stood and said, "Thank you, Ms. Woolsey."

The librarian smiled and went back to her papers. The discussion was over. As Angela said good night and closed the door behind her, the librarian opened the drawer and removed the Jefferson file. She consulted her address book for a phone number.

She felt a thrill of excitement as she punched out the number. It was the first time that she had used it. She had been given the number by a member of the board of directors, since deceased, who had recognized her cold ambition and asked if she would like to take over a job he was no longer able to handle because of his failing health. She would work for an eccentric individual with a fascination for certain subjects. She had only to keep her eyes and ears open for discussion of these topics, at which time she would be required to make a phone call.

The money arrangement was quite generous for virtually no work, and she had used it to furnish her apartment and buy a secondhand BMW. She was pleased to earn her pay at last. She was disappointed to hear a recorded voice which told her to leave a message. She gave the recorder a brief summary of the Jefferson findings and hung up. She experienced a moment of panic when she realized that the call may have ended her service to the unknown paymaster. But after a moment's reflection, she concluded with a smile that the Jefferson file could start her off on a new and lucrative career as well.

She would not have been as sanguine had she known that her call could have far more lethal repercussions. Nor would she have been pleased to know that in another part of the American Philosophical Society building, her assistant sat at her desk making a phone call of her own.

14

AUSTIN WAS HAVING HIS RIBS bandaged by a ship's officer who doubled as a medical technician when the sick bay
door opened and Captain Lange walked in with Carina on his arm.

"I found this young lady wandering about the ship," Lange said
to Austin, who was sitting on an examining table. "She tells me a
knight in shining armor saved her life."

"My armor has a few chinks in it," Austin said. In addition to his
creased rib, his face was bruised and knuckles were lacerated from
the battering he'd suffered during his climb up the pilot's ladder.

"I'm very sorry about your injuries," Carina said.

Carina's face was swollen where the crewman named Juan had
punched her. Even with her lopsided jaw, Carina was a striking
woman. She was long-legged and slender, and had a head-turning
physical presence about her. Her cinnamon-and-cream complexion
set off bright blue eyes under perfectly arched brows. Shoulder-
length sable hair was tied back away from her face.

"Thanks," Austin said, "it's just a scratch. The bullet only grazed
me. I'm more concerned about you."

"You're very kind. I put a cold compress on my face and that reduced the swelling. The inside of my mouth is a little raw, but my teeth are intact."

"I'm greatly relieved. You'll need your all teeth when we have dinner together."

Carina displayed a crooked smile. "We haven't even been properly introduced, Mr. Austin."

Austin extended his hand. "Please call me Kurt, Miss Mechadi."

"Very well, Kurt. Call me Carina. How did you know my name?"

"This gentleman, who is doing such a fine job patching me up, said that you were a passenger on the ship, and that you're with the United Nations. Beyond those sketchy details, you are a mystery, Carina."

"Not mysterious at all. I'm an investigator with UNESCO. My job is to track down stolen antiquities. If *anyone* is a mystery, it is Kurt Austin. You're the one who rose from the sea like a merman and saved the ship and the oil platform after you rescued me."

"The captain deserves most of the credit. He steered the ship away from the rig. If I had been at the helm, we'd all be picking crude oil out of our front teeth."

"Kurt is being far too modest," Lange admonished. "He freed me and my crew. While I steered the ship, he fought off the hijackers and saved a piece from your cargo."

Carina's face lit up. "You saved the *Navigator*?"

Austin nodded. "There's a large object wrapped in canvas sitting on the deck. Might be your statue."

"I'll have it moved immediately to a safe place," Lange said. He called the bridge on his pocket radio and ordered his first mate to round up a work crew.

The mate said that a Coast Guard cutter was on its way and that the shipowners' representatives were flying in. The captain excused himself and the medical technician went with him, after handing Austin some painkillers.

"I'm curious," Austin said. "What's so special about the *Navigator?*"

"That is what's so odd," Carina said with furrowed brow. "The statue is not terribly valuable and may even be a fake."

"In that case, let's talk about things we *do* know about. Like our dinner date."

"How could I forget your unexpected invitation, especially after your sudden appearance? But first tell me where on earth you came from."

"Not on earth. On the *sea*. I was in the neighborhood lassoing icebergs."

Carina glanced at Austin's broad shoulders. She wouldn't have been surprised if he *wrestled* icebergs. She assumed he was joking until he explained what he had been doing on the *Leif Eriksson*.

Carina had encountered scores of memorable men in the course of travels around the world, But Austin was truly unique. He had risked his life to save hundreds of people and property worth millions of dollars, fought off hijackers, even killing one of them to rescue her. Yet he was flirting like an impetuous schoolboy. Her eyes roamed over his hard, tanned body. From the looks of the pale scars marking his bronze skin, this wasn't the first time he had put himself in danger and had paid a price for it.

Carina reached out to touch a circular scar on Austin's prominent right bicep. She was about to ask if it were a gunshot wound, but, just then, the door opened and a slender, dark-complexioned man stepped into the sick bay.

Joe Zavala's eyes widened in surprise, and then his lips turned up at the corners in his trademark half smile. He had heard that Austin was being treated for a wound. No one had told him about the lovely young woman who seemed to be caressing his friend's arm.

"I stopped by to see how you were doing," Zavala said. "From the looks of things, you're doing pretty well."

"Carina, this gentleman is Joe Zavala, my friend and colleague.

We're both with the National Underwater and Marine Agency. Joe piloted the boat that brought me over to the ship. Don't be alarmed by his piratical looks. He's quite harmless."

"Nice to meet you, Carina." Zavala gestured at Austin's bandage. "Are you okay? You both look a little banged-up."

"Yes, we're quite the couple." Carina said. She blushed at the implication in her comment and removed her hand from Austin's arm.

Austin went to her rescue and brought the conversation back to himself. "I'm a little stiff around the ribs. Bad bruising, and scrapes in a few other places."

"Nothing a shot or two of tequila wouldn't help," Zavala said.

"I can see you are in good hands," Carina said. "If you don't mind, I'll go see how the crew is doing with my statue. Thanks again for all you have done."

Zavala gazed at the door after it had closed behind Carina and let out a whooping laugh that was uncharacteristic of his usual quiet-spoken demeanor.

"Only Kurt Austin could find an angel like Miss Mechadi out here in the fogbound reaches of Iceberg Alley. And they call *me* a Romeo."

Austin rolled his eyes. He slid off the table, pulled on a borrowed blue denim work shirt and buttoned up the front.

"Captain Dawe holding up okay?"

"He's reached the end of his joke repertoire and has begun to recycle old ones."

"Sorry about that, old pal."

"He says he'll stand by another day, but then he's got to go chase Moby-Berg. So you're not off the hook yet."

"How'd you get aboard? Last I knew, the pilot's ladder was cut."

"They must have dug up a spare. You had a tough time climbing on board. What happened?"

"I'll lay out the whole sordid tale over a cup of coffee."

They headed for the mess hall, where they poured themselves steaming mugs of coffee and devoured a couple of tall pastrami sandwiches on pumpernickel. Starting with the close call boarding the *Ocean Adventure,* Austin gave Zavala a detailed account of his exploits on the containership.

"Someone went through a lot of expense and trouble to steal this statue," Zavala said, after pursing his lips in a low whistle.

"Seems that way. It takes money to buy helicopters and organization to mount a hijacking at sea. Not to mention the connections needed to put a couple of moles on board to welcome the hijackers."

"They could have simply stolen the statue and run for it," Zavala said. "Why destroy the ship and the oil rig?"

"By getting rid of the ship, they eliminate evidence and witnesses. The oil rig was simply a means to an end. It has a certain clinical neatness about it. The sea claims all."

Zavala slowly shook his head. "What kind of a mind would think up a bloodthirsty scheme like that?"

"A very cold and calculating one," Austin said. "The choppers must have come from an ocean launchpad. We're within helicopter range of land, but the coast is pretty rugged. I can't see them flying any great distance with a heavy weight hanging at the end of a rope."

"A water-launched attack on a moving target makes the most sense," Zavala agreed.

"Which means we may be wasting time," Austin said. "They could still be in the area."

"Unfortunately, there's no air support on this ship," Zavala said.

Austin cocked his head in thought. "I remember Captain Dawe saying that a helicopter was due back on the rig. Let's go see if it's arrived."

He chugged down a painkiller with a final swallow of coffee and led the way out of the mess hall. Captain Lange welcomed them on the bridge. Austin borrowed a pair of binoculars and pointed them at the oil rig. He could see a helicopter on the oil platform.

"This is quite a vantage point, "Austin said."Did you see what direction the hijackers flew in from?"

"Unfortunately, no. It happened very fast." Lange's face flushed with anger at the recollection.

"What do you know about the two Filipino crewmen who were working with the hijackers?" Austin said.

"They were vetted through the usual hiring practices," Lange said. "There was nothing in their records to indicate that they were pirates."

"It's possible that the men who shipped on board weren't the real owners of the papers," Zavala said.

"What do you mean?"

"They either stole the papers from the real crewmen or killed to get them," Zavala said.

"In which case, we can add two more murders to this gang's list of crimes." Austin said.

The captain swore softly in German. "You know, sometimes when you're up here, guiding this big ship across the ocean, you feel like King Neptune." He shook his jowls. "Then something like this happens and you see how impotent you really are. I would much rather deal with the sea than with monsters of my own species."

Austin knew from experience exactly what the captain was talking about, but they would have to postpone their philosophical discussion to another time."I wondered if you would mind getting in touch with the oil platform operators," he said. He told the captain what he and Zavala had in mind.

Lange got on the radio immediately. The rig operators were hesitant to send the helicopter over at first but changed their mind when

Lange said the request was coming from the man who had saved the platform and its crew from destruction.

Twenty minutes later, the helicopter lifted off from the rig and flew the short distance to the containership. The chopper touched down on the wide foredeck. Austin and Zavala ran under the still-spinning rotors. The aircraft was airborne a moment later. They had barely adjusted their intercoms when the pilot said, "Where to, gents?"

The hijackers had a big head start, which meant that it was un-likely they would be anywhere near the ship. Austin asked the pilot, whose name was Riley, to head in any direction for five miles, then go into a low-altitude expanding spiral with the ship at its center.

Riley gave him a thumbs-up and flew the helicopter due west at about a hundred miles an hour.

"What are we looking for?" Riley said.

"Anything big enough to hold two choppers," Austin replied.

Riley gave another thumbs-up. "I got ya."

Several minutes later he put the helicopter into a banking turn and made the first circle. The fog had cleared and visibility was two to three miles. They saw a handful of fishing boats and big chunks of ice, including one which might have been Moby-Berg. The only large ship was a freighter. Its deck was too small to hold two copters and was obstructed by cranes that would have made takeoff and landing impossible.

Austin asked the pilot to make two more circles. On the second circuit, they saw a big vessel silhouetted against the ocean sheen.

"Ore carrier," said Zavala from the backseat.

The helicopter dropped to an altitude of a few hundred feet and paced the black-hulled ship. Rectangular hatch covers that covered ore-storage holds were evenly spaced on the long deck between the tall crew house at one end and the high, raised bow at the other.

"What do you think?" Austin asked the pilot.

"Hell. It'd be easy to land a chopper on that deck," Riley said. "It's like an aircraft carrier."

Zavala agreed. "If you wanted to hide something, there'd be plenty of room in those cargo holds."

"Hafta modify a few things," Riley said. "No big deal."

Austin asked the pilot to check out the ship's name.

The helicopter flew over the ship's wake, offering a clear view of the big white letters on the transom:

SEA KING

The ship was registered in Nicosia, Cyprus. There was a logo of what looked like a bull's head next to the name.

Austin had seen enough. "Let's head home."

The chopper wheeled around and the vessel faded into the haze.

As the *whup-whup* of the rotors faded, a pair of pale round eyes watched from the bridge until the helicopter shrunk to the size of a mosquito. Adriano lowered the binoculars, a tight smile on his lips. The helicopter had come close enough to give him a clear view of the face in the cockpit window.

The hunter had become the hunted.

As the oil platform helicopter approached the container-ship, a Coast Guard cutter could be seen anchored a short distance away. The pilot put the helicopter down on the deck of the con-tainership. When Austin and Zavala stepped out of the aircraft, Captain Lange was waiting for them. He said the Coast Guard had sent over an investigatory team to start interviewing witnesses.

Austin was going on sheer nerve power. His brain was fried. His rib cage throbbed. The last thing he wanted to deal with was a te-dious interrogation. A good night's sleep would be preferable. He knew that the Coast Guard would bring a fresh perspective to the crazy events of the day, but he was just plain weary.

The Coast Guard lieutenant who conducted the investigation in the recreation room was businesslike and efficient. He drew statements from Austin and the others, and said he would work his way through the rest of the crew. Austin must have winced with pain more than once, because the lieutenant suggested that he should have his wound properly tended to in a hospital. The captain said the oil rig helicopter could run him back to the mainland in the morning.

Carina asked if she could go with him. She said she wanted to attend a reception in Washington the next evening and wouldn't worry about her cargo with the Coast Guard cutter escorting the ship. Zavala wanted to get back to prepare for his trip to Istanbul. Austin called Captain Dawe and said they would have to take a rain check on the hunt for Moby-Berg.

"I'm disappointed," Dawe said. "I'll have some new jokes when you come back."

"I can't wait." Austin said.

15

VIKTOR BALTAZAR HAD LISTENED in silence as Adriano told him about the foiled hijacking plot. The bile had risen higher in his throat with each detail of the failed attempt to steal the Phoenician statue. Although he displayed no outward manifestation of his anger except for a vein pulsating in his forehead, Baltazar's fury was like the molten innards of a nascent volcano. When Adriano described how the mineral ship had been shadowed in a helicopter by the same pale-haired man who had prevented the theft of the statue, Baltazar could stand it no more.

"Enough," he growled.

Baltazar squeezed the cell phone in his mailed fist, tightening his thick fingers like a vise, until he felt the satisfying crunch of plastic and metal. He tossed the ruined instrument to the groom holding the reins of a giant gray sorrel. He took a steel helmet from the hands of his waiting squire and lowered it onto the padded cap on his head.

With his sturdy frame encased in gleaming armor from head to toe, Baltazar resembled a hulking robot from a science-fiction film epic. He was far more agile than any metallic monster, however. Even wearing armor that weighed seventy pounds, he easily pulled himself into the stallion's high-backed saddle.

The squire handed Baltazar a fifteen-foot wooden lance. Called a courtesy lance because of the blunt steel tip that distinguished it from a sharp-pointed war lance, the weapon was still potentially lethal when propelled forward by the power and strength of the huge Belgium horse. Baltazar had bred the animal from a long line of great warhorses that were known as *destriers* in medieval times. The animal was twice the size of an ordinary riding horse. Even without its protective armor, his mount weighed more than a ton.

Baltazar rested the lance across the thick, arching neck. The squire handed him a shield that came to a tapering point at the bottom. The head of a bull was emblazoned in black on the white shield. The same bull's-head motif decorated Baltazar's tunic and a flowing cloth that was draped over the horse's body.

With the lance at rest, Baltazar bent forward until he could see through the *occularium,* a narrow horizontal slit set high in the face of the helmet. On his left was a low, solid fence known as the tilt. On the other side of the tilt, at its far end, was a rider, also dressed in full armor, who was mounted on an equally large horse.

Baltazar had singled the man out of his mercenary corps. His practice opponent had a sturdy physique and was an accomplished rider. Like a sparring partner for a professional boxer, he usually came out on the losing end in his jousts with Baltazar. He was paid extra to compensate for his bumps and bruises. Baltazar tended to treat his opponent lightly, not because of any sympathy. He simply didn't want the bother of training a new practice knight. But after learning about the failure of the hijacking, Baltazar was in a murderous mood.

He glared at his unsuspecting opponent with blood in his eyes. He had refrained from unleashing his vicious temper on Adriano. The young Spaniard he had rescued from a murder charge was intensely loyal. Despite Adriano's size and strength, Balthazar's personal assassin was in some ways as delicate as a fine watch. Threatening or scolding Adriano would have sent him into a spell of despondency, and he might have dealt with it by going on a self-destructive and awkward killing spree.

Baltazar clenched his teeth and tightened the grip on his lance. A herald dressed in a gaudy medieval costume raised a trumpet to his lips and blew a single note. The signal to charge. Baltazar raised his lance and put his long gold spurs to the horse's flanks.

The massive animal dug its hooves into the sod and moved out in a deceptively slow amble known as pacing. The smooth ride kept the rider in his saddle where he was better able to aim the lance. Both riders kept their lances pointed toward their left at a thirty-degree angle. Each man kept his head two feet from the tilt and his right hand three feet. The left hand was protected by the raised shield.

The horses accelerated with a thunder of hooves. At the midpoint of the tilt the riders clashed. Baltazar's opponent was the first to score. His lance hit Baltazar's shield dead-on. The fluted breastplate was designed to shunt off a lance head, diluting the force of the impact, but the shaft shattered even before it was deflected to the side. Baltazar's lance found its mark a second later. The blunt tip slammed into his opponent's left shoulder.

Unlike his opponent's weapon, Baltazar's lance stayed intact. Even the blunted lance had a battering ram impact. The force of the moving horse and rider, concentrated on one small spot, knocked his opponent out of his stirrups. He crashed to the ground with a noise like a junkyard avalanche.

Baltazar wheeled his horse around and tossed the lance aside. He slid out of the saddle and drew his sword. His opponent's body was on its back, twisted at an unnatural angle. Ignoring the groans of pain, he stood over the man with straddled legs and held his sword high in both hands. The point was aimed down. He savored the moment, and then he drove the sword into the ground a few inches from the man's neck.

With a snarl of disgust, he left the sword in the ground and strode off toward a tent covered in fabric that repeated the bull's-head design. A medical crew that had been standing nearby hurried out to tend to the injured jouster.

Baltazar's squire helped him remove his armor. Underneath his chain mail suit he wore a protective layer made of Kevlar. His opponent would have worn the more traditional suit of padded cotton, which offered little protection. Baltazar always liked to give himself an edge. His lance contained an alloy core that prevented it from shattering like that of his opponent's wooden weapon.

Still wearing his chain mail, Baltazar got behind the wheel of an Umbrian red Bentley GTC convertible and drove away from the jousting field. He accelerated the twelve-cylinder, twin-turbocharged car to sixty miles per hour in less than five seconds. Although the car could go nearly two hundred miles per hour, he held it at half that speed. He raced along a road for a couple of miles before turning onto a driveway that led past manicured lawns to a vast pile of stone built in the style of a Spanish villa.

He parked the Bentley in front of the mansion and strode to the door. A house the size of Baltazar's would have begged for a large staff, but he employed only one servant, a trusted valet who doubled as a chef of considerable accomplishment. Baltazar lived in a few rooms of the mansion. If he needed chores done, he summoned members of his private army, who lived in a nearby barracks when they weren't patrolling the grounds of the vast estate.

The valet met him at the door. Despite his servant's quiet household manner and skills, he was a master of martial arts and highly trained as an armed bodyguard. Balthazar made his way to his pool house and stripped to the skin. He swam half a mile in the Olympic-sized pool and then soaked in the hot tub, letting the anger ooze out of him. After his bath, he slipped into a white hooded robe similar to those worn by monks.

Even dressed in the loose robe, Baltazar cut an imposing figure. The garment could hide the thick arms and legs, but there was no way to contain the wide shoulders. Baltazar's imposing head looked as if it had been sculpted out of granite that by some miracle of alchemy had been transformed, almost, into flesh and blood.

He left orders with his valet that he not be disturbed and locked himself in his portrait gallery. The walls of the huge room were covered with pictures of Baltazar's forebears going back hundreds of years. Baltazar poured cognac into a snifter, swished the liquor around, and took a sip. He set the glass aside and went over to an eighteenth-century oil painting of a young matron that hung on the wall near the huge flagstone fireplace. He put his face inches from the portrait so that their eyes met. He placed his hands on the carved panels to either side of the painting.

Tiny sensors located behind the subject's eyes probed his retinas and matched the findings with data in a computer database. Hidden scanners in the panels compared his hand- and fingerprints to those in a database. There was a soft click and a section of the wall opened to reveal a stairway.

He descended the stairs to a steel door that opened with a pushbutton combination. Behind the door was a room lined with glass-enclosed cabinets. The airtight cabinets were controlled for temperature and humidity to protect hundreds of thick volumes arranged by date.

The books contained the history of the Baltazar family going back more than two thousand years. The chronicles told of the family's origin in Palestine, its move to the island of Cyprus, where they flourished as shipbuilders. The family provided ships for the Fourth Crusade. They were involved in the bloody looting of Constantinople, where they stole as much gold as they could carry in their vessels.

After the Crusade, the family threw its lot in with the Crusaders.

They moved to western Europe and joined a cartel that used the stolen gold as the basis for a mineral empire. Since then, every birth, death, and marriage, going back to Cyprus, had been recorded. Business dealings. Feuds. Diaries. Each detail, no matter how sordid, embarrassing, or criminally liable, was enclosed between the covers of the gold-embossed volumes.

Baltazar had read every word in every volume, and it was his Crusader past that had stoked his interest in jousting and other trappings of chivalry. A touch screen computer built into the wall was used to make entries and serve as a reference guide.

A stone idol sat on a platform in the center of the room. It was the figure of a man, with his palms up, arms angled slightly downward, as if he were waiting to be handed something. He had a round, bearded face, and his lips were spread wide in a smile that was just short of a leer. Twin horns protruded from the sides of his head. The god Ba'al was given a special place because he was the namesake of the Baltazar family, which had courted his favor and asked it to guard its fortunes since its very beginning.

The idol had been used in unspeakable rites of human sacrifice. It had originally been set up on the edge of a fiery pit. The stone feet were still blackened by smoke and heat. In hard times, priests of Ba'al would sacrifice infants, placing them on the sloping arms, where they rolled into the flames. Instead of a blazing fire, the space in front of the idol was occupied by an altar. Sitting on the altar was a chest made of dark wood and decorated with dozens of precious stones.

Baltazar pushed back the lid and lifted out a smaller, undecorated wooden box. Inside the box were several sheets of parchment, which Baltazar spread out on the altar. His father had introduced him to the contents of the box when the family's main base was still in Europe. The script told of his family's history before it fled to Cyprus. But it was not until he was older and had studied Aramaic that he was able to understand the dark secrets that had resulted in their exile.

As he read the instructions set forth by his ancient ancestor, he could feel the weight of centuries pressing down on his shoulders. After a moment, he carefully replaced the parchment in its twin receptacles and closed the lid.

He lifted eyes that were nearly colorless and saw Ba'al's stony gaze. It was as if the ancient god were looking directly into his soul. Power seemed to flow from the statue into Baltazar's body. He drank in the invisible emanations like a thirsty pilgrim until it seemed as if he would burst.

He backed up to the door, then turned and climbed the stairs to his study. Still shaken by the experience, he finished his brandy to calm his nerves. Then he picked up the telephone. He punched the keys, and his call was relayed to Adriano through a series of connections, each designed to disguise its origin.

Baltazar thirsted for details on the failed hijacking and theft. He wanted to know the identity of the man who had spoiled his plans. Whoever he was would receive the same fate as hundreds of others who had run afoul of the Baltazars: the promise of a long and painful death.

16

FOR A SUPERSECRET GOVERNMENT ENTITY, the National Security Agency is remarkably visible to the world at large. The NSA's headquarters are at Fort Meade, Maryland, between Baltimore and Washington, in two high-rise office buildings, faced in blue-black glass, that look as if they had been created by a cubist in a dark frame of mind.

The office buildings are an illusion. The structures represent only part of an extensive complex said to include ten acres of underground operations. The NSA is the largest employer of mathematicians in the U.S., possibly the world, and the agency's twenty thousand or so employees include the best cryptologists in the country.

Angela Worth, the assistant librarian at the American Philosophical Society, drove past the NSA complex and turned into the parking lot for the National Cryptographic Museum. She had arisen early in the day, called in sick, and driven south from Philadelphia. She found a parking space, grabbed an old briefcase from the passenger seat, and headed for the museum's front door.

She asked the receptionist in the museum's lobby if she could see D. Grover Harris. A few minutes later, she was approached by a skinny, mop-headed young man dressed in jeans. He shook Angela's hand.

"Hi, Angela," he said with a bashful grin. "Nice of you to come all this way."

"No problem, Deeg. Thanks for seeing me."

Angela had met Deeg at a convention of puzzle fans. They had hit it off immediately. They were both geeks. Deeg was pleasant and good-looking, and impossibly bright. And like Angela, he was low on the institutional ladder. He ushered her into his cluttered office and offered her a seat. The space was hardly bigger than a closet, confirming Harris's bottom status on the agency's food chain.

Harris settled behind a paper-covered desk that would have been considered a firetrap by any competent inspector. "You sounded pretty excited on the phone. What's going on?"

Angela unlocked the briefcase. She extracted the Jefferson file copies and handed them over to Harris without comment. He scanned the pages and found the perforated cardboard on the bottom of the stack. He held it to the light and then placed the cardboard over a page.

"This wouldn't be a cipher grille, would it?"

"I was hoping you could tell *me,*" Angela said. "You're the expert on codes and ciphers."

"I'm just an *aspiring* expert who's been taking courses at the National Cryptologic School."

"That's good enough for me," Angela said. The NSA school trained people from all government departments in the fine points of cryptographic analysis.

"Don't sell yourself short. *You're* the one that picked up on this," he said. "What can you tell me about it?"

"I think it was misfiled by subject. It should have gone into a Thomas Jefferson file."

He sat bolt upright in his chair. *"Jefferson?"*

"Uh-huh. I'm pretty sure the handwriting is his. I've compared it to the Declaration, and there's a small TJ in the lower right hand corner of the cover page."

He held the page up to his face and let out a soundless whistle. "Jefferson. That would make sense."

"I'm glad to hear you say that," Angela said with a sigh of relief. "I was worried that I'd be wasting your time."

"Hell, no!" Harris shook his head. "Most people don't know that Jefferson was an accomplished cryptologist. He used ciphers to communicate with James Madison and other government figures. He became proficient at codes and ciphers when he was minister to France." He rose from his chair. "C'mon. I've got something to show you."

He led the way to the exhibition area and stopped in front of a display case that held a brown wooden cylinder mounted on a spindle. The cylinder was about two inches in diameter and eight inches long and was constructed of a series of disks. The rims of the disks were inscribed with letters.

"This was found in a house near Monticello," Harris said. "We believe it's a 'wheel cipher' Jefferson invented when he was serving as Washington's secretary of state. You write your message and rotate the disks to scramble the letters. The person getting the message unscrambles them with a similar device."

"Looks like something out of *The Da Vinci Code*."

Harris chuckled. "Ol' Leonardo would have been fascinated by the next evolution of the wheel cipher."

He dragged her over to another display case containing several machines that looked like big typewriters.

She read the placard. "Enigma cipher machines," she said with excitement in her eyes. "I've heard of them."

"They were one of the best-kept secrets of World War Two. People would have killed for one of these contraptions. They were basically glorified versions of Jefferson's wheel cipher. He was far ahead of his day."

"Too bad we can't use one of these things to decipher his writing," Angela said.

"We may not have to," Harris said.

They returned to Harris's office, where he plopped behind the desk again. He leaned back in his chair and tented his fingers.

"How did you get into codes and ciphers?" he said.

"I'm good at math. I do the crosswords, and I've liked acrostics since I was a kid. My interest in puzzles got me into reading books on the subject. That's where I read about cipher grilles and Jefferson's interest in cryptology."

"Half the cryptologists in the world would have given me the same answer," Harris said. "It was exactly those interests that allowed you to sense the possibility of a hidden message in this stuff."

She shrugged. "Something about it struck me as being funny."

" 'Funny stuff' is what the NSA deals with on a regular basis. Jefferson would have felt right at home in the agency."

"Where does his wheel cipher fit it?"

"It *doesn't*. Jefferson got away from cipher devices later in his career. My guess is that he only used the grille to create a steganograph to conceal the fact that the artichoke info contains a secret message. He would have jotted down the message in the apertures and built sentences around them."

"I noticed that the syntax in the text seemed stilted or just plain weird in some of the lines."

"Good catch. Let's assume Jefferson used this as an extra layer of concealment. First, we'll have to copy the letters exposed by the holes in the grille."

Angela pulled a notebook out of her briefcase and handed it over. "I've already done that."

Harris inspected the lines of seemingly unrelated letters. "Fantastic! That will save a lot of time."

"Where do we start?"

"About two thousand years ago."

"Pardon?"

"Julius Caesar used a substitution cipher to get a message to Cicero doing the Gallic Wars. He simply substituted Greek letters for Roman. He improved on the system later on. He'd take the plain text alphabet and create a cipher alphabet by shifting letters three places down. Put one alphabet over the other and you can substitute those letters on one row for the other."

"Is that what we have here?"

"Not exactly. The Arabs discovered that if you figured out the frequency of a letter's appearance in written language, you could decipher a substitution cipher. Mary, Queen of Scots, lost her head after Queen Elizabeth's code-breakers intercepted the messages used in the Babington Plot. Jefferson developed a variation of a system known as the Vigenere method."

"Which is an expansion of the Caesar substitution."

"Correct. You create a batch of cipher alphabets by shifting so many letters over for each one. You stack them in rows to form a Vigenere box. Then you write a key word repetitively across the top of the box. The letters in the key word help you locate your encoded letters, something like plotting points on a graph."

"That would mean that the letters in your clear text would be represented by different letters."

"That's the beauty of the system. It prevents the use of letter frequency tables."

Harris turned to a computer and, after typing furiously for several minutes, created columns of letters arranged in a rectangular shape. "This is the standard Vigenere box. There's only one problem. We don't know the key word."

"How about using *artichoke*?"

Harris laughed. "Poe's 'Purloined Letter,' out in plain sight? Artichoke was the key word Jefferson and Meriwether Lewis used to unlock the code they agreed on for the Louisiana Territory expedition."

He wrote the word artichoke several times across the top of the square and tried to decipher the encrypted message revealed through the grille. He tried the plural form and shook his head.

"Maybe that was *too* obvious," Angela said. They tried *Adams, Washington, Franklin,* and *Independence,* all with the same disappointing results.

"We could spend all day doing this," Angela said.

"Actually, we could spend decades. The key word doesn't even have to make sense."

"So there is no way a Vigenere cipher can be broken?"

"*Any* cipher can be broken. This one was busted in the 1800s by a guy named Babbage, a genius who's been called the father of the computer. His system looked for sequences of letters. Once he had those, he could figure out the key word. Something like that exceeds my skills. Fortunately, we're within spitting distance of the greatest code breakers in the world."

"You know someone at the NSA?"

"I'll give my professor a jingle."

The professor was in class, so Harris left a message. With Angela's permission, he copied the material. He'd been so intent on the written text that he had paid little attention to the drawing.

Angela saw him studying the lines and Xs. "That's the other part of the mystery. I thought it was a garden layout at first." She told him what she had found on the ancient-languages website.

"Fascinating, but let's concentrate on the main text message for now."

Harris made copies of the papers. Angela tucked the original documents back into her briefcase. Harris walked her to the door and said he would let her know what he learned. Two hours later, he got a call from his professor. Harris started to tell him about the cipher problem. He only got as far as the name Jefferson when the professor told him to come over immediately.

Professor Pieter DeVries was waiting for Harris at the other side of the security check-in. The professor practically dragged Harris to his office in his haste to look at the file.

The professor epitomized the brilliant but absentminded mathematician that he was. He tended toward tweed suits, even in the warmer months, and had the habit of tugging at his snowy Vandyke beard when he was engaged in thought, which was most of the time.

He studied the artichoke file. "You say a young lady from the Philosophical Society brought this to you?"

"That's right. She works in their research library."

"I probably wouldn't have given it a second look if not for the grille," which Angela had let Harris hold on to. He picked up the perforated cardboard, stared at it with disdain, and then set it aside. "I'm surprised Jefferson would have used something as crude as this."

"I'm still not convinced this stuff conceals a message," Harris said.

"There's one way to find out," the professor replied.

He scanned the columns of letters into a computer and tapped the keyboard for a few minutes. Letters arranged and rearranged themselves on the screen until a word popped up.

EAGLE

Harris squinted at the screen and laughed. "We should have known. Eagle was Jefferson's favorite horse."

The professor smiled. "Babbage would have sold his soul for a computer with tenth the capacity of this machine." He typed the key word onto the screen and then instructed the computer to use it to decipher the message he had scanned earlier.

The letter Jefferson had written to Lewis in 1809 came up in plain text.

Harris leaned over the professor's shoulder.

"I can't believe what I'm reading," he said. "This is crazy." Harris dug out the paper with the odd drawings on it. "Angela thinks these words are Phoenician."

"That concurs with what Jefferson's source at Oxford says in his letter."

Harris felt a great weariness. "I've got the feeling that we may have stumbled onto something *big*."

"On the other hand, this fairy tale may be a hoax, the product of a clever imagination."

"Do you really believe that, sir?"

"No. I think the document is for real. The story it tells is another matter."

"How do we handle this thing?"

The professor tugged at his beard so hard it was a wonder that the Vandyke didn't come off.

"Ve-ry carefully," he said.

CHAPTER
17

Traffic was heavy on P Street, where the Republic of Iraq had its embassy in the historic nineteenth-century Boardman House. A stream of limousines and luxury cars passed in front of the three-story Romanesque-style building near Dupont Circle, stopping from time to time to disgorge men in tuxedos, women in gowns, attired for a black-tie affair.

The doorman waved a taxi in to take the place of a departing diplomatic limo and opened the passenger door. Carina Mechadi emerged, her lithe figure sheathed in an ankle-length velvet dress whose black-brown color matched shoulder-length hair that was pinned back in a French twist. The gown's scooped neckline displayed a décolletage that hovered between proper and sexy. An embroidered white shawl covered her bare shoulders and set off her creamy dark skin.

She thanked the doorman with a smile that sent his middle-aged temperature soaring to unhealthy levels and followed the other guests through the arched front entrance. A young male embassy employee glanced at her gilt-edged invitation and checked her name off a list.

"Thank you for coming to our reception, Ms. Mechadi. The Embassy of Iraq welcomes you as our guest."

"Thank *you,*" Carina said. "I'm pleased to be here."

The vestibule echoed with the conversational hubbub created by dozens of chatting guests. Carina glanced around with her bold blue eyes, unsure whether to linger or peel off into a side room. As the other guests became aware of her presence, they turned her way, causing a lull in the level of voices.

Carina was not a tall person, yet she had a compelling physical presence that seemed to demand attention. The women in the room sensed her female magnetism and instinctively gripped the arms of their escorts, relaxing only after a tall, middle-aged man broke off from the crowd and made his way toward the newly arrived guest.

He clicked his heels and bowed gallantly. "Carina Mechadi, the Angel of the Antiquities, if I'm not mistaken."

An anonymous headline writer had given Carina the lofty title in an article published by *Smithsonian* magazine. She smiled graciously and took control of the conversation. "I've never liked that description, Mr.—"

"Pardon me, Ms. Mechadi. My name is Anthony Saxon, and I offer my profound apologies if I have offended you." He spoke in the vaguely British accent that was once cultivated in exclusive American prep schools.

"Not at all, Mr. Saxon." She extended her hand. "How did you recognize me?"

"Your picture has been in a number of journals. It is a great pleasure to make your acquaintance in person." He took her hand and kissed it.

With his distinguished looks and baroque manner of speaking, and well-fitting tux, Saxon seemed like a turn-of-the-century ambassador. He was more than six feet tall and rail thin. His thick ginger-and-gray hair was combed straight back from a devilish widow's peak that came to a point above thick eyebrows. A pencil-thin mustache of the style worn by 1940s movie stars and gigolos decorated his upper lip. His face glowed with its desert tan.

"Are you with the Washington diplomatic corps, Mr. Saxon?"

"Far from it, I'm afraid. I am an adventurer by choice, a writer and filmmaker by need. Perhaps you've read my last book, *Quest for the Queen,*" he said with a hopeful lilt in his voice.

"I'm afraid not," Carina said. Not wanting to hurt Saxon's feelings, she added quickly, "I'm away a lot."

"Spoken with gentle honesty." Saxon clicked his heels again. "It matters not whether you have heard my name, for I have heard of yours, especially in connection with the retrieval of antiquities stolen from the Baghdad Museum."

"You're very kind, Mr. Saxon." She glanced around "I don't suppose you would know where I could find Viktor Baltazar."

Saxon's eyebrows dipped. "Baltazar is about to make his presentation in the main reception area. It would be my pleasure to show you the way."

Carina's lips parted in an amused smile. "You're very much the Victorian gentleman," she said, taking his proffered arm.

"I fancy myself as more of an Elizabethan. Swords and sonnets. But I appreciate the compliment."

He guided her through the milling crowd into a large room decorated with maroon-and-gilt drapes. At one end, a raised dais was flanked by lights, video cameras, and microphones. An enlarged photo of the Iraqi National Museum hung on the wall behind the stage. Rows of plush chairs had been set up in front of the stage.

Saxon headed to a love seat against a side wall. He explained in a conspiratorial whisper that the seat offered a good view of the guests entering the room and allowed for an easy escape if the speakers became too long-winded.

Carina recognized several low-level State Department staffers, politicians, and journalists. A number of men and women who represented a cross section of Middle Eastern antiquities scholarship were familiar to her as well. She became particularly excited when Professor Nasir came into the room.

She stood and waved. The professor strode across the room, a wide grin on his face.

"Miss Mechadi, how wonderful to see you."

"I was hoping you'd be here, Professor." She turned to Saxon. "Professor, this is Anthony Saxon. Mr. Saxon, Professor Jassim Nasir."

Saxon stood to his full height, towering over the Iraqi. "I'm honored to be in your presence, Dr. Nasir. I'm well acquainted with your work at the museum."

Nasir beamed with pleasure.

"Please excuse us," Carina said to Saxon. "Dr. Nasir and I have much to talk about. It's been quite a while since we last saw each other."

"By all means," Saxon said. In a single motion, he snatched two champagne flutes off passing tray and handed one to Carina. "Please let me know if I can be of any further assistance."

Nasir watched Saxon weave his way through the crowd. "Not many people outside of Iraq know I exist," he said, obviously impressed. "How long have you known Mr. Saxon?"

"About five minutes. He ambushed me at the door. More important, how long has it been since you and I last met? Three years at least?"

"How could I forget? It was in Baghdad at the museum. A terrible time."

"I'm sorry I haven't kept in touch with you as often as I should have."

"We've cleaned the place up, and, thanks to people like you, the recovering effort continues. Money has been coming in, but our expenses are phenomenal. And with the continuing instability in our country, it will be a long time before busloads of tourists pull up at our front door."

"All the more reason why this reception must be so encouraging."

"Oh, yes," he said, brightening. "I was thrilled when you called and said you had recovered a major cache of artifacts. The idea for the tour is sheer genius. I never imagined that I would be here with so many of my respected colleagues. There is one of them now. You remember Dr. Shalawa?"

The heavyset woman taking the podium was a leading expert on Assyrian archaeology. Dr. Shalawa was dressed in the traditional Muslim dress down to her ankles. A scarf covered her hair. She cleared her throat to get attention, and, when the audience had settled down, she introduced herself.

"I would like to thank the embassy for hosting this reception and our guests for their financial and moral support. Our first speaker exemplifies the spirit of generosity that will be instrumental in making our museum again one of the world's great cultural institutions. I am honored to give you Viktor Baltazar, president of the Baghdad Museum Foundation."

As Dr. Shalawa led the applause a man rose from the front row and climbed onto the dais to shake her hand.

Carina had no idea what Baltazar looked like; he had a talent for keeping his pictures out of public circulation. She hadn't known what to expect, but it wasn't the powerfully built man in the custom-tailored tuxedo who took his place behind the podium. The massive head reminded her of a mastiff's. As she watched, Baltazar underwent a transformation. The fierce grin became a warm smile and the pale eyes seemed to reach out to every person in the room.

When the applause finally died, he said in a deep, melodious voice,

"It is *I* who am honored for being invited to speak before this august gathering. You were all part of the international effort to recover the antiquities stolen from the Iraqi National Museum in Baghdad."

He acknowledged the second round of applause, and went on.

"My foundation was only a single link in the chain. Thanks to you, many artifacts continue to be recovered. The museum is reestablishing its conservation labs, training its staff, and establishing a database. Additional funding will come from the tour, sponsored by the Baltazar Foundation. I regret that I must leave the reception before I get a chance to thank you all individually, but I look forward to working with all of you in this noble cause."

He blew the audience a kiss, stepped down off the stage, and made his way to the door. Carina hurried from the room and caught her quarry in the lobby.

"Excuse me, Mr. Baltazar. I know you're in a rush, but I wondered whether I could have a minute of your time."

Baltazar's lips widened in an engaging smile. "I would be impolite, and foolish as well, to refuse a simple request from such a lovely woman, Miss—"

"That's very kind of you. My name is Carina Mechadi."

A thoughtful expression came to Baltazar's face. "Miss *Mechadi*! What an extraordinary surprise. From what I have heard about your bulldog persistence, I had envisioned you as a short, stout woman of middle age, with a mustache perhaps." He drew his forefinger across his upper lip.

"Sorry to disappoint you," Carina said.

"No disappointment, except for the fact that I must be on my way. How can I help you?"

"I simply wanted to add my thanks to you and your foundation for aiding my efforts."

"You're welcome. I regret now that I had not met you before and that we were able to communicate only through intermediaries. My business and charitable interests are very demanding."

"I understand completely."

"Then I am relieved. You are apparently quite the detective. Were you trained by the police?"

"I was a journalist originally. I reported on some important Italian art thefts that wound up in European and American museums. I became angrier the more I learned how the academic institutions and museums have become part of the illegal trade. Before long, I was trying to *find* stolen objects instead of writing about them."

"I understand your work is not without its dangers. I heard through Benoir about the hijacking and attempted theft of an artifact. Absolutely outrageous! It's a wonder you weren't hurt."

She nodded. "I would not be here talking to you if not for Kurt Austin."

"I'm not familiar with the name."

"Mr. Austin is with the National Underwater and Marine Agency. He prefers to stay out of the limelight, but he is responsible for saving my life, the ship, and the long-lost Iraqi artifacts. One of the hijackers shot him. He was only wounded, thank goodness."

"Austin sounds like a remarkable gentleman," Baltazar said. "How did he come to be on board the vessel?"

"Pure accident. He was on another ship that happened to be nearby when he heard an SOS."

"Remarkable. I would like to meet him some time so I can thank him."

"I would be glad to arrange it."

"I am amazed that you were able to recover so many of the Iraqi antiquities. How did you do it?"

Carina thought about the countless informants she had cultivated, the bribes she had given freely, and the reluctant government officials she had wheedled without mercy until they gave in to her demands simply to be rid of her.

"It's a long story," she said with a shrug. "Much of my success is simply an accident of birth. I have roots in Europe and Africa, which eased my ability to make contacts on both continents."

"African, you say? Your father was Italian, I take it?"

She nodded. "My grandfather too. He was with Mussolini's army when it invaded Ethiopia, which was where he met my grandmother. My mother never knew his name, only that her father was Italian. When she moved to Italy, where I was born, she gave her maiden name, Mekada, an Italian twist."

"Mekada? That's a lovely name."

"Thank you. I understand it's not uncommon in Ethiopia."

Baltazar paused in thought for a moment before speaking again. "Tell me, Miss Mechadi, what are your immediate plans?"

"I'm going to be busy organizing the tour. The artifacts are at the Smithsonian under guard. I'll be providing provenance data and background information that can be used with the exhibits. I've lined up meetings with people who have offered their help. Tomorrow, I'm going to Virginia to see Jon Benson, a *National Geographic* photographer who was present at the excavation of a statue known as the *Navigator*. Perhaps you can drop by and see the statue and the other pieces in the collection."

"That sounds like a fine idea. I'm a bit of a novice about archaeology, I'll admit, but I own a few pieces. All legal, I might add. I'd be happy to show them to you over lunch or dinner."

"I'd like that, Mr. Baltazar."

"Splendid. Call the foundation when you have some free time. They will have my schedule."

They shook hands, and Baltazar stopped to say his good-nights to the ambassador and several other embassy officials. Carina turned

to go back into the reception room and encountered Saxon. He had
a bemused smile on his face.

"I saw you chatting with Mr. Baltazar," he said.

"Mr. Baltazar is the main reason I came to the reception. He's
quite charming."

"Do you know the source of the money he has been handing out?"

"Only that he owns mining companies."

"That's right, as far as it goes. Baltazar is the head of a mineral cartel that includes the biggest gold-mining conglomerate in the world.
He's quite controversial. His companies have been accused of destroying the environment and messing up the poor locals in half a
dozen countries. What many people don't know is that he owns one
of the biggest private security companies in the world. Mercenaries
for hire."

Carina had come across the unfavorable reports on Baltazar when
she researched his background, but she had been so eager for the
foundation's help that she downplayed their significance. "What I *do*
know is that he's been extremely generous when it comes to the
Iraqi museum."

"I see. Blood money doesn't matter when it comes to the greater
good, and all that."

"I don't need to be lectured on ethics," Carina said, her eyes
blazing.

Saxon felt the heat of her words. "No, you don't. Again, you have
my apologies. I actually wanted to talk to you about the recovered
antiquities, in particular a statue called the *Navigator*."

Carina wondered if Saxon had overheard her conversation with
Baltazar, but she realized he had been out of earshot. "You know
about the statue?"

He nodded. "I know that it's a bronze, nearly life-sized, that
was excavated decades ago in Syria. It portrays a mariner, and is

thought to be Phoenician, but there are doubts, which is why the statue was consigned to the basement of the Baghdad Museum. It languished there for years, until thieves stole the statue during the American invasion in 2003. Its whereabouts since then had been unknown, until you found it recently with a group of other stolen antiquities."

"That's astounding! How do you come to know so much about the statue?"

"I've been searching for the elusive fellow since I first heard him mentioned in my Solomon research. I almost had my hands on it in Cairo, but you were one step ahead of me. Congratulations, by the way."

"Why are you so interested in this particular artifact?"

He raised his palm. "Aha! If you had read my books you would not have to ask that question."

"I'll be sure to put your books on my reading list." Carina didn't hide her displeasure at Saxon's coyness.

"It will be worth your time," he said with a grin.

She had had enough of Saxon's smug attitude. "If you'll excuse me."

"You're excused. But heed my warning. Be careful in your dealings with Baltazar."

Carina ignored the comment and headed over to talk to Professor Nasir.

Saxon watched her go. There was a grin on his face, but there was no mistaking the worry in his eyes.

As BALTAZAR exited the Iraqi embassy, a black Mercedes limousine pulled up to the curb. The driver got out and shouldered aside the doorman to open the car door. The doorman was an ex-marine who was not easily intimidated. Angered at the loss of a tip, he went to protest, but the powerfully built driver shot him a look of such malevolence that the words never left his month. A moment later, the limo took off with a squeal of tires.

"Good evening, Mr. Baltazar," said the driver. "The reception went well?"

"Yes, Adriano. So well that I almost forgot about the debacle off Newfoundland."

"I'm very sorry, Mr. Baltazar. I have no excuse for my failure."

"Perhaps I can provide you with one, Adriano. His name is Kurt Austin. He's with NUMA. Austin is the gentleman who foiled the hijacking."

"How did this Austin know of our plans?"

"He didn't. It was a regrettable coincidence that he happened to be in the neighborhood. Unfortunately for you, this Mr. Austin is quite intrepid. And lucky as well. Your shot only wounded him slightly."

Adriano recalled the quick glimpse of Austin over the sights of his gun and later in the cockpit of the helicopter that had shadowed the mineral ship. "I'd like to talk to Mr. Austin."

"I'll bet you would," Baltazar said with an evil chuckle. "But we have more important matters to deal with. I've learned that there is a *National Geographic* photographer who has some pictures that should not see the light of day. I want you to acquire these photos."

"Would you like me to dispose of the photographer?"

"Only if it becomes necessary, and make it look like an accident. I would prefer that the pictures merely be removed."

"What about the woman?"

Baltazar pondered Carina's fate. He was a man who was capable of extinguishing a human life when it suited him, but there was more to Carina than met the eye.

"We'll keep her alive as long as she proves useful. I want a comprehensive investigation of her background."

"Then can I deal with Austin? We have something to settle between us."

Baltazar let out a heavy sigh. Cruelty didn't bother him in the least. His was the classic psychopathic personality, and, as such, he was devoid of empathy. People existed to be used and tossed aside. But Adriano's suggestion signified independent thought on the part of an employee when what he demanded was obedience. At the same time, he was not without sympathy with Adriano's need for revenge. He too had a score to settle with Austin.

"I want to find out what he knows, Adriano. You can deal with him later. I promise."

Adriano closed his eyes and worked the thick fingers of his hands.

"*Later,*" he said, as if he were cherishing the very word.

18

P ROFESSOR PIETER DEVRIES WAS turning the Jefferson file over in his mind as he waited in a reception area at the State Department's Bureau of Near Eastern Affairs. He had read every line and found no inconsistencies.

The receptionist picked up the buzzing intercom phone and exchanged a few words with the person on the other end.

"Mr. Evans will see you now, Professor DeVries," she said with a smile. "Third door on the right."

"Thank you." DeVries slipped his reading material into a file case, tucked it under his arm, and walked down the hallway. He knocked lightly, then opened the door and stepped into an office. A tall, long-jawed man in his late thirties was waiting to greet him with a hand shake.

"Good morning, Professor DeVries. My name is Joshua Evans. I'm an analyst with the bureau. Have a seat."

DeVries sat down and said, "Thanks for seeing me."

Evans settled his lanky frame behind a desk whose clinical orderliness suggested a compulsive personality. "It's not every day that I get a visit from the NSA," Evans said. "You folks usually keep to yourselves. What brings you to over to Foggy Bottom?"

"As I explained on the phone, I'm a code breaker with the agency. I've come across information that might be of interest to your bureau. I came directly to State rather than go through NSA channels. This is a matter of some delicacy."

"You've got my interest," Evans said.

The professor opened his file case and handed over the folder that held copies of the original Jefferson material and the deciphered version. He gave Evans a capsule account of the file and how he had acquired it.

"Quite a story," Evans said with a lightness of tone that suggested he'd been listening to a Mother Goose tale. He eyed the professor's baggy tweed suit and Vandyke beard. "I'm still not clear why you brought it to Near Eastern Affairs."

The professor spread his hands apart. "Phoenicia was in the geographical area that is the responsibility of your bureau."

"*Phoenicia,*" Evans said with a wan smile.

"That's right. It was one of the greatest seafaring empires of all time. It spread from its original home to the shores of Spain and beyond the Pillars of Hercules."

Evans sat back and clasped his hands behind his head. "That may be so, Dr. DeVries, but Phoenicia longer exists."

"I understand that, but the descendents of the Phoenicians still inhabit the countries of Lebanon and Syria."

"Unlike those two countries, Phoenicia was not a member of the United Nations, the last I knew," Evans said with an indulgent chuckle.

DeVries pasted a grin on his face. The professor was a battle-scarred veteran of the bureaucratic process. He knew that he would have to work his way up the ladder through self-satisfied staff people like Evans.

"I'm a mathematician, not a diplomat like yourself," DeVries said, using a bit of flattery. "But it seems to me that when we talk about such a volatile region, *any* development that shakes deeply held beliefs should be given serious consideration."

"I apologize for seeming dismissive. But artichokes? Secret codes? A long-lost Jefferson file? You must admit that the story is a fantastic one."

DeVries gave a short laugh. "I would be the first to agree."

"And, besides, how do we know that any of this is true?"

"We can't authenticate the content, but the translation of the enciphered message into clear text is accurate. The fact that the material you're holding was produced by the third president of the United States and the author of the Declaration of Independence must give it some weight."

Evans hefted the packet of papers as if they were on a scale. "You've authenticated Jefferson as the source of this material?"

"Some NSA handwriting experts looked at it. There is no doubt that Jefferson wrote it."

A confused look came to Evans's face. DeVries had seen the same panicked expression with bureaucrats who'd been asked to deviate from their normal function, which was to gum up the workings of government. Evans's worst nightmare had come true. He might have to make a decision. The professor offered Evans a lifeline.

"I realize the material I've brought you seems far-fetched. That's why I hoped for guidance from the State Department. Perhaps you could tell your superior about our discussion?"

Passing the buck was a strategy Evans could understand. A relieved look came to the young man's face. "I'll bring it up with my boss, Hank Douglas. He's head of cultural affairs for the bureau. I'll get in touch with you after I talk to him."

"That's very kind of you," DeVries said. "Could you call Mr. Douglas while I'm still here so I won't have to bother you later?"

Evans saw that DeVries was making no attempt to rise from his chair. He picked up his phone and punched out Douglas's number.

He was hoping Douglas was out and was chagrined when his colleague answered the phone.

"Hello, Hank, this is Evans. Wondered if you had a few minutes."

Douglas replied that he had an hour before his next appointment and invited him to stop by his office. "Okay," Evans said. He hung up and said to DeVries, "Hank's busy right now. I'll see him this afternoon."

DeVries stood and extended his hand. "Thank you," he said. "If you ever need anything from the NSA, I'm sure we will be similarly accommodating. I'll call you later today."

After DeVries took his leave Evans stared at the closed door for a moment, then he sighed and picked up the packet of Jefferson material. Passing the buck had its hazards. As he left his office, he thought that he would have to be careful how he handled this hot potato.

DOUGLAS WAS a genial African American in his fifties. The circular bald spot on the top of his head made him look like a tonsured monk. He had been a history major at Howard University, where he'd excelled at his studies. His office shelves were lined with books encapsulating the history of homo sapiens going back to Cro-Magnon times.

He was one of the most respected people in the bureau. He backed up his diplomatic skills with practical knowledge, having spent several years in the Near and Middle East. He was an expert on the region's politics and religion, the two often entwined, and spoke Hebrew and Arabic.

Evans had figured out a face-saving approach: *derision*. He puffed out his cheeks as he stepped into Douglas's office. "You won't believe the odd conversation I just had."

Evans rendered a reasonably accurate description of his talk with

DeVries. Douglas listened intently as Evans did his best to portray himself as the victim of an encounter with a nutty professor. Douglas asked to see the file DeVries had delivered. He studied the pages for several minutes.

"Let me see if I understand what your professor is saying," Douglas said as he finished the last page. "A code expert from the NSA has deciphered secret correspondence between Thomas Jefferson and Meriwether Lewis. The material suggests that Phoenicians visited North America."

Evans grinned. "Sorry to take your time with this. I thought you'd find the story amusing."

Douglas neither smiled nor laughed. He picked up the copy of the artichoke garden layout and gazed at the strange words. Then he reread the translations made so long ago by Jefferson's professor friend. He said the first one out loud.

"*Ophir,*" he said.

"I saw that. What does it mean?"

"Ophir was the legendary location of King Solomon's mines."

"I always thought that was something somebody made up," Evans said.

"Perhaps," Douglas said. "The fact is, Solomon amassed great amounts of gold in his lifetime. The source of that gold has always been a mystery."

"Based on what you say, and this material, Jefferson believed Ophir was in North America. Isn't that crazy?"

Douglas didn't answer. He read the second translation.

"*Sacred relic.*"

"More craziness. What's that supposed to mean?"

"Not sure. The most sacred relic associated with Solomon would have been the Ark of the Covenant."

"You're saying Jefferson's biblical object is the *Ark*?"

"Not necessarily. The sacred relic could be Solomon's *sock.*"

Douglas fiddled with a ballpoint pen. "God, I wish I could smoke my pipe at times like this."

"What's wrong, Hank? Jefferson or not, this thing about the Ark sounds like a fairy tale. There probably isn't a word of truth in this stuff."

"Makes no difference if it's true or not," Douglas said. "It's all about *symbols*."

"I don't understand. What's the big deal?"

"This is trouble any way you look at it. Remember what happened at the Temple Mount in 1969, and again back in 1982?"

"Sure. An Australian religious fanatic set the mosque on the mount on fire, and later a religious group was arrested for plotting to blow it up."

"What would have happened if they had been successful in clearing the mount to make way for the rebuilding of Solomon's third temple?"

"Their action could have provoked a strong reaction, to say the least."

"Now imagine that reaction if the discovery of Solomon's sacred relic is used as an excuse to build a new temple and that the object is in the United States."

"Given the paranoid nature of that part of the world, some people would say that it was another U.S. plot against Islam."

"That's right. The U.S. would be open to charges that it is scheming to clear the Temple Mount of any Muslim presence. Every extremist of every major religion would be brought into this mess."

"Damn!" Evans said. "This stuff *is* hot!"

"Firehouse material," Douglas said.

The color drained from Evans's face. "What do we do with it?" he said.

"We've got to go to the secretary of state. Who else knows about the Jefferson file?"

"Professor DeVries and his student from the NSA museum. Then there's the researcher from the American Philosophical Society. The NSA people know how to keep their mouths shut."

"Nothing stays a secret longer than six months in Washington," Douglas said. "We've got to think of ways to undermine the story so that when it does come out, this country has plausible deniability."

"How do we do that? The NSA says the material is authentic."

"The NSA is a secret organization. It can say it never heard of this stuff. I say we attack the basic premise. That it would be impossible for a Phoenician ship to have made the trip from the eastern Mediterranean to North America. The sailing skills and technology of the day would not have allowed it."

"Do we know that for a fact?"

"No. We'll need a source to help lay the foundation for our argument."

"How about the National Underwater and Marine Agency? NUMA has the experts, the database, and they know how to be discreet. I've got a few contacts over there."

Douglas nodded. "You get busy on that. I'll set up a meeting with the undersecretary. Get back to me in an hour."

After Evans had departed, Douglas reached into his desk drawer and pulled out a pipe and tobacco pouch. Although his office was off-limits to smoking, he stuffed the pipe bowl with tobacco and lit up. With the smoke curling around his head, he leaned back in his chair and let his thoughts drift.

It all still seemed so fantastic. Maybe it was a hoax, as Evans theorized. He dove into the Jefferson file, reading every word this time.

Like many African Americans, Douglas was ambivalent about Thomas Jefferson. He recognized the man's genius and greatness but found it hard to reconcile that with the fact that Jefferson kept slaves. As he reread the file material, he couldn't help connect with its author on a human level. Although Jefferson's correspondence with

Lewis showed him as cool and competent, there was no doubt that the man was worried.

Douglas could have been excused if the hand holding the pages shook slightly.

The potential for chaos in today's world was far greater than Jefferson could ever have dreamed of.

CHAPTER

19

AUSTIN SAT IN HIS STUDY hunting the sea marauders who had hijacked the containership. The magic carpet that carried him over the virtual sea was a satellite-imaging system operated by NUMA. Dubbed NUMASat, the sophisticated system had been developed by the agency's scientists and technicians to provide instantaneous pictures of the world's oceans. Satellites circled four hundred miles above the earth in orbits that allowed their cameras and other remote-sensing equipment to transmit information from any point on the globe.

The satellites transmitted optical or infrared pictures of water surface temperature, currents, phytoplankton, chlorophyll, cloud cover, meteorological and other vital data. The system was available free of charge to anyone with a computer, and was heavily used by scientists and nonscientists around the world.

Austin was sitting in front of a twenty-four-inch-wide computer monitor. He was casually dressed in a Hawaiian shirt, shorts, and sandals. He washed down a couple of aspirin with a beer and punched ENTER on his keyboard. A satellite image of the rugged Newfoundland coast materialized on the screen.

"Okay, Joe," he said into his speakerphone. "I'm looking at St. John's and points east."

"Gotcha." Zavala had the same image on a computer screen in his NUMA office. "I'll zoom in."

A shimmering bluish white rectangle popped up on Austin's screen, superimposing itself on a section of Atlantic Ocean. Zavala expanded the size of the square. Tiny black specks appeared. The specks grew in size and began to assume the long, slim shape of ships. The time and date in the upper-left-hand corner of the screen indicated that the picture had been taken several days before.

"How close can you go?" Austin said.

"Pick a target."

Austin clicked his computer cursor on a blip. The camera seemed to rush at the target. Hundreds of flopping fish filled the screen. Then the camera pulled back to show a fish hold and a deck covered with the booms and winches of an oceangoing fishing boat.

"Impressive," Austin said.

"Yeager used Max to pump some hormones into NUMASat's normal search function. He says it can tell you the color of a sand flea's eyes."

Hiram Yeager was NUMA's resident computer genius and director of the vast computer complex he called Max, which occupied the entire tenth floor of NUMA's green-glass-faced tower overlooking the Potomac River.

"Their eyes are blue," Austin said.

"Really?"

"Kidding. But the resolution is better than anything I've seen."

"Before Yeager beefed up the system, the best we could get was one yard square in black and white and four yards in color. He's got it down to one yard square in color," Zavala said. "What you're seeing on the screen has been enhanced by information coming in from other satellites and military and intelligence systems."

"All done legally and according to Hoyle," Austin said with a wry smile.

"*Mostly.* Yeager considers it tit-for-tat, because the military relies so heavily on NUMASat. They've worked out a deal to blank out images when military operations are under way. I told him I didn't want to know, and he said that was fine with him."

"We're in no position to criticize," Austin said. The Special Assignments Team sometimes operated under the radar of traditional government oversight. "Have you located our friendly ore carrier?" Austin said.

"Watch!" Zavala said.

The image slowly zoomed out. The ships again were displayed as specks. Zavala outlined a target within a rectangle. Austin clicked the computer mouse. The image of a huge ship filled the screen. Austin leaned forward.

"Definitely the ore carrier we saw from the chopper," he said. "There's that weird bull's-head logo on the hull."

"I ran a check on the ship. It belongs to an outfit named PeaceCo. Their website describes them as peace-and-stability consultants."

Austin chuckled. "That's the new jargon for mercenaries."

"They're up front about the ship's conversion from an ore carrier. They advertise it as a mobile-force platform. They claim they can have airborne forces on the ground anywhere in the world within forty-eight hours. The ship is guaranteed to arrive with the full unit within twenty-one days."

"Who's behind PeaceCo?"

"Hard to tell. They've got a roster of retired American and British military people on their board. The ownership is hidden behind layers of shell corporations in several countries of registration. I've got Yeager working to unravel that mess too."

"Sounds like a lead, but what we need is a smoking gun."

"Hell, Kurt, we've got a fully loaded howitzer! I've run a sequential album from the archives, starting shortly before the hijacking. These shots were taken at intervals, so they don't cover every minute."

Images flickered on the screen in a jerky stop-action mode, like pictures in a nickelodeon. Figures were moving around a cargo hatch. The cover slid back until the hold was revealed as a dark square. A platform rose from the ship's innards of the hold like the elevator on an aircraft carrier. Two helicopters could be seen parked side by side on the platform. Men got into the helicopters and the choppers took off.

"Who says time travel is impossible?" Austin said. "That nails down our launch."

"Next I'll show you the containership."

The image changed to show the deck of the *Ocean Adventure.* The choppers appeared as if by magic atop the containers. Figures streamed out of the aircraft. There was little change for several frames until the satellite showed one helicopter hovering above a foaming circle in the ocean where its companion had gone down. Zavala jumped back to the ore carrier. A single helicopter returned to land on the platform. Figures got out of the helicopter, it was lowered back into the ship, and the cargo hold cover slid back over the opening. One of the figures, who was taller than the others, could have been the man who shot Austin, but his back was to the camera.

"That nails it," Austin said. "Where's the ship now?"

"The maritime schedules I checked have her leaving New York a few days before the hijacking, supposedly on her way to Spain. She did a funny little loop around the time of the hijacking, then kept on heading across the Atlantic. I can turn this stuff over to the Coast Guard with a flick of a switch."

"Tempting," Austin said. "She's in international waters, and even if the Coast Guard jumped in now at best we'd snag only the little guys. I want the brains behind the hijacking scheme."

"I'll keep sniffing around. How are you feeling, by the way?"

"A little stiff, but the incident taught me a good lesson."

"That you should avoid men with guns?"

"Naw. That I should move *faster.* Keep me posted if you turn up anything before you leave for Istanbul." Austin heard a knocking. "Got to go. Someone's at the door."

"Having company?"

"The very best kind. *Ciao.*"

The Italian connection dawned on Zavala. "*Ciao?* Hey—"

"*Buona notte,* Joe," Austin said. He was chuckling as he hung up and went to open the front door.

CARINA MECHADI was waiting on the steps. She lifted the wine bottle in her hand. "I believe I have a dinner reservation for tonight."

"Your table is ready and waiting, *Signorina* Mechadi."

"You said *casual.* I hope I'm dressed for the occasion."

Carina was wearing jeans with flowers stitched on them and a sleeveless blouse of turquoise. Her outfit emphasized her feminine curves in the most flattering way possible.

"A queen could not be more fashionably attired," Austin said.

"Thank you," Carina purred. She appraised Austin with equally appreciative eyes. He was wearing white shorts that emphasized his tanned, muscular legs, and his wide shoulders strained against a flowered silk shirt. "And you look quite smashing in that shirt."

"Thanks. Elvis Presley wore the same design in the movie *Blue Hawaii.* Come right in."

Carina stepped into the house, and her eyes took in the comfortable, Colonial-style dark wood furniture that was set off by white walls hung with original paintings by the local artists Austin liked to collect. There were some antique ocean charts and shipbuilding tools, a photo of Austin's sailboat, and a scale model of his racing hydroplane.

"I thought I would see old anchors and stuffed swordfish hanging on the walls. Maybe an old diving helmet or ship models in bottles."

Austin roared with laughter. "I used to drink margaritas in a Key West divers' bar that fits that description."

"You know what I mean," Carina said with a smile. "You work for the world's foremost oceanographic agency. I expected more evidence of your love of the sea."

"I'll guess that your place in Paris has little in it that would indicate to a stranger what your job is."

"I have a few reproductions of classic artworks, but the rest is quite traditional." She paused. "I get your point. It's healthy to have some space from your work."

"I'm not ready to move to Kansas, but the sea is a demanding mistress. That's why the old ship captains usually built their houses inland."

"Nevertheless, this is quite lovely."

"It wouldn't qualify for a photo spread in *Architectural Digest,* but it's a great landside retreat for an old sea dog in between assignments. This building was a fixer-upper when I bought it, but it was it was riverfront property, and close to Langley."

Carina picked up on the Langley connection. "You were in the CIA?"

"Underwater intelligence stuff. Mostly, spying on the Russians. We closed shop when the Cold War ended, and I went over to NUMA, where I work as an engineer."

Despite Austin's denial, his affinity to the sea was subtly evident in the wall shelves filled with the sea adventures of Joseph Conrad and Herman Melville. There were dozens of books on ocean science and history. The most hand-worn volumes were on philosophy. She pulled out a well-thumbed book.

"*Aristotle.* Pretty heavy reading," she said.

"Studying the great philosophers supplies me with profound quotes that make me seem smarter than I am."

"There is more here than bons mots. These books have been much read."

"You're very observant. I'll use a maritime analogy. The wisdom in those pages keeps me anchored when I'm drifting into ambiguous waters."

Carina thought about the contrast between Austin's warmth and the way he had coldly dispatched her attacker. She replaced the book on the shelf. "But there is nothing ambiguous about the pistols over the fireplace."

"You've exposed my weakness for collecting. I've got around two hundred braces of dueling pistols, most stored in a fireproof vault. I'm fascinated by their history as well as the art and technology that went into them. I'm intrigued by what they say about the role of luck in our fates."

"Are you a fatalist?"

"I'm a realist. I know I can't always make my own luck." He smiled. "But I *can* make your dinner. You must be hungry."

"Even if I weren't, the wonderful fragrances coming from your kitchen would make me believe I'm famished." She handed over the bottle of wine.

"A Barolo," Austin said. "I'll open it and let the wine breathe. We're dining al fresco."

While Austin went to uncork the wine, Carina wandered out onto the deck. The table was lit with oil lamps whose colored glass lent a festive appearance to the setting. Lights sparkled along the Potomac, and there was the slightly rank, but not unpleasant, smell of the river. Austin put on a recording from his extensive jazz collection, and the soft piano notes of an Oscar Peterson number floated from a couple of Bose speakers.

Austin came out with two chilled glasses of *Prosecco*. They drank the sparkling Italian wine with an antipasto of *Prosciutto di Parma* over honeydew melon. Austin excused himself and came back with plates of fettucine with cream-and-butter sauce. Carina almost swooned when he blanketed the dishes with shaved white truffles.

"Dear God! Where did you find truffles like this in the U.S.?"

"I *didn't*. A NUMA colleague has been going back and forth to Italy."

Carina devoured the fettuccine, along with the *secondi* course, a sautéed veal chop, and a mushroom-and-cheese salad, again with white truffles. They polished off the bottle of wine. She didn't slow down until she came to *dolce,* or dessert. As she dug into a dish of Ben & Jerry's Cherry Garcia, she said, "This is *magnifico,*" for about the tenth time during the meal. "You have added master chef to your array of accomplishments."

"*Grazie,*" Austin said. He had been amazed at Carina's gusto but not unpleased. A hearty passion for food often revealed appetite in other areas. They finished off the meal with small frosted glasses of *limoncello* liquor.

As they clinked glasses in toast, Austin said, "You never told me how you came to be babysitting an old statue on its journey to America."

"It's a long story."

"I have time, as well as another bottle of *limoncello*."

She laughed softly and stared out at the river to collect her thoughts. "I was born in Siena. My father, a doctor, was an amateur archaeologist who was fascinated with the Etruscans."

"Understandable. The Etruscans were a mysterious people."

"Unfortunately, their art was in great demand. As a girl, I saw a site that had been plundered by *tombaroli,* tomb robbers. There was an arm of pure marble lying in the ground. Later, I went to the University of Milan, then to the London School of Economics, and drifted into journalism. My interest in antiquities was revived by research I did for a magazine article on the role of museums and dealers in art theft. The image of that marble arm stuck with me. I joined UNESCO and became an investigator. Stealing a country's history is one of the worst things someone could do. I wanted to take looting face on."

"That's a pretty tall order."

"As I quickly found out. The trade in illegal antiquities ranks third in international monetary terms behind drug smuggling and weapons sales. The UN has tried to discourage the trade through treaties and resolutions, but the challenges are formidable. It would be impossible to stop the sale of every cylinder seal or tablet."

"You've evidently had great success."

"I work with a number of international agencies such as Interpol and governments trying to track down certain high-profile items, mainly through dealers, auction houses, and museums."

"Is that what brought you to Iraq?"

She nodded. "Weeks before the invasion, we heard rumors that crooked dealers were in touch with the unscrupulous international art dealers and diplomats. They were taking orders for specific artifacts. The thieves were in place, ready to move in as soon as the Republican Guard moved out of the museum."

"Where did the *Navigator* figure in all this?"

"I didn't even know it existed. It was not on the list of artifacts that I tried to recover through an unsavory dealer named Ali. He was murdered, which is no loss to the world, but he knew where the objects were. I left the country after hearing a warning that I was going to be kidnapped as a hostage. Not long after that I was contacted by the Baltazar Foundation."

"That's the organization that is sponsoring your tour?"

"Mr. Baltazar is a wealthy man who was appalled at the Iraq looting. I met him for the first time at the reception last night. His foundation provided the funds to keep after the artifacts that had eluded me in Baghdad. Not long ago, an Egyptian source said the Iraqi objects were on sale in Cairo. I flew to Egypt and bought the cache. The *Navigator* was part of the deal."

"What do you know about the statue?"

"It must have been taken from the museum at the same time as the other loot. Professor Nassir, the director of the museum, remembered the statue as being stored in the basement. He considered it a curiosity."

"In what way?"

"It appears to be a Phoenician sailor, but it's carrying a compass. I'm told there is no evidence that the Phoenicians had the compass."

"That's right. The Chinese get credit for the compass."

"Professor Nassir figured it might have been a copy of the type of trade goods that the Phoenicians sold. Sort of like the classic statues that are sold as souvenirs in Egypt or Greece."

"Did your professor friend know where the statue was found?"

"It came from a Hittite site excavation around Black Mountain in southeastern Syria back in the 1970s. It found its way to Baghdad where its authenticity came into question. I've talked to a *National Geographic* photographer who was on the site."

"Strange that it would suddenly be of interest to thieves, and later to hijackers, after sitting in a museum basement all that time."

"Only a few people ever *knew* about it, which was why I was so surprised when Mr. Saxon mentioned it to me at the Iraqi embassy reception."

Austin's ears perked up at the name. "Not Anthony Saxon?"

"Yes. He seemed quite knowledgeable about the statue. Do you know him?"

"I've read his books and attended a lecture he gave. He's an adventurer and writer with an unconventional views of history not accepted by mainstream scientists."

"Could he have had anything to do with the hijacking?"

"I can't picture it. But it would be worth learning why he is so interested in the statue. I'd be interested in meeting the *Navigator* myself."

"I'm inviting a select few to view the statue. It's at a Smithsonian warehouse in Maryland. Would you like to come tomorrow morning?"

"Wild horses couldn't keep me away."

She drained the last of her *limoncello*. "This has been a wonderful evening."

"I think I hear a 'but' in your voice."

She laughed. "Sorry. I'd love to stay, but I have much work to do on the tour."

"I'm completely heartbroken, but I understand. I'll see you tomorrow."

A thought seemed to occur to her. "I'm going to try to set up a meeting with the *National Geographic* photographer. He lives in Virginia. Would you like to go along?"

"I'm officially on sick leave, but a ride in the country would do wonders for the healing process."

She rose from the chair. "Thank you so much, Kurt. For *every*thing."

"My pleasure, Carina." He walked outside to her car. Austin expected to receive the customary European buss on both cheeks, which was what happened. But she also gave him a warm and lingering kiss on the lips. She tossed a smile over her shoulder, got in the car, and drove off.

Austin had a funny smile on his face as he watched the car taillights disappear down the driveway. Then he went back into the house and went out on the deck to clear away the glasses. He extinguished the lamps, and happened to glance toward the river. A figure was silhouetted against the reflection of the night sky on the rippling water. He knew every inch of the riverbank and was sure he was not looking at a tree or a bush.

He whistled a tune and carried the glasses back into the house. He set the tray aside and went over to a locked cabinet where he kept his Bowen. The flat-topped customized Colt single-action revolver was one of several Bowen models that he collected, in addition to his dueling pistols.

He loaded the gun, grabbed a flashlight, and descended from his living-room study to the first level, where he kept his racing scull and smaller hydroplane. He slid the door aside on well-oiled rollers and stepped out onto the boat ramp.

He let his eyes become accustomed to the darkness, and made his way along the foundation of his house, moving across the lawn where Zavala had found him trying out his new dueling pistols. He stopped and stared at the space between two large trees. The figure had disappeared. He decided against a search on his own and crept back into the house and up the stairs, where he called the police and reported a prowler.

The police car showed up exactly eight minutes later. Two officers knocked on his door. He and the policemen made a thorough search of the area around the house. Austin found a shoe print in the mud near the river, which helped convince the police that he wasn't seeing things. They said they would check back later than night.

Austin made sure the doors of the house were locked and the burglar alarm was on. Rather than sleep in his turret bedroom, he stayed fully dressed and stretched out on the living-room sofa. He was sure that whoever had been watching his house had left. But he kept his Bowen close by his side.

20

THE NEXT MORNING Austin arose early and threw on a pair of shorts and a T-shirt. Slipping into a pair of sandals, he made his way to the river's edge and knelt next to the muddy heel mark. The footprint was still faintly visible. He measured the outline next to his own foot. Big man.

Austin stood for a minute deep in thought, squinting at the silver sheen of sunlight on the Potomac. There was little he could do now; the peeping Big Foot was long gone. He shrugged and headed back to the boathouse. Austin might not have been so complaisant if he had glanced above his head and seen a compact transceiver with a whisker-thin antenna that was attached to the branch of an oak tree.

Austin took a quick shower and changed into slacks and a polo shirt. He filled a travel mug with the Jamaican coffee he favored, slipped behind the wheel of a turquoise Jeep Cherokee from the NUMA motor pool, and headed toward the Maryland suburbs.

He arrived at the Smithsonian Institution's complex of warehouses a half hour earlier than Carina had asked him to come. He wanted time alone with the statue that had caused so much commotion. The security guard at the door checked his name against a clipboard list and waved him into the corrugated-metal building.

Running the length of the building's interior were rows of shelves neatly stacked with labeled cardboard cartons that held overflow from the Smithsonian's massive collections.

A slender man was fiddling with a camera mounted on a tripod that stood next to a bronze statue. The photographer looked up from the viewfinder and frowned.

Austin extended his hand. "Anthony Saxon, I presume."

Saxon hiked a bushy eyebrow. "Have we met?"

"My name is Kurt Austin. I'm with NUMA. I attended your lecture on lost cities a couple of years ago at the Explorers Club. I recognized you from the jacket of your last book, *Quest for the Queen*."

Saxon's frown vanished and he reached out and shook Austin's hand like a pump handle.

"*Kurt Austin*. You found Christopher Columbus. I'm honored to meet you."

Austin hedged his reply. "I was part of a team effort that found old Chris taking a nap."

"Nevertheless, your discovery of the Columbus mummy on a Phoenician ship in a Mayan tomb established the scientific base for pre-Columbian contact in the New World."

"Many people still don't accept it as fact."

"They are Philistines! I used your find as a foundation for my theories. What did you think of my book?"

"Entertaining and informative. The concepts are highly original."

Saxon snorted. "When people call my work *original,* they're often saying that it's nutty. They compare my stuff to those books that brought UFOs, cow mutilations, and space aliens into the debate."

"I didn't think the book was nutty at all. Your theory that the Phoenicians came across the Pacific, as well as the Western Hemisphere, was fascinating. When you stirred the Queen of Sheba into the mix, it was bound to cause controversy. You made a strong case that she is the key that will unlock the ancient puzzle of Ophir."

"The queen has her dainty little prints over centuries of historical record. I've been following her trail for years."

"It wouldn't be the first case of *cherchez la femme*. Too bad an accidental fire destroyed your Phoenician ship replica before you could prove your theory."

Anger flashed in Saxon's eyes. "That was no accident," he said.

"I don't understand."

"It was arson. But that's the past." His charming smile returned. "I've scratched the idea of a Pacific crossing. Too costly and complicated. I'm trying to pull together a more modest expedition. I'd like to sail a vessel from Lebanon to the Americas and back by way of Spain, like the old ships of Tarshish might have done."

"I'd hardly call a two-way transatlantic crossing modest, but good luck."

"Thanks. What brings you here?"

Austin nodded at the statue. "Miss Mechadi invited me to stop by and see this gentleman. And you?"

"I heard through my sources at the Smithsonian that the old boy was in town. Thought I'd say hello."

Judging from the elaborate camera setup, Saxon's interest in the statue apparently was more than casual. Austin touched the *Navigator*'s metal arm. "Miss Mechadi said you were quite knowledgeable about the statue. How old is he?"

Saxon turned to the *Navigator*. "More than two thousand years old."

Austin gazed with curiosity at the dark green statue that had almost cost the lives of hundreds of people. The figure was nearly six feet tall, standing with his sandaled left foot slightly forward. It was wearing an intricately embroidered kilt tied at the top by a wide sash. An animal skin was draped over the right shoulder. Hair hung down in rows from under a conical hat. The smile on the bearded face had an almost Buddha-like peacefulness. The eyes were half closed.

The right hand held a boxlike object at waist height. The left hand was held high, slightly clenched, like Hamlet contemplating Yorick's skull. A skinny, small-headed cat curled around the legs. The artist had cleverly used the animal's legs to give the statue added stability.

"If I hadn't been told this was Phoenician," Austin said, "I'd be hard put to identify any specific culture or period."

"That's because Phoenician art doesn't *have* any particular style. They were too busy trading to create great works of art. The Phoenicians produced goods made to sell, so they imitated the art of their market countries. The statue's posture is Egyptian. The head is Syrian, almost Oriental in style. The natural way the folds of his kilt fall is borrowed from the Greeks. The size is unusual. Phoenician bronzes tend to be small."

"The tabby is an unusual touch."

"The Phoenicians brought cats on board ship to catch rats and to use as trade items. They preferred orange-striped tomcats."

Austin examined the boxlike object in the statue's right hand. It was about six inches across. A circular section on the top was recessed about a half inch. An eight-point star was etched into the circle. One point was larger than the rest. A thick line, pointed at both ends, crossed from one side of the star to the other.

Saxon noticed the intense expression on Austin's face. "Interesting, eh?"

"Carina mentioned the compass paradox. The Chinese supposedly invented the compass hundreds of years after the heyday of Phoenician trade."

"That's the common perception. What do *you* think?"

"I'd keep an open mind," Austin said. "The Phoenician empire stretched along the shores of the Mediterranean and beyond. They would have needed constant contact with their colonies. They had to cross long open stretches of water. From Tyre to the western end of the Mediterranean is more than two thousand miles. That presumes an unparalleled skill at navigation, good charts, and nautical instruments."

"Bravo! I have no doubt that these inquisitive, clever people knew the peculiar properties of the lodestone. They had the technical expertise to mount a magnetized needle on a wind star like this. *Voilà!* A compass."

"Then the statue *is* authentic?"

Saxon nodded. "I'd guess that it was made around 850 B.C., when the Phoenician empire was at its highest peak."

"The compass needle seems to be pointing east and west."

Saxon raised an eyebrow. "What else do you see?"

Austin studied the bronze face. The nose looked as if it had encountered the business end of a sledgehammer. Except for the damage, it was a reasonably good likeness of a young man, with a layered beard. What Austin thought at first was a smile might actually be a grimace. The eyes were tightened in a squint. Austin stood behind the statue and studied the upraised hand.

"I think he's looking into the sun, as if he were navigating with a cross-staff."

Saxon chuckled. "You're downright frightening, my friend."

The camera lens was pointing at the statue's midsection, where a motif was repeated in the sash. Repeated throughout the design was a horizontal line, with a Z facing inward at each end.

"This mark was in your book."

Austin was intent on the detail and failed to see the startled expression on Saxon's face. "That's right. I believe it symbolizes a ship of Tarshish."

"You found similar motifs in South America and the Holy Land."

A furtive expression flickered in Saxon's gray eyes. "My detractors say it's coincidence."

"They're Philistines," Austin said.

Austin inspected the circular medallion hanging from the figure's neck. Engraved in the medallion were a horse head and a palm tree, with its roots exposed. "This was in your book. The horse and the palm tree."

"The horse was the symbol of Phoenicia and the tree symbolized a planted colony."

Austin ran his fingers like someone reading Braille over several raised lumps under the palm tree. A female voice rang out, cutting his unspoken question short.

"How did *you* get in here?"

Carina stood in the doorway, an expression of disbelief on her face.

Saxon tried to deflect her glare with a smile. "I don't blame you for being irate, Miss Mechadi. Please don't take it out on the guard. I showed him my Explorers Club credentials. They're authentic, by the way."

"I don't care if they're tattooed on your *derrière*," Carina said. "How did you know the statue was here?"

"I have sources who knew of my interest."

She came over to the camera tripod. "Photos of this statue will be featured in a book that we will sell during the tour. You have no right to take unauthorized pictures."

Saxon looked past Carina, and his expression changed dramatically. His grin faded. He bared his teeth like an angry pit bull and growled a single word:

"Baltazar."

The minerals magnate had stepped through the doorway. Behind him was a young man carrying a leather case. Baltazar strode over to Carina.

"Good to see you again, Ms. Mechadi." He offered his hand to Saxon. "Viktor Baltazar. I don't believe I've had the pleasure."

Saxon kept his hand by his side. "Tony Saxon. You tried to buy a boat I had built to sail across the Pacific."

"Oh, yes," Baltazar said, unfazed by the snub. "I wanted to give it to a museum. I heard it burned to the waterline. A great pity."

Saxon turned to Carina. "My apologies, Ms. Mechadi. I hope you will remember our conversation at the embassy."

He folded the tripod's legs and hoisted it onto his shoulder. With a final fierce glance at Baltazar, he strode to the door and left the warehouse.

Carina shook her head in frustration. "Sorry if I overreacted. That man is the most infuriating person I've ever met. Well, enough about him. Kurt, I'd like you to meet Viktor Baltazar, whose foundation is sponsoring the tour."

"Very pleased to meet you, Mr. Austin. Miss Mechadi explained your role in thwarting the hijacking. Thank you for saving this remarkable young lady and preserving the collection."

"Carina has told me about the generosity of your foundation," Austin said.

Baltazar dismissed the comment with a wave of his hand and turned his attention to the statue.

"At long last. The *Navigator*. Truly remarkable. I applaud your decision to make him the centerpiece of the exhibition, Miss Mechadi."

"He was the natural choice," Carina said. "Even with the damage to his face, he projects a dignity and intelligence. Then there's his air of mystery."

Baltazar nodded. "What do you think of our mute friend, Mr. Austin?"

Austin thought about his conversation with Saxon. "Maybe he would be more talkative if we could ask him the right questions."

Baltazar gave Austin a strange look and turned his attention back to the statue. He walked around the *Navigator,* his eyes roving over every square inch of bronze.

"Have you had an expert look at the statue?" he asked Carina.

"Not yet. It's going to be transported to the Smithsonian where it can be readied for the tour."

"I've been a bit concerned about security in view of the attempt to steal the statue," Baltazar said. "As Mr. Saxon's unauthorized visit shows, security is lax. The statue might be particularly vulnerable while it is being moved. I've taken the liberty of arranging for a trucking company to come in this morning to move the statue under guard. They should be here in a short while. If you don't mind, of course."

Carina pondered the offer. As more people knew where the *Navigator* was, the less secure it would be.

"That's very kind of you," Carina said. "I'd be glad to accept your offer."

"Good, then. It's done. I know it's early in the morning, but I suggest we celebrate our success with a toast."

He signaled his valet who set the case in his hand on a shelf and unsnapped the lid. Inside the case was a bottle of Moët. The valet popped the cork, poured from the bottle into three champagne flutes, and passed them around.

They clinked glasses, and Baltazar held his high. "To the *Navigator.*"

Austin studied Carina's benefactor over the rim of the glass. He looked as if he had been carved in stone. Under the charcoal pin-striped suit, Baltazar had the powerful body of a wrestler. Even with his wide shoulders, the head that rested on the thick neck still seemed too big for his physique.

Baltazar was unaware of Austin's scrutiny. He couldn't keep his eyes off Carina and seemed to be studying her every move. Austin had detected a veiled hostility behind the warm smile. He wondered if Baltazar was interested in Carina and resented Austin's friendship with the lovely Italian woman.

The valet began collecting the empty champagne flutes. The others were focused on the statue and no one noticed when the valet took Carina's glass and slipped it into a plastic bag, which he tucked into the case. Then he went over and whispered in Baltazar's ear. A moment later, Baltazar glanced at his watch and said he had to go.

Carina ushered him to the door. When she came back, she apologized to Kurt for cutting his visit short but said she had to prepare the statue for the movers. They agreed to stay in touch by cell phone and meet later in the day for their drive to Virginia to see the *National Geographic* photographer.

A BLACK YUKON with dark-tinted windows was parked close to Austin's Jeep. A glance at the license plate told Austin it was a U.S. government vehicle. His conclusion was confirmed when the back door of the Yukon opened and a man in a dark blue suit and sunglasses got out and flashed a badge under Austin's nose.

Holding the door wide, the man said, "Someone wants to talk to you."

Austin didn't take kindly to orders from rude strangers. He smiled. "If you don't take that toy badge out of my face, you're going to end up eating it."

Austin expected a hostile reaction, but, to his surprise, the man laughed, then he spoke to someone in the SUV. "You're right," he said. "Your pal is a hard case."

A loud guffaw issued from the vehicle's interior. A voice Austin hadn't heard for a long time called out: "Don't get too close or he'll bite you."

Austin peered into the car and saw a large man seated behind the steering wheel. He was smoking a cigar and had a wide grin on his broad-featured face.

"Oh, hell, I should have known it was you, Flagg. What brings you here from Langley?"

"Folks at the very highest levels of government asked me to collect you. Get in. Jake here can follow in your NUMA car."

Austin tossed the keys to his Jeep to the other man and got into the Yukon. He had worked with John Flagg on a number of CIA assignments but hadn't seen his former colleague in years. The Wampanoag Indian from Martha's Vineyard worked behind the scenes as a troubleshooter and rarely came to the surface.

They shook hands, and Austin said, "Where are we going?"

Flagg grinned and said, "*You're* going on a boat ride."

THE MOVING VAN ARRIVED at the Smithsonian warehouse twenty minutes after Austin had departed in the Yukon. Carina was relieved to see the unmarked truck back up to the warehouse. She had seen firsthand the ingenuity and determination of the ship hijackers.

The truck's rear doors opened and two men dressed in generic gray uniforms and matching baseball caps climbed out. One man activated the tailgate-lifting platform and the other unloaded a wheeled dolly and a large wooden box. The driver got out of the cab and came around back with a fourth man.

"You must be Ms. Mechadi," he said in a slow Southern drawl. "My name is Ridley. I'm in charge of this gang of gorillas. Sorry we're late."

Ridley was a husky man with a blond marine brush cut. He and his crew carried sidearms in belt holsters and had portable radios clipped to their pockets.

"No apology needed," Carina said. "I just finished wrapping the statue to be transported."

She led the way into the warehouse. Ridley chuckled when he saw the figure swathed from top to bottom in padding and tied with rope. "*Whooee!* Kinda looks like a big sausage."

Carina smiled at the apt comparison. "The statue is more than two thousand years old. It's already been damaged, and I wanted to do whatever I could to protect it."

"Don't blame you a bit, Ms. Mechadi. We'll take good care of it."

Ridley stuck his curled thumb and forefinger between his lips and let out a sharp whistle. His men came into the warehouse, placed the wooden box on the dolly, and lined the container with additional pads. Using straps to keep the statue steady, they lowered it into the box, and moved the loaded dolly out of the warehouse. The tailgate lifted the load to the level of the cargo level and the movers pushed it into the truck.

Two movers got into the back of the truck. One man produced a rifle and sat on the box, as if he were riding shotgun on a stage-coach. The other closed the door, and Carina heard it lock from the inside. The driver got behind the wheel and Ridley came over with a clipboard, which he handed to Carina.

"Have to ask you to sign this form, just to make it all legal."

Carina scrawled her signature across the bottom of the form and handed the clipboard back to Ridley.

"That's my car over there," she said. "I'll follow you to the Smithsonian."

"No need, Ms. Mechadi. We know where to go. We'll take care of things, and you can go about your business."

"This *is* my business," she said with characteristic firmness.

Ridley's eyes grew hard as he watched Carina walk to her car. He swore softly under his breath and climbed into the cab, where he made a quick call on his cell phone. He talked for a few moments and clicked off. He turned to the driver and barked: *"Move!"*

With Carina's car tailing it, the truck pulled out of the warehouse complex onto the road. The vehicles wound their way through suburban Maryland neighborhoods. Carina began to relax. Ridley and his men seemed competent and efficient, almost in a military fashion. Although she didn't like firearms, she was comforted by the fact that the movers were armed. Unlike the defenseless crewmen aboard the containership, they would be able to put up a fight.

Carina was familiar with Washington, but the surrounding bedroom communities were a bewildering maze of commercial and residential. The truck drove past shopping malls, gas stations, and subdivisions. She expected that they would eventually turn onto the Beltway or some other highway that headed into the District and was surprised when the truck pulled over in front of a convenience store.

Ridley got out and ambled back to the car.

"How you doin', Miss Mechadi?"

"I'm fine. Is there a problem?"

He nodded. "Heard on the radio that there's a mess on the highway leading into the city. Truck overturned and traffic's backed up for miles. We're going to use a back way into town. It kinda winds around, so I thought I'd warn you."

"That's very thoughtful of you. I'll make sure to stay close."

Ridley strolled back to the truck as if he had all the time in the world and climbed into the cab. The truck pulled out of the parking lot, with Carina close behind. She hadn't heard any reports of the accident or traffic tie-ups, but maybe she'd been lost in thought. She switched the radio off and paid full attention to the truck.

The moving van turned off onto a secondary highway lined with an unbroken wall of strip malls and fast-food joints. The heavy traffic stopped every hundred yards or so for traffic lights. Carina was grateful, after a couple of miles of stop and go, when the truck's directional lights signaled a right turn.

She was less thankful when they began to pass through a deteriorating neighborhood of seedy apartment houses and run-down commercial areas that looked as if they dated back to the Great Depression. Graffiti were scrawled on every vertical service; litter had washed up along the gutters. The unsmiling people she saw seemed stoned on drugs, as they probably were, given their surroundings.

Minutes later, they passed through an area that looked like a war zone. What had once obviously been a busy commercial area was a deserted neighborhood of abandoned stores, shut-down garages, and padlocked brick warehouses. Vacant lots were overgrown with weeds and cluttered with windblown papers.

Carina was frustrated at not being able to communicate with the truck. She tapped her car horn. Ridley stuck his muscular arm out the window and waved, but the truck showed no sign of stopping. She was looking for a wide place in the road where she could come up alongside, when the truck turned off into a potholed restaurant parking lot. The word PIZZA could barely be made out on the faded sign on the front of the dilapidated brick building.

Carina expected Ridley to come back and tell her that they were lost. When he didn't, she became annoyed, then angry. She clutched the wheel as if she wanted to pull it off. The truck just sat there. She thought about getting out, but one glance around at her desolate surroundings told her that she was in a very unhealthy place.

She reached over to press the lock button on the door. In that instant, a figure materialized from behind an old Dumpster, opened a rear door of her car, and got into the backseat.

"Hello," the man said in a soft, breathy voice.

Carina looked in the rearview mirror. Round eyes stared out of a baby face. She was looking at the hijacker she'd seen as she lay tied up in the ship container. She was gripped with fear, but she had the presence of mind to reach for the door handle. She felt coldness on her neck and heard a low hiss. She lost consciousness, and her head lolled on her chest.

The man got out of the car and went over to the back of the truck. He knocked on the doors, which opened a second later. The guards inside the cargo area offered no resistance when he climbed in and inspected the wooden box. He spoke into a hand radio. A moment later, a truck with a FAST DELIVERY logo pulled around from behind the derelict pizza house. The statue was quickly unloaded and exchanged for four limp bodies that were taken from the second truck.

The baby-faced man went over and gazed at Carina, thinking how beautiful and peaceful she appeared. He flexed the fingers that could still her beating heart in an instant and closed his eyes, taking a deep breath. With his homicidal impulse more or less under control, he climbed into the back of the moving van. The van pulled out of the parking lot, with the delivery truck close behind.

CHAPTER
22

T HE YUKON PULLED INTO the parking lot of a Potomac River marina and Austin got out. The second agent had been following in the NUMA Jeep. He parked the vehicle, tossed Austin the keys, and got into the SUV.

Flagg leaned out the window. "Let's get together for lunch at Langley sometime. We can bore the crap out of Jake here with Cold War stories."

"We were pretty dumb back then," Austin said with a shake of his head.

Flagg laughed. "Damn *lucky* too." He put the vehicle into gear and drove off.

Austin strolled along the line of boats. A few people puttered around, but otherwise the riverside was relatively quiet. He stopped to inspect a vintage motor cruiser.

The white-hulled, wooden boat was about fifty feet long, and the mahogany trim was polished to a blinding shine. The name on the hull was LOVELY LADY. A man was sitting in a deck chair reading a copy of the *Washington Post*. He saw Austin, put his paper aside, and rose from his chair.

"What do you think of her?" the man said.

Austin was fond of classic yachts and their understated air of luxury, which was so different from the garish display of extravagance to be found in some of the modern-day craft tied up at the marina. "Her name says it all."

"Indeed it does."

"I know it's not polite to ask a lady's age, but I was wondering how old she was."

"Don't worry about insulting the old girl, my friend. She knows she's as beautiful as the day she was born in 1931."

Austin ran his eyes over the craft's sleek lines. "I'd guess she came out of the Stephens boatyard in California."

The man raised an eyebrow. "That sounds like more than a guess. Stephens built her for one of the lesser-known Vanderbilts. Would you like to come aboard for a closer look, Mr. Austin?"

Austin's lips widened in a tight smile. It was no accident that Flagg had dropped him off near the boat. He walked up the short gangway onto the deck and shook hands with a man who introduced himself as Elwood Nickerson.

Nickerson was tall and wiry, with the physique of a tennis player. His tanned face was relatively unlined, and he could have been in his sixties or seventies. He was dressed in beat-up, tan canvas shorts, weathered boat shoes, and a GEORGETOWN UNIVERSITY T-shirt that was one thread short of being a rag. His close-trimmed white hair and manicured fingernails, and the tinge of a prep school accent, suggested that he was no boat bum.

He regarded Austin with flinty gray eyes. "Nice to meet you, Mr. Austin. Thank you for coming by. Sorry about the cloak-and-dagger antics. I'd offer you a Barbancourt rum on the rocks, but it's probably too early."

Nickerson knew Austin's current drink of choice. Either he'd been snooping in his liquor cabinet or he had access to government personnel files. "It's never too early for good rum, but I'll settle for a glass of water, and an explanation," Austin said.

"The water I can provide immediately. The answer to your question will take a little longer."

"I've got time."

Nickerson called out to the boat's captain and said they were ready to leave. The captain started the engines while his mate cast off the dock lines. As the boat pulled out into the river and cruised downstream, Nickerson ushered Austin into a spacious deck salon whose centerpiece was a rectangular mahogany table that had been polished to a mirror finish.

Nickerson offered Austin a seat at the table. Then he got a bottle of springwater from the refrigerator and poured Austin a glass.

"I'm with the Near East Section at the State Department, where I preside as chief mucky-muck and general factotum," Nickerson said. "This outing has the blessing of my boss, the secretary of state. He thought it best that he not be involved at this time."

"You've been digging around in my personnel file, which indicates clearance at a higher level than Foggy Bottom."

Nickerson nodded. "When we brought this matter to the attention of the White House, Vice President Sandecker suggested that we go to your boss, Director Pitt. He said to dump this in your lap."

"That was very generous of the director," Austin said. Typical Pitt, he mused. Dirk liked decisions to be made by those most likely to be affected by their consequences.

Nickerson caught the irony in Austin's voice. "Mr. Pitt was being sensitive to our wishes. He has the highest confidence in your abilities. It was my decision to do a background check on you. I have a reputation for being careful."

"And mysterious as well."

"Your file said you have little patience with small talk. I'll get right to the point then. Two days ago, my office received a visit from Pieter DeVries of the NSA. DeVries is one of the most respected cryptanalysts in the world. He brought us information of a startling nature."

For the next twenty minutes, Nickerson described in meticulous detail the discovery of the Jefferson file at the American Philosophical Society and the deciphering of the secret message it contained.

Nickerson wrapped up his presentation and waited for Austin's reaction.

"Let me see if I understand," Austin said. "A researcher at an organization started by Ben Franklin comes across a long-lost file containing a coded correspondence between Thomas Jefferson and Meriwether Lewis. Jefferson wrote Lewis and said he believed that Phoenicians visited North America and hid a sacred relic in Solomon's gold mine. Lewis writes Jefferson and says he is coming to see him. Lewis dies en route."

Nickerson let out a deep sigh. "I know. It sounds absolutely fantastic."

"What does this fantastic story have to do with NUMA?"

"Please bear with me and I'll make my motives clear." He handed Austin a thick loose-leaf notebook. "These are copies of the Jefferson material and the deciphered messages. The information has been labeled and catalogued as to source."

Austin flipped the notebook open and perused Jefferson's tight, disciplined handwriting. After leafing through several pages, he said: "You're sure this is authentic?"

"The Jefferson papers are the real thing. Their historical accuracy will have to be determined."

"Even so, this discovery challenges all assumptions," Austin said. "Any idea as to the nature of the relic?"

"Some of the analysts who have seen this suggested that it might be the Ark of the Covenant. What do you think?"

"There's a good possibility that the Ark was destroyed during the Babylonian Captivity of Jerusalem. I've also heard that it's under piles of rubble in an African mine. The Ethiopians say they have it, but few have seen it. Ark or not, this find will be a historical bombshell."

"You're right. The Ark is probably in splinters by now. We know that whatever was deposited in North America was of great concern to Jefferson."

"You sound equally worried."

"I *am*. Your bombshell metaphor is unfortunate but accurate."

"Are you concerned about treasure hunters?"

"No. We're worried about a conflagration that could start in the Middle East and spread into Europe, Asia, and North America."

Austin tapped the notebook cover. "How would this cause a conflagration?"

"The discovery would be seen as a sign by certain groups that Solomon's third temple must be built to house this relic. Building a new temple would necessitate destruction of the Temple Mount mosque, the third most sacred site in Islam. The mere rumor of the find could trigger a violent reaction from Muslims around the globe. They would see news of the discovery in North America as nothing more than a U.S. plot. The U.S. would be accused of inciting anti-Islamic forces to destroy something that is sacred to Islam. It would make all previous conflicts in that region look like a day at the park."

"Aren't we jumping the gun? You don't even know what this relic is."

"It doesn't *matter*. Perception is everything. A few years ago, a red heifer born in Israel was seen by some as setting off a chain of events that would have ended the world. That was only a bloody cow, for heaven's sake."

Austin pondered Nickerson's words. "Why are you so worried now?"

"Too many people now know about this file. We can do our best to stem leaks, but it's bound to come out eventually. The State Department will pursue diplomatic strategies to soften the blow if it comes, but we have to take other measures."

Austin knew from experience that the government was leakier than a sprung dory. "What can I do to help?" he said.

Nickerson smiled. "I see why Dirk Pitt left this matter in your hands. Our best defense is the truth. We must find what the Phoenicians brought to our shores. If it's the Ark, we'll bury it for a thousand years. If it isn't, we can scotch the story when and if it comes out."

"Finding a needle in a haystack would be easier. NUMA is an ocean-research agency. Shouldn't you be using land-based intelligence agencies?"

"We've tried. Without more information, it's useless. NUMA is in a unique position to help. We'd like to concentrate on the ship and the voyage rather than the artifact. Your past experience with the Columbus tomb makes you the ideal one to lead the effort."

Austin's eyes narrowed. "If we could trace the route of the voyage, that would narrow it down. It's a thought."

"We're hoping it's *more* than a thought."

"We can give it a shot. We're talking about a voyage that happened thousands of years ago. I'll talk to my colleague Paul Trout. He's an expert at computer modeling and may be able to retrace the route."

Nickerson looked as if he'd had a heavy burden removed from his narrow shoulders. "Thank you. I'll tell the captain to turn back."

Austin pondered their discussion. There was something about Nickerson that nagged at him. The State Department man seemed sincere, but his statements were too pat, and he seemed a bit sly for Austin's taste. Maybe deviousness was a tool for surviving at the higher levels of government. He decided to push his doubts aside, but to keep them within reach, and to concentrate on the immediate problem.

Phoenicians again.

He seemed to be encountering these ancient mariners at every turn. He began to plot a strategy. He'd give Trout a call and get him started on the problem. Tony Saxon would be ecstatic if he knew that his oddball theories of pre-Columbian contact in the Americas were about to be vindicated by an international crisis. Austin wanted to take another look at the *Navigator,* only, this time, he'd bring along his own Phoenician expert.

THE CELL PHONE in his pocket was vibrating. He clicked it on and said, "Kurt Austin."

A man's voice said, "This is Sergeant Colby of the District police, Mr. Austin. We found your name in the wallet of a Miss Mechadi."

Austin's jaw muscles worked as he listened to the police officer go through the details in the monotonic, euphemistic language that is peculiar to police.

"I'll be there in thirty minutes," he said. He made his way to the pilothouse. While Austin was urging the captain to crank every possible ounce of speed out of the *Lovely Lady's* engines, Nickerson was in the salon talking on the phone.

"Austin bit," he was saying. "He's taken the assignment."

"From what I know about Austin, I'd be surprised if he hadn't," said the voice on the other end.

"Do you think this scheme will work?"

"It *better.* I'll tell the others," he said and clicked off.

Nickerson put the phone down and stared into space. The secret of three thousand years could be revealed in his lifetime. The die was cast. He went over to his liquor cabinet, extracted a bottle and glass. Damn the doctor's orders to stay away from booze, he thought, and poured himself a stiff shot of brandy.

CHAPTER

23

SERGEANT COLBY WAS WAITING for Austin at the nurses' station of the Georgetown University Hospital emergency room. The police officer was engrossed in conversation with a man wearing a doctor's green frock coat. Colby noticed Austin's purposeful approach and guessed he was the man who had peppered him with questions over the phone.

"Mr. Austin?"

"Thanks for calling me, Sergeant. How is Miss Mechadi doing?"

"Pretty well, considering. Our car was patrolling a war zone of a neighborhood and found her in her car slumped over the steering wheel."

"Anyone know what happened?"

"She didn't make much sense when she regained consciousness," the police officer said with a shake of his head. "I was just talking to Dr. Sid here about the physical evidence."

He deferred to the other man, whose name was Dr. Siddhartha "Sid" Choudary. Dr. Sid was a resident anesthesiologist who'd been called in for consultation. "It appears from your friend's blood test that she was given a dose of sodium thiopental, either nasally or through the skin. It would have knocked her out within seconds."

"We don't think robbery was the motive," Colby said. "Her wallet had money in it, along with her ID and your phone number. We'll have the lab people go over her car. To be honest, that's not going to happen right away. Murders get priority, and there's a waiting line at the morgue."

"I'd like to see her," Austin said.

The doctor nodded. "She's wide-awake now. She'll feel fine as the stuff leaves her bloodstream. It's a bit like having one martini too many. A slight hangover, dizziness, and possible nausea. She can leave as soon as she feels able to walk, as long as she's got help. No driving for a while. Third door on the right."

Austin thanked the two men and then started down the corridor. "I wouldn't get too close," the policeman warned. "She's nail-spitting mad."

Carina was sitting up on the edge of the bed, trying to put a shoe on her foot. She was having a hard time with her hand-eye coordination. She seemed angrier at her foot than anyone in particular.

Austin stood in the doorway. "Need a hand?"

The deep frown on Carina's face vanished. She broke into a wide smile, and grunted in triumph as she pulled the shoe on. She tried to stand, but her legs wobbled. She was sinking to the floor when Austin stepped into the room. He picked her up and deposited her on the bed.

"*Grazie,*" she said. "I feel like I drank too much wine."

"The doctor said the drug should wear off soon."

"Drug? What's he talking about? I didn't take any drug."

"He knows that. You were knocked out with an anesthetic. Either you breathed it in or it was injected through the skin. Can you tell me what happened?"

A look of fear came to her eyes. "I saw the hijacker from the containership. The big man with the face like an evil baby."

"You'd better start at the beginning," Austin said.

"Good idea. Help me sit up."

Austin reached around Carina's waist, gently pulled her to an up-right position, and poured her a glass of water. She sat on the edge of the bed and told her story between sips.

"The movers came for the *Navigator*. A man named Ridley was in charge. I followed the truck in my car. The truck turned into a terrible neighborhood. Stopped. I remember the old pizza sign. The rear door opened. I saw the hijacker in the rearview mirror."

Austin flashed on the oversized footprint in the riverbank near his house. "Go on."

"I heard a hiss. Next thing I know, I'm waking up in this place." A thought occurred to her. "They took the statue. I have to tell the police." She stood and leaned against the bed. "Still a little dizzy."

Austin kissed her on the forehead. "I'll talk to the police officer while you rest."

COLBY WAS FINISHING a phone call when Austin approached and said, "Did she tell you about the truck and a missing statue?"

"Yeah. I thought she was delirious. Just checked into the station. A truck matching the description she gave went off the highway and caught fire. They found four bodies burned beyond recognition."

"Any sign of a bronze statue?"

"No. The fire was pretty hot. Probably would have melted your statue."

Austin thanked Colby and went back to fill Carina in. He didn't tell her about the bodies in the burned-out truck. She glanced at the wall clock. "I've got to get out of this place. I'm going to miss my ap-pointment with Jon Benson, the *National Geographic* photographer I told you about."

"When are you supposed to see him?"

"About an hour." She gave Austin an address. "Can we make it?"

"If we leave now. Depends on how you feel."

"I feel fine." She stood and managed a couple of steps before she wobbled. "I wouldn't mind a helping hand, though."

They hooked arms and shuffled down the hall. Colby had left a note at the nurses' station to call him when Carina was ready for an interview. By the time she had signed the papers checking her out, Carina seemed much stronger. The nurse insisted that she ride down to the lobby in a wheelchair. When Carina walked out the front door, she was weaving only slightly.

ON THE DRIVE to Virginia, Carina tried calling the photographer. No one answered the telephone. She assumed Benson had simply stepped out and would be home at the appointed time.

Carina recovered rapidly thanks to the fresh country air blowing through the car window. She put in a call to Baltazar to tell him about the theft. She got an automated reply and left a message.

"You don't suppose Saxon had anything to do with it, do you?" she said after a moment's reflection.

"Saxon doesn't seem the type. Maybe he can help. We could use the photos he took of the *Navigator* to publicize its loss."

Carina dug into her pocketbook and found the card Saxon had given her at the Iraqi embassy reception. She called the number written on the back of the card and got the Willard Hotel. The desk clerk said Mr. Saxon had checked out. Carina relayed the information to Austin with a self-satisfied smile.

Ten minutes later, Austin turned off the main road and drove down a long dirt driveway to a low-slung, clapboard farmhouse. They pulled up next to a dust-covered pickup truck and went onto the front porch. No one answered repeated knocks on the door.

They checked the barn and then came back to the porch. Austin tried the door. It was unlocked. He pushed it open. Carina stuck her head in and called out.

"Mr. Benson?"

A low moan came from inside the house. Austin stepped inside and followed a hallway to the cozy living room, where he borrowed a fireplace poker. Walking quietly, they made their way to the end of the hallway. A man lay faceup on the floor of a large studio.

Carina knelt by the man's side. The blood had stopped oozing from a head wound that was surrounded by angry blue-black skin.

The studio looked as if it had been hit by a monsoon. Filing cabinet drawers were pulled open. Photos were scattered all over the floor. The computer screen had been smashed. Only the *National Geographic* covers hanging from the walls were undamaged. Austin called 911 and inspected the other rooms. The rest of the house was deserted.

When Austin returned to the studio, Benson was sitting up against the wall. Carina was holding a towel full of ice cubes gingerly against his head. She had wiped the spittle off his lips. His eyes were open, and he was apparently alert.

Benson was a burly, middle-aged man whose skin had been turned to leather by the sun in the exotic places he had worked. His long gray hair was tied back in a ponytail. He wore jeans, a T-shirt, and a film-cartridge vest that was an anachronism in an age of digital photography.

Austin knelt by his side. "How are you feeling?"

"Like crap," Benson said. "How do I look?"

"Like crap," Austin said.

Benson managed a weak smile. "*Bastards*. They were waiting when I came back from my walk to meet with the lady from the UN. Is that you?"

"I'm Carina Mechadi. I'm an investigator with the UNESCO.

Mr. Austin here is with the National Underwater and Marine Agency."

The light of recognition sparkled in Benson's gray eyes. "Did stories on both your outfits years ago."

"Tell us what happened after you returned from your walk," Austin said.

"Saw a car out front. Black SUV. Virginia license plates. I always leave the door unlocked. They were inside going through my stuff." He grimaced. "In case I pass out again, tell the cops there were four of them. All masked. All with guns. One was a real big guy. Think he was the leader."

Austin and Carina exchanged glances.

"Did he say anything?"

Benson nodded. "He wanted all my negatives. I told him to go to hell. He laid the barrel of his gun across my head. Guess I should be grateful he didn't shoot me. Only dazed. Played dead. Saw him and his pals go through my negative cabinets. Dumped all my stuff into plastic trash bags. They get my computer? Laptop."

Austin glanced around. "Looks like they cleared the place out."

"They figured I had done back-up. Every picture I ever took was on disk. Twenty-five years' worth." Benson chuckled. "Jerks. So busy beating up on me they didn't know I had backed up the backup. What the hell did they want?"

"We think they were after photos you took of an archaeological dig in Syria," Carina said.

He furrowed his brow. "I remember. Photographer remembers every shot he ever made. Nineteen seventy-two. Cover story. Hotter'n hell out there."

"The backup disk. Can we borrow it?" Austin said.

"Help catch those bastards?"

"Maybe." Austin lifted his shirt to show the bandage on his ribs. "You're not the only one with a score to settle."

Benson's eyes widened. "Guess they *really* didn't like you." He grinned. "Check my barn. Third stall on the right. Steel door under the hay. Key's hanging in the kitchen labeled BACK DOOR."

Carina said, "There was a big statue excavated in Syria. It was called the *Navigator.*"

"Sure. Looked like a cigar-store Indian with a pointy hat. Don't know what happened to it." His eyes rolled as if he were about to pass out, but Benson pulled himself together. "Check out the living-room mantle."

Austin found the key to the disk-storage safe in the kitchen and went into the living room. The fireplace mantle was crowded with hunks of rock and figurines Benson must have collected on his travels. One figure caught Austin's attention. He picked up a scale model of the *Navigator* about four inches high.

Tires crunched in the driveway. An ambulance was pulling in with its red-and-blue lights flashing. Austin slid the figurine into his pocket and went to welcome the EMTs. There were two emergency medical technicians, a young man and a woman. Austin led them to the studio.

The female EMT glanced around at the chaos. "What happened?"

Carina looked up from her charge. "He was attacked and his studio vandalized."

While the EMT examined Benson, her colleague put a call in to the police. After checking Benson's vitals, and applying a compress, they eased the photographer onto a stretcher and loaded him into the ambulance. They said Benson would be sore for a while, but his excellent physical condition should pull him through.

Austin told the EMTs that he and Carina would wait to talk to the police. As soon as the ambulance drove off, they went out to the barn. They swept aside the hay in the third stall to reveal a metal trapdoor, which Austin unlocked and opened. A short set of stairs led down to a temperature-controlled room about the size of a walk-in closet. The walls were lined with drawers labeled according to year. Austin found the disk inscribed HITTITE DIG, 1972, SYRIA.

Austin slipped the disk into his pocket. He and Carina walked back to the house. Minutes later, the police car came down the driveway. The lanky man in uniform who exited the driver's side was straight out of Mayberry USA. He approached them with a slow, shambling walk, and introduced himself as Chief Becker. He jotted their names down in a notebook.

"EMT said Mr. Benson was attacked."

"That's what he told us," Carina said. "He returned from a walk and found four men in his house. He tried to stop them from stealing his photos and was beaten with a gun."

The chief shook his head. "I knew he was a big photographer with the *Geographic,* but I'd never guess the photos were worth a B and E in the daytime." He paused for a moment, trying to figure out where the exotic woman and her brawny companion fit into the picture. "Mind saying what your business with Benson was?"

Austin said, "I'm with NUMA. Miss Mechadi works for the UN, investigating stolen antiquities. Mr. Benson took some photos years ago of a missing artifact, and we thought he might be able help in its recovery."

"Think that had anything to do with him getting beat up?"

The chief was shrewder than he looked. He was watching their reaction closely. Austin told him the truth. "I don't know."

The chief seemed satisfied with the explanation. "Care to show me where you found Mr. Benson?"

Austin and Carina led the way into the house. The chief let out a low whistle when he saw the studio mess.

"You touch anything?" he said.

"No," Austin said. "Would it have made a difference?"

The chief chuckled. "I'll get the crime scene folks to come out."

He took their personal information down in his notebook and said they might be called later for more questioning.

As Austin turned the car onto the road, Carina said, "You weren't exactly truthful with the chief."

"It might have complicated things if I went into the ship hijacking and the theft of the statue. And the fact that the common denominator is the *Navigator.*"

Carina slumped down in her seat and closed her eyes. "I feel responsible for all this somehow."

"Don't beat yourself up. The only people at fault are the thugs who've been exhibiting antisocial behavior. Who besides us knew about the Benson photos?"

"The only ones I've told were you and Mr. Baltazar. You don't think—"

"Another common denominator."

Carina slumped down into her seat and stared straight ahead. After a few minutes spent deep in thought, she seemed to rally.

"All right. Where do we go from here?"

Austin pulled the disk out of his pocket and handed it over. "We're going on an archaeological dig."

CHAPTER

24

As Austin slotted the Jeep into the reserved space in the underground garage, Carina blinked her eyes open. Traces of the drug must have lingered in her bloodstream because she had dozed off within minutes of leaving Benson's house. The last thing she had remembered was the rolling Virginia countryside.

She glanced around in bewilderment. "Where are we?"

"King Neptune's lair," Austin said with a poker face.

He got out of the car and opened the door on the passenger side. He gently took Carina's arm and led her to the nearest elevator, which swooshed them to the main floor. The doors opened, and they stepped out into the lobby that formed the centerpiece of the imposing, thirty-story NUMA tower of tinted green glass in Arlington, Virginia.

Carina looked around the atrium, with its waterfalls and wall aquariums and the huge globe at the center of the sea green marble floor. The lobby bustled with activity, much of it having to do with milling tour groups that bristled with cameras.

"This is *wonderful*," she said in wide-eyed wonder.

"Welcome to the headquarters of the National Underwater and Marine Agency," Austin said with pride. "This building houses more than two thousand marine scientists and engineers. The people who work here provide the support for another three thousand NUMA people and ships scattered across the world's oceans."

Carina pivoted like a ballerina. "I could stay here all day."

"You're not the first one to say that. Now we'll go from the sublime to the ridiculous."

They got back in the elevator which silently rocketed them to another floor. They stepped out into a thickly carpeted corridor and followed it to an unmarked door. Austin ushered her inside his office with an Alphonse and Gaston swoop of his arm.

Austin's modest corner space was the antithesis of the sweeping open vista that greeted visitors who came through the front doors of NUMA. It was what a real estate salesperson would describe as comfortable but cozy. There was a dark green rug on the floor. Furniture consisted of two chairs, filing cabinet, and a small sofa. A low bookcase held books devoted mostly to technical marine matters and philosophy.

The desk could have been measured in square inches, unlike the standard acre-sized centerpiece of most Washington offices. On the wall were photos of Austin with a rugged-looking older man who could have been his twin but was undoubtedly his father and pictures of various NUMA research vessels. Despite its unprepossessing dimensions, the office had an impressive of view of the Potomac River and Washington.

"My interior decorator is on vacation," Austin said in apology. He got two bottles of springwater from a small refrigerator, gave one to Carina, and invited her to sit in a chair. He sat at his desk and lifted his water. "Cheers."

"*Santé,*" she said, looking around. "This is not ridiculous at all. It's quite functional and homey."

"Thank you. I share a secretary who takes messages for me. I'm away a lot and don't spend much time here except for special tasks, like this one."

He took the photographic disk from his pocket and slid it into the computer on his desk. A *National Geographic* logo came up on the screen, followed by a story headline: "Digging Into the Past of a Forgotten Civilization." The headline accompanied an article on the excavation into the Hittite settlement. Austin called up all the photos on the disk. The screen immediately filled with small rectangles arranged in neat rows.

Benson had taken hundreds of photos. Austin pushed the ALBUM command for three-second internals and swiveled the screen so Carina could see the photographs.

After a few minutes, Carina pointed to the screen. "That's it!"

The photo on the screen showed several dirt-covered day workers standing at the edge of a pit, shovels in their hands. Nearby was the supervisor, a portly European wearing a pith helmet and unsoiled shorts and shirt. Protruding from the dirt at the bottom of the pit was a conical-shaped mound.

Austin went through the sequence of about two dozen photos. The series showed the head of the statue being unearthed. Then its shoulders were cleared until the workers were able to get lines under the armpits and hoist it from the hole. The dirt had been cleaned off in later pictures. Benson had taken several close-ups of the face, with its smashed-in nose, along with front, back, and side shots.

"It certainly *looks* like our statue," Carina said. "Unfortunately, this is all we have. A photograph. We're at a dead end."

Austin reached into his pocket and pulled out the figurine he had taken from Benson's fireplace mantle. He set it on the table in front of Carina. "Maybe not."

Carina took a deep breath. "It's a miniature version of the *Navigator*. Where did you find it?"

"At Benson's house."

She picked up the figurine. "The fact that it exists at all suggests that it was made from the original." She crinkled her brow. "From what we know, the statue was shipped from Syria to Baghdad and never saw the light of day. When could this copy have been made?"

Austin reached for his phone. "Let's ask the man who knows."

Using directory assistance, he found the name of the hospital nearest to Benson's farm and punched in the number. The receptionist connected him to Benson's room. Austin put the phone on speaker. The photographer answered with a furry hello, but he perked up when Austin identified himself. He said that he had suffered a concussion and contusions but no fractures.

"I'll be out of here in a couple of days. Any word on those bastards?"

"Nothing solid. We wondered where you found the figurine on the mantle. The miniature of the statue you photographed at the Syrian dig. Did someone copy the statue at the excavation site?"

"Naw. That one was shipped off right away. Maybe someone copied it from the other statue."

Austin and Carina exchanged blank looks. "*What* other statue?" she said. "We were under the impression that there was only one *Navigator.*"

"Sorry about that. I was going to mention it, but, as you know, I was under the weather when you came by the house. There was a second statue. The German guy who was running the Syrian dig said the statues might have guarded the entrance to an important building or tomb. I took some shots of the old boy, but that was before digital. The film got ruined in the blasted heat."

"What happened to the second statue?" Austin said.

"Got me. I went on to another assignment. The *Geographic* wanted shots of native women with bare breasts, so they sent me to

Samoa. A couple of years ago I was in Istanbul doing a feature on the Ottoman Empire. I found the little figure in a market. Guy who sold it to me was a bandit, but I bought it anyhow."

"Do you remember where the market was?"

"Somewhere in the covered bazaar. Shop had a pile of the statues. Damn. Painkiller's wearing off. Got to call the nurse. Let me know when you find the creeps who bopped me."

"I will." Austin thanked Benson, told him to stay well, and clicked off.

Carina looked as if she were sitting on bedsprings. "A *second* statue! We've got to find it."

Austin pictured the sprawling city of Istanbul as he remembered it from an assignment in the Black Sea a couple of years earlier. The covered bazaar spread out over several acres in a bewildering labyrinth of shops. He remembered Zavala's plans for the Subvette.

"We've got a contingent of NUMA people going to Istanbul to help survey an ancient port. Joe Zavala could check out the bazaar for us."

"And *then* what?" Carina said. "What if he finds the dealer? We are here and he is there. What good will *that* do us?"

Carina had a point. "I'll see if there's a seat on the plane."

"Make that *two* seats." She raised her hand to cut short Austin's reply. "I can be a great help. I know someone in Istanbul who's close to the antiquities market." She shrugged. "Well, he's a smuggler, but only of minor artifacts. I've used him on several occasions to go after bigger fish. He knows every crooked dealer in Istanbul. He could save us time. He will only work through me."

Austin gave her proposal a second's thought. It would be pleasant to have the lovely Italian woman as company, but there were other reasons that had nothing to do with male libido. He was concerned about Carina's safety if she were left alone. Trouble seemed to dog the young woman's footsteps. He'd feel better if he could keep an eye on her. Her informant could save a lot of sweat. Carina had successfully tracked down the *Navigator* where others had failed.

She was putting on an unnecessary display of persistence, showering Austin with other reasons for her to go, stopping only after he put his finger to his lips. He called Zavala and asked if he had room for two passengers. After a short conversation, Austin hung up and turned to Carina, who had been hanging on every word.

"Pack your bags," he said. "The plane is leaving at eight tonight. I'll drive you to your hotel and pick you up at five o'clock."

Carina leaned forward and gave Austin a long and lingering kiss that practically curled his toes. "It will be faster if I take a cab. I'll be waiting for you."

Seconds later, she was out the door, and he could hear her padding down the hallway. He glanced at his wristwatch. He kept a packed duffel bag ready at all times. All he had to do was grab it and go.

On the drive to the boathouse, he called his shared secretary and said he would be away for a few days. Then he called Elwood Nickerson and left a similar message. He didn't go into details. Somehow he didn't feel comfortable telling the undersecretary of state that the key to heading off an international crisis was a doll-sized figure five thousand miles away.

25

"T ODAY'S THE DAY," Paul Trout said with steely determination.

Trout stood wide-legged in a dinghy while he handed fishing tackle to his wife Gamay, who was aboard their twenty-one-foot powerboat. Gamay set the rods into a rack and said, "Ho-hum," bringing her palm to her lips in an exaggerated yawn. "I recall the same male bragging twenty-four hours ago on this very same spot. It was an empty boast, just like the day before."

Trout climbed onto the boat with surprising agility for a man built like a professional basketball player. Although he was six foot eight, he moved with a catlike grace that came from years of experience on boats at the side of his fisherman father. He punched the starter button on the console. The inboard engine came to life with a throaty grumble and a puff of blue exhaust.

"No brag. When you're born into an old Cape Cod family that's caught tons of fish over the decades, you expect an off day once in a while." He stuck his nose in the air like a bloodhound. "That granddaddy striper is waiting in his honey hole for me to hook him."

"Now I know why fishermen have a reputation for telling tall tales." Gamay cast off the mooring line.

Trout gave the throttle a light touch and steered the boat at a slow speed across Eel Pond toward the Water Street drawbridge. They passed a bar whose deck overlooked the pond, and Trout smacked his lips. "I can taste that cold frosty beer."

"Let's jack up the ante," Gamay said. "Loser buys dinner too."

"It's a bet," Trout said without hesitation. "Fried clams go great with beer."

The boat proceeded slowly under the drawbridge and out into the harbor, past the Martha's Vineyard ferry terminal and the research vessel *Atlantis,* which was tied up to the dock of the world-famous Woods Hole Oceanographic Institution, where Trout's interest in oceanography had been stimulated when he was still a boy.

The boat cleared the harbor and Trout goosed the throttle. The bow angled up on plane and he steered toward the Elizabeth Islands, an archipelago that lay in a string southwest of Cape Cod. Gamay puttered about the deck, readying fishing gear.

There were few things better in Trout's opinion than racing over the waves with the salty breeze in his face and the prospects of a full day of fishing. All he needed to make the outing a perfect ten would be to catch a bigger fish than Gamay. He was used to friendly competition with his wife, but he had been quietly annoyed that she had outfished him over the last two days.

As a young girl growing up on the shores of Lake Michigan, Gamay was no slouch when it came to boats and fishing. Although she had grown into an attractive woman, she retained a hint of the tomboy she had once been. Her good-natured taunts at Trout's lack of success ran counter to his understated New England persona. He gritted his teeth. Today damn *well* better be the day or he would never live it down.

Near the low-lying hump that was Naushon Island, Trout pointed the boat toward a cloud of squalling seabirds diving in the water in search of bait being chased to the surface by larger links in the food chain. Amorphous yellow blobs were popping up on the fish-finder screen. There was a fishy scent in the air. He cut the engine and the boat plowed to a stop.

Gamay handed Trout a fishing rod and took the wheel. It was customary for the highliner on the last trip to let the lowliner go first. Trout settled into the swivel chair and let some line out. He started jigging, continuously jerking the rod to keep the lure traveling through the water.

"Fish on!" he yelled.

He cranked the reel and pulled in a thirty-two-inch-long striped bass. After measuring the fish, he threw it back. Gamay quickly caught a twenty-eight-incher. Again they tossed the fish overboard. They took turns catching stripers in roughly the same size range before the school played out, and they moved to another spot that was equally as productive.

They kept a running compilation and were in a dead heat when Trout felt a sharp tug on the line that almost pulled his arm out. This was going to be the tiebreaker. He was barely aware of a cell phone chiming. Gamay put the phone to her ear and, after a moment, said, "Kurt needs to talk to you."

Trout cranked the reel like a man possessed. The silver body of a huge fish flashed near the surface. *Damn*. It was as big as a whale. He tried to concentrate.

"Tell him to wait," he shouted over his shoulder.

"He can't wait," Gamay said. "He and Joe are on their way to Turkey."

Turkey? The last Trout was aware of, Austin and Zavala were off to Newfoundland. In that instant, Trout lost his train of thought, and the fish. The line went slack. Oh, hell. He got up, handed the rod to Gamay, and took the phone in exchange.

"Hope I'm not interrupting anything," Austin said.

"Naw," Trout said. He stared disconsolately at the ripples where he'd last seen the giant striper. "What's up, Kurt?"

"Can you come up with a computer model that will reconstruct a transatlantic ship voyage? I know it's a tall order."

"I'll give it a try," Trout said. "I'll need a date. I can figure in currents, weather, and speed if that information is available."

"Actually, very little is available. This was a Phoenician ship. The crossing was made around 900 B.C."

Trout was more intrigued than discouraged. "Tell me more," he said.

"I've sent you a package by special courier. Should be there by now. It will explain everything. This is urgent. I'll call first chance I get. Bye."

"What was that all about?" Gamay said after Trout clicked off.

He explained Kurt's request. They would have to call it a day. He stared longingly at another cloud of wheeling seabirds. "Damn shame about that fish."

Gamay pecked him on the cheek. "I saw him. It was a monster. I think it's my turn to buy the beer."

THE PACKAGE from Austin was leaning against the front door of the two-hundred-year-old Cape Cod cottage that overlooked a circular kettle pond. Trout had grown up in the broad-roofed house within walking distance of the Oceanographic Institution, whose scientists had encouraged his boyhood curiosity about the ocean.

He and Gamay sat at the harvest table in the kitchen, munching on the ham-and-cheese roll-ups they had prepared for their picnic lunch as they went over the Jefferson file. At one point, Gamay looked up from her reading and blew a strand of dark red hair out of her eyes.

"This is unbelievable!"

Trout took a swig from a can of Buzzards Bay ale. "I'm trying to figure out what we can do. My experience with computer modeling is mostly deep-sea geology. You made the switch from nautical archaeology to marine biology. We could pull something together, but it wouldn't be pretty. We'll need help."

Gamay smiled, showing the slight space between her front teeth, a dental anomaly that somehow looked attractive on her. "Didn't we hear some gossip last night?"

Trout recalled the gentle ribbing he had received from the local barflies who had heard about his fishing contest with Gamay. Then he remembered someone mentioning a familiar name. He snapped his fingers. "Charlie Summers is in town."

Gamay handed Trout the phone and he called the research-vessel dock. He got through to Summers, who was working on a retrofit for the *Atlantis,* and laid out the problem.

"That's a lot more interesting than what I'm doing," Summers said. "Can you come over now?"

Minutes later, the Trouts were walking out onto the research-vessel dock. A stocky man with a square jaw and thinning straw-hued hair greeted them with effusive hugs.

Summers was a well-known naval architect who specialized in the design of research and educational vessels. He often consulted in the design of luxury yachts, and was an expert in the stability of large sailing vessels.

He gave Gamay a big wink. "Thought you two would be out fishing today."

"News of our competition got around fast," Trout said with a smirk.

"It's the talk of the town. You know how gossipy fishermen and scientists are."

"Paul almost beat me today," Gamay offered.

Summers roared with laughter. "Please don't tell me it was the one that got away." He wiped the tears from his eyes. "Now, what's all this about Phoenicians?"

Trout jumped at the chance to change the subject. "We got a call from NUMA this morning. Someone is doing research on pre-Columbian contact and needed help replicating a voyage. We get a lot of odd requests."

"Not odd at all. I've read reams of material on Phoenician ship-building. There's no doubt from a naval architect's point of view that they had the capacity to go almost anywhere they wanted."

"Then you *can* help us plot a course?" Gamay said.

Summers shook his head. "That's a tough one," he said. "The Phoenicians left no maps or charts. They guarded their sea knowl-edge with their lives." Noting the disappointment in Gamay's face, he added: "But we can take a stab at it. Let's go build us a ship."

Summers led the way into a brick building where he had his tem-porary office. He sat behind a computer and clicked off the schematic diagram of the *Atlantis* that had been displayed on the screen.

"I see we're going to build a virtual ship," Trout said.

"That's the very best kind," Summers said with a grin. "They never sink, and you don't have to worry about mutinies." He called up a computer file and a drawing of a square-sailed vessel appeared on the monitor.

"Is that a Phoenician ship?" Gamay said.

"This is one type, based on pictures from vases, sculptures, mod-els, and coins. It's an early design. It's got a keel, rounded hull, oars, and a high seat for the steersman."

"We're looking for something capable of deep-ocean travel," Trout said.

Summers leaned back in his chair. "Their ship designs were modified by need. The Phoenicians graduated from shore coasting and stops at night to long, uninterrupted voyages. I'm going to use a software program developed for some architects doing research in Portugal and at Texas A&M. They created a methodology to test and evaluate the sailing characteristics of ships where no plans were available. The goal was to come up with a comprehensive image. They used Portuguese *naus*, the trade ships that sailed from Europe around Africa to India and back. *Watch*."

Summers bent forward and clicked the mouse. A computer-generated image of a three-masted ship appeared on the screen.

"Looks like a ghost ship," Gamay observed.

"This is only the foundation. They fed the info from a wreck survey into a computer. Using the software, they developed plans for the ship's rigging, sails, and spars. The picture is one of those images. By coming up with a hypothetical reconstruction of the ship's hull, they figured out how the ship performed at sea and in adverse weather. Once they had that mathematical model, they could test it in a wind tunnel."

"And you can do the same for a Phoenician ship?" Trout said.

"No problem. We'll use three known Phoenician wrecks that were found in the western Mediterranean and off the coast of Israel. The ships were upright and perfectly preserved in cold water. We used the *Jason,* the same remote-operated vehicle that photographed *Titanic,* to come up with a photomosaic. I programmed the specs into my computer."

A set of drawings that looked like blueprints for a shipbuilder filled the screen. The drawings showed the ship as seen from above, the side, and head-on.

"The plans indicate the ship is only fifty-five feet long," Trout pointed out.

"This is a composite of the Israel ships. I'll add some length. I tweaked the program so that it will automatically add in design features that would have evolved with the increase in the ship's size."

A skeletal, three-dimensional image appeared, outlining the ship's timbers and other structural elements. The spaces between the timbers began to fill in. Decks, oars, rigging, and sail materialized, along with a ramming beak on the prow. The last feature was a carved horse head on the bow.

"*Voilà!* A ship of Tarshish."

"It's magnificent," Gamay said. "The lines are functional yet graceful."

"She would be around two hundred feet long, as I reckon," Summers said. "That ship could go anywhere in the world."

"Which brings us back to our original problem," Trout said. "How do we figure out that vessel's transatlantic routes?"

Pursing his lips, Summers said, "It's possible to back into a solution like those guys did with the *nau*. You'd need wind, current, and weather patterns, work in the ship's probable speed, figure out the pilot's choices according to ship design, and then factor in historical accounts."

Gamay let out a heavy sigh. "We've got a lot of work to do."

Summers glanced at his wristwatch. "Me too. They want the *Atlantis* ready to sail in three days."

THE TROUTS thanked Summers and walked back along the main street of Woods Hole. "Where do you think we should go from here?" Gamay said.

"Tough to say. Kurt only gave us a few crumbs of information. He's not going to be happy, but I don't think we have enough to pull this thing together. We may need another approach."

Like many married couples, Paul and Gamay had a way of anticipating each other's thoughts. Their work for the NUMA Special Assignments Team, where unspoken communication could mean the difference between life and death, had honed their skills to a sharp edge.

"I've been thinking the same thing," Gamay said. "Every sea voyage starts on land. Let's go through the Jefferson file again. There may be something we missed."

Back at the house, they sat at the kitchen table, read half the file, and then exchanged the sections. They both finished reading at about the same time.

Gamay put the papers down and said, "What pops out at you?"

"Meriwether Lewis," Trout said. "He was on his way to tell Jefferson what he had found when he died."

"That intrigued me too." She riffled through the papers in front of her. "Lewis had *material* evidence he wanted to show Jefferson. I suggest that we try to figure out what happened to it."

"Might be almost as tough as reconstructing a Phoenician voyage," Trout said.

"There's a nexus that might help us," Gamay said. "Jefferson was president of the American Philosophical Society in Philadelphia. He sent Lewis there to prep him in the sciences for his historic exploration. While Lewis was in Philadelphia, Jefferson devised the cipher for them to use."

Trout blinked his large brown eyes in a barely noticeable show of excitement and picked up the thread. "Jefferson wrote to members of the society to tell them about his Indian language research and the theft of his papers. He contacted a society scholar, who identified the words on the vellum map as Phoenician. The artichoke file was found at the society."

"That's better than knowing Kevin Bacon or six degrees of separation," Gamay said. She looked through the file and found a number for the Philosophical Society and the name of the researcher who had discovered the file. She called Angela Worth, identified herself, and made an appointment to meet the next day.

As Gamay hung up, Trout grinned and said, "You realize our vacation has come to an end."

"That's okay," Gamay said. "I think I'm getting tired of fishing."

Trout gave a weary shrug of his shoulders.

"I *know* I am," he said.

CHAPTER
26

WITH A CRUISING SPEED OF more than five hundred miles an hour, the turquoise-colored Cessna Citation X aircraft flew to Istanbul in three hours after a quick refueling stop in Paris. The raked-tail aircraft touched down at Kemal Atatürk International Airport and taxied away from the main terminal. The six passengers went through a special entry gate reserved for VIPs and were politely whisked through customs.

The Subvette had arrived earlier on a special NUMA cargo plane and was being stored in an airport warehouse. Zavala wanted to inspect the submersible to see how it had fared on its journey. He told Austin he would catch a taxi to the excavation after he arranged for the vehicle to be transported to the dig.

Two vans awaited their arrival. One vehicle would take their luggage to their hotel while another went directly to the excavation. The NUMA scientists were eager to get to the site. The team's leader was a veteran nautical archaeologist named Martin Hanley.

On the transatlantic leg of the flight, Hanley had explained the reason for haste. He had made a preliminary trip to Istanbul to see the port which had been built when the city was still known as Constantinople. The port was found in Yenikapi, on the European side of the narrow Bosphorus Straits, when squatter shanties had been cleared to build a new hub railroad station. The site had been named the Port of Theodosius.

The archaeological excavation could delay construction of a tunnel connecting the European and Asian sides of the city. Hanley and the Turkish archaeologists were worried that important finds could be overlooked in the hurry to excavate the site. He had returned to Washington to assemble his team.

The American scientists were greeted warmly by their Turkish counterparts. Round-the-clock shifts were working the muddy excavation.

"Sure you don't want to stick around?" Hanley said. "They've found a church, eight boats, shoes, anchors, lines, and part of the old city walls. Who knows what treasures they'll discover next?"

"Thanks. Maybe after we do some sightseeing."

Austin hailed a cab that took them along Kennedy Caddesi, the busy thoroughfare that runs along the edge of the Bosphorus. An unbroken line of cargo ships was queuing up to pass through the busy connector between the Black Sea and the Mediterranean. Austin turned to Carina and said, "How long have you known your Turkish connection?"

"A year or so. Cemil helped me recover some Anatolian treasures that had been stolen from the Topkapi Palace. He used to be a smuggler. No arms or drugs, he says. Cigarettes, appliances, anything that was covered by high tariffs."

"Is he connected to the Turkish mafia?"

She laughed. "I asked him that. He said that in Turkey *everyone* is in the mafia. He came through for me, but he's . . ." Carina's English failed her for a moment. "How do you say it? Mysterious."

"I had concluded that. You're sure he said to meet him at the 'upside-down woman with the stone eyes'?"

"*Positive.* He likes to talk in riddles. It's quite maddening at times."

Austin asked the cab driver to take them to Sultanamet. They got out of the cab and walked across the busy street. "We'll find your friend right below our feet if I'm not mistaken," Austin said.

"He's not the *only* one who talks in riddles."

Austin went over to a kiosk and bought two admission tickets to the Basilica Cisterns. They went down a flight of stairs. The cool, damp air that brushed their faces felt good after the heat of the city.

They were in a huge, dimly lit vault that resembled an underground palace. Fish darted through the murky green water that covered the floor. Elevated boardwalks ran between rows of columns. Voices echoed in the cavelike chamber. Classical music played in the background. The *drip-drip* of water could be heard from a dozen different locations.

"The Romans had built these cisterns to hold a water supply for the Grand Palace," Austin said. "The Byzantines discovered them when people started catching fish through holes in the floors of their houses. The stone lady is this way."

They walked to the end of a boardwalk and descended to a platform. Two thick columns rested on bases carved into the faces of Medusa. One face lay on its side; the other, upside down. A steady stream of tourists came and went, after pausing to take snapshots of the curiosity.

Finally, the only other person left was a middle-aged man who had been there since they arrived. He carried a camera but hadn't used it. He was wearing dark slacks and a white short-sleeved shirt with no tie, the standard uniform for many Turks. He wore aviator-style sunglasses, although the light was low in the cistern.

"Why do you think the Romans put the heads in this strange position?" he asked Carina, speaking English with a slight accent.

Carina studied the sculptures. "Maybe it's a joke. One face looks at the world as it should be and the other as it is. Topsy-turvy."

"Excellent. Would you be Signorita Mechadi?" the man said.

"Cemil?"

"At your service," he said with a smile. "And this must be your friend, Mr. Austin."

Austin shook hands with the Turk. After hearing of Cemil's underworld exploits, he had expected a Damon Runyon character with a Turkish twist. This man looked more like someone's favorite uncle.

"It's good to meet you after all our dealings, Señora Mechadi. How can I help you?"

"We're looking for a statue that's the twin of one stolen from the Iraq National Museum."

Cemil glanced at a new group of tourists and suggested a walk. As they strolled between rows of columns, he said, "There's been a steady stream of Baghdad merchandise through Istanbul. It's depressing prices. Do you have a photograph?"

Austin handed over the *Navigator* figurine. "This is a scale model. The actual statue is almost as tall as a man."

Cemil produced a loupe-penlight instrument and examined the figurine. He chuckled. "I hope you didn't pay too much for this artifact."

"Do you recognize it?" Carina said.

"Oh, *yes*. Come with me."

Cemil led the way to the exit, and they climbed back into the bright sunlight. The Grand Bazaar was a short tram ride away. The bazaar was a labyrinth of hundreds of shops, restaurants, and cafés, and former caravan-storage depots called *han*s. Politely aggressive proprietors lurked like trap-door spiders ready to pounce on passing tourists and talk them out of their Turkish lira.

They went through the Carsikapi Gate and made their way through the hot, unventilated maze of roofed streets. Cemil navigated the twists and turns as if he were operating on personal radar. He took them deep into the heart of the bazaar and stopped at a small shop.

"Merhaba," Cemil said to a man in his sixties who sat in front of the shop, sipping tea and reading a Turkish newspaper. The shopkeeper smiled broadly. Putting the newspaper aside, he rose from his chair and pumped Cemil's hand.

"Merhaba," he said.

"This is Mehmet," Cemil explained." He's an old friend."

Mehmet brought out comfortable cushions for his guests to sit on and poured tea for everyone. He and Cemil chatted in Turkish. After a few minutes of conversation, Cemil asked Austin for the figurine and handed it to Mehmet. The shopkeeper examined the miniature *Navigator* and nodded vigorously. Using expansive hand gestures, he invited everyone into his shop. Shelves and floor were covered with rugs, jewelry, boxes of tea, scarves, pottery, and red fezes. He walked up to a shelf crowded with pottery and placed the figure next to a row of four identical statues.

Cemil translated his friend's commentary. "Mehmet says he can give you a deal on these. Normally, they go for eight lira, but he's willing to drop the price to five if you buy more than one."

"Does Mehmet remember selling a statue to an American photographer a few years ago?" Austin asked.

Cemil translated the question and the answer. "Mehmet is Turkish. He remembers every sale he ever made. He recalls the photographer very well. Especially with this item, which moves very slowly. But he is old, and memory has not been very good lately."

"Maybe this will help," Austin said, "I'll take all of the figurines."

Mehmet beamed as he carefully wrapped each statue in tissue paper and placed the purchases in a plastic bag, which he handed to Carina.

"Can your friend tell us where he acquired these statues?" Carina said.

Mehmet explained that he had bought the statues in the south where his mother lives. He tells buyers that they are harem eunuchs. The craftsmanship could be better, and the detail was poorly executed, but he likes the old man who made them. He picks up a batch whenever he visits his aging mother, which is about once a month. The artist sells them in the abandoned village, he said.

"Where is that?" Austin said.

Cemil said, "It's called Kayakoy, near the town of Fethiye. It was a Greek village until the Treaty of Lausanne was signed in 1923. The Greeks returned to Greece in the exchange and Turks living in Greece came to Anatolia. Then the Turks left after a big earthquake. It's a tourist attraction now."

Austin asked the artist's name. Mehmet said he was sure he'd remember, but first he suggested that Austin and the lovely lady would like to look around the shop. Austin got the hint. He bought a silk scarf for Carina and a fez for himself, even though no self-respecting Turk would be caught dead in the cylindrical headgear.

Bidding Mehmet good-bye, at Cemil's suggestion they headed to the Haghia Sophia neighborhood for lunch in a pleasantly shaded garden restaurant. While they waited for their food, Cemil said, "I'm sorry you came all this way for nothing."

"*I'm* not sorry," Carina said. "It gave me the chance to meet you in person, and to thank you for all you have done. Besides, we're not through here yet."

"But you have seen that the statues are only a tourist item."

Austin lined up the figurines on the table. "How far is the town where these were made?"

"It's on the Turquoise Coast. About five hundred miles. Are you thinking of extending your visit to Turkey?"

Austin picked up a figurine. "I'd like to talk to the artist who made this."

"So would I," Carina said. "It's quite possible he used a life-sized model."

"This statue must be very valuable."

"Maybe," Austin said. "Maybe not."

"I understand the need for discretion," Cemil said, rising from the table. "Dalyran is only about an hour from here by plane. From there, it's not a bad drive to Kayakoy. If you'll excuse me, I'll be on my way, but if you need any help please let me know. I have a great many connections in Istanbul."

A few minutes after Cemil left, Austin and Carina hailed a taxi to drive them back to the hotel. The desk clerk found two seats on an early-morning plane to Dalyran and made car rental arrangements as well. As they stood in the hotel lobby, Carina said, "Now what, Mr. Tour Guide?"

Austin pondered her question and said, "I think I can do something off the beaten path."

A cab took them back to the archaeological dig. Austin asked Hanley if he needed volunteers. He put them to work shoveling mud through strainers. Carina didn't seem to mind being covered from head to toe with Bosphorus mud. She jumped about like an excited schoolgirl whenever they found a coin or broken pottery from the muck.

They worked until late at night, when the van came by to take the NUMA crew back to the hotel. As they trudged through the hotel lobby, Austin and Carina were so tired they hardly noticed the pair of men sitting in plush chairs reading magazines. Nor were they aware that two pairs of eyes followed them every step of the way to the elevator.

CHAPTER

27

AUSTIN TURNED THE RENTED RENAULT off the Turquoise Coast highway onto a road that twisted and turned
like a spastic snake. The road ran for several miles through cultivated countryside and sleepy villages. As the car rounded a bend,
ruins could be seen on the crest of a hill.

Austin parked next to a cluster of buildings. The abandoned village had become a state-run tourist attraction. The inevitable ticket
seller was waiting to take their modest admission fee. He pointed the
way toward the village, and went to intercept a car with two men in
it that pulled up next to the Renault.

An ascending mule path went past an outdoor restaurant, sou-
venir shop, and several freelance vendors peddling their wares. After
a hike of a few minutes, Austin and Carina had an unimpeded view
of the village.

Hundreds of roofless houses baked under the hot sun. Plaster
had peeled off the outside of the silent structures to expose their
rough stucco walls. A few houses had been taken over by squatters
who had spread their laundry out to dry. The only other sign of life
was a satanic-faced goat that munched contentedly on a weed-
choked garden.

"It's hard to believe that this place was once full of life," Carina said. "People making love. Women crying out in labor. Fathers bragging about their newborns. Children celebrating birthdays and baptisms. Mourning the passing of old ones."

Austin was only half listening to Carina rhapsodize. Two men had stopped on the trail about a hundred feet behind them. One was taking photos of the goat. They were in their twenties, Austin estimated, both dressed in black pants and short-sleeved white shirts. Their arms were thick and muscular. Their faces were shaded by the brims of their caps and sunglasses.

Carina had continued along the mule path. When Austin caught up with her, she was strolling across the courtyard of an abandoned church toward an old man perched on a wall under a shade tree. Decorated bowls and plates were lined up on the wall, which he was using to showcase his wares.

Austin greeted the man and asked if he were Mehmet's friend, Salim.

The man smiled. "Mehmet buys my work for the covered bazaar."

"Yes, we know. He told us where to find you," Carina said.

Salim had the Pablo Picasso look that comes to Mediterranean men of a certain age. The skin on his cheeks and bald head was tanned the color of tanbark and his face was as unlined as a baby's. Good humor and wisdom lurked in big eyes that were as dark as raisins. He gestured toward his wares.

"Mehmet tells you of my souvenirs?" he said.

Austin pulled the *Navigator* figurine from his pocket. "We were looking for something like this."

"Ah," Salim said, his face lighting up. "The *eunuch*." He made a horizontal cutting motion with an invisible knife. "I stop making them. No one buys."

Austin carefully considered the next question. "Does the eunuch have a grandfather?"

Salim gave him a puzzled look and then flashed a big-toothed grin. He drew his arms in wide arcs as if they were describing a large circle. "*Büyük. Big* eunuch."

"That's right. *Büyük*. Where?"

"In Lycée tomb. You understand?"

Austin had noticed the strange Lycian tombs carved high up on the faces of plunging cliffs. The entrances were framed by ornate columns and triangular lintels like classic Greek or Roman temples.

In halting English, Salim said he had always been interested in art. As a young man, he explored the countryside with paper pad and charcoal in search of subjects. On one exploration, he had found a Lycian tomb unknown to the people in his village. The tomb was cut into a cliff above the sea, hidden from view by thick vegetation. He had gone inside and discovered a statue in the cave. He sketched it. When he was looking for a subject later to mold in clay, he went back to the sketch.

"Where is the statue now?" Carina said with growing excitement.

Salim pointed to the ground. "Earthquake." The cliff had slid into the sea.

Carina was visibly disappointed, but Austin persisted. He showed Salim a map of the coast and asked the old man to pinpoint the site of the tomb. Salim tapped the map with his fingertip.

Carina clutched Austin's arm. *"Kurt,"* she said. "Those men were in the hotel last night."

The Turks had paused at the edge of the courtyard and were staring directly at Carina and Austin. Austin remembered the two men he had seen lounging in the lobby. Their arrival at the village was no accident.

"You're right," he said. "They're a long way from Istanbul."

He took a handful of lira from his pocket and dropped the bills next to Salim. He picked up a ceramic plate, thanked the old man for the information, and slipped his arm around Carina's waist. He told her to walk as casually as she was able to the church.

He guided her through the doorway into the vacant building and edged over to a window that had been stripped of glass and framework. Peering around the edge of the doorframe, he saw the men talking to Salim. The old artist pointed to the church. The men broke off their conversation and headed toward the building. They were no longer sauntering and walked quickly with purpose in each step.

Austin told Carina to climb out a window opening on the opposite wall. He followed her through the opening, and they scrambled up a gravelly path to a hill that overlooked the church.

Carina hid in a small chapel perched at the top of the hill and Austin flattened himself to the ground. Their pursuers had separated and set off in opposite directions around the church. They met up again and had a heated discussion. Then they split up and disappeared into the labyrinth of deserted houses.

Austin retrieved Carina from the chapel and led the way down the other side of the ridge. They caught a glimpse of something black moving between them and the main road. One man had come around the bottom of the ridge and was going from house to house. Austin pulled Carina into a doorway.

He was still holding the plate he had bought from Salim. He stepped out of the doorway, curled the plate into his wrist, and snapped it like a Frisbee over a nearby rooftop. There was the sound of the plate shattering and the rattle of gravel kicked up by running feet.

Austin and Carina veered off the main thoroughfare through the village and followed a rocky goat path back to the road. Staying close to the side, they walked about a quarter of a mile back to the village entrance.

They headed for the Renault and saw the car that the two men had driven up in parked tight next to theirs. Austin told Carina to wait and went to the snack bar. He came back a minute later holding a corkscrew in his hand.

"This is no time for wine," she said with a sour look.

"I agree," Austin said. He wiped the sweat from his forehead. "A cold beer would be better."

He asked Carina to keep watch. He ducked down between the cars as if tying his shoe and jammed the corkscrew point into the other car's tire. He worked the point around until he felt a rubbery puff of air on his hand and mangled the valve for good measure.

"What are you doing?" Carina said.

"I'm making sure our friends get the point," Austin said with a wolfish grin.

He slid behind the wheel of the Renault, started the engine, and pulled out onto the road with spinning tires.

AUSTIN DROVE as if he were in the Grand Prix. With Carina map-navigating, they headed toward Fethiye, a coastal market and resort town. He drove directly to the harbor. They walked along the quay past the wide-beamed wooden boats that took tourists out on day trips for fishing and scuba diving.

He stopped at the tie-up for a wooden boat about forty-five feet long. A sign said that the *Iztuzu,* the Turkish name for Turtle, was for hire on an hourly or daily basis.

Austin crossed the short gangway and called out a hello. A man in his forties came out of the cabin. "I'm Captain Mustapha," he said, with a friendly smile. "You want to rent the boat?"

The boat was not new, but it had been well maintained. Metal was free of rust, and the wood was highly polished. Lines were neatly coiled. Austin surmised that Mustapha was a competent mariner.

The fact that he was still in port suggested that he might be hungry for business. Austin pulled out the map he had shown Salim and pointed to the coastline.

"Can you take us here, Captain? We might like to do some snorkeling."

"Yes, of course. I know all the good places. When?"

"How about now?"

Austin agreed to the price Mustapha threw out and waved at Carina to come aboard. Mustapha cast off the dock lines and eased the boat out of its slip. He pointed the bow into the bay. The boat followed the irregular coastline. They passed resort complexes, a lighthouse, and luxurious villas perched in the hills. Eventually, all signs of human habitation disappeared.

Mustapha angled the boat in toward a half-moon cove and killed the engine. He dropped anchor and dug out a couple of beat-up snorkels and masks and fin sets.

"You want to go swimming?"

Austin had been squinting up at a section of cliff where the rock was exposed like an open wound. "Maybe later. I'd like to go ashore."

Mustapha shrugged and put the snorkels away. He hung a ladder over the side and brought the dinghy around. Austin rowed the short distance to shore and pulled the dinghy up on the rocky beach. Within a dozen or so feet from the water's edge, the terrain rose at a sharp angle. Using tree trunks and bushes as handholds, Austin climbed until he was about a hundred fifty feet above the lagoon.

He stood on a ledge that bulged out from the cliff like a Neanderthal's brow. A swath of rock about a hundred feet wide had been sheared off as neatly as if by a giant chisel. Austin guessed that the cliff had been weakened by the tomb, in combination with natural faults, and the violent shaking of the earth had jiggled it loose. Huge boulders lay at the base of the cliff and in the water.

Austin wondered whether the statue could have survived the

crushing fall. Then he waved at Carina, who had been watching his climb, and started down the hill. He was sweating from the heat and exertion, and his shorts and shirt were covered with dirt. He dove into the water fully clothed, giving his body and clothes a quick laundering. When it came to the behavior of foreign tourists, Mustapha was never surprised. He started the engine and headed back to port.

Austin cracked open a couple of bottles of Turkish beer from the cooler and handed one to Carina. "Well?" she said.

He took a deep gulp and let the cold liquid trickle down his throat. "We'll assume that Salim is correct and the statue was still in the tomb at the time of the earthquake. There's no certainty that it wasn't buried between tons of rock. Even if we do find it, the *Navigator* may be too damaged to be of help."

"Then this was all for nothing?"

"Not at all. I'd like to come back for a closer look."

He told Mustapha he wanted to lease the boat for another day.

"Can we come back here tomorrow?" Austin said. "I'd like to do some diving."

"Yes, of course. You're scientists?" Mustapha said.

Austin showed him his NUMA ID. Mustapha had never heard of the agency, but the fact that Austin carried special identification impressed him. Mustapha was glad to get the charter. He had told the boat's owners that if they didn't get him a mate soon he would quit. Austin took a satellite phone from his backpack and punched in Zavala's number. Zavala was at the port excavation, waiting for Hanley to give him the green light on the Subvette.

"You'll have to tell Hanley that the sub's services are needed elsewhere," Austin said.

He gave Zavala his location and rattled off a shopping list. Zavala said if he could work out the logistics he would fly to Dalyran the next morning.

The boat pulled into its slip at dusk. Austin asked Mustapha to recommend a quiet hotel. The captain suggested a resort that was a twenty-minute drive at the end of a twisting road that wound through the wooded hills near Fethiye. The hotel clerk said reservations were usually necessary but that he had one room with a king-sized bed. Austin hadn't given sleeping arrangements any thought. He asked Carina if she wanted to look for another hotel.

"I'm exhausted," she said. "Still suffering from jet lag. Tell him we'll take it."

They had a quiet dinner in the hotel restaurant at a corner table overlooking the sea. Shish kebab and rice. The lights of Fethiye shimmered in the distance like diamonds on a necklace.

"I hate to waste a romantic setting talking business," Austin said. "But there are certain issues we should discuss. Most of all, how did those goons track us down to the abandoned village?"

She looked as if she had been struck by lightning. *"Baltazar."*

Austin smiled faintly. "You told me your benefactor was off-limits to suspicious minds."

"He's *got* to be involved. He was the only one I told about the *National Geographic* photographer. He arranged for the statue to be moved. Saxon warned me about him."

"We knew all that before now. What changed your mind?"

She fidgeted in her chair. "Before we left for Istanbul, I called Baltazar's representative and told him where we were going and why. It was part of our original financing agreement, and I didn't see anything wrong with it at the time. Baltazar was the one who financed the recovery of the Baghdad cache." She realized the implication of her words. "Dear God. Baltazar has wanted the statue all along. But *why*?"

"Let's back up a bit," Austin said. "Assume he was behind the theft. Why would he try to prevent us from tracking down the statue's twin?"

"He obviously doesn't want anyone to see it, for whatever reason."

"Maybe we'll know why after tomorrow." He glanced at his watch. "Sure you're satisfied with the sleeping arrangements? We haven't known each other very long."

Carina reached out and touched his hand. "I feel as if I have known you several lifetimes, Mr. Austin. Shall we call it a night?"

They took the elevator up to their room, and Austin walked out on the balcony to give Carina time to change. He was gazing at the reflection of lights in the sea when Carina came up and slipped her arm around his waist. He felt the warmth of her body against his. He turned and was greeted by a silky kiss. She was wearing a long, white cotton nightgown, but the simple garment did little to disguise her supple figure.

"What about your jet lag?" Austin said.

Carina's voice was low and cool as she wound her arms around his neck. "I just got over it."

28

AUSTIN AWOKE FROM A SOUND SLEEP and grabbed his warbling cell phone from the bedside table. He eased out of bed, wrapping the top sheet around his muscular body like a Roman senator. The sight of Carina's sable hair spread out on her pillow brought an appreciative smile to his tanned face.

He stepped onto the balcony and put the phone to his ear. "The eagle has landed at Dalyran Airport," Zavala announced. "The Subvette trailer is off the plane and ready to go."

"Good work, Joe." Austin said. "I'll meet you in ninety minutes." He gave Zavala directions to the launch site.

"Might take longer, Kurt. I'm standing by the road looking for a tow truck to pull the trailer. Only little cars for rent at the airport. Gotta go. I think I see my ride coming."

Austin didn't doubt for a second that Zavala could pull it off. The soft-spoken Mexican American had a knack for accomplishing the impossible.

The sound of running water came from the bathroom. Awakened by the phone, Carina had slipped quietly out of bed. Austin could hear her singing to herself in the shower.

"I need someone to scrub my back," she called out.

Austin didn't have to be asked a second time. His improvised toga went flying. After their shower, they toweled each other off and got dressed. Austin wore tan shorts and a conservative Hawaiian shirt that Don Ho would have been proud of. Carina pulled on a shift of African sun yellow over her black bikini. After a room-service continental breakfast of rolls, hard-boiled eggs, and coffee, they drove to the marina.

Austin had been honest with Captain Mustapha. Before parting the night before, he had told the captain that he and Carina were hunting for an ancient artifact without permission of the Turkish government. He had no intention of keeping the artifact if they found it, but he wanted Mustapha to be aware of what he was getting himself into. On the other hand, the captain would be paid well for the added risk.

Mustapha said he didn't worry about government rules. Austin had hired the boat. Mustapha would take them wherever they wanted to go. What they did there was their business.

Austin had told the captain he would need a secluded place with a launching ramp. Mustapha had described an abandoned boatyard whose owner had gone into bankruptcy. The boatyard was across the harbor from the marina. Carina would ride with Mustapha and re-join Austin there.

The boatyard was reached by a dirt road with more craters in it than the dark side of the moon. Austin wandered among the wooden skeletons of unfinished boats and inspected the boat ramp. The blacktop was eroded along the edges, but the main part of the ramp was in relatively good shape.

Zavala was fifteen minutes overdue. Austin stood at the edge of the road wondering whether his friend's resourcefulness had been put to the test. He cocked his ear at the rumble of an engine. A cloud of dust and feathers was heading in his direction. A truck lurched through the potholes, gears grinding in protest, its engine coughing asthmatically. The truck skidded to a stop in a haze of purple exhaust smoke and amid a cacophony of clucks from the chicken cages piled precariously behind the cab.

Zavala emerged from the truck and introduced the driver, a brawny Turk with a gold-capped smile and heavy five o'clock shadow.

"Good morning, Kurt," Zavala said. "Meet my pal Ahmed."

Austin shook hands with the driver and walked around behind the truck. The submersible was under a green plastic tarp lashed down with ropes. Zavala had used additional ropes to improvise a backup system for the ancient trailer hitch. "I had to jerry-rig a tow system," Zavala said, gazing with pride at his handiwork. "Not bad for government work."

"Not bad at all," Austin said with a roll of his eyes. The improvised setup must have made for anxious moments on the coastal road's tight curves. He wondered how the NUMA bean counters would react if they knew their multimillion-dollar submersible had been roped to the bumper of a chicken truck.

Ahmed backed the trailer onto the ramp. Motorized rollers moved the launch platform off the trailer and into the water, where it floated on two long pontoons.

Mustapha arrived with Carina. He threw out a towline to Zavala, who tied the other end to the launch platform. Austin peeled off a wad of Turkish lira for the grateful truck driver and thanked him for his help.

Before he left to deliver his chickens, Ahmed tucked the trailer into a corner of the boatyard. Austin and Zavala rowed out to the motor cruiser in the skiff, and Mustapha immediately got under way. The motor cruiser steamed out of the harbor and entered the bay with the submersible in tow.

The fishing boats and pleasure craft began to thin out until only a few distant sails were visible. Austin gathered his friends under the shade of an awning on the aft deck. As they sipped cups of strong coffee, Austin filled Zavala in on the escape from the abandoned village and the previous day's outing with Mustapha.

"You crammed a lot into a short time," Zavala said.

"The secret is time management," Austin said.

The boat slowed as it approached the gray-brown swath of exposed rock where the cliff had fallen into the sea. The captain dropped anchor near the base of the cliff. Austin and Zavala rowed the skiff to the floating platform, climbed aboard, and pulled the tarp off.

Austin ran his eyes over the submersible's gleaming fiberglass body. Zavala had copied every detail of his Corvette convertible except for the color, and added the modifications that allowed it to travel under water.

Austin shook his head with wonder. "It looks like it just rolled off the Chevy assembly line, Joe. How about a five-minute lesson in launch procedure?"

"I can do it in *one* minute. The Launch, Recovery, and Transport vehicle has its own power. External controls on the starboard side. Flood the pontoons. When the platform reaches dive level, pump out water to attain neutral buoyancy. Fine-tune our positioning with the LRT thrusters. Release the securing clamps. I drive off. You can stay below or take the LRT to the surface."

"What about recovery?"

"The same procedure in reverse. I come in like a plane landing on an aircraft carrier. You secure the vehicle on the platform and up we go."

"You're a *genius,*" Austin said. "Crazy, maybe, but still a genius."

"Thanks for the vote of confidence. I worried that the project might be seen as a frivolous expenditure of NUMA resources."

"It's not exactly the ALVIN," Austin said, referring to the tubby submersible that dove to the *Titanic*. "But I'm sure Pitt would approve." NUMA director Dirk Pitt was a passionate collector of vintage cars. Let's take the latest addition to the NUMA undersea fleet out for a spin."

They rowed back to the boat and got into their scuba gear. Austin had asked Zavala to bring along scuba equipment that included an underwater communications setup. The Ocean Technology Systems receivers were attached to the straps of their full face masks.

Mustapha rowed the two men to the submersible platform. They climbed aboard and pulled on their air tanks. Zavala sat behind the Subvette's steering wheel. He had modified the seats to accommodate the tanks. Austin took his station on a folding seat built into the starboard side of the launch vehicle. He punched a button on the control panel to start the battery-powered pumps. The pontoons filled with water, and the platform and submersible slowly sank below the surface.

At a depth of forty feet, Austin reversed the pump action to stabilize the platform in a hover. Other controls allowed him to detach the metal clamps that held the submersible on the LRT. The sub's headlights snapped on. With a whirr of its vertical thrusters, the Subvette rose off the platform and hovered above it.

Austin pushed off from the platform and positioned himself in a sitting position above the submersible. He purged air from his buoyancy compensator and slowly dropped into the passenger seat. Zavala had built extra foot room into the cockpit to accommodate swim fins.

Recognizing the impossibility of working floor pedals with fins on his feet, he had placed the thruster controls on the steering wheel.

Zavala pivoted the submersible around to face inland. Twin cones from the submersible's high-intensity headlights illuminated the scarred face of a rockslide that sloped down to the bottom at a forty-five-degree angle. The collapsed cliff had broken into fragments that ranged in size from rocks no bigger than a head of cabbage to giant boulders that dwarfed the submersible.

"Your *Navigator* would have to be one tough hombre to come out of this mess in one piece," Zavala said. "He'd be crushed down to the size of a beer can."

"The old guy didn't survive three thousand years by being a wimp," Austin said.

Zavala's gargled chuckle came through Austin's earphones. "Can't argue with unreasonable and unjustified optimism. What's a few hundred thousand tons of rock? Where do we begin the search for our hardheaded friend?"

A flat rock, the size and shape of a banquet table, lay several yards out from the base of the slide. "We'll use that slab as a starting point," Austin said. "Work to the right, and move up the slide in parallel tracks until we get near the surface. Then we'll do a reverse search on the left side of the rock. Keep an eye out for columns, a portico, or pediment. Anything that looks man-made."

Zavala drove the Subvette along the base of the slide. Startled at the submersible's approach, schools of feeding fish darted into nooks and crannies. At the outer edge of the rockslide, Zavala put the submersible into a graceful climbing reverse turn. He continued the lawn-mowing pattern, moving back and forth across the face of the slide. Occasionally, he stopped at a promising object and pivoted the submersible so that the headlights could come to bear on the target.

The deep-blue water changed to a shimmering green as they neared the surface.

The submersible dove again and coursed along the base of the slide to the left. Austin saw an object on the bottom that was buried except for an exposed, curved edge. He asked Zavala to blow the surface covering off the object with bursts from the vehicle's thrusters. The technique was commonly used by treasure hunters to uncover a buried wreck. The clouds of sediment eventually settled to reveal the cylindrical shape of a stone column.

"Try going straight up the slope from the column," Austin advised.

Zavala narrowed the back-and-forth area of coverage, and the vehicle ascended the slide. On one turn, the headlights swept across a triangular pediment that rested at a drunken angle on sections of columns. Austin's probing gaze zeroed in on a shadow. He pushed himself out of the submersible and swam closer to the cavelike opening. He flashed the beam of his waterproof torch into the cavity.

A second later, Zavala heard Austin's laughter.

"Hey, Joe, got any kitty treats?" Austin said.

"Talking crazy is a symptom of nitrogen narcosis, my friend."

"This is not a case of rapture of the deep. I'm looking at a bronze Phoenician cat."

A feminine squeal of delight filled their earphones. Carina had been listening to the conversation.

"You've *found* it!"

Austin ran the flashlight beam around the cave's interior. The statue lay faceup, like a corpse stretched out on a funeral bier. The space was about ten feet across and deep, and three or four feet from top to bottom. Austin squeezed through the opening. The figure's conical hat was dented, and the arms were broken off. Unlike the original statue, the nose was intact.

Austin backed out, and curled his thumb and forefinger in the universal okay signal.

"He's in good shape for a crushed beer can. Let's pull him out."

"There's line and lift bags in the portside compartment," Zavala said.

Austin swam to the launch vehicle and pulled a coil of nylon rope from a storage compartment. He tied one end to the rear bumper of the hovering Subvette. Austin tied four open-bottomed lift bags to the line, and went back and attached the free end of the rope to the base of the statue.

He used air from his tank to inflate the bags, then he waved at Zavala, who gunned the thrusters. The line went taut as a violin string. The statue moved several inches. Austin made a throat-slashing motion and swam back to the cavity. The bronze cat attached to the statue's legs was wedged against an overhead outcropping.

Austin wriggled past the statue and into the cave. His air tanks scraped against the rocks, and there was barely enough space for him to turn around and face out. He pushed down on the statue and told Zavala to start pulling.

The statue moved toward the opening and stopped again. The jagged stub of the left arm had caught in some rocks. Zavala stopped pulling. Austin used his sheath knife to pry the arm away from the pediment.

On the next try, the statue came free, and Austin guided it through the opening, bracing his feet against the back of the cave. The statue slowly emerged from its prison—but as Austin tried to follow, he discovered that he was unable to move his right foot. A section of the cave wall had collapsed and caught his fin.

Pebbles fell like hailstones from the roof as he reached back with his knife and cut the fin strap. Falling rocks pelted his legs, and bounced off his head with enough force to jar his teeth. He reached forward and grabbed the statue's head a second before it would have eluded his grasp.

The submersible pulled Austin and the *Navigator* from the cave just before the roof collapsed.

Seeing Austin was clear, Zavala goosed the thrusters. The cave opening disappeared under the disintegrating wall of boulders.

Austin had his hand to his head, where it had been struck by a fist-sized rock.

"Kurt, are you okay?"

"I'd be better if I had a bronze skull."

Disregarding the throbbing in his head, Austin swam to the statue. The *Navigator* hung at an angle, partially buoyed by the lift bags. Zavala powered the sub until the *Navigator* was above the stationary launch vehicle. Austin guided the statue to a platform on the stern end. He detached the line from the submersible. The lift bags kept the full impact of the statue's weight from sinking the launch vehicle.

Austin slipped behind the controls and prepared to bring the launch vehicle closer to the surface. His fingers were poised above the control panel when his sharp hearing picked up the high-pitched whine of a motor, amplified by its passage through water.

"Carina," he called over his communicator. "Do you see any boats?"

"There's one coming straight at us. Very fast."

Speaking calmly, Austin said, "Listen carefully. Tell Captain Mustapha to haul anchor and leave right now."

"We can't leave you," Carina said.

"We'll be fine. Get moving."

The edge in Austin's tone was impossible to miss. Carina relayed Austin's message to Mustapha. Austin heard the captain's muffled reply. Shouts drowned out Mustapha's words. Then came the sharp rattle of an automatic weapon firing.

The line went dead.

Austin swam back to the Subvette. "Douse the lights," he said.

Austin was worried about Carina, but he and Zavala knew better than to react too quickly. At the same time, inaction was alien to both of them.

"What now?" Zavala said.

"Bring us up to check out our uninvited guests."

Zavala elevated the vehicle's long nose and gave the thrusters minimal power. Austin saw a smaller silhouette on the surface next to that of Mustapha's boat and motioned for Zavala to stop. The communicator clicked on. They were in contact with the surface boat again.

A Southern drawl came over the communicator.

"How ya doing, fellas? I can see your bubbles. Whyn't ya join the party?"

"I don't accept invitations from strangers," Austin said. "Who's this?"

"Friend of Ms. Mechadi's. C'mon up. Your air's going to run out eventually."

Zavala unclipped a small slate from his vest and wrote a question mark on it.

Austin paused for a second, thinking. If they did as the stranger wanted, they would get their heads shot off.

He borrowed the slate, and in large block letters he wrote: MOBY-DICK?

Zavala digested what Austin had suggested, and it must have given him a stomachache. He erased the previous message and wrote: OUCH!!

Austin wrote back: SUGGESTIONS?

Zavala shook his head, and scribbled: AHAB, HERE WE COME.

He put the slate away, and dropped the Subvette to the bottom. Zavala spun the submersible around and pointed the nose up at a sharp angle. With a whirr of thrusters, the submersible began its ascent, gaining speed with each foot.

He and Austin braced themselves in their seats.

29

MINUTES BEFORE THE SUBVETTE had begun its ascent, Carina had seen the boat round the headland and speed toward Mustapha's motor cruiser with its bow up on plane, bouncing over the wave tops like a stone skipped across the water.

She had relayed Austin's urgent message to vacate the premises. Too late. The fast-moving boat had closed the distance. The boat swerved seconds before a collision, and the operator throttled back the powerful inboard engine. The craft bumped sideways into Mustapha's boat a few feet from where she stood.

One of the men on board let forth with a burst in the air from his machine pistol. She dropped the microphone to the deck.

There were four men all dressed in uniforms of olive drab, and all armed with short-barreled automatic weapons. Aviator sunglasses hid their eyes, and the floppy brims of their military style hats kept their faces mostly hidden in shadow. Only their tight-lipped mouths were visible.

Three men vaulted over the rail onto Mustapha's boat. The last man to board whipped his hat off to reveal a blond brush cut. Carina recognized Ridley, who had supervised the theft of the *Navigator*. He

grinned broadly, and greeted Carina with a lame Minnie Pearl imitation.

"*How-dee,* Ms. Mechadi."

Her initial shock was replaced by anger. "What are you doing
here?" she demanded.

"Heard you were in the neighborhood, Ms. Mechadi. Thought me
and the boys might drop by for a friendly visit."

"Don't patronize me with that fake hillbilly accent," Carina said.
"Where's my statue?"

Still maintaining his grin, Ridley stepped over to the rail and
stared with flat eyes at the bubbles coming to the surface. "Someone
taking a swim, Miss Mechadi?"

"If you're so curious, jump in and see for yourself." Carina could
feel her temper getting away from her but couldn't help it.

"I got a better idea," Ridley said. He picked the microphone off
the deck, clicked it on, and talked to Austin.

Ridley's grin grew even wider when he saw increased bubble activity on the surface. His hand unclipped a hand grenade on his belt
and hefted it like a baseball pitcher ready to make a throw. Carina
tried to snatch the microphone, but Ridley backhanded her across
the mouth with a blow that drew blood. The other men laughed at
Ridley's violent response, and didn't see the turquoise flicker of
movement in the sea until it was too late.

The submersible shot toward the surface like a breaching whale.
The front bumper slammed into the powerboat with the force of a
battering ram.

The speedboat rose up at a crazy angle. The man at the wheel let
out a startled yelp as he was catapulted into the air with his arms
flailing. He hit the water, went down several feet, and struggled
back to the surface, yelling for someone to help him. His weapon
slipped from his hands.

✦ ✦ ✦

THE SUBMERSIBLE had bounced backward after ramming the speedboat, and Zavala fought to keep the sub under control.

Austin saw legs thrashing in a cloud of foam at the surface. An object was falling through the water. He launched himself out of the cockpit and grabbed the plummeting machine pistol.

He lowered himself back into the cockpit and jerked his thumb toward the surface.

RIDLEY WAS a professional soldier. Quickly getting over his surprise, he pointed at the figure in the water

"Get that idiot!" he barked.

His men slung their weapons on their shoulders and threw a ring-shaped life preserver to their comrade. Ridley clutched the grenade in his hand, ready to drop it over the side like an improvised depth charge. He was probing the water with his cold eyes when he heard what sounded like a car horn. He whipped his head around.

"*Jeezus!*" he gasped.

A turquoise Corvette convertible with a bashed-in bumper was skimming across the water toward Mustapha's boat, Zavala at the wheel. Austin rested the machine pistol on the windshield frame and let off a few bursts, deliberately aiming high.

Ridley's men slipped their weapons off their shoulders, dropped them onto the deck, and threw their hands in the air, leaving the man in the water to fend for himself. Ridley slowly brought his hands up.

Carina was being helped to her feet by Captain Mustapha. Austin was distracted by the sight of blood streaming from her mouth. In the meantime, Ridley had brought his hands together over his head, pulled the pin, and had an arm back ready to toss the grenade at the oncoming vehicle.

Austin's eyes went back to Ridley and his finger tightened on the trigger. He hesitated, fearing that Ridley might drop the grenade to the deck. Captain Mustapha had also seen Ridley arm the grenade. As Ridley brought his arm back in a throwing position, the captain snatched a boat hook from a rack and brought the heavy wooden handle down on Ridley's wrist. The grenade flew from his fingers, hit the rail, and rolled onto the deck.

Reacting with lightning speed, Mustapha dove on the grenade and flipped it over the side.

Ridley roared with pain and rage. He fumbled at his belt with his left hand for another grenade. Austin's gun stuttered and laced Ridley's chest with bullet holes. Ridley pitched over backward into the water as the grenade exploded and sent up a geyser that spattered onto the deck.

Austin swung the gun barrel toward the other two men.

"Jump," he ordered.

He let off a fusillade at the awning. Shreds of canvas rained down like confetti. The men jumped over the side and joined the crewman already in the water. Austin triggered another burst that ripped into the water within inches of the swimmers.

Austin watched the sorry trio swim to land, then scramble onto shore and disappear into the woods. He put more holes in the listing speedboat and then turned his attention to Carina.

Mustapha wrapped some ice cubes in a dish towel and she held the improvised compress against her head. Austin saw that she was not seriously hurt and handed the gun to Mustapha, with instructions to shoot first and ask questions later.

Zavala brought the Subvette alongside the motor cruiser and Austin climbed aboard. The vehicle slipped below the surface and descended to the launch platform. Austin swam to the control console, and Zavala brought the vehicle down on the platform and the clamps locked it in place. Austin activated the pumps to expel water from the pontoons.

The launch platform surfaced near the motor cruiser, and it sat at a steep angle in the water because of the weight of the statue at the stern. Mustapha handed Carina the gun and moved his boat closer to the LRT platform. He threw a towline to Austin and Zavala. Then they slipped into the water and breaststroked to the boat ladder.

Back on board, Zavala peeled out of his wet suit, and glanced toward the wooded shore. "How did those guys find us way out here?"

Austin picked up his shirt and slipped the satellite phone from the pocket. "They may have zeroed in on the phone signal. Let's not take any chances."

He winged the phone as far as he could and watched it splash into the water. Then he thanked Mustapha for his quick-witted work with the boat hook and apologized for putting him and his boat in jeopardy and ruining his awning. The Turk took it in good spirits, but he wondered if he could call it a day and get paid. Austin peeled off enough Turkish lira to choke a horse.

"One more favor. We need to go somewhere we can be undisturbed," he said.

"No problem." The captain tucked the bills into his pocket. "There's a place a few miles from here."

LESS THAN half an hour later, Mustapha steered his boat into a quiet cove and anchored behind an outcropping of land. Mustapha said that local mariners avoided the inlet because the rocks hidden under the surface at the entrance made it tricky to navigate.

Zavala sat in the bow with the machine pistol resting in his lap. Carina gathered up a bag holding art supplies she had bought the day before and got into the skiff with Austin. He rowed to the launch platform, and they climbed aboard.

Carina leaned over the statue. "I feel guilty disturbing his sleep after all these years," she said with undisguised tenderness.

"He's probably glad to have a beautiful lady keep him company," Austin said. "Look at his smiling face."

Carina brushed away the dried marine vegetation clinging to the statue's mouth. The face was that of a young bearded man with a strong nose and chin. Like the original statue, he wore a neck pendant engraved with a horse head and palm tree, a kilt around his waist, and sandals on his feet. The lack of arms gave him the grotesque aspect of a disaster victim.

Carina opened her bag, pulled out two sponges, and handed one to Austin. Working together, they cleaned every square inch of bronze. Carina laid out a brush, a square of cheesecloth, and a jar of liquid latex. She applied multiple layers of latex to the statue's face, pendant, and other sections, then stiffened the layers with cheesecloth. The dried layers were peeled off, labeled with a marking pen, and carefully placed in the bag.

"It's done," she said, peeling off the final mold.

"What about the cat?" Austin said. "He was part of the crew."

"Absolutely right," Carina said with a smile. She applied the latex process to the side and half-turned face of the cat.

After the cast hardened, she removed it. Her work was done, but she was reluctant to leave.

"What should we do with him?" she said.

"We can't bring the statue back," Austin said. "It's too heavy to move without specialized equipment, and transporting it overland would be a major problem. Someone is bound to see us. The Turkish authorities do not look kindly on foreigners who steal the country's antiquities."

Carina had a sad look in her eyes. She gave the statue a kiss on both cheeks. She patted the bronze forehead and got back into the skiff. Back on the boat, Austin asked Mustapha the depth of the water in the cove. The Turk said it was around fifty to sixty feet deep.

Austin and Zavala rowed back to the launch platform and, bracing their backs, shoved the statue with their feet. The statue teetered on the edge. One final push sent it over the side. The *Navigator* plunged into the depths, as if eager to return to the sea, and quickly disappeared from sight.

CHAPTER

30

THOUSANDS OF MILES FROM Turkish waters, the *Navigator*'s twin rotated slowly on a circular pedestal about a foot high, shimmering like an angry god under the battery of lights that bathed its bronze skin in a polarized glow.

A ghostly white, three-dimensional X-ray image of the *Navigator* pivoted on a large wall screen. Arrays of electronic probes surrounded the ancient statue.

Three men sat in leather chairs facing the screen. Baltazar was enthroned in the center. At his right was Dr. Morris Gray, an expert in the use of computed tomography. On Baltazar's left was Dr. John Defoe, an authority in Phoenician history and art. Both scientists had been absorbed into Baltazar's corporate empire with the expectation that the statue eventually would be found.

Gray aimed his laser pointer at the screen. "The X-ray technique we're using here is similar to the CT scans employed in hospitals," he said. "We take photographic slices of the object. The computer renders the photos into a 3-D image."

Baltazar was slouched in his chair, his thick fingers entwined, his gaze fixed on the pale image projected against a dark blue background. He had waited for this moment for years.

"And what does your magic lantern tell us, Dr. Gray?" he rumbled.

Gray smiled slightly. He moved the laser's red dot to a display panel, one of several that ran from top to bottom along the right side of the monitor.

"Each box shows information taken from the probes. This displays the statue's metal composition. The bronze is the standard ninety percent copper and ten percent tin. The other boxes deal with thickness, tensile strength, as well as information that's not pertinent."

"What are those dark areas on the statue?" Baltazar asked.

"The statue was made with the lost wax process," Defoe said. "The artist made a clay form, which was encased in wax, then clay again. The X-ray shows the channels and vents that were drilled in the outer shell to allow wax and gas to escape and molten metal to be poured in. The statue was fabricated in pieces, so we're also looking at rivet points and hammer marks."

"All very interesting," Baltazar said. "But what is inside the statue?"

"The X-ray shows nothing behind the bronze exterior except for a hollow space," Gray answered.

"What about the exterior?"

"A lot more promising." Gray produced a slim remote control from his suit jacket and pointed it at the screen. The ghostly figure disappeared. Filling the screen was a close-up of the statue's face. "I'll let Dr. Defoe deal with this area."

Defoe squinted at the screen through round-framed glasses. "The damage makes it difficult to gauge the subject's age, but, judging from the muscular body, he is probably in his twenties."

"Forever young," Baltazar observed in a rare poetic moment.

"The conical hat is similar to that we see in pictures and sculptures of Phoenician sailors. The beard and hair have me puzzled. The way they are layered denotes someone of upper-class Phoenician society, yet he is garbed in the kilt and sandals of a simple sailor."

"Go on," Baltazar said. There was no discernible change in his expression despite his growing excitement.

The image morphed into a close-up view of the pendant around the *Navigator*'s neck. "This pendant replicates a Phoenician coin design," Defoe said. "The horse is the symbol for Phoenicia. The uprooted palm tree to its right denotes a colony. Here's where things get intriguing."

The red dot jumped to a semicircular space below the horse head and palm tree where there was a horizontal line of squiggles.

"Runes?" Baltazar said.

"That was the common assumption when figures like these were seen on the coins. However, none matched any known Phoenician script. The markings remained a puzzle for years. Then a geologist at Mount Holyoke College named Mark McMenamin came up with a startling new theory. He submitted the symbols to computer enhancement, which I will do here."

The symbols on the screen became sharper and more defined.

"This pattern looks familiar," Baltazar said.

"Perhaps this will help." The shapes on the screen were set off by familiar continental outlines.

Baltazar leaned forward. "Incredible. They're continents!"

"That was McMenamin's conclusion. As a geologist, he recognized the landmasses for what they are. You can make out the rectangular shape of the Iberian Peninsula projecting down at an angle from Europe, which with North Africa encloses the Mediterranean. That's Asia off to the right. Those smaller symbols west of Europe could be the British Isles. North America is the landmass on the left. South America seems to be missing or absorbed into the northern continent. Computer enhancement can be subject to different interpretations. But if McMenamin is right, this pendant indicates the range and scope of Phoenician colonies."

"A bloody map of the world," Baltazar said with a grin.

"Not just *any* map of the world. The gold coins I mentioned were minted around 300 B.C. The bronze in this statue is about three thousand years old, making this the oldest world map we know of. More important, it indicates travel to the New World as early as 900 B.C., when the statue was made."

Baltazar felt a rush of blood through his veins.

"I want to take a closer look at North America," he said.

The enlarged symbol that appeared on the screen looked like an obese saguaro cactus. A pair of thick arms were upraised from a wide trunk.

Baltazar snorted. "You must admit that it takes a stretch of the imagination to see that amorphous blob as the North American continent."

"Maybe this will help," Defoe said. An outline of North America was superimposed over the symbol. "The trunk becomes the main continent. That's Alaska off on the left and Newfoundland on the right."

"Any evidence of trade routes between the Eastern and Western Hemispheres?"

"Not specifically. But that shouldn't come as any surprise given the Phoenician penchant for secrecy, and the fact that ocean routes consisted of astronomical readings that could be committed to memory. But if we look at the compass in the statue's hand," he said with a flick of the remote, "we can deduce that east–west, west–east trade routes are suggested. The position of the statue relative to the north point of the compass rose indicates that he is looking toward the west."

"Toward the Americas," Baltazar said.

"Correct."

"Can you pinpoint a landfall?"

Defoe shook his head. "This statue is the equivalent of the world maps you see in the airline magazines. Informative, but in no way useful to an airplane pilot."

"They would have needed a more detailed chart when close to shore," Baltazar pointed out.

"That's right. Maps had limited value at sea. They would have needed a coastal pilot that showed the location of prominent points, so the travelers could check position. Directions rather than distance become paramount close to shore."

"Is there any evidence of a coastal pilot?"

Defoe shook his head. "I have found nothing that denotes navigational positioning. I did find something else, however."

The screen image changed once more. "This symbol was etched repeatedly in the sash that held up the sailor's kilt."

"It looks something like a boat," Baltazar said. "Rough depictions of the bow and stern."

"The symbol looked familiar to me. I remembered seeing it in a book by Anthony Saxon. He's an amateur archaeologist and explorer who's come up with some outlandish theories."

"I *know* who Mr. Saxon is," Baltazar said, in a tone that dripped with icicles.

"Saxon is a self-promoting showman, but he's been around. He says this is the symbol for a ship of Tarshish. He's found examples in both the Americas and the Middle East, thereby establishing a link between the two regions."

"I'm not interested in half-baked theories put forth by fools," Baltazar said. "Tell me if anything on this statue pinpoints a North American landfall."

"The answer is yes and no."

Baltazar glowered. "I'm a busy man, Dr. Defoe. I'm paying you a great deal for your expertise. Don't waste my time with riddles."

Defoe became uncomfortably aware of the menace behind Baltazar's smooth veneer. "Sorry," he said. "I'll show you what I mean." He clicked the remote and the screen displayed a faint network of curving lines. "We think this is a topographical map."

"Where on the statue did you find it?"

The camera lens drew back to reveal the cat that formed part of the statue's base.

"You're telling me the information I want was written on the side of a *cat*?"

"It's not really that far-fetched. The Egyptians regarded felines as sacred, and the Phoenicians drew upon Egypt for their religious themes."

"What did your computer enhancement show?"

"This *is* the computer enhancement."

"I see nothing."

"It's the best we could do. The surface was worn away for the most part except for a small area which you see here. We'll include what we've found in the final report, but, for all intents and purposes, any information engraved in the metal is gone forever."

"I'll have to concur," Dr. Gray said. "No technology on earth can re-create that which is no longer there."

If not here, elsewhere, Baltazar thought.

"This lost wax process you mentioned. Could it be used to create a duplicate of this statue?"

"It would be no trouble if the sculptor used the indirect process, which forms the wax around a finely defined core."

Baltazar stared at the useless image on the screen, and then he rose from his seat. "Thank you, gentlemen. My valet will show you the door."

After the two men had been ushered out, Baltazar paced back and forth in front of the statue. He brooded about the time and money he had spent to acquire this useless piece of metal. The frozen grin seemed to mock him. Benoir had told him that Carina was going to Turkey to find a replica of the statue. He had ordered his men to intercept her. He was not a man who left things to chance. At the same time, he assumed possession of the original statue would give him an edge.

His dark thoughts were cut short by the chirping of his telephone. The call was from Istanbul. He listened to the caller describe the failed attack. He told the caller that his orders still stood and slammed the phone down.

Austin had more lives than a cat.

Cat.

He glared at the bronze feline at the foot of the statue. He lifted his eyes and saw, in his imagination, not the damaged features of an ancient Phoenician but Austin's face.

Baltazar went over to a mace that was hanging on the wall with other deadly instruments from medieval days. He removed the mace from its rack and let the spiked ball swing at the end of its chain. Then he stepped between the camera stanchions, raised the handle above his shoulder, and swung.

The ball arched down at the end of its chain, slammed into the statue, and bounced off. The impact produced a sound like an off-key gong. A human being on the receiving end of the murderous weapon would have been reduced to a bloody pulp. The ball had made multiple dents in the statue's chest, but the serene smile still lingered.

Uttering a mighty curse, Baltazar tossed the mace aside, stalked from the room, and slammed the door behind him.

CHAPTER

31

THE TROUTS WALKED BRISKLY PAST the line of tourists queuing up for a guided tour, turned down a side street, and headed away from the hustle-bustle around Independence Hall and toward the American Philosophical Library, a two-story brick building facing a quiet park.

Angela Worth was at her workstation in the corner of a reading room. She looked up and raised an eyebrow. The striking couple approaching her desk did not seem like the usual researchers.

The man was several inches over six feet tall, dressed in razor-creased khakis and a blue-green linen blazer over a pale green shirt. A color-coordinated bow tie adorned his neck. The tall woman at his side could have stepped out of the pages of *Vogue* by way of a triathlon. The olive-colored silk pants suit rippled around her athletic body, and she seemed to flow rather than walk.

The woman stopped in front of Angela's desk and extended her hand.

"Ms. Worth? My name is Gamay Morgan-Trout. This is my husband, Paul." She smiled, showing the slight space between her front teeth that didn't diminish her attractiveness.

Angela realized she was slack-jawed. She regained her poise and stood to shake hands.

"You're the people from NUMA who called yesterday."

"That's right," Paul said. "Thanks for seeing us. Hope it's not an imposition."

"Not at all. How may I help you?"

"We understand you were the one who discovered the long-lost Jefferson file," Gamay said.

"That's right. How did you hear about it?"

"The State Department contacted NUMA after the NSA deciphered the file."

Angela had tried to reach her friend at the NSA cryptographic museum. Deeg hadn't returned her call.

"Did you say the *State* Department?"

"That's right," Gamay said.

"I don't understand. Why would they be interested?"

"Do you have any idea of what was in the file?" Gamay said.

"I tried to decipher the material. I'm only an amateur. I gave it to a friend at the NSA. What's going on?"

The Trouts exchanged glances.

"Is there anywhere with a bit more privacy?" Gamay said.

"Yes, of course. There's my office."

Angela's office was small but well organized. She took a seat behind her desk and offered the Trouts a couple of chairs. Paul Trout opened a leather portfolio case and extracted a folder. He placed the folder on the desk.

"This is our only copy, so we'll have to summarize the contents," Trout said. "The material you found indicates that Jefferson shared with Meriwether Lewis his belief that a Phoenician ship had crossed the Atlantic nearly three thousand years ago and that it carried a sacred relic, possibly a biblical object, to North America. The State

Department is worried that the story, true or not, might stir up things in the Middle East."

Angela listened, spellbound, as Paul and Gamay took turns explaining the file's contents. Her mind was awhirl. Her tongue seemed stuck to the roof of her mouth. Her eyes were glassy, like those of a victim of shock.

"Angela," Gamay said. "Are you all right?"

Angela cleared her throat. "Yes. I'm fine. I think." She regained her composure.

Gamay continued.

"We realized we could only go so far delving into an ancient voyage. It seemed to us that the American Philosophical Society was the nexus for many threads of the story. Jefferson was president of the society. Lewis studied here for his great exploration. A fellow member told Jefferson that the vellum contained Phoenician words. The connections go on and on."

"I'm not surprised," Angela said. "Many people don't even know this organization exists. Think of its history. Founded by Franklin. George Washington was a member, along with John Adams, Alexander Hamilton, Thomas Paine, Benjamin Rush, and John Marshall. Its reach extended worldwide: Lafayette, von Steuben, and Kościuszko. Later, we had Thomas Edison, Robert Frost, George Marshall, Linus Pauling. Women too. Margaret Mead. Elizabeth Agassiz. This library has millions of documents and papers, including the original Newton's *Principia,* Franklin's experiments, Darwin's *Origin of Species*. It's simply breathtaking."

"The collection's scope is both a blessing and a curse," Paul said. "We're looking for a needle in an intellectual haystack of enormous size."

"Our cataloguing system is second to none. Just point me in the right direction."

"Meriwether Lewis," Gamay said. "According to the artichoke file, Lewis had important information that he wanted to get to Jefferson."

"I pulled some files on Lewis after talking to you on the phone. There's lots of controversy about his death. Some think it was suicide. Others say it was murder."

"That would fit in with the air of mystery surrounding the Jefferson file," Paul said. "Where do we begin?"

Angela opened a folder. "Even as a boy, Lewis was smart, adventurous, and intrepid. He joined the army, made full captain at the age of twenty-three, and was twenty-seven when he became Jefferson's private secretary. Jefferson found Lewis to be bold, fearless, and intelligent. Three years later, Jefferson picked Lewis to lead one of the greatest expeditions in history. To prep for the journey, he sent him to study at the Philosophical Society."

"Everything Lewis needed to know was contained here," Paul said.

Angela nodded. "The members tutored him in botany, astronomy, geography, and other sciences. He was an apt student. The expedition was a huge success."

"What happened to him after the expedition?" Gamay said.

"He made what might have been the biggest mistake of his life. In 1807, he accepted an appointment as governor of the Louisiana Territory."

"Mistake?" Paul said. "I would think he'd be a natural for the job."

"Lewis was better suited for trekking through the wilderness. St. Louis was a frontier outpost filled with dangerous men, crooks, and fortune hunters. He had to deal with plots, feuds, and conspiracies. He was constantly undercut by his assistant. But he managed to last two and a half years as governor before his death."

"Not bad, considering the difficulties he faced," Paul said.

"It was a sedentary and confining job," Angela said. "But, from most accounts, he did pretty well."

"What were the circumstances leading to his decision to go to Washington?" Gamay said.

"Lewis had repatriated a Mandan chief. There was a five-hundred-dollar cost overrun, and the federal government rejected his claim. There were rumors of a land deal scandal. Lewis said he was in a financial bind, and he had to go back to Washington to clear his good name. He had some important documents to deliver as well."

"Tell us about the trip that ended in his death," Gamay said.

"The whole thing is full of contradictions and inconsistencies," Angela said.

"In what way?" Gamay said.

Angela slid a map across the desk. "Lewis leaves St. Louis at the end of August 1809. He goes down the Mississippi River and arrives at Fort Pickering, Tennessee, on September fifteenth. Lewis is exhausted from the heat and may have a touch of malaria. A rumor circulates that he was out of his head during the trip and attempted suicide. Another rumor says he drank heavily the whole time with old army comrades. That's funny, because he didn't have any army friends at the fort."

"Any truth to these rumors?" Gamay said.

"They were secondhand accounts. Lewis wrote a letter at the fort to President Madison that shows he was pretty clearheaded. He tells Madison he was exhausted but that he is much better. And that he plans to go overland through Tennessee and Virginia. He says he is carrying original papers from his Pacific expedition and doesn't want them to fall into the hands of the British, who were expected to declare war."

"What happened next?" Paul said.

"Two weeks after he arrived at the fort," Angela continued,

"Lewis set off again. He was carrying two trunks that held his papers from the Pacific expedition, a portfolio, memo book, and documents of a private and public nature. The expedition journals are contained in sixteen notebooks bound in red morocco leather."

"It must have been tough carrying all that stuff overland on his own," Paul said.

"Almost impossible. Which is why he accepted an offer of an extra horse from James Neelly, a former Indian agent for the Chickasaw nation. On September twenty-ninth, they left the fort: Lewis, his servant, Pernia, and a slave, and Neelly."

"Hardly the sort of entourage you'd expect of a territorial governor," Gamay noted.

"I can't figure it either," Angela said. "Especially in light of the legend of Lewis's long-lost gold mine."

"The plot thickens," Paul said. "Tell us about this mine."

"It was said that Lewis discovered a gold mine on his Pacific expedition. He told a few friends, and supposedly left a description of the mine so that if he died it might be of some use to the country. I'm sure the gold mine story was generally known. And it was common knowledge along the Trace that the governor would be passing through."

"Lewis would have been in special danger," Gamay said.

"Every bandit along the Trace would have been thinking about the map and how to get it away from Lewis," Angela agreed.

"Wouldn't Lewis have been aware of the risk?" Gamay said.

"Lewis knew the risks of traveling through the wilderness. He had faced danger before and might have thought he could handle it."

"Or," Gamay said, "he could have been so driven to get to Washington that he figured the risk was worth it.'

"Maybe the danger was closer than he thought," Paul said. "Neelly."

"More contradictions," Angela said. "Neelly said later that Lewis was deranged, but the group did a hundred and fifty miles in three days."

"That's a good trek for a crazy man," Paul observed.

Angela nodded in agreement.

"The Fort Pickering commander was disturbed at reports that Neelly had urged Lewis to drink. Lewis's Spanish servant Pernia was pushing booze on Lewis as well. Then Neelly lost two horses and told Lewis to go on ahead with the two servants while he searched for the animals."

Gamay laughed. "If Lewis were deranged, why let him go ahead with the servants?"

"Good question," Angela said. "But they broke up, and Lewis went on to Grinder's Stand with Pernia and his slave servant."

"Grinder's Stand sounds like a place that makes submarine sandwiches," Paul said.

"Lewis would have been better off if it *had* been a sandwich shop," Angela said. "The Grinder place consisted of two cabins. Mrs. Grinder was there with her kids and a couple of slaves. Her husband was away. Lewis stayed in one of the cabins, his servants in the stable. Mrs. Grinder said that about three A.M. she heard two pistol shots— and that Lewis had shot himself in the head and the chest. Mortally wounded, he made it to her cabin, asked for a drink of water, called for help, and died a few hours later. Neelly showed up the next day."

"Convenient," Gamay said.

"*Very*. He talked to Mrs. Grinder and the servants, and a week later he wrote Jefferson and said Lewis committed suicide over his problems with the government."

"Half the population of the country would be dead if they felt that way. Sounds fishy," Paul said.

"It *is*. Lewis had been around firearms his entire life. Yet when he tried to blow his brains out, he only made a furrow," Angela said. "He took a long-barreled flintlock and shot himself in the chest."

"Sounds like someone shot him in the darkened cabin," Paul said. "What do we know about Neelly?"

Angela said, "Neelly was dismissed as an Indian agent after problems with the Chickasaws. The commander at Fort Pickering said he was a liar and a thief. Neelly claimed he loaned Lewis money even though Lewis had a hundred twenty dollars in cash, which was missing after he died. Neelly claimed Lewis's pistols as his own."

"What about Pernia?" Gamay said.

"Pernia was either as a Spaniard or Frenchman. He showed up out of nowhere to travel with Lewis. Later, Neelly sent him to Jefferson with Lewis's horse. He said he'd send the trunks to the family later, which he apparently did. Pernia went to see Lewis's mother, who thought he had something to do with her son's death."

"Was there any kind of an investigation?"

"Mrs. Grinder was the only eyewitness, and she eventually told three different versions of the story. Neighbors suspected her husband had something to do with it, but when Jefferson said it was suicide that pretty much closed the books."

"Didn't you say that Jefferson's finding rested entirely on Neelly's account?" Paul said.

"That's what's so crazy. Jefferson told the world that Lewis was a hypochondriac when he was young, but Jefferson didn't know him back then. He said Lewis was subject to depression, yet he sent him on the Pacific expedition. He said the depression returned when Lewis became governor, but there was no evidence of this. On the basis of hearsay, he said Lewis was deranged at Grinder's. It doesn't fit in with the deliberative character we think of with Jefferson."

"I'll go out on a limb," Paul said. "Jefferson was using the suicide story as a cover-up. He knows it's murder, but there's nothing he can do, and he wants to recover the documents Lewis had for him."

"That's possible. Years later, Jefferson said Lewis was murdered.

There's another legend about the young slave. He died when he was about ninety-five, and, on his deathbed, he said it was murder but didn't name names."

Paul summed up. "So we've got three possibilities for the murderer. Neelly, Grinder, and Pernia. Or all three. Pernia is the strongest suspect. He had motive—Lewis owed him money. And opportunity. There's another possibility. One or all of them were working for someone else."

Gamay said, "Lewis was carrying something important to Monticello. We'll assume that Lewis was murdered to prevent him from carrying out his mission. Let's concentrate on what happened to the documents Lewis was taking to Jefferson."

"If Lewis knew he was in danger," Paul said, "he wouldn't have carried the documents on his person."

Gamay said, "You've *got* it!"

"Thanks, but *what* have I got?"

"Lewis gave the papers to someone *else* to carry. Who would be the least likely to be suspected of having anything of value?"

Angela laughed. "The slave boy."

"*Damn,* I'm good," Paul said. "The slave would have helped Pernia move trunks to Monticello. He'd have a chance to slip the goods to Jefferson."

"What's this about slaves and Monticello?"

Helen Woolsey, Angela's boss, had seen the huddle in Angela's office. She stood in the doorway with a grin pasted on her face.

Angela was fast on her feet. "Oh, hi, Helen. We were discussing the fact that Jefferson had slaves even while he was saying all men are equal."

"Fascinating. Won't you introduce me to your friends?"

"Sorry. This is Paul and Gamay Trout. This is my boss, Helen Woolsey."

They shook hands. Woolsey glanced at the clearly labeled

Jefferson file folder on the desk. "Is that the same material you brought to me the other day, Angela?"

Gamay reached out and retrieved the file, holding it on her lap with her hands on top. "This is *our* folder," she said. "Angela has been helping us with some background on Meriwether Lewis."

"Paul and I are with NUMA," Paul said, figuring a half-truth was better than a whole lie. "We're conducting historical research on the importance of the Pacific Ocean to the United States. We thought we'd start with Lewis, who led the first expedition to reach the ocean."

"You've come to the right place," Woolsey said.

"Angela has been most helpful," Gamay said.

Woolsey said to let her know if she could be of help.

Gamay watched her walk across the reading room. "Cold fish," she said.

Angela laughed. "I call her Miss Smarty-Pants, but I like your name better." Her face grew serious. "Something's up. I gave her a copy of the Jefferson file days ago. She said she was going to tell the board of directors but didn't do anything with it that I know of."

"She zeroed right in on the Jefferson file."

Angela gathered up the Lewis material. "I'll dig into the slave angle. Could you come back in a couple of hours, when Miss Smarty-Pants isn't snooping around?"

"We'll be glad to," Paul said.

Angela watched them leave. She was newly energized. She locked the Lewis folder in her desk and tended to some routine chores, until Woolsey came back into the reading room, obviously checking on the Trouts. When she had gone, Angela got on her computer.

With a few strokes of the keyboard, she turned the clock back to 1809.

CHAPTER

32

ZAVALA FINISHED HIS DETAILED inspection of the Subvette and stepped back from the trailer, his mouth widening in a broad smile. Austin took his friend's expression as a good sign. On the return trip to the abandoned boatyard, Zavala had tried to be upbeat, but he couldn't hide the sadness in his eyes at the damage to his creation.

He said, "I built her like a tank, so the frame is intact, and the propulsion system is in good shape, but the lights are cockeyed and some of the sensors were damaged. She's going to be out of commission until I get back to the States."

Austin put his hand on Zavala's shoulder. "She was wounded in a good cause. We'd be dead meat otherwise. You can always build another and donate this one to the Cussler car museum. Looks like your ride is here."

A tow truck had turned into the boatyard. Austin had asked Mustapha to line up something more suited than Ahmed's chicken truck to the task of towing the submersible trailer back to the airport. The captain had made a few phone calls and found someone willing to do the job. While the truck hooked up to the trailer, Austin thanked Mustapha again for all his help. Zavala rode in the tow truck, Austin and Carina got into their rental car and followed the trailer along the coastal road to Dalyran Airport.

Austin and Carina hitched a ride to Istanbul on the transport plane with Zavala. They parted company at the airport. Zavala would be working late to prepare the submersible for its trip home and planned to stay near the airport. Austin and Carina went back to the hotel, where they had spent their first night in Istanbul. This time, they shared the same room.

THE NEXT MORNING, Austin caught a cab to the Bosphorus archaeological dig and walked down a makeshift wooden ramp that had been set up for wheelbarrow traffic. He wove his way past the hundreds of workers who were hacking away at the exposed sea bottom with picks and shovels.

Hanley knelt in the hardened mud, examining pieces of broken pottery. The archaeologist got to his feet and extended a mud-caked hand.

"Good to see you, Kurt. Ready to get back into some good old Marmara muck?"

"I'll have to take a rain check," Austin said. He surveyed the activity on the site. "Looks like the project is going well."

Hanley's face flushed with excitement. "This is the most fantastic dig I've ever participated in."

"I hope you won't be too busy to do me a small favor," Kurt said.

"I still owe you and the young lady for your volunteer work. Where is Carina, by the way?"

"Freshening up. I'm meeting her for lunch."

"Please give her my best regards. Now, what can I do for you?"

Austin reached into a canvas bag he had borrowed from Captain

Mustapha and pulled out the latex molds of the second *Navigator.* "Could you make plaster of paris casts from these?"

Hanley held a mold at an angle to view the relief. "No problem. It will take a couple of hours for the stuff to dry."

"We'll come by after lunch."

Hanley took the bag and its contents. "Where's Joe?"

"Nursing his submersible. It got a bit banged up on a dive and probably won't be of use to you."

"Sorry to hear that," Hanley said. "It would have helped us explore the site's perimeter, but, as you can see, most of the excavation is dry."

Austin said he would be back after lunch. He hailed a taxi and told the driver to take him to the Topkapi Palace. The sprawling complex of buildings, courtyards, pavilions, and parks dominated Seraglio Point, a hilly promontory at the junction of the Golden Horn, the Sea of Marmara, and the Bosphorus. The Ottoman sultans and their retinues had lived at Topkapi for four hundred years during the heyday of the Ottoman Empire.

The palace grounds had been transformed into a museum. Austin strolled between the twin turrets into a park shaded by leafy trees and teeming with tourists from every part of the world. He passed the treasury, which guarded a fortune in precious jewels, and made his way to the building housing the Konyali Restaurant.

Carina sat at a table in the courtyard, gazing out at the sun-sparkled water. She had changed from the casual outfit she wore on the Turquoise Coast and wore a long-skirted dress of dark russet that complemented her cinnamon-and-cream complexion. Austin wore tan slacks, foregoing his standard Hawaiian color riot for a more-conservative dark green polo shirt.

He pulled up a chair. "The sultans really knew their real estate. Location, location, and location."

She greeted him with a dazzling smile. "It's spectacular!"

"The prices are exorbitant and the food is less than five-star. The service is cafeteria-style. But the dining view is the best in Istanbul. You can't go wrong with the salad or the kebabs."

Austin offered to do the honors. He carried two fresh green salads and lemonades back to the table.

Carina took a dainty bite of lettuce. "An excellent recommendation. Is there any place you *haven't* been?"

"I get to travel a lot in my job."

"What exactly *is* your job?"

"As I said before, I'm an engineer."

She cocked a finely arched eyebrow. "NUMA is world renowned for its study of the oceans. But you and Joe spend most of your time fighting bad men and rescuing maidens in distress, thank you."

"You're welcome," Austin said. "I'm also head of the NUMA Special Assignments Team. It consists of Joe and two others who investigate mysteries on, under, and above the sea, that don't fit easily into any mainstream category."

"And how does this mystery stack up with your past experience?"

Austin gazed off at the queue of cargo ships that stretched off into the distance.

"Looking at events objectively, I'd say that this is a case of someone wanting something, ready to destroy anything or anyone in the way. *Subjectively,* I'm afraid it goes deeper than that."

"What do you mean?"

"You get a sixth sense when you spend a lot of time under water. It's telling me that there is more to this than what we see. There's evil lurking behind the violence."

"As if things weren't strange enough," she said with a nervous smile. "What do we do next?"

"Enjoy our lunch, savor the view and the sunshine, and then check out the plaster of paris casts Hanley is making for us."

"Do you think the casts will tell us anything?"

"That's my hope. Someone didn't want us to find the second statue. I think we've got all we can out of Turkey. The NUMA plane is heading back to the States tomorrow. We can regroup at home. I'd like to look deeper into the Baltazar question."

"And I've got to salvage the pieces of the national tour. *Kurt,*" she said, lowering her voice. "Don't turn around. I think one of those men who attacked us on the boat is sitting at a table."

"Maybe you've got the jitters."

He rose from his seat and came around behind Carina. He put his hands on the back of her chair and quickly scanned the other tables. A man sitting alone saw Austin glance his way and raised a newspaper as if he were reading it.

"You're right. I'll see what he's up to."

Carina looked on in horror as Austin strolled over to the table. He peered over the top of the newspaper directly into the man's face. "Peekaboo!"

The man lowered the newspaper and his lips curled into a snarl.

"We've got to stop meeting like this," Austin said. "I don't even know your name."

"The name is Buck. You won't have to remember it for long. You're dead meat, Austin."

"How'd you get out of the woods?"

"We called in backup."

Austin sized up the husky physique and the military brush cut.

"American accent. Green Beret or Delta Force?"

"Neither one, smart-ass. Navy SEALs," he said with a proud smile.

"That explains why you swam so well. The SEALs are a good outfit. Why'd they throw you out?"

Austin must have struck a nerve with his wild guess because the smile vanished.

"Unnecessary roughness."

"Who are you working for now?" Austin said.

"Someone who wants you dead."

"Sorry I can't oblige your employer."

The man gave him a nasty chuckle. "They want you to suffer, but I'm going to make it quick. I owe you. When you killed Ridley, I became squad leader. Look around."

Austin surveyed the courtyard restaurant. He picked out the other men he had last seen swimming for shore. One lounged against a wall. A third man sat at a table. They stared at Austin as if they wanted him on a dinner platter.

"I see you've brought along the rest of the Turkish swimming team."

"Go along with us. You can make it easy on the lady."

"You'll kill her quick and easy too?"

Buck shook his head. "My employer has other plans for her."

"Nice chatting with you, Buck. I'll explain the hopelessness of our situation to Ms. Mechadi."

Austin sauntered back to the table where Carina sat, her face frozen in fear.

"Good spotting," he said. "There are three of them. They want my hide, but they want you alive."

"Dear God! What do we do?"

"They won't try anything now. It's too public. Let's go for a stroll."

Austin guided Carina in the direction of the palace gate. His pursuers kept pace a hundred or so feet behind. He scoured his memory and tried to recall the layout of Topkapi and the palace grounds, searching for a hidey-hole where they would be temporarily safe.

An idea came to him. Not a total escape, but it might gain them valuable time.

Carina saw the faint smile on Austin's face and wondered if her friend had gone mad.

"What are you thinking?" she said in an anxious voice.

"No time for questions. Just do exactly what I tell you."

Carina was an independent woman who bridled at anyone telling her what to do, but Austin seemed to have the knack of getting them out of tight places. She felt him tug gently on her arm and walked faster to keep up.

Austin guided her through the camera-toting crowds milling in the courtyard outside the treasury. They ducked around the corner of an elegant stand-alone marble building that once housed the sultan's library and broke into a run. They ran through the ornate Gate of Felicity into another expansive courtyard. Austin guided her to the right, dashing through an open chamber where the sultan's viziers used to meet, his eye fixed on a long row of colonnades and a ticket gate for the Topkapi harem.

They were in luck! The ticket taker who normally manned the gate had wandered off to have a smoke.

Hardly breaking stride, Austin pulled Carina past the untended gate to a door. It was unlocked. Austin opened the door, pushed Carina ahead, and stepped through the portal into the sultan's harem. He closed the door behind them.

"What do we do *now*?" Carina said. She was breathless from their last-minute dash. Austin's wound was kicking up again. He put his hand to his ribs.

"I'll let you know just as soon as I figure that out," he said.

33

IN OTTOMAN DAYS, when the Topkapi harem was filled with hundreds of veiled beauties, an uninvited entry into its forbidden precincts would have been met by razor-sharp scimitars in the hands of the African eunuchs who guarded the place.

As Austin and Carina stepped into a long courtyard, the handsome young tour guide stopped his spiel and gave them a steely stare that was almost as cutting.

"*Yes?*" he said.

Austin put on his best Gomer Pyle grin. "Sorry we're late."

The guide frowned. The harem tours were conducted on a strict timetable. No one from the ticket booth had called to say there were two add-ons.

He clicked his hand radio to call the security guard.

Carina stepped over and gave the guard her most beguiling smile. She fumbled in her pocketbook and extracted a hundred-lira bill. "Do we tip you now or later?"

The guard smiled and clipped the hand radio onto his belt. "It is customary to tip at the end of the tour, but only if you are satisfied."

"I'm *sure* I'll be satisfied," Carina said with a flutter of her long eyelashes.

The guide cleared his throat and turned back to the mixture of about two dozen Turks and assorted foreigners clustered around him.

"At one time, the harem housed more than a thousand concubines, slaves, sultan's wives, and the sultan's mother. The harem was like a small city, with more than four hundred rooms. On your left are the quarters of the Black Eunuchs and the chief eunuch, who guarded the harem. Other doors lead to the quarters of the imperial treasurer and the chamberlain. You can go through that door and inspect the apartments of the eunuchs," he said.

The guide gave the same speech in Turkish, and then led the way into the guards' dormitory like the Pied Piper of Hamelin.

Austin held Carina back until they were alone in the courtyard. His blue-green eyes scanned the doors, searching for a possible escape route. He tried one door handle. The door was unlocked. He was hoping they could lose their pursuers in the vast labyrinth of apartments and courtyards.

"*Kurt,*" Carina said.

The Carriage Gate door had opened. Buck stepped into the courtyard with his hard-faced friends and signaled to his men to spread out. They moved three abreast toward their prey.

The guide and the tour group poured out of the eunuchs' living quarters into the courtyard, creating a human barrier of camera-toting tourists. Austin and Carina merged with the group as it went through a door that stood in a vestibule at the far end of the courtyard.

Austin glanced over his shoulder. Buck and his men were shouldering their way through the crowd.

"What should we do?" Carina whispered.

"Enjoy the tour for now, and when I say run, *run.*"

"Run *where?*"

"Still working on that," Austin said.

Carina muttered in Italian. Austin didn't need a translator to tell him she was cursing. He saw her anger as a good sign that she hadn't given in to despair.

The guide led the way through a square-domed chamber. Stopping every few minutes to deliver a speech in Turkish and in English, the guide pointed out where the concubines lived, where the children of the harem went to school, and where the food for the vast complex was prepared.

Austin glanced longingly at the doors and corridors that offered possible escape routes. There was no way he and Carina could break away from the crowd. With each stop, Buck and his friends drew closer.

Austin put himself in the shoes of the pursuers. The three men would move in and separate him from the crowd. Two men would finish him off with their knives. The third would grab Carina.

Buck and his thugs were all former special ops men. Their training would have included knife fighting and assassination. A hand clamped over his mouth to prevent him from calling out. A quick thrust of a blade between his ribs. By the time bystanders realized murder had been done, Austin would be breathing his last. Buck and company would slip away in the confusion that would follow.

If he was going to make a move, he'd better do it soon.

The tour group stepped into a large carpeted room. The walls were decorated in seventeenth-century blue-and-white tile. A wide sofa covered in gold brocade sat on a platform under a gilded canopy supported on four columns. The walls were decorated in a combination of baroque and rococo style. Light filtered through the stained-glass windows in the upper section of the domed room.

The guide said they were in the throne room, or royal saloon. At one end of the chamber was another platform where the concubines, wives, and the sultan's mother sat during affairs of state or to enjoy music and dancing.

The crowd began to break up, removing the human buffer Austin and Carina had been using to fend off Buck and his gang. As the group dissipated, Austin faced the three men with only a few tourists in between them.

Now or never.

Austin whispered to Carina to play along. He took her by the hand and sidled up to the guide.

"Would it be possible for us to leave the tour?" Austin said. "My wife is not feeling well. She's pregnant."

The guide took in Carina's slim profile. "Pregnant?"

"Yes," Carina said with a demure smile. "Only a few months."

Carina spread her fingers across her flat abdomen. The guide blushed and hurriedly pointed to a doorway. "You can go out that way."

They thanked him and headed for the exit.

"Wait!" the guide said. He lifted his walkie-talkie to his lips. "I'll call the guard to escort you."

He spoke into the hand radio. The guard would arrive in a few minutes. He told them to stay with the group in the meantime.

Buck had seen Austin talking to the guide. When the guide spoke into his radio, he assumed that Austin had called for help.

"Let's do it," he said to his men.

Austin was guiding Carina from one part of the room to the other, trying to put space between them and their pursuers. He was learning that hide-and-seek wasn't made to be played in the open.

The three men closed in. Buck was close enough so that Austin could see the murderous gleam in his eye. Buck reached under his jacket.

A burly security guard entered the royal saloon, and the tour guide pointed out Austin and Carina. Austin played his ace card.

Pointing an accusing finger at Buck and the two other men, he roared at the top of his lungs. "PKK! PKK!"

The PKK was short-hand for *Partiya Kerkerên Kerdistan,* or

Kurdistan Workers' Party, a Marxist-Leninist guerrilla organization that wants to set up an independent Kurdish state in south-eastern Turkey. The PKK had been staging a violent campaign against the Turkish government since 1978, attacking government property and tourist areas and, in the process, killing thousands.

The guard's amiable expression vanished, and he fumbled for the revolver in its belt holster. In Turkey, shouting PKK was the equivalent of throwing gasoline onto an open fire. The guard had finally got his gun out.

The guard saw the knife in Buck's hands. Holding the revolver with two hands, he shouted in Turkish. Buck turned and saw the muzzle pointed at his chest. The knife clattered to the floor, and he raised his hands in the air.

One of Buck's men was aiming a pistol at the guard. Austin threw a battering ram shoulder block into the man's midsection, and the gun went flying. They crashed to the floor, and Austin drew his arm back and nailed the man with a short punch to the jaw.

The throne room had emptied out. The tour guide had ducked into a doorway and was calling for reinforcements on his radio.

Buck slipped his hand under his jacket and came out with a gun. It was a fatal mistake. The middle-aged guard was a Turkish army veteran. Although he was thick around the middle, he remembered the discipline that had been drilled into him. Austin got to his feet, yelled "PKK" again, and pointed at Buck.

The guard turned, calmly aimed at Buck's torso, and squeezed the trigger. The bullet caught Buck square in the chest and sent him crashing onto the sultan's divan.

Austin scrambled to his feet, grabbed Carina, who had been frozen in place, and guided her toward the exit door. They flew along a corridor, made a blind turn, and retraced their steps to a small room that had a door in the corner. The door led out onto a terrace that was drenched with sunlight.

Standing on the terrace were the two men who had chased them through the abandoned village. Austin stepped in front of Carina to protect her. As the men started toward Austin and Carina, the harem door burst open and Buck's men stepped out into the open with guns in hand. They blinked in the bright sunlight and didn't see the Turks reach under their jackets for guns, which had silencers attached. The guns coughed simultaneously. Buck's men crumpled to the deck.

While one Turk kept his gun trained on the door, the other took Austin's arm.

"Come," he said. "It's okay. We're friends." He gave Austin a friendly pat on the back and winked at Carina.

The other man took up the rear. He was talking on a cell phone and frequently glanced over his shoulder to see if they were being followed.

The Turks hid their guns when they entered the public area and led the way through a maze of buildings and courtyards to the palace gate. A silver Mercedes waited at the curb with its engine running. The lead Turk opened the passenger door.

Austin and Carina got into the backseat and discovered it was already occupied.

Their old friend Cemil smiled and gave a soft-spoken order to the driver. The Mercedes pulled away from the palace complex and merged with the Istanbul traffic flow.

"Those were *your* men?" Carina said.

"Don't worry. They are not angry about the tire your friend ruined. It was their own fault. I told them to keep watch on you, but they got too close."

"I'll pay for a new tire," Austin said.

Cemil chuckled. As a Turk, he explained, he could not refuse the offer.

"I apologize if my men frightened you," he said.

He explained that after he had seen them in the cisterns, he had heard disturbing rumors. Hard-eyed mercenaries had arrived in town. They had come into the country unarmed so as not to attract attention and had acquired weapons from a local dealer, who was a friend of Cemil's. More worrisome, they had arrived the same day as Carina and Austin and were staying in the same hotel.

He had sent his men to keep an eye on his friends. After his men had been ditched in the abandoned village, they had returned to Istanbul and kept an eye on the hotel, figuring Austin and Carina would come back for their luggage. They had followed Austin from the archaeological site to Topkapi only to lose him when he and Carina had ducked into the harem. They had seen Buck and his men go in after them and had run around to the exit.

Carina planted a big kiss on Cemil's cheek. "How can we ever thank you?"

"There is one way. I made a bad business decision that has come to the attention of the international authorities. It would be helpful if you vouched for my character should the situation become awkward."

"It's a *deal*," Carina said.

Cemil's cheerful manner changed. "Your hotel is no longer safe. My men will pick up your luggage and move you to an inn where you will be okay for the night. I have a lot of friends in Turkey, but people are easily bought and sold, and I could not guarantee your safety indefinitely"

"I think Cemil is saying the climate here is no longer healthy," Austin said.

"Your friend puts it very well," Cemil said. "My advice is to get out of Istanbul as quickly as possible."

AUSTIN WASN'T one to disregard good advice. But he had unfinished business to attend to. The Mercedes dropped them off at the

Bosphorus dig, and arrangements were made to pick them up in two hours.

Hanley was in a shed that had been set up as a conservation laboratory. The plaster casts were laid out on a table. They were dark gray in color.

"I painted the ridges and raised areas to make them stand out," Hanley explained. "Fascinating stuff. Where did you say you got it?"

"These designs were etched into a Phoenician statue. We'll run them by an expert when we get home," Austin said.

Hanley bent over the plaster of paris replica of the cat that had been entwined around the *Navigator*'s legs. "I've got three cats back home, so I got a big kick out of this," he said.

Austin was looking at the swirling lines that were the cat's stripes when his eye began to see patterns that didn't seem random. He held a magnifying glass over the cat's rib section. Almost lost in the feline's stripes was an opposing *Z* symbol. Unlike the others, which were horizontal, this one was upside down.

He handed the glass to Carina, who studied the mark and said, "What does it mean?"

"If this *is* a symbol for a ship, it's either sunk or sinking." Austin stared at the pattern of lines and whorls. "I think this is more than artistic whimsy. We're looking at a *map*. Those lines depict a coastline. The indentations are bays and coves."

He borrowed a digital camera and a tripod. Carina held the casts at a vertical angle. Austin shot dozens of photos and downloaded the pictures on a borrowed laptop computer and sent them to a NUMA e-mail address.

While Hanley and Carina wrapped the casts in plastic foam, Austin put a call in to Zavala at the airport. Zavala said he would meet them the next morning for the flight back to the United States. The damaged Subvette had been loaded onto its cargo plane.

The Mercedes arrived with their baggage and took Austin and

Carina to a small hotel that overlooked the Bosphorus. They turned in early, too tired to enjoy the view, and fell asleep as soon as their heads hit the pillow. When they arose early the next morning, the Mercedes was waiting to take them to the airport.

Zavala welcomed them on board with a fresh pot of coffee.

Less than an hour later, the Citation was airborne and heading west at five hundred miles an hour.

"How was Istanbul?" Zavala said as the plane sped over the Aegean.

Austin told him about the encounter with Buck and his gang at Topkapi, the mad dash into the harem, and the rescue by Cemil and his men.

"The *harem*! Wish I could have been there," Zavala said.

"Me too. We could have used you when the shooting started," Austin said.

"That's not what I had in mind. I wish I could have been there when the harem was full of beautiful women."

Austin should have known better than to expect any sympathy from his womanizing friend.

"I understand there's an opening for a eunuch," Austin said.

Zavala clamped his knees together. "Ouch," he said. "Thanks but no thanks. I think I'll go up and chat with the pilot."

Austin grinned at his partner's discomfort. His light mood only lasted a moment. Buck and Ridley were dead and their cohorts neutralized, but if Austin's suspicions about Viktor Baltazar were correct there would be more hard-eyed men in his future.

Even worse, the baby-faced killer was still on the loose.

CHAPTER

34

ANGELA FELT AS IF someone had walked over her grave.
There was no reason for the icy coldness between her shoulder blades. She often stayed after hours and had never felt nervous about working alone; there was something comforting about being surrounded by the wisdom of the ages.

She thought she had heard a voice call out. She wasn't sure. She had been focused on the Meriwether Lewis material.

The only other person in the building was her boss. Perhaps Helen Woolsey had said good night.

Angela sat back in her chair and breathed a sigh of relief. She had been playing a waiting game, hoping Woolsey would leave the building by the time the Trouts returned. She could barely contain her excitement. She had much to tell them.

She cocked her ear. Silence. Something didn't seem right.

Angela rose from her chair and walked across the silent reading room. She stepped into a darkened corridor and flicked on the light switch. The hall remained in darkness. She'd have to call the building superintendent in the morning. She started down the corridor, walking toward the glow that seeped out around the edges of Helen's door.

She stopped and knocked softly. No reply. Helen must have forgotten to turn off her light. Angela opened the door and entered the office, only to freeze in midstep.

Woolsey was still at her desk, her hands folded neatly on her lap, her head angled back like a broken doll. Her mouth was wide open, and dead eyes stared at the ceiling. Reddish purple bruises marred her pale throat.

A silent scream echoed inside Angela's skull. She put her hand to her mouth and fought the impulse to vomit.

She slowly backed out of the office. Her instinct was to run toward the front door. She stared down the unlit corridor, but a primeval sense of danger stopped her from bolting into the gloomy shadows. Instead of heading for the entrance, she sprinted back into the interior of the building.

Adriano's hulking figure stepped from the gloom. He had jammed the light switch with a pocketknife and had expected the young woman to panic and rush into his arms. But she had turned and run the other way like a rabbit retreating into its warren.

Adriano's blood was up after killing the Watcher. That had been easy. The thought of a challenge cheered him. The kill was much more enjoyable when it came at the end of a hunt.

He passed Woolsey's office and glanced in at his handiwork. Woolsey had been the latest in a long line of Watchers embedded in the Philosophical Society. The Watcher system went back centuries. Watchers were quietly engaged in centers of learning around the world, their only job to sound the alarm at the first hint that the Secret had been uncovered.

Two centuries before, another philosophical society Watcher had warned of Jefferson's findings. The Watcher was one of the academics Jefferson had asked to translate the words on the vellum. The destruction of Jefferson's papers was supposed to have ended his quest, but the connection to Meriwether Lewis was discovered and that loose end had to be tied up by assassins dispatched to the Louisiana Territory.

Woolsey could not have known that her first call as a Watcher had set in motion the chain of events that would lead to her demise. Her job was to report any serious queries about Phoenician voyages to America. She had dutifully relayed news of the Jefferson file. By the time she received instructions to turn the file over to a courier, a State Department representative had come by to collect the Jefferson material. She angrily put the blame on her assistant, but was told not to mention the incident to Angela. When she called again to report the Trouts' visit to Angela, she sealed her death warrant.

Woolsey was told to make sure Angela stayed late. Adriano had showed up at the museum after hours, dispatched the librarian, and unsuccessfully tried to ambush her assistant.

He continued along the corridor, methodically trying each door. The offices were all locked. He came to a four-way intersection and sniffed the air like a keening hound.

Click.

The sound of a latch closing was barely audible. Adriano's senses were at their height during a hunt. He turned to his right, follow-ing the passageway to a door, which he opened, and stepped into a dark room.

Adriano had never been in the library but knew its layout well. After Angela had discovered the file, he had sent people to scout out the building. He considered himself a professional and wanted to ac-quaint himself with a potential killing field.

He knew that the darkened room housed thousands of books stacked on tall bookshelves that were laid out in parallel rows.

Angela had ducked between two rows when she heard the door open and close. She had been headed toward an exit at the rear of the room. She was sure the pounding of her heart would give her away.

Adriano hit the wall switch and the room was flooded with light.

Angela dropped to her hands and knees and crawled to the end of the row, then along a narrow aisle between the ends of the shelves and the wall.

Adriano's hunter's ears picked up the shuffle of knees and palms brushing the floor.

He strolled along the aisle. He took his time, pausing to peer between the rows of bookshelves before going on. He could have found Angela in a second, but he wanted to prolong the hunt and increase the terror of his prey as long as he could.

After checking out several rows, he saw an object on the floor and walked between shelves for a closer look. It was a shoe. Another lay a few feet away. Angela had slipped into her stocking feet to muffle the sound her movement.

Adriano chuckled softly and flexed his fingers.

"Come to me, Angela," he crooned like a mother calling for its child.

At the unexpected sound of her name, Angela scrambled to her feet and ran for the exit door. Quick steps padded behind her. A hand reached out and grabbed the back of her blouse. She screamed and pulled free. Adriano had purposely let her go. He liked to play with his victims.

Angela ducked between stacks and plastered her back against a bookshelf.

Adriano turned down the next row of shelves and his baby face peered over the tops of the books.

"Hello," he said.

Angela turned and saw the round blue eyes. She tried to scream, but the sound was caught in her throat.

"Angela."

A woman's voice had called her name.

Adriano's first instinct was to attack the intruder. He advanced toward the sound of the voice. He would batter the newcomer to the floor, quickly dispose of her, and then return to Angela.

He rounded a corner and saw two people near the door. A red-haired woman and a man who was even taller than Adriano. They seemed startled by his appearance but rallied quickly.

"Where's Angela?" the woman said.

He said nothing. But there was an audible whimper from the stacks. Angela.

They showed by their aggressive posture that they had no intention of yielding. The man started toward him. The woman was circling around behind.

Adriano wasn't used to resistance. The situation was becoming complex. He feinted toward the man, then turned and ran for the exit door. He hit a light switch and fled the room.

"Angela, are you okay?" Gamay said. "It's the Trouts."

"Be careful," Angela warned. "He's after me."

The room lights came on again.

Angela rushed out and threw her arms around Gamay. Her body was wracked by sobs.

Paul made a quick survey of the room. Then he opened the exit door and stepped out into the hallway. All was quiet. He returned to the stacks room. "He's gone. Who *was* that creep?"

"I don't know," Angela said. "He killed Helen. Then he came after me. He knew my name."

"The front door was unlocked," Paul said. "We got lost trying to find your office and heard your scream. You say he killed your boss?"

Although she hated to go back to the murder scene, she led them along the corridor to Woolsey's office. Trout pushed the door open with his toe and stepped inside. He went to the desk and put his ear close to Woolsey's gaping mouth but neither heard nor felt her breath. He hadn't expected her to be alive after seeing the angle of her head and the marks on her throat.

He stepped back into the hallway. Gamay had her arm around the young woman's shoulders. She saw the grave expression on her husband's face and called 911 on her cell phone. Then they went outside and stood near the front stairs to wait for the police.

The patrol car showed up within five minutes. Two Philadelphia police officers got out of the car and, after talking to the Trouts and Angela, they called for backup. They drew their guns. One went inside while the other walked around the building.

Adriano slipped out from behind the shelter of a tree growing in a small park across from the library entrance. The red-and-blue lights from the police car reflected off his soft features. He stared with curiosity at the tall man and the red-haired woman who had interrupted his hunt.

Another cruiser screeched to a halt and two more policemen got out.

Adriano melted back into the shadows and left the library grounds without being seen. He was a patient man. He knew where Angela lived. And when she came home that night, he would be waiting.

CHAPTER

35

AUSTIN WAS IN THE NETHERLAND between sleep and consciousness when he sensed a change in the Citation's attitude and speed. He opened his eyes and peered out the window. He recognized the tapestry of lights spread out below as Washington and the densely populated Virginia suburbs.

Carina was asleep, her head resting on his shoulder. He tapped her arm. "We're home."

She woke up and yawned. "The last thing I remember, we were taking off from Paris."

"You were telling me about your plans for the exhibition."

"Sorry." She rubbed the sleep out of her eyes. "I'll go back to my hotel and get a good night's rest. Tomorrow morning I'll take the train to New York. I have to talk to the people at the Metropolitan Museum of Art about the opening."

"You're going ahead with the tour even without the *Navigator?*"

"I don't have much choice. Looking on the bright side, the news about the statue's theft may bring in more people."

Austin groped for words that wouldn't make him sound paternal. "In view of past events, do you think it's a good idea for you to be traveling on your own?"

She kissed him on the cheek. "Thanks, Kurt, but only a few people will know my plans." She yawned again. "Do you think I'm still
in danger?"

Austin compressed his lips in a tight smile. He didn't want to
scare Carina, but she needed to be aware that she had a bull's-eye
painted on her back.

"Our friend Buck said that you were a kidnapping target. The
people he worked for have a long reach. We saw that in Turkey."

Carina tilted her stubborn chin up at an imperious angle. "I'm not
going to let *anyone* make me spend the rest of my days hiding in
a closet."

"Don't blame you. I'd like to offer a compromise," Austin said.
"Stay at the boathouse tonight. I'll prepare a sumptuous dinner of
Thai takeout. Sleep off your jet lag and get a good start in the
morning."

"I'd like that," Carina said without hesitation.

The pilot announced that the plane was making its approach to
Dulles Airport and would be on the ground in fifteen minutes.
Austin glanced across the aisle. Zavala looked like a dead man sleeping. He could fall asleep on a bed of nails and be up at a moment's
notice, ready to spring into action.

Austin removed the cell phone from Zavala's jacket and put in a
call to the Trouts. Paul answered. Austin said he was back from
Turkey and asked if he and Gamay had received the Jefferson file.

"We've read it," Paul said. "We've got a good rendering of a ship
of Tarshish, but need more information to plot a course. But you
need to know something, Kurt: We followed a lead to the American
Philosophical Society and stumbled into a real snake pit."

"I have a problem imagining that venerable institution of learning as a nest of vipers."

"Times have changed. Shortly after we visited the library, a librarian was killed. Her assistant would have met a similar fate if Gamay and I hadn't showed up and chased the killer away."

"Did you get a look at him?"

"Yeah. Big guy, with a baby face and round blue eyes."

"I've met the gentleman. Is the assistant okay?"

"Still a bit shaky. We persuaded her to get out of Philadelphia after the police finished interviewing her. She wanted to stop by her apartment. We insisted that she come directly to Georgetown. Gamay loaned her some clothes that fit, more or less."

"I'd like to meet her. How about seven o'clock tomorrow?"

"We'll bring the doughnuts and coffee. You haven't told me about your trip to Istanbul."

"Turkey has a snake infestation problem too. See you in the morning."

The thump of the plane's landing gear on the tarmac woke Zavala up from his sound sleep. He looked out the window. "Home so soon?"

Austin handed the cell phone back. "You dreamed your way across the Atlantic."

Zavala puffed out his cheeks. "I was having nightmares about eunuchs, thanks to you."

The plane taxied away from the general aviation area to a special NUMA hangar. The three passengers debarked and carefully loaded the plaster casts along with the baggage into a Jeep Cherokee from the NUMA motor pool. Austin dropped Zavala off and drove to his boathouse after stopping to pick up an order of Thai food.

Dinner was on the deck, with selections from Austin's collection of progressive jazz in the background. He and Carina sipped brandy to the music of John Coltrane and Oscar Peterson and agreed not to discuss the mysteries surrounding the *Navigator*. They talked about their work instead. Carina matched every NUMA adventure with a fascinating episode of her own.

The combination of brandy and hours of travel took its toll, and Carina started to nod off. Austin showed her to the bedroom in the Victorian turret, and, unable to sleep, he went back down to his study. He stretched out in a comfortable leather chair and studied the amber liquor in his glass as if he were looking into a crystal ball. In his mind, he went over every detail, starting with the SOS from the oil rig.

He was hoping his ruminations would produce a picture with the clarity of a Rembrandt, but what he got was a Jackson Pollock abstract. He rose from his chair, went to a bookcase, and found Anthony Saxon's book. He settled back into his chair and began to read.

ANTHONY SAXON was a true adventurer. He had hacked his way through the jungle to discover long-lost South American ruins. He had narrowly escaped death at the hands of nomadic desert tribesmen. He had rummaged through countless dusty tombs and made the acquaintance of numerous mummies. If only a tenth of what he wrote was true, Saxon was cut from the same mold as such famous explorers as Hiram Bingham, Stanley and Livingstone, and Indiana Jones.

Several years before, Saxon had launched what could have been his greatest adventure. He intended to sail a replica of a Phoenician ship from the Red Sea to the coast of North America. The Pacific Ocean crossing would have proven his theory that Ophir, the fabled site of King Solomon's mines, was in the Americas. However, the ship burned to the waterline one night under mysterious circumstances.

Saxon believed that Ophir was not a single place but the code name for several sources of Solomon's wealth. He theorized that

Solomon launched two fleets under the direction of Hiram, the Phoenician admiral. One flotilla left from the Red Sea. The other flotilla crossed the Atlantic, after passing through the Straits of Gibraltar.

Saxon had found a strange glyph in a Peruvian ruin that matched similar symbols inscribed on tablets in Lebanon and Syria. He called the glyph the Tarshish symbol, and thought it might have been short-hand for "Ophir." There were several photos of the glyph in his book.

Austin stared at the pictures.

The symbol was a horizontal line with back-to-back Zs at each end, identical to the mark carved into the *Navigator*'s kilt and the side of the bronze cat.

Saxon had exhausted every avenue of research on Solomon and Ophir. Then, in a chapter entitled "Epiphany," he described how he'd hit upon the idea of searching for the Queen of Sheba. No one was closer to Solomon than Sheba. Maybe they shared pillow talk. His quest for Ophir took a backseat to the search for Sheba's tomb.

Saxon had spent years and traveled thousands of miles in his quest for the Queen of Sheba. He had become infatuated with the dead queen. Saxon believed that Sheba was real, not a legend as some experts contended; that she was dark-skinned, and probably from the Yemen area. He recounted the legend of Solomon and Sheba. Curious about the stories she had heard about Solomon's wisdom, she went to visit him. Their attraction for each other blossomed; they had a child. Eventually, she returned home, to tend to her own kingdom. Their son was thought to have become king of Ethiopia.

A dark-skinned beauty with links to Ethiopia, Austin mused. He glanced toward the stairs leading to the turret bedroom.

Austin finished the last chapter an hour later and put the book down. He checked the doors, turned off the lights, and quietly ascended the spiral staircase to the bedroom. He undressed, slid under the sheets without awakening Carina, put his arm protectively around her warm body, and quickly fell asleep.

CARINA'S VOICE woke him up early the next morning. She had brewed a pot of coffee and was on the phone making train reservations and arrangements with the Metropolitan Museum of Art. After they showered, dressed, and had breakfast, Austin drove Carina to Union Station. She planted a kiss on his lips and said she would return to Washington that night. She would call him when the train left New York.

From Union Station, Austin drove to the NUMA tower. He took the elevator from the underground garage to the fifteenth floor, followed a corridor, and stepped through a doorway into a large, dimly lit space. A wide, curving wall was lined with glowing television screens that projected information collected by NUMASat.

The all-seeing system had gained it the nickname as the "Eye of Sauron" among the more literary-minded at NUMA. Jack Wilmut, the keeper of the eye, bore no resemblance to the fearsome creatures from a Tolkien saga. Wilmut was a mild-mannered man in his forties who supervised the NUMASat system from an elaborate console in the center of the room.

On both sides of the console were smaller computer workstations. Satellite interpreters fielded the dozens of queries that came in from scientists, universities, and ocean-related organizations from around the world.

Austin wondered why geniuses tended to be eccentric when it came to hair. Einstein. Beethoven. Mark Twain. Superman's nemesis Lex Luthor. NUMA's bearded computer whiz, Hiram Yeager. Wilmut, a plumpish man in his forties, affected a double comb-over parted just above the ears.

Austin came up behind Wilmut and in his deepest voice said, "Greetings, O all-seeing Sauron."

Wilmut spun around in his chair and grinned with delight.

"*Greetings,* Mortal. I was expecting you."

"The Eye of Sauron sees all, knows all," Austin said.

"Hell, no," Wilmut replied. "I got your e-mail and pictures from Turkey. Pull up a seat and tell me how I can help."

Austin plunked down in a swivel chair. "The photos show plaster casts made from the markings on an ancient statue. I think the squiggly lines are the contours of a map. Possibly a location on the East Coast. I wondered if the map could be compared to satellite photos."

In answer, Wilmut clicked the computer mouse. The picture Austin had taken of the *Navigator*'s cat appeared within a rectangle. The image was sharper than on the original photo. "I've enhanced the picture," Wilmut explained. "Got rid of the gray areas, fuzzy edges, and miscellaneous garbage. The borders help in the visualization."

Austin tapped the screen with his forefinger. "This symbol may denote a sunken ship. The problem is, I don't know if that square is one mile across. Or ten. Or even a hundred."

"The image is similar to a fingerprint," Wilmut said. "Prints are matched according to ridge characteristics called Galton details, points of identity or minutiae. You ID prints by comparing minutiae points. Ridge characteristics. Islands. Bifurcation. I've created an algorithm that will match the points on the primitive map with satellite photos. I'll have the NUMASat computer look at each one of those possibilities. It will take a little while."

Austin told Wilmut he would be in conference but to call when he had some news, and took the elevator down to another floor. He met Zavala in the hallway and they walked to the conference room together. The walls were hung with pictures of sailing ships. The centerpiece was a long oak conference table that seemed to float like a ship at sea on the thick blue carpet.

The Trouts sat at the table with a serious-faced young woman Austin assumed was Angela Worth. Angela was still in something of a state of shock. In the space of a few hours, she had met the Trouts, her boss had been murdered, and an attempt made on her life. She was still reeling from those events when she was drawn into the very heart of NUMA, an agency whose exploits she had only heard about.

Then the door opened, and the two men who came into the room could have stepped out of an adventure novel. The husky man with the piercing blue-green eyes and strange pale hair came over and introduced himself and his darkly handsome friend. She was practically speechless.

They sat at the table and Paul handed them copies of the computer-generated ship of Tarshish. "We think this is the type of vessel that would have sailed to North America. We didn't get far on the transatlantic route, so we tried another avenue. We noticed a series of connections to the Philosophical Society and followed it up. That's when we met Angela."

"Congratulations on finding the Jefferson file," Austin said with a friendly grin that put her at ease.

"Thank you," Angela said. "It was dumb luck, really."

"Angela has had *more* dumb luck," Gamay said. "Please tell Kurt and Joe what else you've found."

"We think that Meriwether Lewis was murdered to stop him from bringing some vital information to Thomas Jefferson."

"I'd be interested in how you reached that conclusion," Austin said.

Angela pulled a file folder out of a battered leather briefcase.

"I dug into the files looking for information on Lewis's slave, a young man named Zeb. The records show that he arrived at Monticello several weeks after Lewis died. It's possible he had gone along with a man called Neelly, who traveled to Monticello with news of Lewis's death. Neelly would have needed help with Lewis's belongings and brought along the slave. I wondered what became of Zeb after that."

"In those days the slave would have been considered part of Lewis's estate," Austin said.

"That's what I thought. He would have been delivered with other property to Lewis's family. On a hunch, I went through Monticello's slave population. I found something quite fascinating."

She handed Austin a sheet of paper with the names of slaves, their sex, age, and job. Austin perused the roster and passed it along to the table without comment.

Gamay said, "Zeb is listed as a *freeman*. He was assigned to the house."

"How did he become free at age eighteen?" Austin said.

"I think it was a reward," Angela suggested.

"That makes sense," Austin said. "It was Jefferson's way of thanking the young man for a service he had performed."

"The Lewis material," Gamay said. "I'll bet he delivered the goods to Jefferson."

"Do you know what happened to him?" Austin asked Angela.

"He stayed at Monticello, working in a prize position inside the house. He vanished from the roster years later, but that's not the end of the story."

She produced a copy of an old newspaper clipping.

Gamay read the clipping. "Our freeman?"

"It says he worked for President Jefferson," Angela said.

Gamay passed the clipping to Paul. "This is dynamite. He's in his nineties, and was interviewed shortly before he died. On his deathbed, he says flat out that Meriwether Lewis was murdered."

"What are the chances he told Jefferson the same thing?" Austin said.

Paul said, "We think Jefferson knew it was murder all the time but pushed the suicide story, even though it diminished the reputation of his old friend."

"Jefferson was not above chicanery, but he must have had a good reason," Austin said.

Paul picked up the ship rendering. "We think he didn't want to call attention to the fact that he knew about *this*."

"I think our next step is clear," Gamay said. "A trip to Monticello to see if we can learn more about young Zeb."

Austin was about to say he agreed with the suggestion when he excused himself to answer a phone call. It was Wilmut.

"I've *got* it," Wilmut's excited voice said.

"You've found the ship's position?"

"Even better, Kurt. I've found the *ship*."

36

AUSTIN STOOD ON THE DECK of his catboat and gazed out at Chesapeake Bay. The bay was familiar territory to Austin. He had gunkholed nearly every cove and inlet on both shores in the twenty-four-foot-long shallow-draft sailboat he had restored. Despite its wide beam, the catboat was surprisingly fast and maneuverable, living up to its reputation to come about as "quick as a cat." Austin had a penchant for speed, and liked nothing better than sailing tight to the wind with the big gaff-rigged sail close-hauled in a brisk breeze.

But not today. Austin climbed out of the sailboat and walked back to the parking lot. He helped Zavala unload their bags from the Jeep. After the meeting at NUMA, they had picked up some gear and drove to the boatyard south of Annapolis. Austin had called ahead to arrange with the boatyard manager for the loan of a twenty-foot fiberglass powerboat.

Zavala carried the duffel bags that held their scuba gear. Austin took charge of two plastic cases. They hauled the equipment out onto the slip dock and stowed their gear on board the powerboat. Then they cast off the lines and headed south into the bay. Zavala manned the wheel. Austin consulted the chart and handheld GPS.

Chesapeake Bay is the largest estuary in the United States, stretching two hundred miles long from Havre de Grace, Maryland, where the Susquehanna River empties into the bay, to Norfolk, Virginia. The bay ranges in width from about thirty-five miles wide near the mouth of the Potomac River to less than four miles near Aberdeen in Maryland.

Zavala scanned the wide expanse of sun-sparkled water. "What's the wreck tally on the bottom of the Chesapeake?" he asked, raising his voice to be heard over the buzz of the motor.

Austin looked up from the chart. "About eighteen hundred at last count. They range from a sixteenth-century wreck of Tangier Island to the *Cuyahoga,* a Coast Guard cutter that went down after a collision. But the historian at NUMA was clueless about the target the satellite picked up."

"What kind of depth are we talking about?"

"The Chesapeake's pretty shallow, for the most part," Austin replied. "Averages about twenty-one feet, although it's laced with troughs that reach nearly two hundred feet." He tapped the chart with his finger. "From the looks of it, our target sank into one of these deep holes."

The powerboat continued south, skimming over the tops of two-foot seas past oyster boats and sailing craft. There was a steady stream of traffic in both directions along the Intercoastal Waterway, which ran down the middle of the Chesapeake.

Less than an hour after leaving the boatyard, Austin again glanced at the GPS and signaled to Zavala, who backed off the throttle and steered the boat to follow Austin's pointing finger. When they were on-site Austin pointed down toward the water and yelled:

"*Here.*"

The boat plowed to a stop and Zavala killed the motor. Austin set the GPS aside and threw the anchor over the side. The boat rocked in the waves a few hundred yards from a small island. The boat's depth finder indicated that the water under their hull was forty-six feet. He and Zavala pored over the satellite photo Wilmut had provided. The faint outline of a ship was clear. It should be right under their hull.

Austin opened a plastic case and lifted out a SeaBotix Remote-Operated Vehicle that was about the size and shape of a canister vacuum cleaner. NUMA had ROVs that were as big as a car, and Austin could have drawn upon an array of the sophisticated remote sensing devices, but he wanted to move fast. He had decided against a time-consuming magnetometer or side-scan sonar survey in favor of a shallow-water vehicle that was portable and easily transported.

At one end of the bright red plastic housing was a high-resolution color camera and halogen lights. At the other end was a pair of powerful thrusters. The ROV had a lateral thruster that could shift it sideways and a vertical thruster for up and down. Metal frameworks on each side of the vehicle served a dual purpose as runners and housing protection.

Zavala snapped open the lid on the other case, which contained the ROV's eight-inch television monitor and controls. He was a skilled pilot, and the single-stick control would be easy to use. He and Austin connected the three-hundred-foot-long low-drag umbilical to the vehicle and control box. Austin lifted the ROV by the handle in the top of the housing and dropped it into the water. Zavala put the vehicle through a few tricky maneuvers to get a feel for the controls. Then he pointed the ROV toward the bottom in a shallow dive and powered the thrusters.

The ROV quickly descended to forty feet. Zavala leveled the vehicle off and checked the TV monitor. Twin cones of light illuminated the muddy bottom. There was no sign of a wreck. He had the vehicle execute a series of parallel lines, as if he were mowing a lawn. Still no wreck.

"I hope our target wasn't a NUMASat hiccup," he said. He turned to Austin, who had been peering over his shoulder.

"Not a chance," Austin said. "Set up a new search pattern to starboard. Keep it tight."

Zavala activated the lateral thrusters and shifted the mini-ROV to the right. He started a new pattern with twenty-five-foot-long parallel turns. Halfway through the new search, the ROV's lights picked out a dark, curving line that protruded from the bottom.

Zavala brought the vehicle to a hover. "That's either a sea serpent rib or a ship's timber."

The image on the monitor brought a grin to Austin's face.

"I'd say we've got ourselves a wreck," he said. "Remind me to sacrifice a Hobbit to the Eye of Sauron."

Zavala powered the ROV so that it moved past the object. More ship's ribs came into view. The skeletal outlines of the wreck could be discerned. The timbers gradually diminished in size as the ROV passed nearer the bow section.

"The wood is pretty well preserved, except for the upper ends, where it seems to be charred," Zavala said.

"That would account for the sinking. She burned to the waterline."

"How long do you figure her to be?"

Austin squinted at the screen. "A hundred fifty feet. Maybe more. What's that, off to the right?"

Zavala put the ROV into a quick turn. The lights picked up what looked like a long wooden animal snout. The upper part of the head was burned beyond recognition.

"Looks like part of a big hobbyhorse," Zavala said.

Austin's pulse quickened. He reached into his duffel bag and pulled out a waterproof folder of transparent plastic. Inside was the computer-generated ship rendering that the Trouts had given him.

He held the picture close to the screen. The horse snout on the monitor and in the picture were almost identical.

"Guess again, amigo. We may be the first people in more than two thousand years to set eyes on a Phoenician ship of Tarshish."

Zavala's face lit up. "I'd trade a case of *anejo* tequila for a glimpse of this lady when it was still afloat."

He moved the vehicle slowly along the port side of the wreck.

Austin saw a dark round shape lying about dead center in the hull. He tapped the screen. "What's this?"

Zavala cautiously powered the vehicle inches forward.

The ROV's lights picked out a metal grating partially covered by marine growth. He turned the vehicle around and used the force of its thrusters to clear away the sand around the object.

Austin said, "It's a diver's helmet."

"I know the Phoenicians were clever, but I didn't know they were into hard-hat diving."

"They *weren't*. Someone beat us to the wreck, and from the looks of it he's still down there."

Zavala put the ROV in a hover that would keep the helmet in view. Austin laid his scuba gear out on the deck. He stripped down to a bathing suit and got into a neoprene wet suit, boots, gloves, and hood. He pulled on his fins. Zavala helped him with his weight belt and air tank. Austin did a quick gear check and tested the regulator. Then he brought a mask down over his eyes and clamped the mouthpiece between his teeth. He sat on the gunwale and rolled backward into the water.

Austin sank several feet in a cloud of bubbles. He felt a quick chill before the cold water seeping between skin and suit warmed to body temperature. With powerful kicks of his muscular legs, he powered himself down through the darkening water toward the silvery green glow from the ROV lights.

Austin came down practically on top of the vehicle, then swam around in front of the ROV's camera lens and gave a thumbs-up. Zavala tilted the front of the ROV up and down as if it were nodding. Austin waved back and swam over to examine the ribs. The wood was definitely charred.

He was turning back to the helmet when he saw a rectangular object lying nearby. He picked up what appeared to be a stone or clay tablet, about eight inches square and a couple of inches thick. Lines were cut into the surface on one side.

Austin slipped the tablet into a stuff bag attached to his buoyancy compensator and gave the helmet his full attention. He cleared the vegetation from around the base. The helmet was still attached to a breastplate. He dug into the muck. Shreds of rotting canvas could be seen fringing the outer rim of the breastplate.

Austin felt a chill that was not entirely due to the water temperature.

He unhooked a waterproof flashlight from his BC, snapped it on, and pointed the beam through the grate. Staring back at him were the empty eyes of a human skull.

Austin pondered his next move. Like most men who follow the sea, he had the deepest respect for watery graves. He could surface and report the find to the authorities. But the heavy hand of police divers could destroy whatever secrets the wreck might have yielded.

He wrapped his arms around the helmet and carefully wrestled it free. The skull dropped out of the bottom and landed upright. Austin took comfort in the fact that the dead diver was still grinning.

He avoided the baleful eye sockets and took a lift bag from a pouch. He tied the lines from the bag to the helmet's neck and inflated the lifter with air from his tank. He inflated his buoyancy compensator, grabbed the helmet, and slowly ascended to the surface.

Zavala had watched the primitive salvage effort on the ROV's monitor. He saw Austin's head pop up at the surface and threw him a line. Austin tied the line to the helmet so it wouldn't sink. He handed Zavala his air tank, weight belt, and fins, and then he climbed a ladder into the boat.

They bent their backs to the line and hauled the helmet onto the deck.

Austin pulled his hood off and knelt next to the helmet. "This is an old-timer," he said. "Probably been down there for years."

Zavala examined the air hose fitting and the ear plates and face-plates. He ran his fingers over the metal dome. "The workmanship is incredible. It's made of brass and copper." He tried to lift the helmet and the attached breastplate. "This baby must weigh more than fifty pounds. The guy who wore this thing must have been as tough as nails."

"Not tough enough," Austin said.

"I suspected that was the case," Zavala said with a glance over the side. "I wonder who he was."

Austin scraped growth away to reveal an oval piece of metal, engraved with the helmet's manufacturer, that was riveted to the front of the breastplate. The engraving said that the helmet had been made by the MORSE DIVING EQUIPMENT COMPANY, of Boston. Underneath the manufacturer's name was a serial number.

"Maybe this will tell us."

He used a cell phone to call the maritime history division at NUMA. He identified himself to a researcher, who said her name was Jennifer, and gave her the information from the manufacturer's plate. Jennifer asked for the numbers on the brail straps as well, and said she would run a search and call him back.

Zavala had returned to the ROV control and brought the vehicle back to the surface. He hoisted the compact vehicle out of the water, and Austin coiled the umbilical and laid it neatly on deck, which was when he noticed his stuff bag. He opened the bag and pulled out the tablet. It had been greenish gray under water, but it turned to more of a brown color as it dried. Several intersecting straight lines were incised about a half inch deep on one side. He handed it to Zavala.

"I found this near the helmet. I thought the lines were natural strata variations, but now I'm not so sure."

Zavala held the tablet at different angles to test the light on the surface. "These lines are too regular and deep to be natural," he said. "The parallel sides are perfectly even. Definitely man-made. How's your Phoenician?"

"Pretty rusty," Austin said. He retrieved the tablet and slipped it into the bag.

They reran the pictures taken by the ROV on its initial pass over the wreck and came up with a new estimate for the length of the ship. After his dive, Austin put it more at two hundred feet.

"One thing's sure," Zavala said. "This was no rowboat."

Austin's cell phone jingled.

"Looks like you snagged yourself a real prize," said Jennifer, the NUMA researcher. "You've got an authentic twelve-bolt, four-light navy MK diving helmet. Morse was a Boston brassware company that started fiddling around with helmet designs during the Civil War."

"This looks much newer," Austin said.

"It *is*. Your helmet was made in 1944. The MK design has been around since the turn of the century. They improved it through the years. It was a real workhorse for the navy, used for all submarine recovery work during World War Two."

"Does that mean it was last used during the war?"

"Not necessarily. Someone could have found it at a surplus warehouse or store. If it's in good shape, it could bring serious money on the collectors' market."

"Too bad we don't know who the owner is," Austin said.

"I can't tell you who the diver is, but I tapped into naval records and found out who used it during the war. Navy diver named Chester Hutchins. Navy records say he bought the helmet as surplus after the war. Hometown listed as Havre de Grace, Maryland."

Austin was familiar with the waterfront town near the mouth of the Susquehanna River. "I know the place. Thanks. Maybe his relatives still live there."

"At least one does. A Mrs. Chester Hutchins. Got a pen handy?"

Austin found a ballpoint in a box of spare parts and jotted the number down on the margin of the chart. He thanked Jennifer and relayed the information to Zavala.

"Sounds like a solid lead," he said.

"About as solid as they get," Austin said. He dialed the number. A woman answered the phone. Austin hesitated. He didn't want to give anyone a heart attack. But there was no gentle way to break the news.

He asked if she were related to Chester Hutchins.

"I am. I mean, I *was*. He's been dead for many years. Who is this, please?"

"My name is Kurt Austin, with the National Underwater and Marine Agency. A friend and I were diving on a wreck in the Chesapeake today and we found a diving helmet. We traced it to your husband."

"Dear God," she said. "After all this time."

"Would you like us to bring you the helmet, Mrs. Hutchins?"

"Please, yes. I'll give you my address."

They spoke a few more minutes before Austin hung up.

Zavala had been listening to the conversation. "Well?" he said.

Austin crooked his forefinger and thumb.

"Bingo," he said with a grin.

CHAPTER

37

CARINA FELT AS IF she were walking on clouds.

The lunch with two exhibition organizers in the Metropolitan Museum of Art garden café had gone far better than she had expected. Things were going her way. *Finally.*

The organizers had enthusiastically embraced her suggestion that the well-publicized theft of the *Navigator* would bring people into the museum. They could barely contain their excitement as she traced her long search for the statue, described the attempted theft and the successful one.

The organizers had tossed ideas back and forth like table tennis players and jotted notes down in their electronic organizers.

The *Navigator* would have its own room. It would be an exhibition within an exhibition, filled with giant *National Geographic* photographs of the statue being excavated in Syria. Photos of the Iraqi museum. The Egyptian Pyramids. The containership. The Smithsonian. All pieces of the puzzle. The centerpiece would be an empty stage, reserved for the statue, adding an air of mystery.

The exhibition's theme was a natural: *Missing.*

The show would be the supreme achievement in museum parlance. A *blockbuster.*

As Carina took the elevator down from the roof café she smiled inwardly. *Americans.* They may have their problems competing in a global economy, but they hadn't lost their ability to sell air.

The thought of Americans reminded her to call Austin.

She was tempted to explore some of the museum's impressive exhibitions, but a glance at her watch told her that the luncheon meeting had gone longer than expected.

She walked briskly through the Great Hall and out the main entrance. She stood between the tall columns at the top of the wide stairway that spilled down to Fifth Avenue and dug her cell phone out of her purse. She scrolled down but stopped short, as she remembered Austin throwing his phone into the Turkish sea.

Carina called directory assistance and asked for the main NUMA number. She was pleased when a real person answered the phone. Admiral Sandecker had hated automated voice mail, and NUMA was probably the only government agency in Washington that still used human telephone receptionists.

She left a message on Austin's answering machine, saying that she was about to take a cab to Penn Station and would call from the train or when she arrived in Washington. She left the same message at the boathouse. If they couldn't make contact, she would take a taxi to her hotel and wait for Austin to call.

As Carina made her phone calls, her every move was being watched from the front seat of a Yellow Cab parked near the museum's main entrance.

Keeping his eyes glued to his target, the driver spoke into a hand radio.

"Picking up fare at the Met."

Carina tucked the phone back into her purse and descended the stairs.

The taxi moved slowly forward, and the driver lit the roof sign switch to show that the cab was free. With precise timing, he stopped in front of Carina just as she reached the curb.

She couldn't believe her good luck.

Carina opened the door and got in the backseat. "Where to, ma'am?" the driver said over his shoulder.

"Penn Station, please."

The driver nodded and slid shut the plastic window divider that separated the front seat from the back. The cab pulled away and joined the busy traffic flow along Fifth Avenue. Carina gazed out the window at the street scene. New York was one of her favorite cities. She loved the city's energy, its culture and power, and its endless variety in people.

Sometimes she worried about her lack of a home base. She was a child of Europe and Africa, with a foot on each continent. Paris was where she lived and worked, but she spent more time on the road than at home. She looked forward to staying at Austin's boathouse again. She liked the fearless and handsome American, and envied the way he had balanced globe-trotting and home. She would have to talk to him about how he managed to achieve the best of both worlds.

Carina became aware of a sweet fragrance, as if a heavily perfumed woman had gotten into the car. The odor was making her giddy. She tried to open a window but the lever wouldn't work. The smell had grown in strength. She felt as if she were being smothered. She slid across the seat and tried the other window lever. Stuck.

She was becoming dizzy. She would pass out if she didn't get some fresh air. She knocked on the divider to get the driver's attention. He didn't respond. She glanced at the driver's ID card and thought that the photograph didn't match the driver's face. Her heartbeat accelerated, and she broke into a cold sweat.

Must . . . get . . . out.

She pounded with her fists on the plastic window. The driver glanced in the rearview mirror. She could see his eyes. Uncaring. The reflection in the mirror began to blur.

Her arms seemed made of lead. She was unable to lift her fists. She stretched out on the backseat, closed her eyes, and passed out.

The cabdriver looked in the mirror again. Satisfied that Carina was unconscious, he flicked a switch on the dashboard to shut off the gas flow to the backseat. He turned off Fifth Avenue and drove toward the Hudson River.

Minutes later, he drove the taxi up to a guardhouse at the entrance to a fenced-off area. The guard waved him through to a helipad at the edge of the river. Two tough-faced men stood near a helicopter whose rotors spun at a lazy speed.

The taxi parked next to the helicopter. The men opened the doors to the backseat, extracted Carina's limp body, and loaded her on the helicopter.

One man got into the pilot's seat and the other sat next to Carina holding a canister, ready to administer another whiff of knockout gas if she started to regain consciousness.

The rotors began to spin into a blur. The helicopter lurched, then lifted off the pavement. Within moments, it was only a speck in the sky.

I AM HAPPY NO PLACE ELSE," Gamay said, quoting from the guidebook. "Jefferson was unequivocal about his love for Monticello."

"Do you *blame* him?" Paul pointed through the windshield toward the familiar columned portico and rotunda on a distant hill high above the green rolling Virginia countryside.

It had been at least a year since the Trouts had last visited Jefferson's fabled retreat on one of the back-road motor treks they enjoyed in their Humvee. Paul usually drove. Gamay navigated and provided local color, drawing on a pile of guidebooks to recite little known facts. *Ad nauseam.*

"*Aha!*" Angela said.

Trout winced. Angela, who was sitting in the backseat, was proving to be Gamay's equal in travel trivia. Since leaving Georgetown that morning, the two women had been taking turns reciting facts and factoids about Jefferson and Monticello.

"Too late," Paul said in an attempt to cut the young woman off at the pass. "We're here."

"This is *important,*" Angela said. She had her nose buried in a

thick paperback entitled *The Life and Times of Thomas Jefferson.*
"This deals with the Jefferson material that was stolen on the riverboat trip to Monticello."

Trout's ears perked up. "Read on."

Angela didn't have to be prodded. "Jefferson is writing to his
friend Dr. Benjamin Barton about the loss of his Indian vocabularies. Barton was a naturalist, and a member of the Philosophical
Society. Jefferson calls the theft an 'irreparable misfortune.' Over
thirty years, he had collected fifty Indian vocabularies, but had put
off printing them because he hadn't digested the stuff Lewis had
collected. He thought some of the Indian words were common to
Russian. He retrieved a few pages from the river, including some
Pani Indian words Lewis collected, 'and a little fragment of some
other,' which I see is in his handwriting, but no indication remains
of what language it is."

"I wonder if those fragments are similar to the words identified
on the map as Phoenician," Gamay said.

"Possible," Paul said. "Maybe Jefferson wrote to Lewis and told
him about the Phoenician words on the map. Lewis recognized the
words as being similar to some other stuff he had collected in his
travels but not given to Jefferson."

"Why would he hold the material back?" Gamay said.

"He didn't recognize their significance. After he got the missive
from his old boss, he dropped everything and headed for Monticello
with something he wanted to show Jefferson."

"That means the map is quite significant," Gamay said. "It makes
the Phoenician connection, and shows the location of Ophir."

"Tantalizing, but useless without more information," Trout said
with a shake of his head. "A compass rose. Measure of distance.
Landmarks. Data like that would help."

Angela opened her briefcase, rummaged through the Jefferson

file, and pulled out the page with the squiggles, dots, and Phoenician words.

She waved the paper in the air. "We all agree that some of the details of the map are cut off," she said.

"That's right," Paul said. "It appears to be part of a larger diagram."

"If that's true," Gamay said with growing excitement, "it's possible that what Lewis was carrying to Jefferson was the other half of the map. Lewis supposedly found a gold mine on his Pacific expedition."

"Wow!" Angela said. "That means if our theory about the young slave holds true, Jefferson *knew* where the Ophir mine was."

"Hold on a second," Paul said with a grin. "We may have given you the wrong impression. Gamay and I tend to toss ideas around, but we can't forget we're scientists. That means we operate on the basis of *fact*. We're making guesses based on assumptions that haven't been proven."

Angela looked crestfallen. Gamay tried to cheer the young researcher. "You'll have to admit it's an exciting suggestion, Paul, even with all the questions."

"I'd be the first to agree that it is plausible," Paul said. "Maybe we'll start to find the answers here."

He pulled the Humvee into a parking lot next to the Jefferson Library, an imposing, two-and-a-half-story, white-clapboard building about a half mile to the east of Monticello's main entrance. They went into the lobby, gave the receptionist their names, and asked to see the archivist they had talked to on the phone. A few minutes later, a tall man in a tan suit strode into the lobby and extended his hand.

"Nice to meet you," he said with a broad smile. Speaking in a soft-edged Virginia drawl, he said, "My name is Charles Emerson. Jason Parker, the archivist you talked to, referred your query to me. Welcome to the Jefferson Library."

Emerson had a deep voice and the courtly manners of a Southern gentleman. His mahogany skin was virtually unlined, except for laugh crinkles at the corners of his eyes. He filled his suit with the sturdy physique of a believer in exercise, but the steel gray color of his hair suggested he could be in his sixties.

Gamay introduced Paul and Angela. "Thank you for seeing us," she said.

"No problem. Jason told me that you're with National Underwater and Marine Agency?"

"Paul and I work for NUMA. Miss Worth here is a researcher with the American Philosophical Society."

Emerson raised an eyebrow. "I'm *honored*. NUMA's accomplishments are well known. The Philosophical Society is one of this country's scholarly jewels."

"Thank you," Angela glanced around the lobby. "Your library is pretty impressive as well."

"We're very proud of our building," Emerson said. "It cost five and a half million dollars to build, and opened in 2002. We have shelf space for twenty-eight thousand volumes, and all sorts of reading and multimedia areas. I'll give you a tour."

Emerson showed them the library reading and research areas and then led the way to his spacious office. He invited his visitors to take a seat and settled behind a big oak desk.

"I'm not sure how the library can help you folks from NUMA," he said. "The Virginia hills are pretty far from the ocean."

"We noticed," Gamay said with a smile. "But you may have more to offer than you think. Meriwether Lewis led an expedition to the Pacific Ocean on the orders of Thomas Jefferson."

If Emerson thought the explanation was wide of the mark, he didn't show it. "Meriwether Lewis," he said thoughtfully. "A fascinating man."

Angela couldn't contain herself. "Actually, we're more interested in his servant. A young man named Zeb Moses, who was with Lewis when he died."

"Jason said you asked about Zeb when you called. It's the reason he turned your query over to me. Zeb was an amazing man. Born into slavery. Worked at Monticello nearly his entire life. Died in his nineties, having lived long enough to read the Emancipation Proclamation."

"You sound pretty knowledgeable about him," Paul said.

Emerson smiled. "I *should* be. Zeb Moses was my ancestor."

"That's a wonderful coincidence," Paul said. "It makes you the perfect person to answer a question that's been nagging us."

"I'll do my best. Ask away."

"Do you know how Zeb obtained his free slave status so soon after arriving at Monticello?"

Paul had a habit when deep in thought of inclining his head slightly and blinking his large brown eyes as if he were peering over the tops of invisible glasses. It was a deceptive idiosyncrasy that sometimes caught people off guard. Emerson was no exception.

He seemed to lose possession of his bland expression of geniality for an instant. His smile melted into a half frown, but he quickly recovered. He snapped the ends of his lips up in a broad grin.

"As I said, my ancestor was a remarkable individual. How did you learn that Zeb was a freeman?"

"We checked the Monticello database," Paul said. "The word 'free' is written next to Zeb's name in Jefferson's handwriting."

"Well, Jefferson *did* free some of his slaves," Emerson said.

"Not very many," Angela said. "Jefferson had his reservations about slavery, but your own website says he always owned at least two hundred at a time. He sold more than a hundred, gave away eighty-five to his family. He only freed five of them in his will, and three of them, including your ancestor, while he was still alive."

Emerson laughed. "Remind me not to cross intellectual swords with you, young lady. You're absolutely right. But it goes to show that he *did* free slaves, although that was, regrettably, infrequent."

"Which brings us back to my question," Paul said. "Why was Zeb freed and given a preferred house job so soon after joining the workforce at Monticello?"

Emerson leaned back in his chair and tented his fingers. "I haven't a clue. Do you folks have any idea why?"

Paul turned to Angela. He wanted to make up for the scientific lecture he'd given the young woman. "Miss Worth can explain."

Angela jumped in. "We believe that Lewis was on a secret mission to deliver important information to Jefferson. Lewis was murdered because of it, but Zeb Moses traveled to Monticello to complete the mission. Jefferson rewarded Zeb with a job and freedom."

"That's quite a tale," Emerson said with a shake of his head that implied skepticism without being rude. "What sort of information could have been entrusted to young Zeb?"

Gamay didn't want to tip their hand. She interjected before Angela could answer. "We think it was a map."

"A map of what?"

"We have no idea."

"That's a new one to me," Emerson said. "Tell you what, though. I'll look into it. You've got me really intrigued. I never dreamed Zeb was involved in cloak-and-dagger machinations." He glanced at his watch and rose from his chair. "I'll have to apologize for cutting short this fascinating discussion but I have an appointment with a potential donor."

"We understand completely," Paul said. "We appreciate your time."

"Not at all," Emerson said as he showed his guests to the door.

Emerson may have been through but Angela wasn't.

"Oh, I almost forgot, Mr. Emerson," she said. "Have you ever heard of Jefferson's Artichoke Society?"

Emerson stopped with his hand on the doorknob. "No," he said. "Never. Something to do with gardening?"

"Maybe," Angela said with a shrug of her shoulders.

"I'll have to look that that subject up too."

Emerson watched from the entrance as his visitors got into the Humvee and drove off. His face wore an expression of utmost concern.

He walked briskly back to his office and punched in a number on the phone.

A man's voice answered. Dry and brittle. "Good morning, Charles. How are you today?"

"I've been better. The people who called yesterday and inquired about Zeb Moses just left the library. A couple from NUMA and a young woman from the Philosophical Society."

"I take it that you used your well-developed conversational skills to put them off."

"I thought I was doing well until the young woman asked me about the Artichoke Society."

For several seconds there was only silence at the other end, then the cold dry voice said: "We had better call a meeting of the others."

"I'll get right on it," Emerson said.

He hung up and stared into space for a moment, and then he snapped to attention and punched in the first of a list of phone numbers from memory.

As he waited for the first person to answer, an image materialized in his mind's eye. It was a giant ball of yarn unraveling.

"FIRST IMPRESSIONS," Paul said as they drove past Monticello.

"Smooth, but not entirely forthcoming," Gamay said.

"He's hiding something," Angela agreed.

"I was watching his reaction when you mentioned the Artichoke Society," Paul said. "Classic deer caught in the headlights."

"I noticed that too," Gamay said. "Angela's question definitely got his attention. Maybe we should dig deeper into this little society. Anyone know an expert on artichokes?"

Angela said. "I know someone who's researching a book about artichokes. I'll give him a call."

Stocker was at home and delighted to hear from Angela. "Are you okay? I heard about the murder at the library and tried to call you at home."

"I'm fine. I'll tell you about it later. I have a favor to ask. In your research, did you ever come across any mention of something called the Artichoke Society?"

"Jefferson's secret club?"

"That's the one. What do you know about it?"

"I found mention of it in an article on secret societies at the University of Virginia. I didn't follow through because it didn't seem like a big deal."

"Do you know who wrote the article?"

"A professor at UVA. I'll give you his name and number."

She jotted the information down, told Stocker she would be in touch, and relayed her findings to the Trouts. Gamay wasted no time getting the professor on the phone.

"Good news," she said after hanging up. "The professor would be glad to see us between classes, but we'll have to hurry."

Trout pressed the accelerator and the wide-bodied vehicle picked up speed.

"Next stop, University of Virginia."

39

THE WIDOW OF THE DEAD wreck diver lived in a square, three-story house that may have once been elegant before years of neglect took a toll. The antique yellow paint was flaked and peeling. Shutters hung off at drunken angles. The air of dilapidation stopped at the freshly mowed front lawn and the neat flower beds along the foundation.

Austin pressed the front doorbell. Hearing no chimes, he rapped his knuckles on the door. No one answered. He knocked as loud as he could without breaking the door down.

"Coming!" A white-haired woman emerged from around a corner of the house. "Sorry," she said with a bright smile. "I was out in the garden."

"Mrs. Hutchins?" Austin said.

"Call me Thelma."

She brushed the dirt off her hands and extended one to Austin and then to Zavala. Her palm was calloused and her grip surprisingly firm.

Austin and Zavala introduced themselves.

She narrowed her flinty blue eyes in a squint. "You didn't tell me when you called that you were good-looking," Thelma said with a grin. "I would have gussied up instead of looking like an old mud hen. So you found Hutch's helmet."

Austin pointed to the Cherokee parked in front of the house. "It's in the back of the Jeep."

Thelma strode purposely down the walk and opened the car's hatch. The marine vegetation had been removed, and the brass and copper gleamed in the sunlight.

Thelma caressed the top of the helmet with her fingers. "That's Hutch's brain bucket, all right," she said, brushing a tear from her eye. "Is he still down there?"

Austin remembered the grinning skull. "I'm afraid so. Do you want us to notify the Coast Guard so they can bring his remains up for burial?"

Thelma said, "Let the old coot be. They'd plant his bones in the ground. He'd hate that. I've had two husbands since then, bless their hearts, but Hutch was the first and the best. I couldn't do that to him. C'mon out back. We'll have our own memorial service."

Austin exchanged an amused glance with Zavala. Thelma Hutchins was not the frail old lady they had expected. She was a tall woman, with erect posture and little of the shoulder stoop that often comes with age. Her walk was brisk rather than doddering as she led Austin and Zavala to a weathered wooden table under a fading CINZANO umbrella. Thelma said she'd be right back.

The house looked even worse from the rear, but the yard was as neat as a putting green. There were flower beds everywhere, and a healthy vegetable garden big enough to feed an army of vegans. A slob of a Labrador retriever came over and drooled on Austin's knee.

Thelma came out of the house carrying three bottles of beer and apologized for the cheap brand.

"I'll start drinking Stella Artois when they increase my Social Security. This panther piss will have to do for now." She glanced at the dog. "I see you've met Lush." She poured some beer into a dish and grinned as the dog trotted over and lapped up the foaming brew. Then she raised her bottle. "Here's to Hutch. I knew someone would find the old pirate after all these years."

They clinked bottles and took a swig.

"How long has your husband been gone?" Austin said.

"My *first* husband." She slugged down a swallow of beer and pursed her lips. "Hutch croaked in the spring of 1973. Where'd you find him?"

Austin unfolded the chart he had brought and pointed to a penciled-in X.

"*Damn!*" Thelma said. "That's miles from where I thought the treasure wreck was."

"Treasure wreck?" Zavala said.

"That's what Hutch called it, the fool. It's what killed him."

"Can you tell us what happened?" Austin said.

A far-off look came to her eyes. "My husband was born and raised on the bay. He enlisted in the navy during World War Two and became a diver. A darn good one, from what I hear. He bought out his equipment when the war ended. We got married, and he did some commercial diving on the side to keep his hand in. Mostly, he ran a fishing boat, which is how he found the wreck. Snagged it on a net. The wreck really stumped him."

"Why is that, Thelma?" Austin said.

"Hutch knew every wreck in the area. He'd dived on a number of them. He was an amateur historian. He did a pile of research. There was no record of any ship going down at this location."

"He never told you where the wreck was?" Zavala said.

"My husband was as tight as a Chesapeake oyster. He was real old-fashioned. Thought women were natural gossips. He said he would tell once he brought up some gold for me."

"What made him think there was gold on the wreck?" Austin said.

"Lots of people don't know that there were gold mines all around here at one time. Maryland. Virginia. Up into Pennsylvania."

"It's not surprising. I only learned last year that the area around the Chesapeake was major gold-mining country," Austin said. "I came across a Gold Mine Café in Maryland and found out it was named after a defunct mine nearby."

"Your husband guessed that some of that gold found its way onto the ship?" Zavala said.

"It was more than a guess, Handsome." She tugged at the chain around her neck. Hanging from the chain was a gold pendant in the shape of a horse head. "He found this on his first dive. Gave it to me with the promise of more." She sighed heavily. "Oh, Hutch," she said. "You were worth more to me than any treasure."

"Sorry to bring these memories back," Austin said.

The bright smile came back. "Don't worry, Kurt. I apologize for losing it."

Zavala had a question. "Kurt and I had some trouble hoisting the helmet out of the water. It's even heavier with the breastplate attached. I was wondering how your husband got in and out of his diving rig on his own."

"Oh, he wasn't alone. He was working with a crewman named Tom Lowry when he found the wreck, so he had to bring him in on the secret. Tom became his dive tender. Hutch promised to split anything they found fifty-fifty."

"Is Tom still alive?" Austin said.

"The wreck killed him too," Thelma said. "Coast Guard figured that Hutch ran into trouble below. Maybe his air hose got tangled. Tom was as strong as an ox but one beer short of a six-pack, if you catch my drift. He was intensely loyal to Hutch. My guess is that he dove over the side without thinking, got into trouble, and drowned."

"Wouldn't the Coast Guard have found the boat anchored at the wreck?" Austin said.

"A squall came up. The boat broke free and floated away. Tom's body and the boat were found miles from the dive site. I sold the boat to one of Hutch's friends, whom I later married."

"Did you ever tell anyone about the treasure?"

She gave a vigorous shake of her head. "Not even the Coast Guard. That bad-luck wreck already killed two men. I didn't want to make a widow out of myself or any other woman in town."

"How many dives did Hutch make?" Zavala said.

"He went out twice." She fingered the chain around her neck. "The first time, he found the pendant. The second time, he must have dove again after he found that jar."

Austin put his beer down. "What jar is that, Thelma?"

"An old clay thing. Kinda green and gray, sealed at the top. I found it in a boat storage bin where Hutch and Tom must have put it. Still covered with seaweed. It was too light to contain gold, but I never had any desire to open it. I figured more bad luck would come pouring out. Just like Pandora."

"May we see the jar?" Austin said.

Thelma looked embarrassed. "I wish you had come earlier. I gave it away a couple of days ago to a guy who stopped by. Said he was writing a book and heard scuttlebutt around town about Hutch and his wreck. When I told him about the jar, he asked if he could borrow and have it X-rayed. I said he could have it."

"Was his name Saxon?" Austin said.

"That's right. Tony Saxon. Good-looking guy, but not as handsome as you. Do you know him?"

"Slightly," Austin said with a rueful grin. "Did he say where he was staying?"

"Nope," she said after a moment's thought. "I didn't give away anything valuable, did I? This house needs lots of work."

"Probably not," Austin said. "But the helmet is yours, and it's worth a lot of money."

"Enough to get this old joint fixed up and painted?" she said.

"You might even have enough left over for a couple of cases of Stella Artois," Austin said.

He declined the offer of another beer to celebrate. He and Zavala carried the helmet from the Jeep and set it in the living room. Austin told Thelma that he would have a nautical appraiser get in touch with her. She thanked them both with a peck on the cheek.

Austin was about to get into the Jeep when he saw a slip of paper wrapped around the windshield wiper. He unrolled the paper and read the message written in ballpoint.

Dear Kurt. Sorry about the amphora. I'll be at the Tidewater Grill until 6 p.m. I'll buy the drinks. AS

Austin handed the note to Zavala, who read it and smiled.

"Your friend says he's buying," Zavala said, getting into the Jeep. "Doesn't get any better than that."

Austin slipped behind the steering wheel and drove toward the waterfront. He'd seen the sign for the Tidewater on the way into town and remembered how to find the restaurant that overlooked the bay. He and Zavala stepped into the bar and found Saxon engaged in a discussion about fishing with the bartender. He smiled when he saw Austin and introduced himself to Zavala. He suggested a locally brewed ale. They carried their mugs to a corner table.

Austin was a hard loser but not a sore one. He lifted his mug in toast.

"Congratulations, Saxon. How did you do it?"

Saxon took a sip of ale and wiped the foam from his mustache.

"Shoe leather and luck," he said. "I've been meaning to focus on this area. I turned my attention from the west coast of North America to the east after my replica was torched."

"Why do you think it was arson?" Austin said.

"A few days before the fire, I got an offer to buy the boat from a broker. I said the replica was a scientific project and not for sale. Later that week, the boat was set on fire."

"Who was the buyer?"

"You met him at the unveiling of the *Navigator*. Viktor Baltazar."

Austin recalled the angry look in Saxon's eye when Baltazar had entered the Smithsonian warehouse.

"Tell us how you were drawn to the Chesapeake," Austin said.

"I've always considered the Chesapeake region a remote possibility for Ophir because of the gold mines in the area. The Susquehanna has intrigued me as well. A number of years ago, some tablets with possible Phoenician writing were found up the river in Mechanicsburg, Pennsylvania."

"What led you to Thelma Hutchins?"

"After the *Navigator* was stolen, I was devastated. I didn't know what to do, so I came here and haunted dive shops and historical societies. Thelma's husband, or, more likely, his crewman, may have spilled the beans to someone. I began to pick up rumors of a treasure wreck. I heard about Thelma and tracked her down. She suggested I take the amphora. She succumbed to my charm, obviously."

"Obviously," Austin said. "How did you find us?"

"If NUMA wants to remain inconspicuous, I suggest that you paint your vehicles a less-distinctive color than that wonderful turquoise. I was on my way to a late breakfast and saw your car. I followed you to the boatyard, watched you unload your gear, staked out your car, and trailed you to Thelma's house. Now, may I ask you a question? How did *you* learn of the wreck?"

Austin told Saxon about the duplicate *Navigator* in Turkey and the map engraved on the statue.

Saxon chortled. "A bloody cat! I always suspected that there was more than one statue. Possibly a pair guarding a temple."

"Solomon's temple?" Austin said, recalling his conversation with Nickerson.

"Quite likely." Saxon furrowed his brow. "I wonder why the people who stole the original statue haven't tracked down the wreck."

"Maybe they are not as smart as we are," Austin said. "You've got the amphora. What do you plan to do with it?"

"I've opened the amphora. I'm studying its content."

"You didn't waste any time. What was in it?"

"The answer depends on you, Kurt. I'm hoping we can work out an arrangement. I could use NUMA's resources. I'm not interested in gold or treasure. Only knowledge. I want to find Sheba more than anything else. I readily admit that I am truly obsessed with the lady."

Austin drew his lips down in a deep frown and turned to Zavala. "Think we should make a deal with this slippery character?"

"Hell, Kurt, you know what a sucker I am for romance. He's got my vote."

Austin had already made up his mind. NUMA's help would be a small price to pay for Saxon's expertise. He admired the man's ingenuity and perseverance as well.

He leveled a steady gaze at Saxon. "I'll make it unanimous, on two conditions."

Saxon's face fell. "What's your first condition?"

"That you tell me what you found in the amphora."

"I found a papyrus," Saxon said. "Condition number two?"

"That you buy another round."

"Egad! Austin. You are a hard man to take advantage of someone so desperate," Saxon said, twirling the end of his mustache.

Then he grinned, called over to the bartender, and held three fingers in the air.

CHAPTER

40

BALTAZAR'S VALET MADE HIS WAY along the dark-paneled corridor and stopped at a thick oak door. Balancing a tray on one hand, he knocked softly. No one answered. His lips parted in a faint smile. He knew Carina was in the room because he had carried her unconscious body there from the helicopter.

The valet dug a key out of his pocket, unlocked the door, and pushed it open.

Carina was standing across the threshold, her face contorted in a mask of fury. She clutched the heavy brass base of a shadeless table lamp in two hands as if it was a war club. She had been prepared to crown the first person she saw. She hadn't expected someone holding a fine china teapot and cup on tray.

Without lowering the lamp, she demanded: "Who undressed me?"

The valet said, "A female member of the house staff. Your clothes were being washed. Mr. Baltazar felt you would be more comfortable wearing something clean in the meantime."

"You can tell Mr. Baltazar that I want my clothes back right away."

"You can tell him yourself," the valet said. "He's waiting for you in the garden. No hurry, he says. Come when you feel up to it. May I set this tray down?"

Carina glared at the man, but she stepped aside and let him into the bedroom. He put the tray down on an end table. Keeping his eye on the lamp, he backed out of the room, leaving the door open.

Carina had awakened minutes before to find herself in a strange bed. She remembered the sweet smell in the back of the taxi. She had thrown the covers off and discovered she was clad only in her underwear. She searched around the luxurious bedroom for her clothes. All she found, hanging in a closet, was a long white cotton shift with a scoop neck.

Holding the shift in her hand, she had glanced around. Except for the bars on the windows, the chamber was like a bedroom in a fine hotel. She went over to a window and was looking out at a manicured lawn when she heard the knock. She had thrown the shift on and grabbed the lamp.

After the valet left, she stepped out into the corridor and watched him disappear down another corridor. She went back into the bedroom and slammed the door behind her. Her hands were trembling with tension. She set the lamp down, settled into a plush chair, and began to cry.

The inner anger that had given her the courage to prepare for an assault on the valet had ebbed. She wiped her eyes and went into the bathroom, where she washed her face and combed her disheveled hair. She took a deep gulp of tea, stepped out into the corridor, and followed in the valet's footsteps to a set of open patio doors. She stepped out into brilliant sunshine and looked around. She was in a courtyard garden. Water bubbled in a fountain whose centerpiece was a nude woman surrounded by naked cherubs. But her eyes went to Baltazar, who was clipping flowers from one of the beds that ringed the fountain.

Baltazar was dressed casually in white slacks and a black short-sleeve shirt. He wore espadrilles, rope sandals, on his feet. He smiled as she entered the courtyard and stepped over to offer her the bouquet of flowers.

Carina folded her arms. "I don't want your flowers. Where am I?"

He lowered the bouquet and set it down on a marble bench. "You are my guest, Miss Mechadi."

"I don't *want* to be your guest. I insist that you release me."

Still smiling, Baltazar gazed at Carina as if he were a butterfly collector who had captured a rare specimen. "Imperious. Commanding. Much as I would expect from the Mekada line."

The answer confused Carina. Her anger gave way to confusion. "What are you talking about?"

"I'll offer a proposition." He gestured toward a round marble table with service settings for two. Join me for a drink and tapas, and I will tell you the story."

Carina glanced around the garden. A couple of men dressed in black uniforms stood near a door that might have led out of the courtyard. Escape was impossible. Even if she made it out of this place, then what? She had no idea where she was. It would be better to bide her time. She walked over and sat at the table with her back rigid.

The valet magically appeared with a pitcher and filled their water glasses. Several dishes followed. Carina planned to pick at them rather than accept Baltazar's hospitality, but she discovered that she was famished. She ate what was in front of her, rationalizing that she would need her strength. She didn't touch the rosé wine. She wanted to have a clear head to deal with what might lie ahead.

Baltazar seemed to be reading her thoughts. He was a shrewd judge of character, and made no conversation during the meal other than to ask if the food was to her liking. When she had enough, she drained her water glass and pushed her dish away.

"I have fulfilled my part of the proposition," she said.

"So you have." Baltazar nodded. "Now I will fulfill mine. The story begins three thousand years ago with Solomon."

"*King* Solomon?"

"The one and only. The son of David, king of the lands that include what we now know as Israel. According to biblical references, Solomon receives a visit from the queen of a place called Sheba. She has heard of Solomon's wisdom and is curious. When she arrives, she is impressed not only with his wisdom but by his wealth. They become smitten with each other. He even writes a series of erotic poems that some believe were to her, at least in part."

"Song of Songs," Carina said.

"That's right. The woman in the poems introduces herself: "I am black, but beautiful, daughters of Jerusalem.""

"She came from Africa," Carina said.

"That seems to be the case. Her mention in the Bible is a brief one. The Koran expands on the story, and the Arab and later medieval chroniclers picked up the thread. Sheba and Solomon are married; she bears him a son, and then returns to her homeland. He has many wives, concubines, and children. She becomes even more powerful and wealthy."

"And the son?"

"The legend says he returns to Africa and reigns as a king."

"A lovely fairy tale," Carina said. "*Now* may I be allowed to dispense with your hospitality and leave this place?"

"But that's only the first part of the story," Baltazar said. "The liaison between Solomon and Sheba's handmaiden also produces a son. He dies at an early age, but his progeny live on. They move to Cyprus, where they establish a shipbuilding business, and make contact with the Fourth Crusaders. They move to Western Europe after the sack of Constantinople and take a Spanish name."

"Baltazar," Carina said.

"Correct. Unfortunately, I am the last remaining male descendant of the Baltazars. When I die, the family dies with me."

And none too soon, Carina thought. She let out an unladylike laugh. "Are you saying that you are descended from Solomon?"

"Yes, Miss Mechadi. And so are you."

"You are far more insane than I have imagined, Baltazar."

"Before you pronounce judgments on my sanity, hear me out. The son of Solomon and Sheba became king of Ethiopia. His family ruled for centuries."

"I was born in Italy, but my mother told me the story of King Menelik of Ethiopia. What of it?"

"Then you know about the *Kebra Nagast*. The holy document tells the story of Sheba and Menelik."

Carina was on less sure ground. "I've heard the name, but I have never read it. I was raised Roman Catholic."

"The *Kebra Nagast* was supposedly found in the third century A.D., in the Santa Sophia library of Constantinople. It may have been written later, but that doesn't matter. If you had read it, you would know that the book tells the story of Solomon and Mekada, Queen of Sheba. I submitted Mechadi to an expert in onamastics, the study of names. Verified that your family name is derived from *Mekada*."

"That proves nothing! That would mean every boy named Jesus or Christian can claim ties to the Messiah."

"I would agree with you, except for one thing. The cup you drank from when you had the *Navigator* on display contained traces of your DNA. I had the samples analyzed by three different laboratories so there would be no doubt. The results were the same in all instances. Your DNA, and mine, both contained the same DNA. I believe it goes back to Solomon. You through Sheba. I through her handmaiden. I'll have the lab results sent to your room and you can see them for yourself."

"Laboratory reports can be forged."

"That's true. But these were not." He smiled again. "So don't consider this an incarceration. It is more of a family reunion. At our first meeting you said you'd like to have dinner with me. We dine at six."

As Baltazar walked away, Carina called out: "Wait!"

Baltazar was unused to commands. He turned and a flicker of anger flashed across his face. "Yes, Miss Mechadi?"

She plucked at her gown. If Baltazar thought she was descended from a queen, she would act like one. "This is not to my liking. I want my own clothes back."

He nodded. "I'll have them sent to your room."

Then he walked away and disappeared through one of the doorways into the house.

Carina stood in stunned silence, unsure of what to do. The valet came out and as he cleared the dishes, he said, "Mr. Baltazar says you are free to return to your room."

The reminder that she was a prisoner shocked her out of her trance.

She spun on her heel and strode through the door, down the corridor and into her room. What had been a prison a short while earlier now seemed a safe haven.

She shut the door and leaned against it, shutting her eyes tight, as if by doing so she could transport herself to another place.

There was no way she shared the same blood with that repellent snake of a man.

His mere presence revolted and frightened her.

But even more frightening was the possibility that his story was true.

CHAPTER

41

PROFESSOR MCCULLOUGH GREETED HIS VISITORS on the steps of the University of Virginia rotunda, the domed, red-brick building based on the Jefferson designs that echoed Monticello and the Pantheon in Rome. The professor suggested a stroll along the tree-bordered cloisters whose columns enclosed the great terraced lawn.

"I can give you twenty minutes before I have to scoot off to my ethics class," said the professor, a big, heavyset man whose full gray beard resembled a clump of Spanish moss. His cheeks were apple red, and he effected a rolling gait more like a retired merchant seaman than an academic. "I've got to tell you, I was intrigued when you called and asked about the Artichoke Society."

"It's apparently something of an enigma," Gamay said as they strolled past the pavilions that framed the green space.

McCullough stopped in midstep. "It's a *mystery,* all right," he said with a shake of his head. "I stumbled on it while I was preparing a paper on the ethics of belonging to a secret society."

"Interesting topic," Paul said.

"I thought so. You don't have to be part of a conspiracy to take over the world to have your ethics questioned. Even membership in the *innocent* organizations can present undesirable potentials. Exclusiveness. Them versus us. The strange rituals and symbols. The elitism. The *quid pro quo* among members. The belief that only *they* know the truth. Many are male-only. Some countries, like Poland, for instance, have banned secret societies. At one end of the spectrum, you've got frat houses; at the other, you've got Nazis."

"What got you interested in secret societies?" Paul asked.

McCullough continued on his stroll. "The University of Virginia is famous for its covert ops. We've got nearly two dozen secret societies on the campus. And those are the ones I *know* about."

"I've read about the Seven Society," said Angela, who seemed to have an inexhaustible supply of arcane information at her fingertips.

"Oh, yes. The Sevens are so secret that we know someone has been a member only when he dies and his obit appears in the campus publications. His grave will be adorned with a black magnolia wreath in the shape of the numeral seven. The university chapel bell tower chimes every seven seconds for seven minutes on the seventh dissonant chord."

"Was Jefferson a member of any of these groups?" Gamay said.

"He joined the Flat Hat Society when he attended William and Mary. It became the Flat Hat Club later on."

"Unusual name?" Gamay said.

"In the old days, students wore mortarboard caps all the time, not just at graduation."

"Like Harry Potter," Angela said.

McCullough chuckled at the allusion. "No Hogwarts that I know of, but the Flat Hats had a secret handshake. They used to meet and talk on a regular basis. Jefferson admitted, in his words, that the society had 'no useful object.' "

Gamay steered the professor back on topic.

"Could you tell us what you know about the Artichoke Society?" she said.

"Sorry for going off on a tangent. I was researching my paper in the university library and came across an old newspaper article. A reporter claimed that as he rode up to the mansion hoping for an interview with the ex-president, he had seen John Adams getting out of a carriage in front of Monticello."

"A reunion of the Founding Fathers?" Paul said.

"The reporter couldn't believe his eyes. He went to the door of the mansion and talked to Jefferson himself. Jefferson said the reporter was mistaken. He had seen a local plantation owner who had come by to discuss new crops. Asked what kind of crops, Jefferson smiled and said, 'Artichokes.' He reported the conversation, noting that Jefferson's friend *looked* like Adams."

"Who first suggested that the Artichoke Society actually existed?" Angela asked.

"I'm afraid *I'm* the culprit." McCullough had a sheepish expression on his ruddy face.

"I don't understand," Gamay said.

"I did a 'What if?' Suppose there *had* been a meeting as described. Why would the Founding Fathers get together? Travel wasn't easy back then. I wrote a humorous article for a university publication based on the story and the UVA penchant for secret societies. I had pretty much forgotten about it when your writer friend called last week. He had come across a Jefferson paper on artichokes at the American Philosophical Society. A Google search turned up my article."

"Angela works for the Philosophical Society," Gamay said. "She's the one who discovered the paper."

"Quite a coincidence," McCullough said. "I told Mr. Nickerson the same thing."

"Who is Mr. Nickerson?" Gamay said.

"He said he was with the State Department. He's a Jefferson history buff, and he had read my article, wondered what else I knew. He was going to look into it, but he never got back to me. Stocker called last week. Then you." He checked his watch. "Damn. This is fascinating stuff, but it's almost class time."

Paul handed him a business card. "Please give us a call if you think of anything else."

"I will."

"Thanks for your help," Gamay said. "We won't delay you any longer."

McCullough shook hands all around and rolled off to his class.

PAUL WATCHED the professor make his way across the lawn.

"In the file Kurt sent us at Woods Hole, he mentioned that he had been asked to look into the Phoenician puzzle by a State Department guy named Nickerson. He met him on an old Potomac River yacht."

"I recall the name. Think it's the same person?"

Paul shrugged and flipped open his cell phone. He scrolled down the index until he found the number of a State Department staffer he had worked with on ocean jurisdiction issues. Moments later, he hung up.

"Nickerson is an undersecretary. My pal at Foggy Bottom doesn't know him personally but says Nickerson is an insider and a survivor. He's considered brilliant but eccentric, and he lives on an antique yacht on the Potomac. He gave me the name of the marina but not the yacht. How about making a quick stop along the Potomac on the way home?"

"Wouldn't it be easier if we knew the boat's name?" Angela said.

"If we liked doing things the easy way, we wouldn't be working for NUMA," Paul said.

✦ ✦ ✦

THE SEARCH FOR Nickerson's boat was tougher than the Trouts had anticipated.

A number of boats could have qualified as old, but only one—a white-hulled motor cruiser named *Lovely Lady*—that fit the bill as an antique.

Paul got out of the SUV and went over to the boat. The deck was deserted, and there didn't seem to be any signs of life on board. He walked up the boarding plank and called hello a couple of times.

No one answered from the yacht, but a man popped his head out of a cabin cruiser in the next slip.

"Nick's not on board," he said. "Took off awhile ago."

Paul thanked him and headed back to the car. On the way, he glanced at the boat's name again and noticed that the transom was whiter than the rest of the hull. He went back to Nickerson's neighbor and asked if the yacht's name had been changed.

"As a matter of fact, it has," the man said.

Minutes later, Paul slid behind the steering wheel. "No Nickerson," he said.

"I saw you checking out the boat's name," Gamay said.

"Just curious. Nickerson's neighbor said the yacht used to be called *Thistle*."

Angela's ears perked up. "Are you *sure*?"

"Yes. Why?"

"Artichokes."

"Come again?" Trout said.

"It's something I came across when I was pulling files for my writer friend. The globe artichoke is a *thistle*."

42

S AXON UNLOCKED THE DOOR to his rented cottage near the bay and snapped the light on. Flashing a toothy grin, he said: "Welcome to the Saxon archaeological conservation lab."

The chairs and sofa in the musty living room had been pushed back against the walls to make space for a plastic trash barrel and two folding picnic tables set up end to end. Stacked on the tables were layers of thick paper sandwiched between top and bottom plywood sheets.

The amphora lay on the sofa in two pieces. The mottled green surface of the slim, tapering container was pitted with corrosion. The sealed top had been severed from the main part at the neck and lay a few inches from the body. Austin picked up a hacksaw from the table and examined the greenish dust caught in the teeth.

"I see that you used the finest precision instruments."

"Home Depot, actually," Saxon said. He looked embarrassed. "I know you're thinking that I'm a vandal. But I've had extensive experience in artifact conservation under primitive conditions and I didn't want a nosy conservator asking questions. There was a risk, but I would have gone bloody bonkers if I had to wait to find out what's in that jug. I was very careful."

"I might have done the same thing," Austin said, setting the hacksaw down. "I hope you're telling me that the patient died but the operation was a success."

Saxon spread his arms wide. "The gods of ancient Phoenicia were smiling on me. It succeeded beyond my wildest dreams. The amphora contained a largely intact papyrus rolled up inside it."

"It's been under water a long time," Zavala said. "What condition was it in?"

"Papyrus thrives best in a dry climate like the Egyptian desert, but the amphora was tightly sealed and the papyrus encapsulated in a leather case. I'm hoping for the best."

Austin lifted the lid off the trash container. "More high-tech?"

"That's my ultrasonic humidification chamber. The pages were too brittle to be unwound without damage and had to be humidified. I put water in the bottom of the receptacle, wrapped the roll in sheets of blotting paper, placed it inside a smaller plastic container with holes cut out of it, and clamped the lid on tight."

"This contraption actually works?"

"In *theory.* We'll have to see." Saxon glanced toward the plywood sandwich on the tables.

"And that must be your super-duper ion dehumidifier," Austin said.

"When the moistened roll became pliable, I sandwiched it between sheets of blotting paper and Gore-Tex, which absorbs the dampness. The weight of the plywood will flatten out the pages while the papyrus cooks."

"Did you see any writing on the papyrus?" Austin said.

"Light can darken a papyrus, so I unrolled it with the shades drawn. I glanced at it using a flashlight. It was hard to make out much writing because of the surface stains. I'm hoping that they will have lightened with drying."

"How soon before we can take a look at it?" Zavala said.

"It should be ready now. In *theory*."

A chuckle came from deep in Austin's throat. "Mr. Saxon is going to be a perfect fit for NUMA, Joe."

"I agree," Zavala said. "He's innovative, ingenious, isn't afraid to improvise, and is skilled in the fine art of CYA."

"Pardon me?" Saxon said.

"That's Spanish for Cover Your Ass," Zavala explained.

Saxon tweaked the end of his mustache like a silent-film villain. "In that case, I'm glad you are here. If I foul things up, we can share the blame." He switched off the pole lamps. "Gentlemen, we are about to prove that the Phoenicians reached the shores of North America centuries before Columbus was born."

Austin slipped his fingers under the edge of the plywood. "Shall we?"

They carefully lifted the top plywood from the pile and set it aside, then removed the Gore-Tex and blotting-paper layers. The papyrus was about fifteen feet long, made up of individual sheets approximately a foot high and twenty inches wide.

The ragged-edged pages were amazingly intact. The papyrus was darkly splotched over much of the mottled brown surface. Script was visible in places, but much of the writing had blended in with the stains.

Saxon looked like a child who'd gotten a pair of socks for his birthday. "*Damn!* It's covered with mold."

His full-speed-ahead exuberance had crashed into a wall of reality. He gazed with stony eyes at the papyrus, then went over to a window and stared out at the bay. Austin wasn't about to let Saxon come apart. He went into the kitchenette and poured three glasses of water. He came back, gave one to Zavala, another to Saxon, and raised his own.

"We haven't toasted the man who gave his life to bring this papyrus up from Davy Jones's locker."

Saxon got the point. His disappointment was nothing compared to the fate of the diver who had found the wreck and salvaged it. "To Hutch, and his lovely widow," he said to the clink of glasses. They gathered once more around the papyrus.

Austin advised Saxon to focus. "Ignore the writing for now, and tell us about the physical qualities of the papyrus."

Saxon picked up a magnifying glass and peered through the lens.

"Papyrus was made from giant sedge plants native to the Nile region," he explained. "These sheets are of the best quality, probably made from slices that came from the heart of the plant, pounded and shaped into strips that were cross-laminated. The ink was of excellent quality as well. The glue was starch based. They used pigment and gum, and wrote with a reed pen, which gives the writing its run-on, unbroken look."

"Now, tell us about the script," Austin said. "It's definitely Phoenician?"

Saxon calmly appraised the papyrus. "No doubt about it. The Phoenician twenty-two-letter alphabet was the single greatest contribution their culture gave to the world. The word *alphabet* itself is a combination of the first two letters. Arabic, Hebrew, Latin, Greek, and eventually English all trace their ancestry to the Phoenicians. They wrote from right to left, continuously, because they used all consonants. Vertical strokes act as punctuation to divide sentences and words."

"Forget what we *can't* read," Austin said. "Start by reading what you *can*. Even the Rosetta stone was missing some text."

"You should have gone into motivational therapy," Saxon said.

He picked up a spiral-bound notebook and a pen and bent over one end of the papyrus. He licked his lips, scribbled in his notebook, and went on to the next text fragment. Sometimes, he studied a single word; other times, several lines of writing. He mumbled to himself as he worked his way down the length of the papyrus.

At the end, he looked up with triumph gleaming in his eyes.

"I could *kiss* you, old boy!"

"I make it a habit not to kiss anyone with a mustache. Man *or* woman." Austin said. "Tell us what it says, please."

Saxon tapped the notebook. "The first fragment is written by Menelik, who describes himself as the favorite son of King Solomon. He talks about his mission."

"Menelik is the son of Sheba as well," Austin said.

"Don't be surprised that she's not mentioned. Solomon had many wives and girlfriends." He pointed to a few lines of text. "Here he says that he is grateful for the trust. He repeats this theme a number of times, which I find extremely interesting."

"In what way?" Austin said.

"The legends say that when Menelik was young, he and a half brother, the son of Sheba's handmaiden, stole the Ark of the Covenant from the Temple and took it to Ethiopia to establish the Solomonic line of kings. Some say it was done with Solomon's knowledge, and a copy built to take its place. One story has him spirit the sacred Ark off to Ethiopia. In another, he redeems himself. Plagued by guilt, he returned the Ark, and Solomon forgave him."

"Solomon practiced motivational therapy as well," Austin said. "Who better to trust than someone trying to make up for a past misdeed?"

"Solomon's reputation for wisdom was well deserved. There are writing fragments on the papyrus that indicate Menelik was transporting a cargo of great value."

"Nothing more specific?" Austin said.

"Unfortunately, no. The rest of the papyrus is basically a ship's log. Menelik is the author, which means he must have been the captain. I found the word *Scythians,* repeated a couple of times. The Phoenicians often hired mercenaries to guard their ships. There is reference to a 'Great Ocean,' some weather observations, but the main part of the log is obscured by mold."

"Now it's your turn to cheer *me* up," Austin said with a shake of his head.

"I think I can do that," Saxon said. He pointed to several un-stained sections. "The roll was wrapped very tight here. The mold couldn't get in. These lines describe a landfall. The captain talks about sailing into a long bay, almost like a small sea, where he could no longer smell the ocean."

Austin came to attention. "The Chesapeake?"

"It's a thought. The ship anchored near an island at the mouth of a wide river. He describes the water as more brown than blue."

"I noticed the muddy quality of the water when we set out today," Zavala said. "We passed an island near Aberdeen Proving Grounds."

Austin still carried the Chesapeake Bay chart in a plastic map pouch. He unfolded the creases and spread the chart out on the floor. Borrowing a grease pencil from Saxon, he marked an X near Havre de Grace at the mouth of the Susquehanna. "We've got our Phoenicians cooling their heels here. What did they do with the cargo?"

"Maybe they hid it in a gold mine," Saxon said.

"Your book suggested that Ophir was located in North America. Are you saying that this thing was hidden in King Solomon's mine?"

"When I first started looking for Solomon's mine, I concentrated on the area around the Chesapeake and Susquehanna," Saxon said. "There was extensive gold mining within walking distance of Washington a hundred years before the big California Gold Rush of 1849."

"We know that," Austin said.

"Thelma Hutchins mentioned that her husband was aware of the gold mines," Zavala said.

Saxon nodded. "There were more than a half dozen mines along the Potomac, from Georgetown past Great Falls, around the turn of the century. At least fifty mines operated in Maryland on both sides of the Chesapeake. The gold was found in rocks from the Piedmont Plateau, which runs from New York to South Carolina."

"That's a lot of territory to cover," Austin said.

"Agreed. I started looking for evidence of Phoenician contact. I found it not in Maryland but farther north, in Pennsylvania. A cache of stones with Phoenician writing on them was discovered near the state capital at Harrisburg. "

"What sort of stones?" Austin said.

"A man named W. W. Strong collected around four hundred stones found near Mechanicsburg in the Susquehanna River valley. Dr. Strong interpreted the markings on them as Phoenician symbols. Barry Fell thinks the writing is Basque. Others say the markings are natural."

"Hold that thought," Austin said. He went out to the Jeep and returned with the stone he had retrieved from the wreck. Saxon's jaw dropped to his Adam's apple.

"Where on earth did you get that?"

"I brought it up from my dive on the shipwreck."

"Astounding!" Saxon said. He took it from Austin, holding it as if it were made of glass, and traced the inscribed line with his finger. "This is *Beth,* the Phoenician symbol for house, later to evolve into the Greek *B.* It ties the wreck into Mechanicsburg."

Austin drew a second X at the wreck site in the bay, and a third at the mouth of the river. He connected the Xs with a line and extended it up the river.

"The trail grows cold at Mechanicsburg," he said.

"Not exactly. I've studied this area for years. Trekked a good deal of it on foot and by vehicle. If any location holds promise, it is this."

He drew a quick circle around an area north of Harrisburg. "St. Anthony's Wilderness has always intrigued me because of the stories of a long-lost gold mine. There's even a Gold Mine Road that runs through it. The area is rife with legends of abandoned towns and mining villages. It's extremely rugged. It's one of the few stretches of territory that hasn't been developed."

"Legends are one thing," Austin said. "Facts are another."

Saxon turned his attention back to the papyrus. "There's an unstained section here that has the only mention of a mine. The surrounding words have been blotted out by mold, except for a phrase that describes a horseshoe river turn." Saxon's long finger traced the river to a prominent U-shaped bend in the Susquehanna. "St. Anthony's Wilderness is east of the bend." He shook his head. "It's a huge area. We could search for years without finding anything."

Austin slipped a piece of paper from the chart pouch and placed it next to the map. A curving line on the paper matched the river bend on the map. Other squiggles denoted mountains and valleys to the east of the river. "This is a copy of a Phoenician map of Solomon's mine. It was found with some Thomas Jefferson papers."

"Jefferson? That doesn't make any sense."

"We're hoping it will in time. What do you think of the map?"

Saxon read the Phoenician writing on the paper. "This shows *exactly* where the mine is in relation to the river."

"Before we get too ecstatic, I have to point out a problem with this," Austin said. "The Susquehanna is a mile wide and a foot deep, as the locals say. It's studded with rapids and islands. There's no way a ship of Tarshish could have made its way upriver."

"But cargo could have come *down,*" Saxon said. "The river would have been deep enough for a boat to come down during the spring snowmelt."

"Tricky, but possible with the right kind of boat," Austin admitted.

"The right kind of boat was called a Susquehanna Ark," Saxon said with a smile. "They started running them in the 1800s from Steuben County, New York, downriver to Port Deposit, Maryland. They were basically big pontoon rafts, seventy-five feet long and sixteen feet wide of beam. They came down in the spring flood tide as the snow melted, carrying produce to market. The arks would be dismantled, their lumber sold, and the crews walked home. It took eight days to float down and six to walk back. They carried millions of dollars in cargo before the railroads put them out of business."

"A simple but brilliant concept," Zavala said. "The Phoenicians could have used the same technique to transport gold."

Saxon let out a hearty laugh. "Rider Haggard will be spinning in his grave. He and the rest of the world have assumed King Solomon's mines were in Africa."

Zavala had been looking at the maps. "I have a problem of my own. There's a body of water covering the site pinpointed on the old map."

Saxon's eyes followed Zavala's pointing finger. "So it is. That complicates matters."

"Only a little bit," Austin said. "I suggest we pull the Special Assignments Team together for a water-search operation tomorrow," Austin said. "It's a short hop to St. Anthony's Wilderness by helicopter. We can be there first thing in the morning."

"Splendid!" Saxon said. I'll go over the papyrus again, and dig into my research, in case I've missed something."

Austin pinched his chin between his thumb and forefinger. "Solomon went through a lot of trouble to hide this relic from mankind's eyes."

Zavala sensed the seriousness in his colleague's voice. "I think you're saying we may be grabbing a tiger by the tail."

"In a manner of speaking. Let's say we find this object. What do we do with it?"

"I never thought of that," Saxon said. "Religious artifacts have a way of stirring people up."

"My point exactly," Austin said in a flat tone that caused Saxon's brow to crease. "Solomon might have been a lot wiser hiding this thing than we are looking for it."

CHAPTER

43

C ARINA WAS STRETCHED OUT on the bed, staring at the
ceiling for lack of anything better to do, when she heard a soft
knock. She investigated and found that someone had left a wicker
basket with her clothes outside the door. She picked up the note
from on top of the neatly folded pile.

*Dear Miss Mechadi. Please join me for dinner at your conven-
ience. VB*

"How absolutely *civilized*," she murmured as she shut the door.

Carina couldn't get the white dress off fast enough. Wearing her
own clothes gave her a sense of control. She knew that it was only
an illusion, but it felt good anyhow. She reread the note. She would
have preferred not to spend another second with Baltazar, but she
knew that he held the key to her fate.

She threw her shoulders back and marched down the deserted
hall to the courtyard. A guard was waiting to escort her to the other
wing. She was ushered into a spacious dining room done in a Spanish
motif. The walls were pale stucco, edged with colorful tile, and
decorated with wall hangings. Tall terra-cotta urns were tucked into
the corners.

The valet appeared and seated Carina at a leather-topped table

with wrought-iron legs. The table was set for two, and illuminated
with ornate iron candelabra.

Baltazar arrived a minute later, dressed in black tie, as if for a for-
mal ball.

"Miss Mechadi, how nice of you to join me," he said with the
warmth of old acquaintance.

Carina smiled without humor. "Did I have a choice?"

"We *all* have choices, Miss Mechadi."

Baltazar snapped his fingers, and the valet filled their wineglasses
with a hearty rioja. He raised his glass in a silent toast and didn't
seem bothered when she ignored the gesture. She picked at her salad
and the fragrant paella that was the main course. She pushed away
the flan dessert but sipped at her espresso.

They ate their meal in silence, like an old married couple with
nothing left to say to each other. Baltazar asked how she had enjoyed
the meal and the wine. Carina answered with a grunt.

"Good," he said. He produced a thin cigar, which he lit, keeping
his eyes on Carina the whole time. "I have a question," Baltazar said,
his head hidden behind a cloud of purple smoke. "Do you believe in
divine destiny?"

"I don't know what you mean."

"I'm talking about the concept that the course of our lives is dic-
tated not so much by our acts but by our *fate*."

"Predestination is not a philosophy that is original with you." She
looked him straight in the eye. "I believe that we are *all* responsible
for the consequences of our behavior. If you jump out of a window
of a tall building, the consequence will be your death."

"You are quite correct. Our acts do affect our lives. But I must ask
you to ponder the unfathomable forces that would make me *want* to
jump out of a window."

"What are you getting at?" Carina said.

"It's very difficult to put into words. I can show you better than tell you."

"Do I have a choice?"

"In this case, no," he said, rising from his seat. He snuffed the cigar out in an ashtray and came around to pull her chair back. Then he escorted her to the portrait gallery.

"These are some of my forebears," Baltazar said. "Do you see the family resemblance?"

Carina gazed at the dozens of paintings that hung on the walls of the large room. Most of the men had been painted wearing decorative armor. While the faces in the portraits often differed physically, many, including the women, possessed Baltazar's wolfish gleam in their eyes, as if predatory instincts had been passed on in their genes.

"Yes," she said. "There are definite family characteristics."

"This lovely lass was a countess," he said, going over to the eighteenth-century oil of the young matron. "She's quite special."

He put his face inches from the portrait and pressed the carved panels to either side. Carina thought he was kissing the painting. Noting the bewildered expression on Carina's face, he explained about the eye and hand scans. He guided her down the stairway to the steel door, with its combination lock.

The door swung open. Carina was surprised to see the glass-enclosed cabinets that lined the walls. "It looks like a library," she said.

"This room holds the family archives of the Baltazars. These volumes contain our history going back for more than two thousand years. This is a treasure trove of intrigue in Europe and Asia during that time."

He went to the far end of the library and opened another door. He removed a torch from a wall sconce and lit it with his cigarette lighter. The flare from the torch illuminated the curved stone walls of a circular room. Carina stepped into the room and saw the statue beckoning at her with outstretched arms.

"Dear God! What *is* that thing?"

"It's an ancient offering statue. It has been in my family for thousands of years."

Her eyes took in the pointed nose and chin and the leering mouth, features made even more prominent by the leaping shadows from the fluttering torch.

"It's *hideous*."

"Some people might think so. But beauty is in the eye of the beholder. It's not the statue I wanted to show you; it's this volume."

Baltazar stuck the torch into a tall metal stand and went up to the altar. He lifted the lid of the gem-studded chest and opened the wooden box inside it. Then he removed the bound sheets of parchment.

Carina didn't want to satisfy Baltazar by showing interest, but she couldn't contain her curiosity.

"They look very old," she said.

"Nearly three thousand years old. The language is Aramaic. The pages were written in the time of King Solomon."

"Who was the author?" Carina said.

"The founding matriarch of the Baltazar family. Her name is lost in time. She refers to herself, and is referred to by others, as 'Priestess.' Would you like to hear what she wrote?"

Carina shrugged. "I have nothing better to do."

"I can recite the contents by heart. She introduces herself here on the first page. She was a pagan priestess who was a favored concubine to Solomon. They gave birth to a boy child who was named Melqart. As I said before, Solomon was a fickle man. He became smitten with Sheba."

"*My* ancestor," Carina said.

"That's right. They had a boy whom they named Menelik.

Solomon gave the priestess to Sheba to be her handmaiden. She had little choice but to obey. The boys grew up together, but Menelik remained the favored son. When they were teenagers, Melqart, at the bidding of his mother, persuaded his half brother to steal a treasured object from the Temple. Menelik eventually returned it, and both boys were forgiven by their father, but he enlisted them into the Phoenician navy through his friend Hiram."

"What was this treasured object?"

"The Ark of the Covenant. More important, the original Ten Commandments that were contained in the Ark."

"The clay tablets Moses brought down from the Mount?"

"No. These were of gold. In the Bible they are referred to as the Golden Calf. Moses is said to have destroyed them, but that was not the case."

"Why would he want them destroyed?"

"The tablets were written when the old religions were in flux. The tablets would have caught people's attention before Moses could sway them in the direction of the religion he was preaching."

"Apparently, the tablets were not destroyed."

"They were hidden until the time of Solomon. He saw them as potential trouble but feared destroying such sacred objects. He worried that the tablets might be stolen again. He told Menelik to take the Ten Commandments to Ophir and hide them. The priestess sent Melqart to retrieve the golden tablets. The half brothers fought. Menelik killed his half brother, took over his ship, and made it home to tell his father of the battle. Solomon banished Melqart's mother, whom he suspected of stirring up his subjects against him and reviving the old pagan religion."

"Where does the *Navigator* come in?"

"The priestess learned through her informants that Solomon ordered two statues of Menelik cast and inscribed the bronze statues with maps that would show the way to Ophir and the tablets. A more-detailed map, written on vellum, was lost during the brotherly battle."

"Why *two* statues?"

"Solomon was cautious as well as wise. He had them placed at the gates to his temple. Hidden in plain sight."

"And the priestess?"

"In exile, she seethed with anger at the death of her only son at the hands of Menelik, Sheba's offspring. She felt that she should have been the wife of Solomon, and that the Ten Commandments, and the power they brought, were rightfully hers. She entrusted Melqart's son with the task of recovering the treasure and exacting revenge on the descendants of Solomon and Sheba. He failed, but passed the instructions down to the next generation. As the years passed, the prime goal became recovery of the tablets before anyone knew of their existence. A system of Watchers was set up worldwide to prevent the secret from being discovered."

"What is your role in all this?"

"My father passed the task on to me. As the last of the Baltazars, it falls on my shoulders to carry out the pledge made centuries ago."

"So, *that's* it. You will take your revenge for this priestess, who is now a bag of dust. You believe I am descended from Sheba and intend to kill me."

"I would rather not. I have a proposal. I wish to carry on the Baltazar bloodline. What better way to do it than to merge our two bloodlines into one?"

A stunned expression came to Carina's blue eyes. "You can't be serious. You think that I—"

"I'm not talking about a love match," Baltazar said. "Consider it a business proposition."

"And will you make it your business to kill me once I have produced your so-called heir?"

"That depends entirely on you."

"Then kill me now. The thought of your touch revolts me." She attempted to get by him. He stepped in to bar the way. She turned instinctively, looking for a place to run; her glance fell on the statue's face, which was illuminated in the flickering torchlight.

"The *statue*. I remember now. I saw one like it in Rome. It was taken from Carthage during the Punic Wars. The Carthaginians used it to sacrifice children to Ba'al when the Romans attacked the city. *That's* why your sainted priestess was exiled. She practiced human sacrifice."

"Solomon was a hypocrite," Baltazar snapped. "He worshipped the old gods, but when his priests rose up against him he gave in to them."

"I don't want anything to do with you or your vile gods. I want you to let me go."

"That's not possible."

A wicked gleam came to Carina's eye. She snatched up the torch from its stand and stuck it in Baltazar's face. He laughed at the show of defiance.

"Put that thing down before I take it away from you."

"If you won't let me go, I will destroy your wonderful priestess."

She whirled around and brought the torch close to the bound parchment pages on the altar.

Baltazar's hand moved with the speed of a cobra. He snatched the torch from her hand before the dry pages caught fire, and his fist slammed her in the face. She crumpled to the floor, unconscious.

Baltazar looked up at the statue. The slanting almond eyes glittered in the light. The arms reached out as if they wanted to embrace him.

He glanced down at Carina's limp body, then up at the silent statue again. He cocked his head as if he were listening.

"Yes," he said after a moment. "Now I understand."

44

AUSTIN DROPPED THE DUFFEL BAG with his dive equipment just inside the entrance to the boathouse and walked into the study. The red light was blinking on the phone. Two messages. He pressed the button. The first message was from Carina.

"Hi, Kurt. Leaving the Met around one-thirty. Meeting was a *great* success! Can't wait to tell you about it. Hope the computer enhancements of the *Navigator* worked out. Catching a cab to Penn Station. I should be back in D.C. by late afternoon. Will call when I'm on my way. *Ciao.*"

He glanced at the wall clock. It was past ten o'clock. The beep signaling the start of the second message broke into his thoughts. Maybe it was Carina calling again. The phone message was short and chilling.

"Good evening, Mr. Austin," a metallic voice said. "We are holding the Italian property for you to view. Call this number back."

A voice changer made the caller sound like a robot. The phone number listed on the caller ID said the caller was OUT OF AREA. Austin remembered Buck's words when Austin had confronted him at Topkapi Palace.

My employer has other plans for her.

Carina had never made it to Penn Station. Austin pursed his lips. He mentally retraced Carina's steps that day, hoping that he'd recall a clue to her disappearance. Carina had told no one else of her plans to go to the Met. He remembered overhearing her making last-minute plans with the museum people that morning on his phone.

Austin picked up the phone to call Zavala, but his hand froze in midair. He put the phone down as if it had turned into a rattlesnake and went out onto the deck.

The air carried a rank but not unpleasant smell of mud and rotting vegetation. Lovelorn frogs croaked soft love songs against the insect chorus. The river was a pale ghost in the light of a half-moon. He remembered the prowler who'd watched the house the night of his first dinner with Carina. The tall oak tree where he had found the footprint was silhouetted against the dull sheen of the river.

The prowler had done more than *prowl*.

Austin went back through the house and out to the car. He drove to the end of the long driveway, turned onto the road, and drove five miles before stopping. He removed the cell phone from its dashboard holder and punched in a number from memory.

A deep voice answered: "Flagg here."

"I could use your help," Austin said. "Can you come by my house? Bring a fumigator."

"Twenty minutes," Flagg said and hung up.

Flagg was probably at Langley. Austin didn't know where his old colleague lived. Maybe he didn't have a home other than the CIA headquarters, where he spent most of his time between troubleshooting assignments that took him around the world.

Austin drove back to the boathouse. He was angry at himself for not insisting that Carina stay out of view, although it probably wouldn't have done any good. Carina was fearless when it came to her own safety.

Two vehicles pulled into the drive exactly twenty-five minutes after Austin called. Flagg got out of a Yukon. A slim young man wearing coveralls emerged from a panel truck that had the name of a pest control company painted on the doors.

The fumigator introduced himself as the Bug Man. He set an aluminum case on the study floor and snapped the lid open. He removed a gadget that looked like a Buck Rogers ray gun and pointed its flared barrel at the walls as he swiveled on his heel.

Working quickly, the Bug Man surveyed each room on the ground level and then climbed up the spiral staircase to the turret bedroom. He came down a few minutes later and went to repack his electronic gear.

"No infestation here," he said. "The whole house is clean."

"What about *outside* the house?" Austin said. He jerked his thumb toward the deck.

The Bug Man tapped his right temple with a forefinger. "Duh. Of *course*."

He went out on the deck and returned seconds later.

"I'm getting something from the direction of the river," he said.

"I think I know where," Austin said. He got a flashlight and led Flagg and the Bug Man down the deck stairs to the base of the tall oak tree. "There was a prowler out here a few nights ago," he said. "I found a footprint under this tree."

The Bug Man pointed his ray gun up toward the network of branches. Numbers appeared on the small LED display screen, and the gun let off a series of electronic pings.

He borrowed the flashlight and asked Flagg and Austin to give him a hand. They hoisted him up to the lowest branch, and he climbed halfway up the tree. He dug into a thick limb with a pocketknife, then climbed back down to earth, and he held his hand out in the beam of the flashlight. A black plastic box the size of a deck of cards rested in his palm.

"State-of-the-art. Maybe even beyond that. Voice-activated. Solar-powered. This little gadget picked up every phone call you made, whether on the regular line or cell phone, and transmitted the conversations to a listening post. Your phone conversations could have been relayed anywhere in the world. What do you want me to do with this thing?"

Flagg had watched the debugging process without talking, but now he offered a suggestion. "I'd put it back. It might come in handy if you want to spread some disinformation around."

"I was thinking of using it to send a few choice words to the listening post," Austin said, but he knew Flagg's suggestion was a good one.

The Bug Man climbed back into the tree. Flagg glanced up into the branches and said, "Somebody went through a lot of trouble to butt into your business. I thought that all you had to worry about since going over to NUMA was counting fish."

"You wouldn't believe the size of some of the fish in the ocean," Austin said. "When your friend is through, I'll crack open a couple of beers and tell you all about it."

The fumigator dropped out of the tree after reinstalling the electronic bug. He gathered up his tools and took off in his truck. Austin got two bottles of Sam Adams from the refrigerator, and he and Flagg settled into leather chairs in the study. For the next hour, Austin filled Flagg in on the events that had transpired since the hijacking of the containership.

Flagg allowed his wide mouth a slight smile in his otherwise impassive face. "King Solomon's mines! Compared to you, Austin, my job is about as exciting as sorting mail." He grew serious again. "You're up against some real heavyweights. You think this Baltazar character has your lady friend?"

"Baltazar's signature as been all over this thing since the very start."

"What can I do?"

"Try to find out where Baltazar spends his time."

"I'll get right on it. Anything else?"

"Stand by." Austin picked up the phone, put it on speaker, and punched in the number left by his anonymous caller.

"We've been waiting for you," said the weird voice.

"I was out of town. What's this Italian property you told me about?"

"You know her as Carina Mechadi. She's in good shape. For *now*. I can't vouch for her future health."

"What's your asking price?"

"Not what. *Who*. We would exchange her for you."

"Guaranteed?"

"In a perfect world. Yours is very imperfect right now."

"What are the terms?"

"Be out in front of the Lincoln Memorial in exactly ninety minutes. Have no one with you. Don't try to bring any positioning devices. You will be scanned."

Austin glanced at Flagg. "I'll be there."

The line went dead.

"She must be quite a woman," Flagg said. He rose from his chair. "You'd better get moving. I'll try to run Baltazar to ground."

Austin told Flagg to use Zavala as his contact. After his friend had left, Austin picked up the phone and called Joe, holding back the temptation to hurl some choice epithets at the unknown listener.

"Hi, Joe. Kurt. I won't be able to meet with you tomorrow. Pitt called and wants me to meet him tonight."

"Must be pretty important."

"It *is*. I'll give you a call later."

Austin made the second call to Zavala fifteen minutes later during the drive along the Beltway toward Washington.

"I was waiting for your call. Didn't see how you'd meet with Pitt tonight. Last I heard, he was on the Sea of Japan."

"Sorry for the runaround. Someone was listening to every word."

Austin told him about Carina and his intention to comply with the kidnapper's orders.

"I'll go along with anything you say, Kurt, but do you think going into this will help Carina?"

"I don't know. It may put me close enough to her to help. The fact that I have a lead on the location of the mine might give me some leverage."

"Hate to rain on your parade, but what if they're simply after your hide and don't want to bargain?"

"I've given that possibility serious consideration. I'll have to take that chance. Meanwhile, I want you to find the mine. It could be a trump card. Speed is of the essence."

"I've already arranged for a chopper and talked to the Trouts. We'll hook up with Saxon at first light. Good luck in the meantime."

"Thanks," Austin said. "I'll need it."

Austin told Zavala that Flagg would be in touch with him and hung up. He parked the Jeep in the NUMA underground garage and caught a cab to the Lincoln Memorial. He got there a minute before the ninety minutes had elapsed. Seconds after the taxi pulled away, a black Cadillac Escalade SUV pulled up to the curb and the rear door opened. A man got out and pointed to the backseat.

Austin took a deep breath and got into the car. The man slid in behind him, wedging Austin between another occupant. The SUV sped away from the memorial and joined the traffic stream.

The man to his left reached under his jacket. Austin saw the gleam of metal. He couldn't tell whether it was a knife or a gun. He cursed his bad judgment. They weren't taking him anywhere. They were going to kill him immediately.

He brought his arm up to protect himself.

Something cold pressed against his neck and he heard a soft hiss.

Then someone pulled a blackout curtain down over his eyes.

His body went limp, his eyes closed on their own, and his head lolled. Only the presence of the men on either side of him prevented him from falling over.

Before long, the SUV was on the outskirts of the capital, moving as fast as the speed limit allowed, in the direction of the airport.

45

THE McDONNELL DOUGLAS MD 500 utility helicopter darted through the sky high over Chesapeake Bay, its turquoise fuselage bathed in the soft light of dawn. Joe Zavala was at the controls. Gamay was in the passenger bucket seat. Paul Trout's long form was stretched out on the rear bench seat, which he shared with bags of dive gear.

Zavala squinted through the tinted bubble canopy and jabbed his forefinger downward. "That's where Kurt and I dove on the wreck," he said. "Havre de Grace coming up."

The white spike of the Concord Lighthouse came into view. Then the railroad bridge at the mouth of the Susquehanna River.

Zavala followed the course of the river as the muddy waterway headed in a northwesterly direction. The Susquehanna's flow was broken here and there by scraggly islands. Rolling agricultural fields out of a Grant Wood painting flanked both shores.

Cruising at a speed of one hundred fifty miles per hour, the aircraft quickly covered the distance to Harrisburg. Traffic on the roads was still light. About ten miles north of the Capitol dome, the helicopter veered east, away from the river and toward a range of mountains. The helicopter passed over dense woodlands and farms, finally dropping down through the early-morning mists to land at a grassy airstrip.

Saxon's secondhand Chevy Suburban was parked at the edge of the tarmac. As the helicopter's skids touched the ground, Saxon started the engine and drove across the field. The Suburban pulled up next to the helicopter and Saxon bounded out. He strode under the spinning rotors to greet Zavala and the Trouts with vigorous handshakes. He was decked out for an African safari in cargo pants, a cartridge vest, and a bush hat with the brim curled up on one side.

"Where's Kurt?" Saxon said.

"Called away unexpectedly," Zavala said. He hid his misgivings about Austin's mission with a cheerful smile.

"Damn shame," Saxon said with disappointment. "Kurt's going to miss all the fun when we find the mine."

"You sound pretty confident," Paul said.

"Joe knows from experience that I tend toward grandiose pronouncements. Showmanship goes with my occupation," Saxon admitted. "But I would swear on Sheba's grave that we have the mine within our grasp. I'll show you."

Saxon went over to his car and dropped down the tailgate. He snapped open his battered suitcase and extracted a thick wad of papers.

"You've been busy," Zavala said.

"I'm bleary-eyed from staying up all night doing research," Saxon said. "But it's been worth it. This is a topographical map of the area of interest. And this diagram shows the old railroad that used to service the coal mines. Joe has probably filled you in," he said to the Trouts, "but what drew me to this place were the persistent rumors of a legendary gold mine and Indian burial caves. There's the Gold Mine Road, which winds through the mountains, and an abandoned village called Gold Mine."

Trout surveyed the woods surrounding the quiet airstrip. His large brown eyes blinked, as they often did when his brain went into ponder mode.

"You'll have to pardon my scientific skepticism," he said with typical New England bluntness, "but it's hard to believe that Phoenicians sailed from halfway across the world and found a gold mine in this pretty Pennsylvania countryside."

"Skepticism is healthy," Saxon said. "You have to look at the context. We see walking trails, sleepy villages, and farms. But this land was once inhabited by at least five tribes who lived in twenty villages. In 1600, when the Europeans rediscovered the place, there were nearly seven thousand Susquehannock Indians living in these hills and valleys."

"What's your theory on first contact?" Gamay asked.

"I believe a Phoenician scouting ship in search of copper heard about the gold from the Indians. With their skill at organization, the Phoenicians could have hired the locals to open the mine, refine the gold, and established land and sea routes to transport it home."

"Difficult but not impossible," Trout said with a nod of his head. "Did I understand you to say that you can actually lead us to the mine?"

"I can lead you to where I *think* it is. Hop in the car and we'll go for a ride."

They shifted their bags from the helicopter to the Suburban. Saxon drove from the airport onto a winding country road. After a few miles, he turned off the road and followed a pair of ruts into the woods.

"Welcome to St. Anthony's Wilderness," Saxon said as the vehicle bumped in and out of cratered potholes. "This is the second-largest roadless area in Pennsylvania. The Appalachian Trail runs through it. You've got fourteen thousand acres of woodlands between First and Second mountains."

"I wasn't aware that St. Anthony visited North America," Gamay said.

"He *didn't*. It was named after a missionary named Anthony Seyfert. The locals know it as Stony Valley. It's as quiet as the grave around here now, but in the 1800s hundreds of men and boys toiled in the coal mines. Rail lines came into the village of Rausch Gap, and later served the Cold Springs resort. Almost everyone left when the mines played out."

"You said *almost*," Zavala said.

Saxon nodded. "Some smart developers figured out a way to profit from the gold mine legend. They built a place called the Gold Stream Hotel. Tourists stayed at the hotel, and took boat rides into a cave—Pennsylvania is loaded with them. The highlight was the opportunity to pan for gold."

"They actually found gold?" Gamay said.

"Enough to make the tourists happy. The hotel sold lockets to hold your gold dust. The hotel went out of business after the railroad pulled out."

"There must have been a source for that gold dust," Paul said.

Saxon grinned. "Absolutely right. That's why I think the hotel is the key to unlocking this whole mystery."

"How is that?" Zavala asked.

"*You'll* see," Saxon said mysteriously.

As the Suburban penetrated deeper into the woods, Saxon launched into a description of the wars between the Indians and the settlers, and pointed out ruins of the old mining camps and towers that marked mine shafts. The road ended abruptly at the shores of a lake. Saxon brought the Suburban to a stop.

"Welcome to the Hotel Gold Stream," he said.

They got out of the car and followed Saxon down a gradual slope to the edge of a lake. Hardly a ripple marred the mirrorlike surface.

"The hotel is under the lake?" Zavala said.

"The hotel used to be in a valley," Saxon said. "After the place was abandoned, gold hunters came in looking for the source. They had more dynamite than brains. They blew up a natural dam, and allowed the waters of a nearby creek to fill the valley and cover the hotel."

Zavala walked over to the water's edge and gazed out at the lake. He judged that it was about a mile wide and two miles long, and surrounded by thickly wooded hills. "How deep is it?"

"Nearly a hundred feet at its deepest point," Saxon said. "The lake is spring-fed."

"Standard dive procedure is to plan the dive and dive the plan," Zavala said. "It's a big lake. Any idea where we should start?"

"I'll show you," Saxon said.

Back at the Suburban, Saxon extracted a file marked HOTEL GOLD STREAM from his bag and handed Zavala a yellowed brochure that touted the features of the hotel, shown as a two-story flagstone building.

A walkway led from the hotel to stairs that went down to the cave entrance, where the tour boats were lined up. A sketch showed people in Victorian attire panning sluiceways for gold. Zavala looked from the hotel layout to the lake, trying to visualize what lay under the surface.

"No one could find the mine when the hotel was high and dry," he said. "What makes you think it will be any easier under water?"

"The same question occurred to me," Saxon said. "I was about to call off the expedition when I came across a magazine article about the lost hotel. One of the former kitchen staff described a trapdoor in the kitchen. It had been locked, but the kitchen staff broke the lock and dropped something down to see how deep it was. No one could hear it hit bottom. The management put a stronger lock on the trapdoor because the kitchen people were dumping peelings down the shaft."

Paul said. "The air shaft could have been dug to ventilate a mine."

Saxon opened a sketch pad to a page where he had made a reasonable copy of the hotel from the tourist brochure. Double vertical lines marked the air shaft.

"I think the hotel was built *over* the mine," he said. "The cave may have been part of the mine entrance before the ceiling caved in. The cave-in blocked access but not the flow of gold-laden water. If we go down that shaft, we can get into the mine. Do you think it's doable?"

Zavala studied the drawing for a moment, going through each step of the dive in his mind. "Any idea how big the shaft opening was?" he asked Saxon.

"No dimensions were given in the article."

Zavala was a careful diver. He proposed a two-stage plan. He and Gamay would explore the cave first, then check out the shaft. Gamay was a highly skilled diver who had explored many wrecks in the Great Lakes and, later, worked as a nautical archaeologist. With their slim builds, they might be able to navigate the shaft.

While Paul inflated a rubber raft, the divers got into their scuba gear. Saxon had charted out the hotel location on a topographical map enclosed in waterproof plastic.

Trout paddled Gamay and Zavala out into the lake. They dropped a weighted marker buoy into the water. All was ready. The divers rolled over the sides of the raft and disappeared into the depths, with only ripples to mark their passage from one world to another.

46

AUSTIN WOKE UP FEELING as if he'd been mugged. He had foolishly expected to be fully conscious until the time he met with Baltazar. Instead, he'd let himself be sucker-punched.

A man's face came into focus less than a yard away. The face was heavily bandaged on the right side.

"Feeling better?" the man said in a disinterested tone that suggested he didn't care one way or the other.

Austin's head ached, his tongue was fuzzy, and his vision was blurred.

"Compared to roadkill, not bad," Austin replied. "Who are you?"

"You can call me Squire. I work for Baltazar." He offered Austin a glass of clear liquid. Seeing Austin's hesitation, he spread his lips in a crooked grin that showed missing teeth. "Don't worry. If Baltazar wanted you dead, you'd be pushing up daisies. It will counteract the effect of the chemical they used on you."

Austin took a sip. The liquid was cold and had an artificial sweetness. The pounding in his head lessened, and his eyes regained their focus. He was lying on an army cot. His newfound friend sat on a folding chair. They were in a large rectangular tent. Sunlight filtered through the translucent red-and-white stripes.

"I've been unconscious all night," Austin said.

"You must make them nervous. They gave you enough happy juice to knock out a steer."

Austin drained the glass and handed it back. The man had the husky build of a professional wrestler and wore blue denim coveralls. A pair of aluminum crutches leaned against his chair.

"What happened to your face?" Austin said.

The left-hand side of the man's mouth jerked downward in a half frown. "*Stuff* happened to it," he said. "Get up."

Squire used his crutches to push himself to a standing position. He leaned on the crutches and watched as Austin slowly swung his legs over the side of the cot and got to his feet. Austin was slightly dizzy, but he felt his strength rapidly returning. He clenched and unclenched his fingers into fists.

Squire caught the subtle motion. "In case you're thinking about trying something funny, there are two guards outside the tent, and they're not friendly guys like me. Mr. Baltazar gave me the authority to have them work you over. Understand?"

Austin nodded.

Squire gestured toward the door. Austin stepped outside and blinked in the bright sunlight. The guards were posted on either side of the door. The medieval tunics they wore didn't match the automatic weapons pointed at Austin. The men had a deceptive lazy look in their eyes, as if they would be glad if Austin gave them a chance to relieve their boredom.

The tent was one of a dozen drawn up in two rows on a large open field bordered by woods. At the center of the opposite row was a raised reviewing stand. The structure was roofed, and closed in on the sides. The corners were built in the shape of towers. Pennants bearing a bull's-head emblem snapped in the wind.

An open space around fifty feet wide separated the lines of tents. A low wooden rail divided the space in half for most of its length.

At each end, separated by the rail, two men in full armor were mounted on gigantic horses. They held wooden lances that had blunt metal points. The huge animals were equally covered with armor, which reflected the morning sunlight.

Someone in the stand waved what looked like a green handkerchief. The armored men spurred their mounts and charged toward each other with lowered lances. The earth shook from the impact of the hooves. The riders met at midpoint with a mighty crash of spears against shields. The wooden lances shattered. The horsemen rode to the end of the rail, spun their horses around, and charged each other with upraised swords. Austin didn't see the second phase of the fight because his guards herded him between two tents.

He glanced around and saw fields and woods. A flicker of red materialized at the edge of the trees. It was a car moving at a high rate of speed. At the last minute, the driver hit his brakes and the Bentley skidded to a halt, with the heavy bumper inches from Austin's knee.

The door flew open, and Baltazar got out from behind the steering wheel. The sunlight gleamed dully off the coat of mail he wore under a tunic emblazoned with a bull's head. He had a wide grin on his broad face. "Nerves of steel as usual, Austin."

"I'm just moving slowly after the cocktail your men gave me, Baltazar."

Baltazar clapped his hands. The Squire brought over two leather-covered chairs, which he placed so they were facing each other. Baltazar sat in one and offered the other to Austin.

"What do you think of our little joust?" he said.

Austin gave Baltazar's armor and tunic the once-over. "I thought I was on the set of *A Connecticut Yankee in King Arthur's Court.*"

"Consider this as time travel," Baltazar said. "I've re-created every detail here as it would have been at a fifteenth-century French tournament."

Austin glanced at the car. "The Bentley too?"

Baltazar greeted Austin's jibe with a frown. "In the days of chivalry, the tournament served to train men for war and separated the bold from the not-so-bold. I use it here for a similar purpose with my mercenaries. I take it very seriously."

"I'm happy you have a hobby, Baltazar, but we both know why I accepted your invitation. Where's Carina Mechadi?"

"Safe for now, as I said on the telephone." He stared at Austin as if he were a lab specimen. "You must think a great deal of the young woman to allow yourself to be taken prisoner."

Austin smiled. "I missed your face, Baltazar. This way I got a free ride to see you."

Baltazar thrust his oversized jaw forward. "Then *talk,* Mr. Austin. I'm eager to learn if you have anything worthwhile to say."

"To begin with, I know what it will take for you to let Carina go."

"Ah, a *proposition.* What do you have to offer?"

"The location of King Solomon's mine."

"You're bluffing, Austin." Baltazar said with a sneer. "Besides, I have the original *Navigator,* with its map. Why would I need to bargain with you?"

"Because if you knew the mine's location, there would have been no need to kidnap Carina and use her as bait to catch me."

"Maybe I did it to swat an annoying fly, Austin. But I'll indulge you. Tell me about the mine. Perhaps you can use the information as a bargaining chip."

Austin grimaced as if he were making a painful choice. "The patterns on the bronze cat were a map. Computer enhancements showed the location of a Phoenician shipwreck. An amphora salvaged from the wreck contained a papyrus with details of the mine."

"And do you know the author of this fabulous papyrus?" Baltazar said.

"His name was Menelik, son of Solomon."

"Menelik?" It came out as a hiss.

"That's right. He transported a sacred relic to North America."

Baltazar's reaction was more subdued than Austin expected.

"Your attempt to shock me with your knowledge only displays your lack of understanding of the situation. Do you have any idea what this sacred relic is?"

"Maybe you can fill me in."

Baltazar smiled. "It's the original Ten Commandments, inscribed on tablets of solid gold."

"I'm not buying, Baltazar. The original Commandments were *clay.*"

"Your words betray your ignorance. There were supposedly three versions of the Decalogue, all made of clay. But there were actually *four.* The first one predated the others. That version was based upon the pagan beliefs of my ancestors but was deemed too controversial. Supposedly, the tablets were destroyed. The truth is, they were hidden, and passed down to Solomon, who decided to transport them to the farthest reaches of his empire."

"You're richer than Croesus," Austin said. "What's a few more pounds of gold to you?"

"Those tablets rightfully belong to my family."

"You don't seem like the family type, Baltazar."

"On the contrary, Austin, this is very *much* a family matter. You look around and see the ritualized violence and think that's all there is to the Baltazar family. We're no worse that the world's governments. Why do you suppose we have just as many conflicts as before the end of the Cold War? The vast military infrastructure not only survived, it prospered after the Cold War ended."

"Which is good for so called peace-and-stability companies like yours," Austin said.

"Fear and tension are in our business interests."

"And when there is no fear or tension, you *create* it."

"We have no need to stir human passions," Baltazar said. "People would kill each other whether we existed or not. There is a great deal more at stake here than meets the eye. The discovery of the tablets will sew doubts about the underpinnings of the world's governments and religions. There will be unrest everywhere."

"Starting in the Middle East."

"Starting, but not ending, there."

"Bringing you great riches and power. What next, Baltazar, the world?"

"I have no intention of taking over the world like some James Bond villain," Baltazar said. "It would be far too difficult to govern."

"What do you want then?"

"A monopoly on the world's security business."

"You've got a lot of competition. There are dozens of companies in the so-called peace line, to say nothing of the world's armies."

"We will push aside or absorb them until there is only one of any consequence. PeaceCo. Our security arms and mineral companies will feed each other. The industrial nations can keep their precious armies and navies. Our private forces will be hired to provide security in exchange for the natural wealth of poor nations in Africa, South America, and Asia. I will build an economic-military empire without equal."

"Empires come and go, Baltazar."

"This one will endure for many years. Since I have no heirs, perhaps I will pass on my legacy to Adriano. He is like a son to me."

"You're an evil man, Baltazar."

"Simply a businessman who looks forward to many small wars without end. A *Pax Baltazar*. But first things first, Austin. We need to find the tablets."

"Then we may have a deal. The location of the mine in exchange for Ms. Mechadi."

Baltazar raised his gloved hand. "Not quite yet. Tell me what you know. I'll have someone check on it."

Austin laughed. "I'm not a fool, Baltazar. You'll kill me once you confirm the mine site."

"Tut-tut. You have a suspicious mind. I'll offer a compromise then. A chance to escape my fiendish clutches. You have taken up the cause of a lady. Under the laws of chivalry, you are her champion and must act as such."

Austin considered the turn of phrase and decided that Baltazar was quite mad.

He forced a smile. "Tell me what you have in mind."

Baltazar rose from his seat. "I'll *show* you. Get in the car."

Baltazar opened the passenger door of the Bentley for Austin and then slid behind the steering wheel. He started the powerful engine, and accelerated to nearly a hundred miles per hour along a straight road.

MOMENTS LATER BALTAZAR SLOWED, touched his brakes, and the car came to a stop a few yards from the edge of a deep gorge.

Spanning the gorge was a bridge of interlocking steel about forty feet long and twenty feet wide. There were no guardrails. A wooden fence ran up the center line. The wood was new, as if the fence had recently been erected.

They got out of the car and walked to the edge of the chasm. The steep sides dropped down for about three hundred feet to a rock-strewn stream.

"This is what the locals call Dead Man's Ditch," Baltazar said. "I had the bridge built to connect pieces of my property. I made some modifications in anticipation of your visit."

"You didn't have to go through all the trouble," Austin said.

"Not at all. Here's my proposition. I will place my car with Miss Mechadi in it on the other side of the ditch." He pointed to the grassy field across the gorge. "I will be in the middle, playing the role of the mythical dragon. We will joust for the favor of the fair lady."

Austin turned and looked at the pair of SUVs that had followed them. "What about your goons?"

"I will instruct my men to stay on this side."

"You will allow us to escape?"

"I will give you a sporting chance, which is more than you have now."

"And if I decline your invitation?"

"I'll have you thrown into the gorge before your lady's horrified eyes."

"I don't see how I can pass up a generous offer like that, Baltazar."

Baltazar grinned unpleasantly and gestured for Austin to get back into the car. They drove at breakneck speed back to the main jousting area. He stopped to let Austin off in front of the tent. Squire was leaning on his crutches in front of the tent's portal.

"Your man will see that you are properly outfitted," Baltazar said. "We'll be wearing only chain mail and a helmet. It wouldn't be chivalrous to burden you with full armor. You will have a shield and a lance. The horses will be unarmored, which will make things go faster. See you at the tilt." He gunned the engine and took off, with his tires spinning on grass.

Squire watched Baltazar drive away and told Austin to get in the tent. He helped him on with a coat of mail and handed him a tunic with no emblem on it. The chain mail hood had an opening for Austin's face. Squire placed a knitted skullcap on Austin's head and tried the helmet on for size. It was a little loose but would have to do, he said. He buckled a sword around Austin's waist and fitted him with spurs. He handed him a kite-shaped shield.

Surveying Austin, he spread his lips in a jagged grin. "You're no

Sir Lancelot, but you'll have to do. Sit down and I'll give you some pointers."

Austin removed the helmet and sat on his bunk.

"Listen carefully. Baltazar likes to do things in threes. He plays with you on the first pass. Misses you completely. On the second, he'll deliver a glancing blow. Probably on the shield. The third time is the money shot. He'll spit you on his lance like a pig. Any questions?"

"Tell me where I can pick up an AK-47."

Squire snorted. "You won't need one. Baltazar uses a lance with a metal core. He makes sure his opponents get the wooden lance, which will shatter on his armor and can be deflected by the shield."

"That doesn't seem chivalrous," Austin said.

"It *isn't.* This time, *you'll* have the one with the metal core. I'll give him a German-style lance made of heavier wood. Hopefully, he'll be so anxious to kill you that he won't notice the difference in weight."

"Why are you doing this, Squire?"

The man brought his hand up to his bandaged face. "The bastard did this to me with his bogus lance. The doctors say I'll look like Quasimodo. There's not a pill in the world that will kill the pain from the damage to my legs. *Forget* me. Third pass is the money shot. He'll go for your shield, thinking the lance will go through the leather and wood. Aim for his midsection. It's the biggest target. Don't miss."

"What happens to you if I do?"

"It's nothing to me. Either way, I'm outta here. Maybe I can get a job with a bank."

A guard poked his head into the tent. "Time."

AN SUV was parked outside the tent. Accompanied by another vehicle carrying guards, Squire drove Austin to the bridge crossing, where a carnival atmosphere prevailed. Bull's-head pennants fluttered from temporary flagpoles. Word of the impending joust had spread among Baltazar's mercenary corps. In addition to the ever-present guards, the edge of the gorge was lined with men in medieval costume who had gathered to see Austin speared or thrown to his doom.

"You didn't tell me we were going to a party," Austin said.

"Baltazar likes an audience." Squire pointed to a couple of huge horses being led from their trailers. "Gray horse is Baltazar's. The dappled one is yours. Name is Valiant. Baltazar wanted you on a nag, but I made sure you got a good mount. Val's steady and sure. Won't balk on a charge."

Squire pulled up near the horse trailers. Austin got out of the SUV and went over to introduce himself to his mount. The animal seemed as big as an elephant up close. Austin patted the animal's side and whispered in its ear. "Come through for me this one time, Val, and I'll feed you all the sugar you can eat."

The horse snorted and tossed its head, which Austin took for a yes. He went over to inspect the jousting bridge. Two horses passing each other on the narrow span would make for a tight squeeze. There would be no margin of error if he were knocked from his saddle.

Austin heard a cheer from the assembled crowd. The Bentley was speeding toward the gorge. It continued across the bridge, trailed by a black Escalade, and stopped around a hundred yards from the canyon. Baltazar got out of his car and opened the SUV door.

A figure wearing a white dress got out, accompanied by two guards. The figure got off a brief wave before being hustled to the passenger side of the Bentley. Baltazar and his guards drove back across the bridge.

Baltazar strode over to Austin. He pointed to the Bentley. "There's your lady. I have fulfilled my part of the bargain. Now it's your turn."

Austin stuck his hand out. "The car key."

Baltazar lifted the helmet tucked under his arm. A key ring dangled from one of the two metal horns that protruded from the crown.

"Yours for the taking, Austin. We don't want to make this too easy."

Austin said, "I'll need a pen and paper."

Baltazar snapped an order. One of his men ran to the nearest SUV and came back with a dashboard pad and attached ballpoint. Using the car's hood as an improvised writing desk, Austin jotted down a series of directions and sketched out a map. He underlined the words Gold Mine.

Baltazar held his hand out. Austin stuffed the paper into his helmet.

"As you said, Baltazar, we don't want to make this too easy."

Austin knew Baltazar could order his men to rush him, grab the mine map, and toss him into the gorge. He gambled that Baltazar's insane ego would not do anything to spoil the show he had arranged for his men.

"Time to prove your mettle, Austin."

With a glower so hot it could have sparked a forest fire, Baltazar spun on his heel and marched over to his horse. He vaulted into the saddle with unbelievable ease. Baltazar's squire was holding the reins. He was a big man, dressed in a scarlet hooded costume, with his back toward Austin. He turned and looked at Austin, who recognized Baltazar's baby-faced killer. Adriano smiled and pointed to the Bentley.

The implication was clear. If Austin failed, Carina was Adriano's for the taking.

Baltazar spurred his horse. He galloped across the bridge and wheeled his mount around to face Austin.

Austin went over to Val and pulled himself into the saddle. Austin was unaccustomed to the weight of the chain mail and was considerably less agile than Baltazar. Squire handed his helmet and told him to keep his head bent forward so he could see through the narrow eye slits.

Next he handed up the shield and the lance and instructed Austin how to hold them.

"Watch the pennant near the lance head," Squire said. "It will tell you where the point is."

"Any other words of advice?" Austin's voice echoed inside the helmet.

"Yeah," Squire said. "Let your horse do his work, remember the third tilt, and pray for a miracle."

He gave the horse a light slap on its flank and the giant animal lurched forward. Austin tried walking the horse in a circle. Val responded well to knee nudges. The weight and fighting equipment were awkward, but the saddle was high in the back and offered some support.

The brief rehearsal was about to come to an end.

A man dressed in the Lincoln green costume of a herald at arms blew a blast on his trumpet. The signal to get ready. Austin brought his horse around to face Baltazar. The second trumpet blast was the alert to lower lances. The third blast followed a second later.

Baltazar dug his spurs in ahead of the signal.

Austin was only a second behind.

The horses accelerated to a rolling gallop that sent clods of earth flying into the air like startled birds. The ground shook as the massive animals and the metal-skinned creatures on their backs flew toward each other in a thundering charge.

CHAPTER

47

USING THE BUOY LINE as a guide, Gamay and Zavala had powered their swift descent with practiced scissors kicks. The lake's surface clarity had been deceptive. The greenish brown tint had deepened into an opaqueness that cut visibility to a few murky yards. The soupy gloom quickly absorbed the twin cones of light from their electric torches and muted the bright yellow of their wet suits.

Several feet from the bottom they hovered to keep from stirring up a cloud of blinding silt. They consulted a compass, and swam west until a shadowy mass loomed in the murk. Their flashlight beams touched a vertical surface. Glimpses of flagstones were visible in the spinachlike growth carpeting the exterior of the two-story hotel. Fish darted through the glassless windows that stared out vacantly like eye sockets in a skull.

A Donald Duck voice crackled in the headset of Zavala's underwater communicator.

"Welcome to the friendly Hotel Gold Stream," Gamay said.

"Every room comes with a water view," Zavala said. "Must be off-season. No one's around."

Although the building was not huge, the mansard roof and stone construction gave it grandeur beyond size. They glided over the wide front porch. The portico had collapsed. Green slime covered the rotting wood where guests of a bygone era once sat in rocking chairs to take in the fresh country air.

They peeked through the entrance. The darkness was almost impenetrable, and the cold emanating from the hotel penetrated their wet suits. They swam around to the rear of the building. Zavala pointed his light at a one-story addition built onto the backside of the hotel.

"That could be the kitchen and service area," Zavala said.

"Good call," Gamay said. "I think I see a stovepipe sticking out of the roof."

They glided down a gradual slope, whose lawn had been replaced with freshwater marine vegetation, to a wide set of stone stairs. At the base of the stairs was a stone apron where the cave boats used to be kept. The granite mooring posts were still in place. The two divers plunged into the open maw.

The stalactites and stalagmites inside the cave had been worn down like the teeth of an old dog, and marine vegetation dulled their once-brilliant colors. Fantastic rock formations hinted at the strange world that once had greeted the eyes of turn-of-the-century tourists.

After swimming about a quarter of a mile against a slight current, they came to the end of the cave. The way was blocked by huge boulders. A cavity in the ceiling appeared to have been the source of the rockfall. Unable to explore farther, they returned to the mouth of the cave, making good time with the current behind them.

Minutes later, they were out of the cave and back behind the hotel. Zavala went along the outside of the service building until he came to a wide doorway. He made his way in, with Gamay right behind. The interior space was big enough to have been the dining room. Zavala swam along the walls until he found a door, and they entered the room. Their lights picked out empty cupboards and large slate sinks. A pile of rust in the corner might have been a cast-iron stove. They examined every square inch of floor. Nothing resembling a hatch cover came to their attention.

"I wonder if we've been 'shafted,' literally," Zavala said.

"Don't give up yet," Gamay said. "The old kitchen worker was pretty specific. Let's try that room."

She swam through an opening into a space around a quarter the size of the kitchen. Shelves lined the walls, indicating the room had been a pantry. She dropped down until her face mask was inches above the floor, and, after searching for a short time, she found a rectangular raised section. She brushed away the silt and found hinges and a rusty padlock.

Zavala reached into a waterproof bag attached to the D ring of his harness and pulled out an angled pry bar around a foot long. He inserted the bar under the trapdoor cover only to have the rotten wood break into pieces. He pointed his light down the shaft. The blackness seemed to go on forever.

"I don't hear you saying 'Me first,'" Gamay said.

"You *are* slimmer than I am," Zavala said.

"Lucky me."

Gamay's reluctance was feigned. She was an intrepid diver and would have gladly arm-wrestled Zavala for the chance to find the mine. At the same time, she had done enough diving to realize she had to be extracautious. Cave diving requires an uncanny calmness. Every move must be deliberate and well thought out in advance.

Zavala tied a length of thin nylon line to the leg of a cabinet and the other end to his pry bar. He lowered the bar into the shaft, but it didn't touch bottom, even after fifty feet were played out.

Gamay examined the wood-covered sides of the shaft. The wood was soft, but she thought it would hold. The shaft opening was about a yard square, which would allow just enough room for her tank.

Gamay glanced at her wristwatch. "Going in," she said.

Her supple body slithered over the lip of the opening and she disappeared into the square black hole. The tanks gonged against the sides, dislodging pieces of wood, but the shaft remained intact. Zavala watched the glow fade as Gamay descended.

"What's it like down there?" Zavala said.

"Just like Alice in Wonderland down the Rabbit Hole."

"See any rabbits?"

"Haven't seen a damned thing—hello."

Silence.

"Are you okay?" Zavala said.

"*Better* than okay. I'm out of the squeeze. I'm in a tunnel or cave. C'mon down. There's a ten-foot drop after you exit the shaft."

Zavala slid into the opening and joined Gamay in a chamber at the bottom of the shaft.

"I think this is a continuation of the boat cave," Gamay said. "We're on the other side of the rockslide."

"No wonder the hotel management was upset. The river would have carried the kitchen slops into the boat cave."

Zavala took the lead again. He swam into the cave, playing his flashlight beam on the walls. The rock formations disappeared after a few minutes.

"We're in a mine," he said. "See the chisel marks?"

"This could be the source of the gold that the hotel guests panned for."

Zavala probed the darkness ahead his light. *"Look."*

A tunnel opening had been cut in the wall to the left.

They left the main cave to explore the tunnel. The passageway was about ten feet high and six wide. A barrel ceiling arced overhead. Alcoves had been cut in the wall for torches.

After about a hundred yards, the tunnel intersected with another at a right angle. The discussion of their next step was short but intense. They could be dealing with a labyrinth. Without a lifeline, they could quickly lose their way. The limited amount of air in their tanks could make the wrong decision a fatal one.

"Your call," Zavala said.

"The floor on the right-hand passageway is more worn than the others," Gamay said. "I say we follow it for a hundred yards. If we don't find anything, we'll head back."

Zavala crooked his forefinger and thumb in an okay signal, and they plunged into the passageway. They swam without talking to conserve air. Both were aware that each fluttering kick brought them closer to danger. But curiosity spurred them on until the tunnel ended, and they broke into the open after swimming about fifty yards.

The passageway had ended in a large chamber. The ceiling and opposite walls were beyond the range of their lights. They had come to the most hazardous part of their dive. It would be easy to become disoriented in a large open space. They decided to confine their exploration to no more than five minutes. Gamay would stay at the mouth of the tunnel. Zavala would do the actual exploration. At no time would one diver be out of sight of the other's light.

Zavala struck out into the darkness, keeping close to the wall.

"Far enough. I'm losing you," Gamay cautioned.

Zavala stopped.

"Okay. I'm swimming away from the wall. The floor is smooth. This room may have seen a lot of traffic. Nothing to indicate what it was used for."

Gamay issued another warning. He turned back and homed in on her light. He followed a zigzag pattern that would cover the maximum about of ground.

"See anything yet?" Gamay said.

"Noth—wait!"

He swam toward an amorphous shape.

"You're moving out of sight," Gamay said.

Gamay's beacon had become a smudged pinpoint. It would be suicide to proceed much farther, but Zavala couldn't stop now.

"A couple more feet."

Then silence.

"Joe. I can barely see you. Are you all right?"

Zavala's excited voice came over the communicator. "Gamay, you've got to see this! Leave the torch to mark the tunnel and follow my light. I'll wave it."

Gamay estimated they had just enough air to navigate the tunnel, rise up the shaft, and make their way to the surface. "We don't have much time, Joe."

"This will only take a minute."

Gamay was known to use salty language, but she kept her thoughts to herself. She placed the flashlight on the floor and swam toward the moving light. She found Zavala next to a circular stone dais about three feet high and around six feet in diameter. The surface of the platform was covered with rotten wood and pieces of yellow metal.

"Is that gold?" she said.

Zavala held a yellow piece of metal close to her mask. "Could be. But this caught my attention."

In brushing away the wood, Zavala had exposed a metal box around a foot long and eight inches wide. Raised lettering on the top of the box was partially obscured by a black film, which came off with a wipe of Zavala's glove. He murmured an exclamation in Spanish.

Gamay shook her head. "It *can't* be," she said.

But there was no denying the evidence of their eyes. A name was embossed on the box lid:

THOMAS JEFFERSON

CHAPTER

48

THE HORSE THUNDERED TOWARD the gorge like a run-away battle tank. Austin fought to stay in the saddle. He was top-heavy from his weapons and armor. One foot had slipped from a stirrup. His steel-encased head bounced like a bobble-head doll's. His shield was sliding off his arm. The long lance pointed every-where except where he wanted.

Val's hooves clattered onto the metal bridge. Through the eye slits, Austin caught a blurred glimpse of a gleaming spear tip and the bull's-head emblem on Baltazar's tunic. Then the horses were off the bridge and back on the grassy turf.

Austin let out the breath he'd been holding and tightened the reins. He slowed the horse and brought it around to face Baltazar, who was on the other side of the gorge calmly watching Austin's dis-array. Baltazar lifted the helmet from his head and held it in front of his chest.

He shouted: "Good joust, Austin. But you seem to be having some trouble keeping things together."

Laughter rippled through the crowd of onlookers.

Austin removed his helmet and wiped the sweat from his eyes

with the back of his mailed glove. He ignored the pain from his half-healed rib wound and called back in defiance. "I was distracted by thoughts of my new Bentley."

Baltazar plucked the car key from the helmet and held it high above his head. "Don't count your Bentleys before they hatch," he taunted.

Austin reached into his helmet for the folded paper and held it in a Statue of Liberty pose. "Don't spend your gold before you find it."

Maintaining his frozen grin, Baltazar hooked the key back onto the horn and lowered the helmet onto his head.

Austin turned in his saddle and glanced at the lone figure in white sitting in the Bentley. He waved and the figure waved back. The gesture gave him renewed encouragement. He stuffed the paper into his helmet and lowered the steel pot onto his shoulders.

The trumpet blew its warning clarion.

Austin balanced his shield against the saddle and elevated the spear a few times to get a feel for its balance. He tilted his head forward and watched through the eye slits as Baltazar called Adriano over and bent down from the saddle to speak to him.

The second trumpet blast shattered the air.

Austin angled the lance to his left so the point would be in the path of the oncoming rider.

The trumpet sounded for a third time.

Austin apologized to Val and dug his spurs in. Baltazar's figure grew larger in the vision vents. Austin crouched low behind the shield, keeping his lance aimed at Baltazar's chest as Squire had advised. His hard breathing sounded like a steam engine inside the helmet.

At the last second, Baltazar raised his lance. The point caught Austin's helmet under the eye slits and levered the steel pot off his head.

Then they were over the bridge.

Austin wheeled his horse around in time to see his helmet hit the ground near where the bridge joined the edge of the gorge. Adriano ran out and snatched up the helmet. He handed the helmet to Baltazar, who extracted the paper with a flourish. He read the words Austin had written and gave the paper to his hired killer. Adriano headed for an SUV, but before he drove off he handed off the helmet to a jouster, who ran over and tossed it up to Austin.

"Bad luck, Austin," Baltazar yelled. "But you can still save the woman."

The trumpet drowned out Austin's suggestion that Baltazar jump off the bridge.

Both men barely had time to get their helmets back on when the herald sounded the signal to lower lances.

Squire had called the third tilt the money shot.

Austin was rattled at the ease with which Baltazar had placed the lance point. At the same time, the metal-cored spear would give him an advantage. Austin intended to use it. He gritted his teeth and lowered his head.

The trumpet sounded again.

The horses charged. Baltazar was hunkered behind his shield so that only the helmet horns were visible. Austin aimed directly for the shield. Baltazar's lance hit Austin's shield dead center. As Squire had predicted, the shaft broke behind the point.

Austin's lance penetrated Baltazar's shield as if it were made of air. The sharp point would have neatly skewered Baltazar if Austin's aim had been better. The point caught a corner of the shield, tore through the leather-and-wood frame, and levered Baltazar out of his stirrups.

He crashed down on the steel bridge and disappeared over the edge.

Austin cursed as only a sailor can. He had zero sympathy for Baltazar. But Baltazar had taken the car key with him.

Then Austin swore again, this time with joy. The twin horns on Baltazar's helmet were rising above the bridge. Baltazar was trying to pull himself up. The weight of his chain mail and helmet compounded the difficulty. The shield still hung from his arm.

Austin pulled his helmet off and threw his lance aside. He slipped out of the saddle and ran out on the bridge.

Baltazar had one shoulder up. He saw Austin bending over him. "Help me," he pleaded.

"Maybe this will lighten your load." Austin plucked the car key from the horn.

Austin was tempted to send Baltazar to oblivion with a shove of his foot. But Baltazar's men had recovered from the shock of seeing their leader unhorsed and were running for the bridge.

Austin turned and loped toward the car.

As he drew near, he saw that Carina had her head against the dashboard as if she had been unable to watch the tilt. He called her name. The figure in the passenger seat lifted its head. The unshaven face of one of Baltazar's men leered at him from under a head covering.

"Thanks for rescuing me," the man said in a falsetto imitation of a female voice. He reached under the folds of his dress for a gun but got tangled up.

Austin hauled back his mailed right fist and channeled his fury into a crashing blow to the man's chin that knocked him cold. He pulled the unconscious man from the car. He slipped behind the steering wheel and muttered a prayer that Baltazar hadn't switched keys. The engine started.

He decided not to head away from the bridge into unknown territory. The woods he saw in the distance might be a dead end.

Baltazar's men had pulled him back onto the bridge. He screamed at his men to get Austin. Half a dozen guards advanced across the bridge. Austin retrieved the lance he had discarded. He angled the point out as if he were in a tilt, drove away from the gorge, then spun the wheel around and aimed for the bridge.

Baltazar saw the Bentley speeding toward him and ducked behind the tilt barrier, but the lance swept his men from the bridge like crumbs being brushed off a table.

When Austin had gained the other side, he discarded the lance and nailed the accelerator. The wheels spun on the grass, but Austin kept the fishtailing car under control and drove onto the road that led back to the tents.

He glanced in his rearview mirror. An SUV was on his tail. Someone had radioed ahead because another SUV came directly at him. Austin aimed the Bentley at the oncoming vehicle and pressed his hand down on the horn.

The SUV driver must have figured the heavier vehicle would win the game of chicken. At the last second the Bentley swerved aside. The SUV crashed head-on into the chase vehicle.

Austin breezed past the entrance to a driveway that led to a big house in the distance. He stayed on the road for another mile until he came to a gate and guard post. He slowed the car, in expectation that a guard would pop out of the shelter, but he drove up to the gate without being challenged. Austin guessed that the gate guards had been given permission to desert their post for the joust.

He got out of the car and went inside the hut, where he punched the button that would open the double cast-iron gates.

As he stepped out of the guardhouse, Austin heard the sound of motors. A convoy of black SUVs was speeding toward the gate. He drove through the open gates, stopped the car, and went back into the guardhouse. Then he closed the gates, picked up a heavy chair, and hammered the controls with the chair leg until they were useless.

The convoy was less than an eighth of a mile away.

Austin climbed a tree and crawled out onto a thick branch that extended over the fence. He dropped to the ground, knocking the wind out of his lungs, but quickly recovered. He scrambled back into the Bentley and mashed the accelerator in a jackrabbit start.

He was speeding along an open road flanked by green pastures and agricultural fields. Farm silos rose in the distance. No one was on his tail. He glanced at the cloudless blue sky, and it occurred to him that Baltazar might have access to a helicopter.

The bright red car would make an easy target from the air.

He turned onto a narrow lane. The closely grown trees on either side formed a thick canopy that shielded the car from above.

He noticed a car pulled over onto the shoulder. A man in a dark suit was leaning against the fender, and he looked up from the map as the red car blasted his way. As Austin flew by, he caught a fleeting glance of the man's face. He hit the brakes, put the car into a fast backup, and slammed to a reverse stop.

"Hello, Flagg." Austin said.

The CIA man looked out of place in his dark suit and tie. When he saw Austin, a half-moon grin crossed his face. His heavy-lidded eyes took in the Bentley and Austin's mail jacket.

"Fancy wheels. NUMA must be paying you big bucks. Suit's nice too."

"They're not mine," Austin said. "I borrowed them from Baltazar. What are you doing here?"

"I found out Baltazar's got a place around here. I was nosing around."

Austin jerked his thumb to the rear. "It's back there a few miles. Where are we?"

"Upstate New York. What about your lady friend?"

"I couldn't get to Carina. How fast can you line up some muscle?"

"Police might be faster."

"The local gendarmerie wouldn't stand a chance against Baltazar's mercenaries."

Flagg nodded and pulled a phone out of an inside pocket. He punched in a number and talked for a few minutes before hanging up. "Got a 'go' team coming out of Langley. They'll be here in two hours."

"Two *hours*!" Austin said. "It might as well be two years."

"Best they can do," Flagg said with a shrug. "How many bad guys you say there were?"

"About three dozen, counting Baltazar."

"Odds are about right for a couple of tough old company men," Flagg said. He opened the door to his car and reached under the seat to pull out a Glock 9mm pistol, which he handed to Austin. "This is a spare." He patted his chest. "I'm already carrying."

Austin remembered that Flagg was a walking arsenal.

"Thanks," Austin said, taking the weapon. "Hop in."

Flagg slid into the passenger side of the Bentley.

"Damnit, Austin," Flagg said. "I had forgotten until now how boring my life had become since you left the company."

Austin levered the gearshift into low and put the car into a tight U-turn.

"Hold on to your hat," he said over the squeal of spinning tires. "Life is about to become very interesting."

CHAPTER

49

"Shouldn't they be up by now?" Saxon said, sounding a note of concern.

"Don't worry. They're both experienced divers," Trout said.

He and Saxon sat in the rubber raft near the marker buoy. Trout was more worried than he let on. He had glanced at his wristwatch a few minutes before Saxon spoke. Gamay and Zavala were pushing their air supply to the limit, especially if they needed decompression stops. Dire scenarios materialized in his imagination. He could picture the divers lost or their tanks entangled in the unknown passages below the hotel.

Trout had been staring at a blue heron skimming over the lake when he saw a disturbance on the surface.

He pointed at the mounding bubbles. "They're *up*!"

He grabbed his paddle and told Saxon to do the same. They dug in and were only a few yards from the first head to break the surface. Gamay. Zavala surfaced seconds later.

Gamay inflated her buoyancy regulator and floated on her back. She pulled the regulator mouthpiece from between her teeth and took gulps of fresh air. Trout tossed a rope to his wife.

"Hey, beautiful, how about a ride?" he said.

"That's the best offer I've heard all day," Gamay said in a weary voice.

Zavala hitched onto the line behind Gamay. Trout and Saxon towed the two tired divers into shallow water. The divers removed their tanks and fins and slogged onto shore. They dropped their weight belts, climbed to the edge of the grassy banking, and sat down to rest.

Saxon hauled the raft onto shore. Trout opened a cooler and passed around cold bottles of water. He was unable to contain his curiosity. "Don't keep us in suspense. Did you find King Solomon's mine?"

A faint smile came to Zavala's lips. "He's *your* husband," he said to Gamay. "Maybe you should break the bad news."

Gamay sighed. "Someone beat us to it."

"Gold prospectors?" Trout said.

"Not exactly," Zavala said. He got to his feet and retrieved the carrying bag from the beached raft. He pulled out the pewter box, which he handed to Trout. "We found *this* in the mine."

Paul's eyes blinked rapidly as he stared with speechless disbelief at the name embossed on the lid. He handed the box to Saxon.

Saxon was less restrained. "Thomas Jefferson!" he burst out. "How can that be?"

Gamay slipped a small knife out of a leg sheath and gave it to Saxon. "Why don't you do us the honors?"

Despite his excitement, Saxon exercised extreme care as he picked away at the rusted fastener. The lid had been sealed with wax, but it opened easily. He gazed into the box for a few seconds, and then lifted out two soft squares of vellum, wrapped in stiff waxed paper and marked with lines and Xs and tightly written script. He put the squares together where their ragged edges matched.

"It's the rest of the Phoenician map," he whispered. "It shows the river and bay."

Gamay took the vellum from Saxon's trembling hands and studied the markings without comment before passing them to her husband.

"The plot thickens," she said.

"*This* plot is as thick as clam chowder," Trout said with a shake of his head. "Where exactly did you find this stuff?"

Gamay described their dive into the cave and down the shaft. Zavala picked up the narrative, laying out their exploration of the cave tunnels and the chamber where the box rested on a stone platform.

Saxon had recovered from his shock and put his mind to work again.

"Fascinating," Saxon said. "Any indication of gold?"

"Nothing that we could see," Gamay said.

Saxon's eyes narrowed. "Either there *was* gold and you didn't see it or the mine had been played out and abandoned."

"In either case, how does what they found fit in with the stories of King Solomon's fabled gold mine?" Trout said. "Is this Ophir or not?"

"Yes and no," Saxon said. He chuckled at Trout's puzzled expression. "Some people believe Ophir was not a specific location, but the name given to several different sources of the king's gold. This may have been *one* of his mines."

Gamay stared out at the placid surface of the lake. "What better place to hide something than an abandoned mine with nothing of value in it?"

"Which brings us back to the Phoenician expedition," Saxon said. "Its purpose was to hide a sacred relic."

"Which raises the question of what happened to that relic," Trout said.

Gamay picked up the metal box. "Maybe we should ask Mr. Jefferson."

Saxon had been holding the vellum squares. He held them up for a better look at the markings and said, "*This* is interesting. I believe the map is a palimpsest."

"A palim*what?*" Trout said.

"It's a term for vellum that has been used more than once," Saxon said. "Byzantine monks perfected the practice of washing and scraping writing from vellum so it could be used again, but the process could be much older. See there, when you hold it to the light, faint writing is visible."

He passed the vellum around for the others to examine.

"Too bad we can't retrieve the original message," Trout said.

"Maybe we *can,*" Saxon said. "The curators at the Walters Art Museum in Baltimore recently deciphered a thousand-year-old message that had been hidden in a palimpsest. They may be able to do something with this. I wish Austin were here to share these wonderful discoveries. When will he be back from his errand?"

Zavala had been thinking about Austin even in the subterranean depths of the lake. Austin was a survivor, but by allowing himself to be kidnapped by the ruthless Baltazar, he was jumping into the abyss. As he got to his feet and prepared to collect his dive gear, he said, "Soon. *Damn* soon, I hope."

CHAPTER

50

AUSTIN AND FLAGG SAT IN the Bentley with the motor running, eyeing the entrance to Baltazar's estate.

"I thought you said these folks were unfriendly," Flagg said. "Looks like they're expecting us."

"That's what I'm afraid of," Austin said.

They had spent the last hour trying to find another way into Baltazar's estate but encountered heavy woods and electrified fence. They got lost in the maze of dirt roads around the property and found themselves back at the main gate. It was wide-open.

Austin leaned on the steering wheel. "This must be what goes through a lobster's mind before he crawls into the trap. Carina's *my* friend, not yours. We can still wait for reinforcements."

"Reinforcements will just get in the way," Flagg scoffed. He produced a third pistol. "Go slow. I'll watch the bushes for redskins."

Austin put the car into gear and drove through the gates. Flagg sat up on the back of the seat with a gun in each hand. No one tried to stop them. The road broke out of the woods, and Austin headed for the jousting field. The tents had all been leveled. The fabric was ripped and covered with tire tracks. The reviewing stand was unchanged, except for an added feature.

As they neared the stand, Flagg tensed. "What the hell is *that*?"

A human figure was hanging from the front of the stand, its chin touching its chest. Arms and legs dangled loosely.

Austin clutched the Glock in one hand and drove closer.

"Aw, hell," he said.

"Anyone you know?"

"I'm afraid so," Austin said.

It was Squire. A lance pinned him to the stand like a butterfly in a display case.

Austin continued on past the reviewing stand and its macabre decoration and came to the SUV he had played chicken with and the vehicle it had crashed into. Both were heavily damaged.

"What happened here?" Flagg said.

"Demolition derby," Austin said. He continued on to the gorge.

The field that had been crowded with vehicles and Baltazar's men was deserted. Even the horses and their trailers had vanished. There were deep tire tracks in the grass, indicating intense truck activity.

Austin described his joust with Baltazar and his encounter with the Carina stand-in. Then he turned around and drove back to the reviewing stand. He told Flagg that he owed Squire a favor. They pulled the lance out and gently wrapped Squire in a piece of tent fabric. After placing the body in the reviewing stand they explored some side roads and came upon a vacant hangar and airstrip, which explained Baltazar's fast escape.

They decided to check out the house. Austin turned up the driveway to the mansion. The two-story hacienda looked as if it had been plucked from the Spanish countryside. The walls were light brown smooth stucco. Rounded parapets decorated the corners of a roof covered in red tile. Arched windows framed a large, intricately carved porch.

Austin parked in front of the house. Still no opposition. He and

Flagg got out of the car and made their way through a courtyard to a tall double door of dark-paneled wood. Austin opened the doors. No one blew his head off, so he stepped into the spacious entry hall.

He and Flagg took turns covering each other as they went through the lower level room by room. Next they searched the second story. They found the room with the balcony. It was a study, with a large desk and leather chairs. Austin went out on the balcony. He had a view of the surrounding lawns and fields. Nothing moved within his field of vision except for a few crows.

"Hey, Austin," Flagg called. "Your pal left you a note."

Flagg was pointing to a sheet of Baltazar's stationery taped to a re-mote control on a side table. Below the bull's-head logo were the words: Dear Austin, Please watch the video. VB

"Too polite. Might be a booby trap," Flagg said.

"I don't think so. Baltazar likes to torture before he kills."

Flagg's expression mirrored his doubts, but he picked up the re-mote and pressed the ON button.

A section of wall disappeared to reveal a wide television screen. Baltazar's smiling face appeared on the screen. The video had evi-dently been shot in the study, because behind Baltazar was the door leading to the balcony.

"Greetings, Austin," Baltazar said. "I apologize for this hasty mes-sage, but I had family business to attend to. Miss Mechadi is with me. You didn't know that she is the direct descendant of Solomon and Sheba. I must carry out my family mission and offer her to Ba'al. I had plans to spare her, but Ba'al sent you as a scourge who would re-mind me to return to my family roots. Adriano will be disappointed, but he has become quite obsessed with you. I suggest that you keep looking over your shoulder. Thank you, Austin. It was a pleasure jousting." He smiled. "You can keep my car. I have others."

The picture faded.

Flagg frowned. "Guy's a real nutcase."

"Unfortunately, he's a *lethal* nutcase. And he's got Carina. You found this place. Any luck locating other holes where he might go to ground?"

"It was hard enough to locate *this* shack," Flagg said with a shake of his head. "We're still working on it, but with all the dummy corporations he's got set up it's tough. Who's this Adriano?"

"The stuff of nightmares." Austin stuck his hand out. "I need to borrow your phone."

ZAVALA WAS CLIMBING into the helicopter cockpit when he heard "La Cucaracha" jangling in the pocket where he kept his phone. He put the phone to his ear and heard a familiar voice:

"You're still answering calls, so I guess you didn't run off to Mexico with Solomon's gold," Austin said.

Zavala grinned broadly.

"And Baltazar must have gotten sick of your wisecracks because you're still making them."

"Something like that," Austin said. "Did you find the mine?"

"Yup. No gold, Kurt, but we found another treasure hidden in the mine. The other piece of the vellum map in a box apparently owned by Thomas Jefferson."

"*Jefferson* again. I'm going to let you and the Trouts work on that one. Baltazar's still got Carina. I need to talk to Saxon."

Zavala passed the phone to Saxon, who said, "Kurt, can you *believe* it?"

Austin cut him short. "I'm interested, but not now. Baltazar left me a message. I'm going to let you hear his exact words. If there is any hint of his plans, no matter how slight, I want you to tell me."

Austin clicked the television remote and held the phone up so Saxon could hear Baltazar's chilling good-bye.

There was a stunned silence at Saxon's end, then he said, "He believes Carina is descended from Solomon?"

"Apparently so. What's the reference to Ba'al mean?"

He quickly regained his composure.

"He said he's going to offer Carina to Ba'al. It can only mean one thing. He's going to *sacrifice* her to the god Ba'al. The bastard! We've got to find her before it's too late."

"You've known the man longer than I have. Any ideas where could he have taken her?"

"Not specifically."

"His company owns a mercenary ship. Is that where he's taken her?"

"I don't think so. He mentions his family *roots*. That implies dry ground. He could be talking about Spain, where the Baltazars moved after the Crusades. Although their ancestral home was on Cyprus. That's where they prospered for many years. It's either Spain or Cyprus. I'd stake my life on it."

"Make up your mind, Saxon. It's not *your* life I'm worried about."

"Sorry. Um—wait. After my boat was torched, I learned what I could about the Baltazars. A shadowy bunch. But I found references to them in the history of the Knights Templar. The Baltazars were connected to the Templars but apparently broke off or they would have been wiped out with the rest of the Knights. The order's symbol was the bull's head, which can also represent one of the incarnations of Ba'al."

The bull's head.

Austin let his mind drift back to the helicopter flight he and Joe had taken after the containership hijacking. The chopper had come in low over a mineral ship and he had seen the bull's-head symbol for the first time. Below the ship's name was its port of registration.

Nicosia. Cyprus.

"Thanks, Saxon. You've been a great help. Tell Joe I'll keep in touch."

Austin clicked off and relayed the substance of his conversation to Flagg.

"Cyprus," Flagg said. "That's the other side of the world."

"Close to the Turkish coast. If I had known Baltazar might be headed that way, I would have stayed in Istanbul. Do you have anyone there?"

"We've got a guy in place who grew up on the island. We've got additional assets in that region. I could spring a few guys to give the gentleman a big surprise."

"Baltazar's dangerous. He's not going to let anyone get in the way of his family destiny. He'll kill Carina before anyone can get to him. Have your guys track him down and move in only if they have to. I'll see if I can commandeer a NUMA plane in the meantime. I'll only be a few hours behind him." Austin shook his head. "Unfortunately, he can cause a lot of trouble in that time."

"That's why I was thinking you might get there *ahead* of him."

Austin was in no mood for jokes. "I didn't know the CIA had mastered teleportation."

"Nothing that sophisticated. I was thinking of the Blackbird."

Austin was well acquainted from his CIA days with the avian nickname for the SR-71, a high-speed, high-altitude aircraft that had flown secret reconnaissance missions for the CIA before it was succeeded by drone aircraft and satellites in the late 1990s. The legendary plane could make a transatlantic crossing in two hours.

"I thought they retired the whole flock of Blackbirds," he said.

"That's the cover story," Flagg said. "We kept one to transport personnel in emergencies."

"I'd say this qualifies as an emergency," Austin said.

"Great minds think alike," Flagg said. He flipped open his cell phone. He worked his way through the bureaucracy, and was still talking when the *whup-whup* of helicopter rotors could be heard.

Austin went to the balcony and saw two helicopters flying in low circles over the mansion.

"The cavalry has arrived," Austin said.

Flagg tucked the phone in his pocket. "I always cheered for the Indians, but I'll make an exception because I'm in a good mood. Just spoke to a mucky-muck. It wasn't easy, but you've got a first-class ticket on the Blackbird."

Flagg's news was good, but Austin was a realist. He was facing long odds.

His eyes hardened. If Carina were harmed, Austin would devote every sinew and synapse in his body to a single goal.

And that was to send Baltazar to hell.

F RED TURNER WAS DOWN on his knees behind the bar, stacking beer mugs. He heard the door open and close. A frown came to his ruddy face. Probably a regular customer looking to start his happy hour early.

"We're *closed*," Turner growled.

No one answered. Turner stood up and saw a large man in the doorway. The stranger's round features were soft and childlike. Turner was a retired policeman, and his cop's instincts sensed an unspoken menace behind the unthreatening façade. He stepped closer to the shotgun he kept near the cash register.

The stranger simply looked around and said:

"Where did the name of this place come from?"

Bender chuckled at the unexpected question. "People think I named it after an Old West saloon. But when I bought the place, I remembered reading that there were gold mines around here in the old days."

"What happened to the mines?"

"Closed them years ago. Didn't find enough gold to keep them open."

After a moment in thought, the man said, "Thank you," and left without further comment. Turner went back to stacking glasses, muttering to himself about the odd people who come into bars.

Adriano sat in his car in the parking lot and reread the directions and map Austin had jotted down on the sheet of notepaper. He gazed up with a bland expression on his face at the neon sign on the flat roof of the low-slung building: GOLD MINE CAFÉ. Then he ripped the paper to shreds, started the car, and drove out of the parking lot onto the Maryland back road.

After leaving Baltazar's jousting contest, Adriano had driven from Upstate New York to New Jersey and then to Maryland. Austin's directions had directed him to a rural area not far from Chesapeake Bay and taken him down a series of back roads that had ended in the Gold Mine Café.

He picked up his telephone and called on the direct line that connected him to Baltazar.

"Well?" His employer's voice came on the phone.

Adriano told Baltazar about the Gold Mine Café. "Too bad Austin is dead," Adriano said. "I would have made him tell us what we want to know."

"Too late," Baltazar snapped. "He escaped. We had to leave the estate. Don't go back there."

"And the woman?"

"I have her. We'll deal with Austin later. I want to see his face when I tell him what I did with his lovely friend."

Adriano had hoped he would be the last to talk to the woman, but he kept the disappointment out of his voice.

"What do you want me to do?"

"I'll be back in a few days. Go to ground in the meantime. I'll call you when I return. You'll have much work to do. I want NUMA and anyone associated with it destroyed. You'll have every resource you'll need."

Adriano was smiling when he hung up. He had never attempted large-scale killing and looked forward to the challenge mass murder offered.

Life was good, he thought. Death is even better.

CHAPTER

52

THE BOEING 737 MARKED with a bull's-head logo on its fuselage touched down at Larnaca International Airport and taxied to an area reserved for private corporate jets. The mechanics who normally worked on the planes had gone home for the night. Baltazar had planned his arrival with great care, and it was unlikely anyone would have had more than mild curiosity at the figure being carried down the steps of the plane in a stretcher.

Bandages covered the person's face except for the eyes and nose. Men in white medical jackets loaded the stretcher into a waiting helicopter. Seconds later, Baltazar descended to the tarmac and got into the helicopter. The helicopter lifted into the air moments later and headed west.

The aircraft landed in a small airport near the coastal city of Paphos. A waiting ambulance drove off as soon as the stretcher was loaded aboard. Baltazar and his men followed in a Mercedes sedan.

The two-vehicle convoy skirted the edge of the city and turned onto a main highway. Eventually, it left the highway for an ascending mountain road. The road narrowed to two lanes, as it traversed a series of switchbacks, passing through quiet mountain villages and past derelict hotels that had once been fashionable summer resorts before people started to spend more time at the seashore.

The countryside grew more rugged and less populated the higher the ambulance and its companion climbed. Dark piney woods crowded in on both sides. With the Mercedes close behind, the ambulance turned onto a dirt lane that was almost hidden by overgrowth.

The vehicles lurched along the cratered road for about a half mile. The road came to an abrupt end without warning. Silhouetted against the starry sky was a squat two-story structure. Baltazar got out of the Mercedes and breathed in the cool night air. The only sound was the moaning of the wind through empty rooms of the old Crusader castle. Baltazar soaked in its ancient aura, gaining strength by his proximity to the ruin that had housed his forebears.

The government had once tried to acquire the historic structure and turn it into a tourist attraction. The plan disintegrated after supporters received death threats, which was just as well for those who knew the fearsome history of the place. The locals still whispered about the unspeakable horrors associated with the moldering ruin.

Baltazar hadn't visited the castle since the last offering to Ba'al. He remembered the stark defensive architecture of the building. It was built as a fortress originally. The roof was crenellated to provide shelter for defenders. The only openings in the otherwise blank façade were arrow slits for archers. But mostly, he remembered the Room.

He climbed a short set of stairs to the entrance. Using an antique key, he unlocked the door, which swung open with a mournful creak. The empty rooms were like refrigerators that kept out the heat of the day and preserved the cold. Baltazar called out to his men to bring the stretcher in and to place it in front of a fireplace big enough for a man to stand in.

There were six mercenaries, all culled from his security company. Their major attributes had been obedience, cruelty, and the ability to keep their mouths shut. He told them to take up guard posts. As soon as he was alone, he pressed a combination of stones on the mantle. The procedure unlocked a door hidden in the back of the fireplace.

He switched on an electric torch, ducked through the fireplace door, and descended a flight of stone stairs.

A miasma of air more foul than dragon's breath flowed up from below. The musty tomblike odor carried memories of pain and terror and was heavy with an oily smell. But to Baltazar it was as sweet as perfume. He stopped to light a wooden torch in a wall sconce and used its flames to ignite wall torches that lined a short passageway. At the end of the corridor was a perfectly round room about a hundred feet in diameter.

Plaques set into the walls marked the ancestral resting place of scores of Baltazars who'd been buried in the castle before the family was forced to flee to Cyprus. Figures of Ba'al in the god's various incarnations ringed the room.

In the center of the chamber was a bronze statue that resembled the stone one in the basement of his mansion in the United States. Like the other, it was a sitting figure whose arms were outstretched with the palms up. It was at least four times as large, sitting on a pedestal around six feet tall. Narrow stairways ran up both sides of the pedestal. The face on the smaller statue was almost benign compared to the visage of the larger one. It was more hideous than the ugliest gargoyle.

Baltazar climbed the stairs. He stood on a small platform behind the statue. The ancient priests took their post here, speaking into a voice tube that they had used to instill even more fear in their hapless victims.

He removed the family book from its bag and placed it on a ledge specially made to hold it. Reading the rituals from the book, he wrapped his fingers around a lever that protruded from between the shoulder blades of the seated figure. He pulled the lever down. There was a grating noise as a system of weights and pulleys came into play and doors slid open to reveal a circular pit in the floor directly in front of the statue.

He lifted the lever. The statue's arms dropped down at the elbows and snapped up almost as quickly.

He descended the stairs and checked the pit with his light. It had been refilled with oil after the last time it had been used, when the family fortunes were on the wane and it had been necessary to make an offering to Ba'al.

A young Eastern European woman with no family had been lured to Cyprus with the promise of a well-paying job.

All was ready.

He went back for Carina. The bandaged figure on the stretcher stirred. Good, Baltazar thought. He wanted Carina to see the fate that awaited her. He undid the straps that held her on the stretcher and slung her over his shoulder fireman-style.

Baltazar heard a moan from Carina's lips. She was coming to.

He smiled. Soon she would be in the loving arms of Ba'al.

CHAPTER

53

THE VOICE OF THE BRITISH TORNADO FB fighter pilot
crackled over the intercom.

"Welcome to the beautiful island of Cyprus, birthplace of
Aphrodite, goddess of love."

Austin sat behind the pilot in the seat normally occupied by the
supersonic plane's weapons system operator. The plane made a circle over the British Air Force base near the old Roman city of
Curium before it dropped out of the sky in a quick descent. As the
jet's landing gear thumped on the tarmac, Austin gazed out at the
runway lights after the ninety-minute flight from England and wondered at how small the planet had become.

Hours earlier he had hitched a ride on a CIA helicopter to Albany.
From there, an executive jet transported him to Andrews Air Force
Base in Maryland, where the Blackbird was housed in a special
hangar, and flown only at night.

The SR-71 had been developed as a long-range strategic reconnaissance aircraft that could fly at speeds of more than Mach 3.2 and
reach an altitude of eighty-five thousand feet. The flattened fuselage,

bluer than black, was more than one hundred feet long, excluding the five-foot-long nose probe. Two vertical stabilizers rose from the rear of the plane like twin shark fins. One of the 32,500-pound thrust engines could power an ocean liner.

Austin was given a high-protein meal of steak and eggs, a medical exam, and fitted out for a special suit similar to those used on the space shuttle. As he suited up, he breathed in pure oxygen to filter gases out of his body. A van took him to the barn where the plane was kept and he was buckled into a specially built passenger seat. The plane rendezvoused with a tanker seven minutes after taking off. Less than two hours later, it landed at a British RAF base in England.

Flagg had arranged for the fighter to transport Austin on the last leg of the trip because it would be less obvious than a U.S. Air Force plane in Cyprus, where the British had long maintained a military foothold.

A car drove out onto the tarmac and paced the fighter jet until it stopped. Three men dressed in black slacks, turtlenecks, and berets got out of the car to greet Austin as he climbed from the plane.

"Good evening, Mr. Austin," said the group's leader, a swarthy Greek American who identified himself as George. He said he had been brought in from Athens to rendezvous with agents from Cairo and Istanbul. A fourth man, who was attached to the American embassy in Nicosia, and was familiar with the island, had gone ahead to scout out the situation.

"Are you armed?" George said.

Austin patted a bulge in the front of his jacket. While Austin was flying to Maryland, Flagg had had someone from Langley pick up a change of clothes and the Bowen revolver from Austin's boathouse and deliver it to Andrews.

George smiled. "I should have known better than to ask an

ex–company man. But these might come in handy." He handed Austin a pair of night vision goggles and a beret.

Austin was bundled into the Land Rover. An air force car escorted them to the exit, and a guard waved them through the gate. They traveled along a darkened highway at speeds of nearly a hundred miles an hour for a time before the driver braked and turned off onto a road that ascended into the mountains.

George handed Austin a satellite photo and a flashlight. The photo showed a perfectly square building whose remote mountaintop location was accessed by a single road.

George's phone chirped. He listened for a few moments and clicked off. He turned to Austin. "A car and an ambulance just arrived at the castle."

"How long will it take us to get there?" Austin said.

"Less than an hour. It's slow going on these mountain roads."

"This is a matter of life or death," Austin said.

George nodded, and told the driver to pick up the pace. The car accelerated, and went through a series of g-force turns around the hairpin switchbacks.

As they neared their destination, George got a second call from his advance man. He had seen the car ascending the hill below and asked the driver to blink his headlights to identify himself. The driver hit the dimmer switch a couple of times. Seconds later, someone signaled with a flashlight from the side of the road.

The car pulled over and George rolled his window down. A man's face was framed in the other car's window.

"The road is about fifty yards ahead," the man said.

"We'll go on foot from here," George said to the advance man. "You lead the way."

Austin got out of the Land Rover and slipped his night vision goggles over his eyes. He and the others followed the advance man along the edge of the road in a distance-eating trot.

✦ ✦ ✦

BALTAZAR CARRIED Carina up the stairs and lowered her onto the statue's upraised arms.

The drugs that had kept her unconscious for hours were wearing off. She awakened with an oily smell in her nostrils. As her vision cleared, she saw the hideous bronze face of Ba'al. Her arms and legs were bound in bandages, but she was able to move her head. She craned her neck and saw Baltazar standing at the base of the statue.

"I'd advise you not to struggle, Sheba. You're on a precarious perch."

"I'm *not* Sheba, you demented fool. And I want you to let me go."

"Your queenly haughtiness betrays you," Baltazar said. "You are Sheba's descendant. You have Sheba's blood in your veins. You tempted me as your ancestor tempted Solomon. But Ba'al sent Austin to remind me of my family duty."

"And you are a madman as well as a fool."

"Perhaps," Baltazar said.

He studied the elements of the scene like an artist contemplating a potential subject. He was reaching for a wall torch when he heard what sounded like gunfire.

AUSTIN HAD halted at the edge of the access road and dropped down on one knee.

A match had flared ahead, and the breeze carried cigarette smoke his way. He could see a figure pacing back and forth in the grainy green vista produced by the night vision goggles.

George tapped Austin on the arm. He pointed to himself and then to the sentry.

Austin gave him an okay signal. George bent low and crept up on the unsuspecting guard. Austin watched as the figures merged.

There was a grunt, and the guard dropped to the ground. George waved the others on.

"Sloppy," George said as he stood over the unconscious guard. "Sorry about that."

Some of the guards had heard the sentry's grunt and came running to investigate. Shouts were coming from every direction. George was illuminated by light from an electric torch. He raised his hands to shield his eyes. Austin threw a flying block that knocked George out of the path of the fusillade that came next.

George scrambled to his feet and unleashed a short burst from his machine pistol. The light went out, followed by screams of pain.

Austin sprinted toward the castle and ran across the bridge over the dry moat. The mercenary guarding the door was trying to make sense of the shouts, moving lights, and gunfire. Unlike Austin, he didn't have the advantage of night vision. He didn't see the figure racing toward him with shoulders lowered until it was too late.

Austin hit the man like a bowling ball. The guard crashed backward, and his head snapped against the castle's wall. He slumped unconscious to the ground.

Austin opened the heavy door and stepped into the coldness of the castle. With his Bowen extended in both hands, he quickly searched the first level and found the room with the big fireplace. The door at the back of the fireplace had been left open slightly, allowing a sliver of torchlight to escape.

Tossing his night vision goggles aside, Austin kicked the door open and ran down the stairs. He stepped through an arched portal and took in the scene. The circular room with its grotesque statuary. The heavy smell of oil. Carina on the upraised arms. And Baltazar, who stood calmly beside the statue as if he had been expecting Austin.

"Austin!" he said, his face contorted into a mask of fury. "Somehow, I knew it was you."

As a start, Austin wanted Baltazar away from Carina. He aimed the Bowen. "Fun's over, Baltazar. Come down from there."

Baltazar ducked behind the statue and spoke into the voice tube. The hollow voice seemed to issue from the open mouth of the statue.

"Too late, Austin. Sheba rests in the arms of Ba'al."

Austin heard a grinding noise underfoot and stepped back as the trapdoors slid open to reveal the oil pit.

Clenching his teeth in concentration, he stood with his feet wide apart, aimed the Bowen at the statue's face, and squeezed the trigger. Chunks of metal went flying. The statue's nose disintegrated, to expose its hollowed interior. Austin let off another round. The heavy bullet took off a cheek. Then he methodically shot out the rest of the statue's evil face.

There was a shriek of pain, and Baltazar stepped out from behind the statue. His face was bloodied from flying metal. He reached out and grabbed a torch from the wall. Austin snapped off a wild shot. It missed, but in his haste to seek cover, Baltazar dropped the torch on the stairs.

Baltazar descended the stairway to retrieve the flaming torch. Austin's gun was empty. He tucked it into the holster and sprinted up the stairs.

Baltazar snatched up the burning brand and stuck it in Austin's face. Austin ducked and threw his shoulder into Baltazar's midsection. Baltazar dropped the torch but he was a physical match for Austin, and his rage gave him added strength. They struggled for a moment, lost their footing, and rolled down the staircase to the edge of the pool.

Baltazar head-butted Austin, got to his feet, and kicked Austin in the ribs. He aimed another kick at Austin's face. Austin ignored the searing pain, grabbed Baltazar's boot, and twisted. Baltazar stood on one foot, trying vainly to maintain his balance, and then fell head-first into the pool.

Austin scrambled to his feet and saw Baltazar trying to swim in the thick liquid. His head and face gleamed with the black oil.

"Get back, Kurt!"

The bandages that held Carina had stretched during her travels. She had freed herself and climbed off the statue's arms. Now she stood on the stairs, holding the torch in her hand. With her white dress, and lovely features contorted in anger, she looked like an avenging angel.

"Wait," Austin said. He started up the stairs.

Carina hesitated. She started to lower the torch. Then she saw that Baltazar was trying to climb out of the pool, a task made difficult by the oil on his hands. He struggled at the edge like a reptilian monster emerging from the deep. Carina raised her arm back and threw the torch. It arced through the air ahead of a trail of embers and landed in the middle of the oil pit.

There was a loud *whoof*.

Austin raced up the stairs and grabbed Carina around the waist. He pushed her into the space behind the statue and threw his body on top of hers.

Although the statue shielded them from the searing heat, they were in danger of choking from the cloud of greasy black smoke that billowed up to the ceiling. Even with smoke escaping through the vent in the ceiling, the chamber was filled with toxic fumes within seconds.

Austin was wrapping his arm tighter around Carina's slim body when he felt a handle on the wall. He pulled the handle and a section of wall slid back. Cold air flowed from the rectangular opening. Austin was barely able to get the words out but he shouted at Carina to crawl through the opening. Then he followed her and slid the wall section shut.

Austin dug a penlight out of his jacket and flashed it around. They were in a room barely bigger than a closet. The air was musty but free of smoke. He guessed that it had been built to protect Baltazar's ancestors when they were making sacrifices to Ba'al.

They stayed behind the statue until the oil burned itself out. Austin slid the door open a crack. The air was foul but mostly free of smoke. They used some of Carina's gauze bandages to fashion makeshift smoke masks. Then they crawled out from behind the statue and made their way down the stairs to the door.

As they passed the smoking fire pit, Carina averted her eyes. Austin glanced into the pool as if he expected Baltazar to crawl from the depths. But all he saw was the noxious blackness of the abyss.

54

AFTER HIS QUICK PHONE CALL to Baltazar, Adriano had driven to New Jersey to work on his plans for NUMA.

He stayed in a cheap motel, where he devised an intricate plan for NUMA that involved multiple assassins, car bombs, biological agents, and old standbys, such as high-powered rifles. He methodically plowed through staff listings and gave priority to targets that would gut the agency. He moved on the next day and stayed in another motel. By the third day, he had put the finishing touches on his scheme for mass death and destruction. Then he waited for word from Baltazar.

After two days, Adriano tried to call Baltazar but got no answer. He hung up on the busy signal and punched in another number that connected him with the recording device he had planted in Austin's tree.

"Hello, Joe," Austin's voice said. "How's your research going?'

"We've got the mine pinned down," Zavala said. "The papyrus told us exactly where to find it."

Adriano raised an eyebrow and listened intently.

"Terrific! Feed me the details."

Zavala told him about the hotel submerged under the lake in

St. Anthony's Wilderness, and went into great detail about the shaft leading from the kitchen into the mine. He gave Austin the GPS coordinates.

"How soon can we make an exploratory dive?" Austin said.

"I'm pulling together a dive team now. We can be on site in forty-eight hours."

"Good work. We'll go over the details tomorrow."

The two men hung up after some unrelated chitchat.

The call had been made earlier that day. Adriano read the notes he'd written down. He checked out of his motel room and drove to a storage unit, one of several he maintained near Washington. The unit contained weapons and ammunition, money, changes of clothing and identity, and, for his immediate purposes, a complete set of scuba gear, which he loaded into the trunk of his car.

The next morning his car was bumping along the dirt road into St. Anthony's Wilderness. He parked at the edge of the lake, got into a wet suit, and slipped into his buoyancy compensator and tank. Adriano was an accomplished diver, having learned his skills from the SEALs who'd been on Baltazar's payroll.

He swam to a buoy floating in the lake, glanced at the reading on his portable GPS, and dove down to the hotel with powerful flutter kicks. He made his way to the kitchen and found the shaft. He dove into the opening without hesitating. Even if he hadn't been anxious to get to the mine, it was doubtful he would have noticed the block-shaped plastic objects buried in the rubble within a few feet of the shaft opening.

When Adriano got to the bottom of the shaft, he was surprised to see a waterproof slate with an arrow drawn on it and the words: THIS WAY.

He followed the direction the arrow was pointing and came to another slate indicating a tunnel off the main cave. He followed it to an intersection. Another slate, another arrow. He came to the end of the tunnel. A fourth arrow pointed the way into the large mine chamber with the dais.

As ADRIANO followed the arrow on the slate, two figures slipped quietly from the woods and made their way to the water's edge. Austin checked his watch. "It's been thirty minutes," he said.

"That would put him down the shaft and into the mine," Zavala said.

The phony telephone conversation had been set up as bait. Time to spring the trap. Austin waded into the water up to his waist. He was holding a transmitter protected in a waterproof case. He waited a few minutes, then lowered the transmitter into the water and pressed a button. Seconds later, multiple mounds of foam disturbed the surface of the lake.

Austin watched, tight-lipped, until the expanding ripples washed against his chest.

Then he turned and sloshed his way back to shore.

He was met by a grim-faced Zavala, who gave him a folder he'd found in Adriano's car. The folder was marked NUMA.

FAR BELOW THE SURFACE of the lake, Adriano heard the explosions as a series of thuds.

He considered turning back but decided to keep on. Adriano had a robotlike sense of purpose, which made him an effective assassin, and he was determined to find the mine and its gold.

Following the arrow, he swam into the altar room. His pulse quickened at the sight of the raised dais, where the Thomas Jefferson box had rested.

Nestled in the shreds of wood was a diver's slate with the words:

WHEN YOU GET TO HELL, ADRIANO, GIVE MR. BALTAZAR OUR REGARDS.

Austin again.

Adriano stared at the message, then threw the slate aside and swam with all his strength along the route that would take him back to the shaft. When he got there, he discovered a pile of rubble that was the only evidence of the collapsed shaft.

He glanced at his air gauge. He had minutes left. Even if there was a way out, he didn't have enough air to search for it. Adriano sat on the pile of rubble until his air ran out completely. The last in the line of Spain's official garrotters died, in a twist of irony, of asphyxiation.

55

A HOY, MR. NICKERSON," Austin said. "Request permission to come aboard the *Lovely Lady*."

Nickerson poked his head out the open door of the salon and smiled when he saw Austin. "Permission granted."

Austin went up the gangway and shook hands with the State Department man.

He tapped a black plastic pouch. "I have something to show you, if you've got a few minutes."

"I *always* have time for you, Mr. Austin. Come below, and I'll brew up some coffee. I'll mix in something to chase away the chill."

"It's eighty degrees, Mr. Nickerson."

"No matter. It's chilly *some*where," Nickerson said.

They went into the cabin, and Nickerson made a pot of strong coffee, which he laced with slugs of Kentucky bourbon. They clicked glasses, and Nickerson said, "Well, now, what do you have for me?"

Austin opened the pouch and produced the squares of vellum. He handed one to Nickerson. "This is the piece Jefferson acquired from an Indian. Meriwether Lewis came across the other vellum in his travels. Together, they form a map showing the location of Solomon's mine in Pennsylvania."

"Wonderful! I knew you could do it. Have you explored the mine?"

"Yes, we have. That's where we found the vellum sections. They had been placed there by Thomas Jefferson."

"That's beyond belief! And what of the relic?"

"The gold Ten Commandments? I think you might know the answer to that question."

"I'm not sure what you mean."

"There was another text written under the map. It's apparently a set of the Ten Commandments that's quite a bit different from the original. Probably what's on the gold tablets."

"Go on, Mr. Austin."

"These commandments were handed down by several pagan gods, including one who demanded human sacrifice. Now I know you know why you were so worried. The Mideast situation wasn't the real reason for your concern."

"Indeed. The Ten Commandments are supposed to be infallible moral guides, declared by a monotheistic god. They provide the foundation for religions followed by millions of people and the underpinnings of Western governmental thought. Some people say they are the inspired source of the legal systems of all Western countries. If the original Ten Commandments were based on pagan writings this frail foundation could be eroded further."

Austin remembered Baltazar's predictions.

"Bringing the world yet another source of unneeded conflict," Austin said.

"Right on the mark. No one knows who had the commandments inscribed on gold instead of clay, but their existence implies validity. Solomon wanted the gold tablets as far away from him as possible.

They contained the possibility of instigating unrest in his day. Much as they do today, I might add."

"You knew when we first talked that the tablets were not in the mine."

"I'm afraid I did."

"Then why did you send me on this wild quest?"

"We know where the tablets *are,* not where they *were.* The ancient writings say that a Navigator will show the way to Ophir. When we heard about the attempted theft of the *Navigator* statue and the discovery of the Artichoke file, we feared that someone would track down the mine and that would lead them to the tablets."

"*We,* meaning the Artichoke Society."

"That's correct. We learned of your role in the hijacking, heard about your team's reputation, and thought you'd be best qualified for the job."

"You owe me an introduction to these Artichokes, Mr. Nickerson."

"Yes, I'm afraid I do."

He reached for a telephone. After a short conversation, Nickerson said. "How soon can you assemble your team?"

"Almost immediately. Where shall I tell them to meet?"

Nickerson smiled. "A little place called Monticello."

LATER THAT DAY, Austin, Zavala, and the Trouts, with Angela, walked between the columns at the entrance to the Jefferson mansion. Emerson and Nickerson were waiting to greet them and ushered them over the threshold.

Emerson waited for a tour group to pass. "I apologize for being devious about this matter," he said.

"Apology accepted," Gamay said. "If you fill in the blanks."

Emerson nodded. "You were close. Meriwether Lewis had come

across the missing half of the mine map in his travels. He had assumed that it was for a western location. He realized his mistake, and was trying to get it to Jefferson when he was murdered by those who wished to keep the mine a secret. Zeb carried the missing piece to Monticello. With the full map in his possession, Jefferson found the mine, and the tablets. He left the map in the mine. Like Solomon, he decided the tablets were best kept out of sight, and formed an organization to ensure this was the case."

"The Artichoke Society you said didn't exist?" Angela said.

"As a member of the society, I'm sworn to secrecy. The original Artichokes consisted of some of the country's founders. As they aged, they recruited new members to take their place. You might be surprised at the names of current members."

Austin gave a shake of his head. "I'm not surprised at *anything* having to do with the subject," he said. "What happened to the tablets?"

"Jefferson formed a work party that included my ancestor Zeb," Emerson said. "They found the mine and brought the tablets back here."

"To *Monticello*?" Angela said. She glanced around as if the tablets were in plain sight.

Emerson tapped the floor with his shoe. "Under our feet. Preserved in a secret room."

There was a stunned silence, broken when Trout asked, "Do you think the world will ever be made aware of their existence?"

"That's up to the Artichokes," Emerson said. "Maybe future members of the society will decide the time is ripe."

Nickerson said, "We're always looking for new members. Anyone on your team would be welcome."

"Thanks, but we're away a lot," Austin said. "But I know someone who would bring youth and intelligence to your group."

He glanced at Angela, who had wandered off, and was staring at the floor as if she could see through it.

A smile crossed Nickerson's face.

"Yes. Thank you for the suggestion. And for all your help. I hope it wasn't inconvenient."

Austin glanced around at the members of his team. "Not at all. We enjoyed ourselves, didn't we?"

Paul Trout blinked his eyes a few times. Keeping a poker face, he said, "I can't wait to write 'What I Did on My Vacation.' "

EPILOGUE

AUSTIN HAULED IN THE MAINSHEET on his catboat, keeping the big sail tight to the wind, while Carina handled the tiller. She pointed the wide bow toward a turquoise research vessel anchored near a Chesapeake Bay island. As the sailboat came up on the vessel, she made a quick turn into the wind, and the sailboat plowed to a stop.

"Nicely done!" Austin said.

"Thanks. I owe it to my teacher."

Anthony Saxon leaned over the rail of the NUMA vessel. He cupped his hands to his mouth. "Come aboard. We've got lots to show you."

They dropped anchor and got into the catboat's dinghy. Austin rowed them over to the turquoise vessel, a smaller version of NUMA's giant research ships used mainly for shallow-water and coastal projects.

As they were going aboard, Zavala surfaced and climbed onto a dive platform attached to the boat. He saw Austin and Carina, slipped his scuba gear off, and came aboard to greet his friends.

"Good morning," Zavala said. "Here to do some wreck diving?"

"Not today," Austin said. "We came by to see what you've found."

"*Wonderful* things," Saxon said.

He led them to a tank where at least a dozen amphorae were submerged in water to preserve them. "We've done preliminary X-rays. These jars are loaded with scrolls. This is bound to be a treasure trove of information. The Phoenicians sailed all over the world. I'm hoping we'll find charts showing where they traded and descriptions of their voyages."

"Sounds as if we're going to have to rewrite the history books," Austin said.

"We've only scratched the surface, Kurt," Zavala said. "The wreck is loaded with artifacts."

Austin glanced at the water. "How's Mrs. Hutchins taking all this commotion?" he said.

"When we told Thelma about the salvage, she admitted that Hutch might be getting waterlogged," Zavala said. "She agreed to have his remains transported to land, where she could be closer to the old guy."

Austin offered his congratulations all around. Then he and Carina rowed back to the catboat. As they hauled anchor and set sail, Saxon called out: "See you Saturday, Carina."

She waved in acknowledgment, and minutes later the sailboat was gliding across the bay under the influence of a steady southwest breeze. They stopped for lunch in a quiet cove. Austin went into the cabin and came back out holding a bottle of champagne and two glasses. He poured out the bubbly, and they clinked glasses.

"I've got something to tell you," Carina said.

"I gathered that from Saxon's comment."

"Saxon has found new clues to Sheba's tomb in Yemen. He wants me to help him search for it. I still can't believe I'm Sheba's descendant, but I'd love to find her resting place. She was a remarkable woman. I said yes."

"I'll miss you, but it sounds like a fine adventure," Austin said. "When will you be leaving?"

"We fly out three days from now."

"Any suggestions how I should treat Your Royal Highness in the meantime?"

"You've got seventy-two hours to find out," Carina said with an intriguing smile. "That should give you *more* than enough time."

Austin set his champagne down and took her glass from her fingers. He gestured toward the cabin.

"No time like the present," Austin said.